CHRISTMAS
Unwrapped

Exciting, sensual stories from
Maureen Child, Sandra Hyatt,
Vicki Lewis Thompson, Jennifer
LaBrecque and Rhonda Nelson

CHRISTMAS
Unwrapped

Maureen	Sandra	Vicki Lewis	Jennifer	Rhonda
CHILD	HYATT	THOMPSON	LaBRECQUE	NELSON

MILLS & BOON

Mills & Boon, an imprint of Harlequin (UK) Limited, Eton House, 18-24 Paradise Road, Richmond, Surrey TW9 1SR

CHRISTMAS UNWRAPPED
© Harlequin Enterprises II B.V./S.à.r.l. 2012

The Wrong Brother © Maureen Child 2010
Mistletoe Magic © Sandra Hyatt 2010
It's Christmas, Cowboy! © Vicki Lewis Thompson 2011
Northern Fantasy © Jennifer LaBrecque 2011
He'll Be Home for Christmas © Rhonda Nelson 2011

ISBN: 978 0 263 90244 0

009-1212

Harlequin (UK) policy is to use papers that are natural, renewable and recyclable products and made from wood grown in sustainable forests. The logging and manufacturing processes conform to the legal environmental regulations of the country of origin.

Printed and bound in Spain
by Blackprint CPI, Barcelona

CONTENTS

THE WRONG BROTHER

MAUREEN CHILD

Maureen Child...

For my mom, Sallye Carberry,
who loves Christmas more than anyone else I
know. You always made the magic for us, Mom.

Maureen Child was born and raised in Southern
California and is the only person she knows who
longs for an occasional change of season. An avid
reader, Maureen looks forward to those rare rainy
California days when she can curl up and sink into
a good book. Or two. When she isn't busy writing,
she and her husband of twenty-five-plus years
like to travel, leaving their two grown children
in charge of the neurotic golden retriever who is
the real head of the household. Visit Maureen's
website at www.maureenchild.com.

1

ANNA CAMERON ducked behind a tinsel-draped potted plant and peeked through the lacy fronds at the mingling crowd. The Cameron Leather company Christmas party was in high gear. People she'd known most of her life were here, laughing, talking, drinking. She wished she were out there in the middle of them enjoying herself.

Instead, she was hiding from her stepmother. Not that Clarissa Cameron was an evil woman or anything. But she'd had a little too much to drink and now all she wanted to do was corner Anna and try to convince her to win back her former boyfriend, Garret Hale.

"As if I'd take him back," Anna muttered, pulling aside a tinsel-decorated frond to scan the crowd in front of her.

They'd gone out only a few times when Garret's older brother Samuel told him to drop her. He'd actually had the nerve to suggest that Anna was doing exactly what Clarissa now *wanted* her to do. Using Garret to help her father's company. Okay, fine, a merger with Hale Luxury Autos would probably save Cameron Leather, but she wasn't a bargaining chip. And even if she had been, it wouldn't have worked.

Because Garret had backed away from her so fast that he'd left sparks in his wake. He hadn't stood up for her to his snooty, suspicious older brother. He'd called Anna to tell her they couldn't see each other anymore because the Great Sam Hale had decreed it. He'd threatened to cut Garret off financially if he hadn't stopped seeing Anna.

"No loss," Anna reassured herself. So despite what Clarissa wanted, Anna wouldn't have Garret back on a platter. She hadn't even been that interested in the man in the first place. One kiss had told her everything she needed to know about him. She hadn't felt the slightest tingle of expectation when he kissed her. Hadn't seen a single star. She had known then that he was not the man for her.

She wanted the *magic*.

Of course, the fact that he'd wimped out for the sake of his big brother and his wallet didn't exactly endear him to her either. And her life might have been easier if she could just admit to Clarissa what had happened. But she had a *little* pride after all.

Clarissa kept urging her to do exactly what Garret's brother had assumed she was up to in the first place— marry the man and bring a nice merger to the family business.

"Anna, honey, is that you in there?"

She jerked, startled and turned to look guiltily into her father's eyes. "Um, hi, Dad."

"What're you doing behind a plant, sweetie?" Dave Cameron's green eyes were smiling, but Anna couldn't help but notice that there was a glimmer of worry there, too.

How to explain that she was hiding from his wife? Nope, couldn't do it. It wasn't anyone's fault, but Clarissa and Anna had never been as close as her dad wanted them to be. Until ten years ago, it had been just her and her father. Her own mother had died when Anna was two, so all she really had were photographs and her dad's stories.

When Clarissa came into their lives, Anna was seventeen. She hadn't been interested in acquiring a new "mother," and at the time had really resented having to share her father's affections. She and Clarissa had finally gotten to the point where they could be friends, if not mother and daughter, but Anna knew her father still worried about their relationship.

So, instead of blurting out the truth, Anna ran her fingertips across the top of the big blue ceramic pot. "Just checking to make sure everything's tidy. Yep, no dust."

He laughed and took her arm, drawing her out from behind the palm. "Housekeeping has never been one of your interests, so what's really going on?"

The music was too loud for any deep conversation and Anna wasn't interested in having one anyway. So she simply smiled, kissed her father's cheek and said, "Nothing, Dad. Everything's great. The party's wonderful."

"So wonderful you're hiding in the shrubbery?"

"Honestly?" she said, mentally crossing her fingers for the tiny lie she was about to tell, "Darren Shivers has had one beer too many and wanted to tell me all about how he won the high school football game back in the seventies."

"Oh, he's not telling that story again, is he?"

"You know Darren," she said, telling herself that really, it wasn't much of a lie. Any time the man had more than three beers, he cornered someone and forced him or her to relive his glory days with him. Still, couldn't hurt to change the subject. "Looks like everyone's having fun."

"Seem to be," he mused, swiftly scanning the crowd

that was even now dancing to the music and gathering in knots to try to talk. "Your stepmother's done a fine job."

"Yes, Clarissa's very good at this sort of thing," she said, meaning it. She and her stepmother did have common ground after all. They both loved Anna's dad.

Her dad sent her a sidelong glance. "Is there something going on between you two?"

"Absolutely not," she said, unwilling to put her father in the middle of all this. Besides, Anna knew that Clarissa's tipsy attempt at matchmaking was only because she was worried about her husband.

Hard to fault her for that when Anna was worried, too.

Cameron Leather company was in trouble and despite this wonderful party, the truth was, if something great didn't happen soon, her dad was going to lose the company he'd built up from nothing. But Dave Cameron was an "old school" kind of man. He treated the women in his life like princesses and didn't want them "fretting" about company concerns. Her dad was sweet and old-fashioned and she loved him fiercely.

She forced a smile on to her face and said, "Don't worry about Clarissa and me. We're fine. And it's a great party, Dad. Why don't you go enjoy it?"

"Good idea." He took a step, stopped and asked, "You're not going back behind that plant are you? You're too beautiful to hide away."

She held up one hand. "I swear. I will have a good time. Now go, dance with your wife."

And keep her off my trail, she added silently.

By the time her father had slipped back into the crowd, greeting old friends with a forced holiday cheer, Anna had disappeared from the ballroom. As a child, she'd explored every inch of the big house, so she knew all the nooks and crannies to disappear into.

She was stopped a dozen times to talk to someone or answer a question from the catering staff. The music jumped into a wild dance beat with a tune from the forties and the drumbeats seemed to echo in the headache behind her eyes.

"Clarissa's looking for you," someone said and Anna smiled and kept moving. *Just nod,* she told herself. Smile and keep walking.

She was almost at the long hallway leading to the front door when she heard, "Anna!"

She stopped again with a barely restrained sigh. Not an easy thing to do at all, she thought, slipping out of a party where she knew everyone. She turned to chat yet again with one of her father's employees.

Eddie Hanover was short, round and sported a wispy gray comb-over. He was one of the guys Anna had grown up around and she loved him like a second father. "Hi, Eddie. How's it going?"

"Going great, Anna. Trust your dad to hold to traditions even when times are hard," he said with a grin.

True. Her father hadn't wanted to even discuss canceling the annual Christmas party. The company might be in trouble, but her dad wouldn't "cheat" his employees out of something they looked forward to all year.

"Have you seen Clarissa?" Eddie's wife Trina asked. "She's been looking all over for you."

"Well, I'll go look for her." In the driveway. Inside her own car.

"Just wanted to say howdy, let you know we all appreciate the Camerons throwing the party," Eddie told her, then grabbed Trina's hand and dragged her off in the direction of the music.

She nodded, but the pair were already lost in the mingling crowd. Then she caught a flash of something bright red out of the corner of her eye. When she glanced over, she saw it was Clarissa, headed her way.

Think fast, she told herself. If only she were dating someone else, she thought frantically. Then Clarissa would have to give up on the whole "marry for the sake of the family" idea and she'd drop the subject of Garret Hale for good.

Unfortunately, there was no man in Anna's life and no prospects for one anytime soon. Her gaze scanning the room, frantically trying to find an escape route, she eventually spotted something even better.

A tall man with no woman clinging to his arm, standing beneath a red ribbon–bedecked sprig of mistletoe.

With Clarissa hot on her heels, Anna sprinted toward him, moving in and out of the ever-shifting crowd like a race car driver on a complicated course. When she was right behind him, she tapped him on the shoulder and shouted to be heard over the pounding music.

"Kiss me and save my life!"

2

He spun around, his lake-blue eyes fixed on her. Then he smiled, reached for her and said, "My pleasure."

She barely had time to take a breath before his mouth came down on hers. He wrapped his arms around her, held her tight and kissed her as she'd never been kissed before. Long and hard and deep, he sent sparks of something wonderful shooting through her system. His tongue tangled with hers as he tasted her completely and Anna found herself melting into him, giving herself up to the incredible glory of what he was making her feel.

The magic she used to dream about was here. Finally here. In the arms of a man she'd never met before.

Who was her newfound hero anyway?

"Oh, Anna!"

Clarissa's voice penetrated the lovely glow surrounding her and Anna reluctantly broke the kiss, pulling back just enough to stare up into her rescuer's blue eyes.

Really, the man was drop-dead gorgeous. No, better. He was bring-the-dead-back-to-life gorgeous. Lake-blue eyes, night-black hair, a strong jaw and shoulders wide enough to belong to a professional football player.

The music was playing, the steady roar of conversations continued to roll on, but she felt as though she and her mystery man were all alone in the world. Until Clarissa piped up again.

"You should have told me!"

"What?" she asked, still looking into those deep blue eyes. "Told you what?"

Clarissa moved in close, gave Anna a tight hug and said, "You should have told me that the reason you stopped seeing Garret was because you were involved with his *brother!*"

Brother?

"*You're* Anna Cameron?"

"*You're* Sam Hale?"

"This is *wonderful,*" Clarissa said on a satisfied sigh.

THIS WAS A NIGHTMARE, Sam Hale told himself, looking down at the pretty woman who had just knocked his socks off.

He didn't belong there and he knew it. Didn't matter that he'd been invited to the Cameron Christmas party. Hell, it looked as if half of Crystal Bay, California, was crammed into the ballroom of Dave Cameron's big house on the sea.

But he wasn't there for the warm holiday celebration, he'd come to get an up close look at Dave's daughter. Of course he'd seen pictures of her, but he hadn't had the time to recognize her before that mind-numbing kiss. The woman he'd heard so much about from his brother, Garret. The same woman who was now looking at him as if he'd just crawled out from under a rock.

He was here to find out if maybe he'd been wrong about the woman. It was no secret that Cameron Leather was in trouble. And the fact that Dave Cameron's daughter had been dating *his* brother had just seemed too coincidental to Sam. He'd figured that some wily, sneaky, money-hungry woman had latched on to Garret for one reason only.

Cash.

But Garret was still pissed about this, so Sam had decided to see for himself if his suspicions were true. If he was wrong about her, he could try to smooth things over between this woman and his brother.

He was off to a hell of a start.

"I can't believe you kissed me!" she accused.

"You asked me to," he reminded her. And there was nothing he'd like better at the moment than to kiss her again. As soon as that thought hit his brain, his blood started humming. He was ready and willing and all too damn eager to give in to his desires. So, he clung to the threads of his anger and used them to fight back the growing rush of want.

She pointed to the arched doorjamb above his head. "You're standing under mistletoe. And I didn't know it was *you,* now, did I?" the redhead with the beautiful eyes argued.

"Anna, you two shouldn't bicker," Clarissa lowered her voice and leaned in to make sure she was heard. "It's a party."

"This isn't what you think it is," Anna said, still glaring at him.

What he should do is leave. Distance himself from this whole mess. But he couldn't quite make himself walk away from her. At least, not yet.

"Lovers' quarrels," the older woman said, "happens to everyone, dear."

"Oh, God," Anna whispered.

Then she licked her lips and Sam's insides tightened. His focus was narrowed on her. This woman was nothing like what he'd expected. The kind of woman his brother usually went for was—*less* than this one. This woman had fire inside her and a mind of her own. She clearly wasn't an empty-headed party girl looking for a good time. The question was, was she a mercenary woman looking for a fat wallet?

"I can't believe this," she muttered.

Damned if he'd stand there and be accused of being a lecher or something. "You know, I was just standing there minding my own business…"

"Have you met my husband?" Clarissa asked.

"You should have introduced yourself," Anna told him.

"Before or after you propositioned me?" he countered.

She gasped, outraged. "I did not!"

"You said, 'Kiss me and save my life,'" he reminded her with a grin. "What did you expect a man to do?"

"Okay, yes, I did. But I didn't know it was you."

"We covered that already," he said.

"I'll just find Dave," Clarissa said, tipsily oblivious. "He'll be so happy to know about the two of you!"

"Don't!" Anna spoke up quickly, but it was too late, the older woman was already disappearing into the crowd. "Oh, for heaven's sake."

"Now that we're alone, want to move back under the mistletoe?"

"No!" She flushed, though, and he knew she was lying. She stared helplessly after her stepmother for a long minute. Then whipping back around to glare at him again, she said, "You have to leave."

He'd been thinking the same damn thing a second ago.

But now that she was practically ordering him out, Sam wasn't about to leave. "Hey, I was invited. Why should I leave just because you're suddenly regretting trying to seduce me?"

She hissed in a breath and her cheeks flamed with hot color. Amazing. He hadn't thought there were still women around who actually *blushed*. Sam was more intrigued by the minute—and even less inclined to leave than he had been.

"I did not try to seduce you," she said through gritted teeth. "It was a blip. An emergency situation."

He was starting to enjoy himself. "An emergency make out session?"

"We didn't—" She stopped, took a deep breath and closed her eyes briefly. "You know what? I'm not doing this anymore. If you're not going to leave, I will."

She turned around so fast that her long, auburn hair swung out behind her like a flag. She was wearing a sleeveless silver top that clung to her breasts and a short, black silk skirt that hugged her behind and defined every curve. Her long, lean legs looked as smooth and pale as fresh cream and the three-inch black heels she wore had a cutout at the toes that spotlighted dark red nails.

His gaze dropped to her behind as she hurried away from him and he had to admire the indignant sway of her hips. But damned if he was going to let her walk off and leave him standing there still buzzed from that kiss.

Sam caught up to her in a few long strides. Grabbing her arm, he stopped her, then swung her around to face him.

She looked pointedly at his hand on her arm. "Excuse me?"

He laughed but let her go. "Does that snotty queen-to-peasant tone usually work on men?"

Her eyes widened. "I'm not the one who tells people how to live their lives," she told him flatly. "That would be *your* specialty, remember?"

A couple of guests wandered through the hallway and before he could suggest it, Anna pointed down the hall and he followed her. She was clearly looking for some privacy to finish this conversation. She led him to a pair of French doors that opened into a garden with a stone pathway laid out between the flower beds. She started off down the path and Sam was right behind her.

A glance to his left showed him bright lights spilling from the ballroom to lay across a wide, brick patio. The music was muted at a distance and the rush of people talking sounded like the sea, rising and falling in rhythm.

Only twenty or so feet away, it was as if he and Anna were alone in the world. There were no lights decorating this tidy garden, just the moonlight covering everything in a pale glow. She kept walking and Sam stayed close, until she stopped beside a stone bench encircling a small fountain in the shape of a dolphin.

The white noise of the falling water drowned out most of the party, but truth to tell, Sam was so caught up in the woman in front of him that he wouldn't have noticed a train blasting through the yard.

Satisfied that they were alone, Anna continued her rant as if she hadn't been interrupted.

"How is it you get to decide what people do and who they date?"

Irritated, he snapped, "I don't remember filling out your social calendar. As for my brother…"

"Did you or did you not tell him to stop dating me because I was—" She stopped and tapped her chin with the tip of one finger. "Let me see if I can get this just right. *She's using you to get to my money to save her father.*" She narrowed her eyes on him. "That about cover it?"

Hearing his own words tossed back at him caused him to wince. Figured that his brother would be fool enough to actually tell her what Sam had said. He should have known.

Most of his life, Sam had been taking care of Garret. He'd seen him through school, bailed him out of trouble occasionally and waited for him to grow up. Hadn't happened yet, though.

He moved in closer to her and had the satisfaction of seeing her eyes widen slightly at his nearness. Good to know he wasn't the only one still affected by that kiss.

"He shouldn't have repeated that to you."

"You shouldn't have said it in the first place."

"I'm looking out for my family."

"And what? I'm a threat?"

Looking at her now, Sam thought she was only a threat to a man's sanity. But how could he be sure she wasn't simply an excellent actress? If she was feigning insult, though, she was doing a damn good job of it.

"Babe, I don't know what you are. All I know is I do what I have to for my family—why shouldn't I expect you to do the same?"

"So you don't even deny saying it—and don't call me 'babe.'"

He scraped one hand across the back of his neck. "No, I don't. Can you deny that your father's company's in trouble?"

She took a deep breath and helplessly, Sam's gaze briefly dropped to the deep V of her shirt. When his eyes met hers again, he noted fresh fury sparking in her grass-green eyes.

Lowering her voice, she said, "Are you in the Middle Ages or something? You really believe I would *barter* myself to save my dad's company?"

"People have done a lot more for a lot less," he mused.

"Well, I don't," she told him. "And I really think you've insulted me enough for one night, don't you?"

"Yeah," he said, edging closer, "I think we've *both* done enough talking."

Staring down into her eyes, he reached for her and waited to see if she would pull away. She glared at him. He pulled her in closer, until her breasts were pillowed against his chest and he could feel the heat of her body sliding into his.

"This isn't a good idea," she said, tilting her head back to look up at him. "I should be kicking you."

"Yeah," he said, his gaze moving over her features as if trying to burn her image onto his brain. "But doesn't seem to matter. I've got to taste you again."

"Really not a good idea," she whispered, going up on her toes to meet him as he lowered his head to hers.

His lips brushed hers and he felt that zip of something amazing scatter through him. Her mouth opened under his and he swept inside, losing himself in her heat, her acceptance. He felt her heartbeat pounding against his chest and knew that his own heart was matching that wild rhythm.

She leaned into him and he swept her up, nearly lifting her off her feet to get her closer to him. He wanted more. Wanted bare skin beneath his hands. Wanted to ease her down on that damn bench and—

Close by, a raucous burst of laughter shattered the

night as people started wandering out into the garden. The intrusion was enough to tear them apart instantly.

Sam took a step back from her, just for good measure, and he didn't think it was far enough. Her taste still filled his mouth and his blood was pumping through his veins as hot and thick as lava.

"This is crazy," she whispered, shaking her head as if she couldn't believe what was happening between them.

Sam knew exactly how she felt. "Doesn't seem to matter," he said, as he took a step closer to her.

An uneasy laugh shot from her throat. "We are not doing that again."

"Why not?" Yeah, he knew this was trouble. But he didn't really care.

"Because…" She mentally searched for a good reason and apparently came up empty. Still struggling for breath, she added, "We're just not going to, trust me. And if you won't leave, then I will."

She swept past him, chin lifted, head held high.

"Good night, Anna Cameron," he said softly.

She stopped, looked over her shoulder at him and said pointedly, "Good*bye,* Sam Hale."

3

SAM DIDN'T LEAVE.

Instead, he wandered through the party, listening to snippets of conversation even as he tried to get her out of his mind. She wouldn't go, though. Instead, he kept seeing her eyes, filled with fury and dazzled with passion. He heard her voice, standing up to him as no one had dared do in years. She hadn't backed down. She'd stood her ground and challenged him. Argued with him.

And then kissed him senseless.

Why the hell had a woman like her ever dated Garret? he asked himself. She was way too much woman for his younger brother. Which led him back to his original thought, that she had only been dating Garret to try to help her father's company.

But if that were true, why wouldn't she have tried to snag *Sam?* Why not go for the head of the business?

He accepted a glass of wine from a passing waiter, had a sip, then set the flute down again on a nearby table. His gaze scanned the crowd, noting the decorations, the Christmas tree that had to stand ten feet tall and the mountain of small gifts beneath it, tokens for their guests, all wrapped in bright paper and festive ribbons.

Sam didn't know whether to admire Dave Cameron for going ahead with a party when times were so bad for his company, or to pity him for being a fool. The snippets of conversations he'd heard throughout the place told him that everyone in the room knew about Dave's troubles, so this party wasn't fooling anyone. Why do it, then?

"Having a good time?"

The voice behind him caught Sam off guard and his shoulders stiffened. He should have known that Dave Cameron would come and find him. Especially considering the man's wife had probably reported seeing Sam and Anna kissing like teenagers in the backseat of a car.

Turning, he held out his hand. "It's a good party, Dave."

"Glad you could come," the other man said, shaking his hand. "Don't recall seeing you here last year."

Or any other year. Sam didn't usually get involved in community activities. The only reason he was here this year was because he'd wanted a look at Anna. Now, he wanted another, longer look at her. "You know how it is," he said, "never enough time to relax."

"You should take the time," Dave told him. "There's more to life than business."

"So I hear."

The older man watched him thoughtfully. "Clarissa tells me you and Anna have...*met*."

Uncomfortable, Sam hedged. No doubt, the story of that mistletoe kiss had already made the rounds, thanks to Clarissa. As it was, he felt the stares of at least a dozen people. Small towns were notorious for gossip, and Sam knew he and Anna were going to be the hot topic for at least a few days.

"Yeah. That's a long story, though," he said and gave a quick look around at the surrounding crowd. "Not really the time for it now."

Nodding, Dave said, "I'll look forward to hearing it."

"Right." Not a conversation Sam wanted to have. "Well, I only stopped by to wish you a Merry Christmas, so I think I'll be going."

"No need to rush off," Dave told him. "Stay, enjoy yourself."

The only way that would happen is if he could get Anna to himself again. And because the chance of that was slim, there was really no point in sticking around.

"I appreciate it. Another time." He took a step, then stopped and added, "Say good night to Anna for me."

Let her explain the situation to her father, he thought with an inner smile.

"NOW THAT'S A GORGEOUS Christmas tree."

Anna stepped back to admire her own handiwork and smiled at her best friend, Tula Barrons. Her real name was Tallulah, but heaven help you if you actually called her that. Tula's blond hair was cut short, close to her head. She wore silver hoop earrings, a blue tunic sweater and black jeans with navy blue boots.

"Thanks," Anna said. "I like a lot of lights."

"Yeah, they'll probably be able to spot that tree from space." Tula grinned as she carried in the lattes she'd gotten at the corner coffee bar.

Anna studied the tall Douglas fir. There were only four strands of a hundred lights on it. "Can you really overdo Christmas?" she wondered aloud. "I don't think so."

Tula handed her one of the lattes and took a long look

at the tree herself. After a second or two, she nodded. "I think you're right."

"Plus, it looks great in the front window and maybe it'll draw in some holiday business." She could use it, Anna thought. Her shop, Faux Reality, had been all too quiet for the last couple of weeks.

But then, people weren't really thinking about faux finishes or trompe l'oeil paintings on their walls right now. They were too busy buying presents and baking. All good, she told herself, because Anna, too, loved the Christmas season. But she could do with a really big job about now, so she could go and do some Christmas shopping herself.

Tula took a sip of her latte and looked at Anna over the rim. "Is business that bad?"

Anna sighed. As a writer of children's books, Tula had her own worries, but at least she understood that making a career out of the "arts" was usually feast or famine. "Bad enough that I took a couple of quickie jobs painting storefront windows. Art is art, right? I mean, Christmas trees on windows is still painting."

"Absolutely." After taking another sip, Tula nodded and said, "So, I heard all about the big mistletoe *kiss* last night."

Anna choked on a gulp of hot latte. "You heard? How? Where?"

"Are you kidding?" Her friend laughed. "You've lived in Crystal Bay your whole life, just like me. You know the grapevine in town works faster than a Google search."

"Oh, God." Suddenly, the brightly lit tree wasn't uplifting her spirits quite so much anymore.

"Oh, yeah," Tula said, walking to the front counter and dropping onto one of the high-backed stools. "So spill.

Tell me everything. Word is you and Sam Hale were lip-locked so completely that steam was lifting off the tops of your heads."

"Oh, this is perfect," Anna muttered.

"Sure sounded like it," Tula agreed, then asked, "still, I'm dying to know…wasn't it weird kissing the brother of the guy you used to go out with?"

Weird wasn't the word she'd use, Anna thought. Hot. Passionate. Intense. Crazy, even. All good words. Weird? Not so much.

"I really don't want to talk about this," she said, moving to hang one of her antique ornaments from a high branch of the tree.

"Nice attempt at evasion," Tula told her with a laugh. "But no way are you getting out of this. I left the party early, so I didn't see the show you two put on. But according to Kate, down at Espresso Heaven, people clear across the room from you guys were going up in flames."

"Just shoot me." Anna looked out the front window onto Main Street and imagined everyone in their shops taking about her. Just great.

"Come on, give a little," Tula whined. "I haven't had an actual date in six months and the least you could do is let a girl live vicariously."

"Just what I want to do."

"Was it great?"

"Are you going to let this go?"

Tula laughed. "Have you met me?"

Anna had to laugh, too. She and Tula had been best friends since junior high. They'd gone to college together and had planned to move to Paris and be famous. They never had made it to France, though, instead coming back to Crystal Bay. Anna had opened her own shop and Tula was making a name for herself as the author of the popular *Lonely Bunny* books.

Tula was loyal, a great friend and profoundly nosy. Anna knew darn well that her friend was never going to let this go.

"Fine," she said on a sigh. "It was incredible. Happy?"

"Not nearly. If it was so incredible, why do you look so bummed?"

Anna shook her head. "Hello? Don't you remember that Sam Hale is the guy who told his brother to dump me?"

Tula frowned and pointed out, "Yeah, and I remember that *Garret* Hale was the giant weasel dog who did the actual dumping."

"True." What kind of grown man took orders from his big brother? Anna wondered. But on the other hand, what kind of guy was Sam to step in and try to take over his younger brother's life?

"So, how'd you happen to bump into Sam's luscious mouth?"

Anna glared at her. "What makes you think it's luscious?"

"I'm not blind, you know. I have seen the man from a distance."

And one look would be enough for most women to curl up and whimper at his feet. Not that she was going to be doing any whimpering, thanks very much. "It was an accident."

"So you slipped and fell onto his mouth. Sure. As your friend, I'm happy to buy that lame explanation." Tula took a sip of latte and leaned back against the counter. "The question is, why are you so touchy about it?"

"Because he was an ass and because I liked that kiss too much."

"Ah, that I get," Tula said, then straightened up, a look of horror on her face. "Oh, you never slept with Garret, did you?"

"Of course not!" Anna practically recoiled at the idea. The few kisses she'd shared with Garret hadn't exactly started a fire inside. "We only went out a few times."

"Good," Tula said with a chuckle, "because that could have been awkward. No guy wants to think you're comparing him to his own brother."

Remembering that long, amazing kiss under the mistletoe had Anna practically sighing. "Trust me when I say, there is no comparison."

"Aha!" Tula crowed. "You're all gooey-eyed and you just admitted that Sam's a better kisser than Garret. The plot thickens."

Anna laughed a little. Impossible to be mad at Tula, especially when she was right. "There is no plot. He still thinks I set out to deliberately trap his precious brother into marrying me so I could save Dad's company."

"Well, then, I don't care how great a kisser he is—he's an idiot."

"Thanks, pal," she said.

"You bet." Tula watched her for a second or two, then apparently decided a change of subject was needed. "I've got to drive down to Long Beach to see my cousin Sherry."

Since Crystal Bay was in northern California, going to Long Beach in the southern half of the state was at least a seven-hour drive.

"Why are you going? You guys aren't exactly close. Heck, it's been six years since you've seen her."

Tula shrugged and took another sip of her latte. "Yeah, but we're all the family either of us has…"

"You've always got me."

"I know," she said with a smile. "And thanks. But Sherry called and said she really needs to see me."

"And she can't come up here."

Wrinkling her nose, Tula said, "You know Sherry. Afraid of freeways, afraid of driving, afraid of flying… afraid, period. So I'm driving down today. Should be back in a few days. Want to have dinner when I get back?"

"Sure, just be safe and call if you need to. I know how Sherry gets to you."

Tula grinned. "I'm going to do a chant for patience all the way down the coast."

"Good idea," Anna said, realizing how grateful she was that Tula had stopped by this morning. Just being around her friend made her feel more herself. She'd spent most of the night before thinking about Sam Hale and those two amazing kisses. And she so didn't need to be thinking about him or his mouth, Anna told herself firmly.

She was back to normal—despite being the topic of gossip all over town.

She pushed that thought aside and tried to focus on work.

"Did you call that Mrs. Soren back?"

There had been a message on the answering machine when she arrived this morning. A woman wanted her to come out and give her an estimate on what it would cost to do a mural on her living room wall.

"Yep," Anna said. "I've got an appointment to see her at one today. Fingers crossed it works out. Her house is on the bluff."

"Ooh," Tula said softly. "So it's probably one of those mansions like your dad's."

Anna nodded, but she knew all too well that a fabulous house didn't necessarily mean a lot of extra cash.

Her own father's house had been built more than thirty years ago. Looking at it, anyone would assume that the Cameron family's financial health was in great shape. Nothing could have been further from the truth. A twist of worry for her dad hit her hard and fast and for a second or two, she almost felt guilty for not falling in with Clarissa's plan to snag a rich husband.

4

A FEW PHONE calls were all it took to give Sam all of the information he needed on Cameron Leather. Yes, the company was in trouble, but it wasn't in its death throes just yet. Dave Cameron had expanded when he should have been more cautious, but with a little judicious input of capital, the company would be back on its feet.

Didn't make him feel any better to realize that. All it told him was that the odds of Anna being exactly as mercenary as he suspected her to be just went a lot higher.

He leaned back in his desk chair and stared out the window at the backyard. Working from home had its perks. Even though Hale Luxury Autos had a full-size shop on the outskirts of town, Sam also had a specially built garage here at home. At the shop, his master mechanics, artists and upholsterers had free rein and he rarely stepped in. Here, he had his own setup and indulged himself whenever he felt the need to get his hands dirty.

His gaze fixed on the manicured lawn and garden that ran down a slope to the ocean below. Sam took a minute to realize just how far he'd come. He'd started out small, building custom cars for people with more money than taste.

Now, Sam had people flocking to him for his expertise and he spent most of his time trying to rein in the near-constant stream of paperwork involved.

"Mr. Hale?"

"Yes, Jenny?" He turned when his housekeeper opened the door and called to him.

"I made the call. Ms. Cameron will be here at one."

He smiled. "Excellent. Thanks."

When she left again to go back to the main house, Sam let his smile widen as he imagined the look on Anna's face when she arrived to give Mrs. Soren an estimate, only to find out *he* was the one who had initiated the call. She wouldn't be happy, but Sam needed to know her. If only to prove to himself he'd been right to break up her and his brother.

Smiling to himself, Sam stepped out of the multi-bayed garage. He studied the view and let his mind wander to the green-eyed redhead whose memory was torturing him.

"THE LIVING ROOM is this way."

Anna followed the fiftyish woman down a parquet hallway to an arched doorway that opened into a huge room. Clearly masculine, the decor was mostly big leather chairs, heavy tables and brightly colored rugs scattered across the inlaid wood floor. A stone fireplace took up most of one wall and floor-to-ceiling windows displayed a view of the wide front lawn.

A huge, beautifully decorated Christmas tree stood in one corner, with wrapped gifts beneath it. Which reminded Anna just how much she needed this job.

"It's lovely," she said, meaning it. But she couldn't help wondering, "This is your husband's lair, isn't it?" she asked with a smile.

"My husband?" The woman laughed and waved one hand. "Oh, my, no. My husband died twenty years ago. This is my employer's house."

She was the housekeeper? Anna frowned and looked around the room, as if searching for a hint to the owner's identity. When she found nothing, she said, "I'm sorry. I thought you wanted to talk to me about painting a mural in here."

"No," a deep, familiar voice said from behind her. "Mrs. Soren made the call, but I'm the one who wants to hire you."

Anna went completely still. A setup. And she'd walked right into it. Turning around slowly, she looked up into Sam's blue eyes and, keeping her voice cool, she said, "I'm sorry. There's been a mistake."

He scowled at her. Small consolation, she knew, but she was pleased that she'd disrupted whatever plan he'd concocted.

Shifting his gaze to the other woman in the room, he said, "That's all, Jenny. Thanks."

"Yes, sir," she answered and nodded at Anna as she left.

"You had her lie for you. That's just low."

"She didn't lie."

Anna tipped her head to one side and tapped the toe of her boot against the floor. "So you want to hire me? Please."

His eyebrows arched high on his forehead. "Are you always this crabby with a prospective customer?"

"You're not a customer, prospective or otherwise," she said firmly and clutched her portfolio closer to her chest.

He walked into the room and Anna couldn't help but notice how at home he looked in faded black jeans and the dark red T-shirt that clung to his broad chest. His black work boots hardly made a sound as he walked across the deep blue and green rug to stand in front of her.

"Business that good, then?" he asked. "You can turn down customers?"

"In my shop, I can do what I like."

"True, but seems shortsighted to turn down a job just because you're embarrassed about kissing me."

"What?" Her eyes widened and her jaw dropped. "Are you delusional?"

He smirked. "You seem a little sensitive."

"I'm not sensitive. I'm insulted."

"Don't know why. It was a great kiss."

True. Damn it.

"Look," Anna said, clinging to every stray fiber of her dignity, "we're wasting each other's time here and even if you can afford it, I can't."

"You agreed to give me an estimate on a wall mural," he reminded her. "The least you can do is keep your word."

Anna glared at him and the dirty look she gave him had zero effect on the man. If anything, he looked supremely pleased with himself. Well, fine. She'd keep the appointment and then when she quoted him an outrageous price, he'd tell her no and she'd leave. All she had to do was take control of this situation.

"Fine, then," she said. "What did you have in mind?"

He gave her a wide smile that tugged at something deep inside her. The man was a walking hormone party.

Anna gave herself a stern, if silent, talking-to. There would be no more kissing. No more flirting.

No *anything* with Sam Hale.

"Actually," he said, spreading his arms wide to encompass the room, "I'd prefer to hear your opinion. What kind of murals do you usually suggest?"

Anything would look fabulous in the opulent room, but Anna wouldn't give him the satisfaction of saying so. She gave a quick look around and fixed her gaze on the wide, empty space above the fireplace.

"A window and garden scene would look nice there."

"A *window?*"

"Trompe l'oeil," she told him patiently.

"Optical illusion?"

"You could call it that," she said and in spite of what she was feeling, she found herself warming to her theme. She loved faux finishing. Loved the trompe l'oeil murals that mimicked reality so completely, she'd once seen a man try to pick up a marble that had been painted onto a tabletop.

"A close translation of the French name means *trick the eye*. With the right artist, you can pretty much remodel your entire home without lifting a hammer."

"And you're the 'right' artist?"

"I'm really good," she said simply.

"I bet you are."

She flushed a little and hated herself for it. But she would defy any woman in the world to remain completely cool and unruffled with *this* particular man focusing all of his attention on her.

He watched her. "Explain what you mean about the painting."

She didn't know what he was up to, but as long as she

was there anyway, she couldn't resist talking about her favorite kind of work. "For instance, on that long wall over there, I could paint a set of French doors opening onto an English garden. It would look real enough to convince you that you could step outside and smell the flowers." She looked back at him. "Or I could give you an ocean scene complete with crashing waves and seabirds overhead. I could really, within reason, give you anything you wanted."

Oh, boy, that had come out a lot different than it sounded in her head. He must have been thinking the same thing, because something hot and wicked flashed in his eyes.

"And what do you charge for this amazing service?"

She cleared her throat, inhaled sharply and told herself that he didn't really care. He wasn't actually interested. So she gave him a price well above what she would normally charge for a mural.

He didn't even blink.

"I'll give you twice that if you can have it done before Christmas."

"Are you serious?" He couldn't be, she told herself. This was all part of some twisted game. He'd brought her here for his own purposes, whatever they were, and now he was dangling a great job in front of her like bait.

The hell of it was, it was working.

"Yes, I'm serious," he told her, and walked toward her with slow, measured steps.

"Why?" Anna stared up into his deep blue eyes and didn't flinch from the gleam of passion she saw shining at her. "Why would you hire me? Why would you offer so much money?"

"Does it matter?"

She wrestled with that question for a second or two. Her mind raced with arguments, pro and con. One part of her wanted to throw his offer in his face and march out the door, head held high. The other, more practical side of her was shrieking, *Are you crazy? Take the job!*

In a couple more silent seconds, she had already tallied up the bills she could pay if she took the job he offered. It had been a slow couple of months in the world of faux finishing and with this one job, she could cover her expenses for another two months. Not to mention the Christmas presents she could buy if she took this commission.

The downside was obvious.

She'd be spending a lot of time with a man who both infuriated and excited her. Who needed that kind of irritation on a daily basis? Not to mention the fact that her body tended to light up like a fireworks display whenever he was within three feet of her. That couldn't end well.

"So what'll it be?" he asked, a sly smile on his face as if he knew she was arguing with herself. "Stay or go?"

His satisfied expression told Anna that he was completely sure of himself. He thought he had her pegged. That she was just another woman ready to grab the money and run.

She should go. She knew it. She'd love to be able to look into his eyes and say, "No, you can't buy me." But as satisfying as that sounded, she knew she wasn't going to walk away.

She couldn't afford to.

"Fine," she muttered. "I'll take the job."

"Thought you might."

To keep from saying something she would no doubt regret, she bit her tongue. The man was more irritating than he was gorgeous, which was really saying something. She'd work for him, Anna told herself, but she wasn't going to let him insult her for her trouble either.

"Just so you know," she told him with a patient tone she was proud of, "I'm only taking this job because I really need the work. But so we're clear...I don't like you."

His eyebrows winged up. "And yet, you're staying. So money talks?"

Make that even *more* irritating than he was gorgeous. He'd already told his younger brother to dump her because he thought she was after his money. Now, he was no doubt convinced that he'd been right about her, which just made her furious.

"Easy to say money doesn't matter when you have plenty of it," she pointed out.

"Yeah, it is." Then he said, "Not the point of this, though. The point is, even though you hate me personally, you're more than willing to take my money."

"Less willing every second," she muttered.

"That I don't believe."

Anna narrowed her gaze on him and asked, "Are you trying to make me quit before I've even started?"

"Nope, just waiting to see how long you could hold on to your temper."

"Not much longer," she admitted. Taking a breath, she said, "If it's all right with you, I'll start tomorrow."

"Fine. I'll expect you at eight."

"Fine."

"Fine."

"Well," she said after a simmering few seconds, "this is childish."

"I'm sort of enjoying it."

"Color me surprised," she told him. "But believe it or not, some of us have other, more important things to do."

He grinned and Anna took a breath. Why was it *this* man who got to her so easily? Where was the indifference she'd felt for his brother? Why did the *wrong* brother feel so right?

If this was some sort of test of her morals, Anna thought, she was already failing badly. It was taking every ounce of will she possessed to keep from finding more mistletoe and dragging this man under it. She didn't want to be interested, but she couldn't seem to help herself.

How was she ever going to be able to hold her ground against Sam Hale?

SHE HAD *It's a Wonderful Life* playing on the TV, and the lights on the tree were the only illumination in the room. Anna took a sip of her cold, white wine and told herself to relax already.

Unfortunately, it wasn't working. Her mind kept turning to Sam Hale and what he might be up to. Since leaving his house that afternoon, she'd been trying to figure him and his plan out. So far, she had nothing.

When the doorbell rang, she groaned, pried herself off the couch and went to answer it. One glance through the peephole had her briefly resting her forehead against the door. Then she surrendered to the inevitable and opened it. "Hi, Clarissa."

Her father's wife scurried inside, fingers clutching at her shoulder bag. She glanced around the room, frowned, then reached over to flip the light switch. Anna blinked at the sudden blast of light.

"Oh, Anna," Clarissa said, "I just wanted to tell you how sorry I am for behaving so foolishly at the party. I didn't mean to embarrass you or anything."

"It's okay. I understand."

"I know you do, dear." The older woman patted her hair as if searching for a strand out of place. She was doomed to disappointment. Clarissa's short, bright red hair was, as always, perfect. "I'm just so worried about your father."

Which was the only reason Anna was willing to overlook Clarissa's panicky attempts at matchmaking. "Dad will be fine. The company's had rough times before."

"Not like this." Clarissa reached out, snagged Anna's wineglass from her hand and downed what was left of it in one long gulp before handing it back. "Thank you. But now that I know you're actually interested in Samuel Hale, I'm resting easier."

Here it comes, she thought. "Clarissa, there's nothing going on between—"

"No, no, I don't want to invade your privacy," she said with a careful shake of her head. "I just wanted you to know that I understand completely. It was so wise of you to move from Garret to Sam. After all, it's *his* company. Garret's just the younger brother."

Anna felt a headache coming on and wished for more wine to drown it. "I'm not *after* either of them. Sam…"

"Oh, we all saw the kiss," Clarissa assured her, letting her gaze sweep around the small living room of Anna's bungalow cottage. She stared at the brightly lit tree for a moment and smiled before adding, "Your father is pleased, too. Though he does want to talk with Sam."

"No," Anna said quickly, imagining her father asking Sam's "intentions." "No talking. Clarissa you have to tell Dad that I'm not dating Sam."

"Why ever would I do that?" Clarissa smiled conspiratorially. "He only wants to know that you're happy, dear."

"Clarissa…"

"Oops," she said, with a quick check of her watch. "I really have to run. I'm meeting your father for an early dinner before we go to the community theater. They're doing *A Christmas Carol*."

"Clarissa," Anna tried again, but her stepmother was already halfway out the door. "It's not what you think. Honestly, there's nothing between Sam and I."

She laughed. "Darling, I *saw* that kiss. Along with half the town, I might add. Whether you want to admit it or not, there's definitely something between you!" She leaned in, brushed a kiss on Anna's cheek and said, "Your tree's lovely, by the way!"

Then she was gone and Anna was left alone with her disturbing thoughts and an empty wineglass.

5

SHE WASN'T GOING to be painting in that wonderful room she had seen the day before.

Anna drove around to the back of Sam's house, following the long, wide driveway around the house to a sprawling lawn and what looked like a five-car garage. Trees lined one side of the property and the lawn sloped down toward the cliff and the ocean below. A white rail fence meandered along the cliff's edge and boasted a few late blooming chrysanthemums at its base.

Storm clouds hovered on the horizon, looking as though they were gathering strength to make a rush toward shore. A cold wind rattled through the boughs of the pines and snatched a few orange leaves from a huge maple tree. Winter in coastal northern California didn't mean snow after all. It meant fall-colored trees long into January.

It really was lovely, but why she was back here, she didn't have a clue. The housekeeper had directed her to the back of the house and now, she wasn't sure what to do next. Anna got out of her car and looked around, pushing the wind-twisted tangle of her hair out of her eyes.

She walked back to the trunk of her small SUV and lifted the hatch, displaying all of her tools. Yardsticks, paints, transfer papers, charcoal sticks and painter's tape. Her brushes were standing straight up in empty coffee cans and she used a plastic caddy to hold a selection of pencils along with painters' rags and tightly closed jars of clean water.

Movement at the corner of her eye caught her attention and Anna turned to look. She hated the fact that her heartbeat jumped in her chest at first sight of Sam Hale striding from the garage toward her. Faded blue jeans hugged his legs, and he wore a dark green sweater and black boots.

She hadn't expected to have to deal with Sam while working here. Didn't he have things to do? Cars to build? Universes to run?

"What are you doing here?"

"I live here, remember?"

"Yes," she said on an irritated sigh, "I meant…"

"I know what you meant." He glanced into the trunk of her car. "You need *all* of this to paint a picture?"

"It's a faux finish, not just a picture," she told him, then added, "and yes, I do."

One corner of his mouth lifted and Anna hated to admit even to herself what kind of impact even that tiny half smile of his had on her.

"Okay, then," he said, reaching into the trunk to pick up most of her equipment. "Follow me."

She didn't have much choice, Anna thought, trotting behind him in an attempt to keep up with his long-legged stride. He led her toward the garage and headed directly for an open doorway. She followed him inside and glanced down the long open space at the cars parked in separate bays. There were two of them and they were really just shells. No tires, no engine, no window glass.

"You couldn't afford one with an engine?"

He grinned at her and the solid slam of that smile hit her hard enough to momentarily dissolve her balance.

"Those are great cars," he pointed out after he set her supplies down onto a neatly organized workbench.

"If you say so."

"I thought artists had great imaginations," he taunted.

"I use it for painting, not for driving."

"When I get that Bentley and the Cobra up and running, you'll change your tune."

Confused, she looked again at the skeletal cars. She hadn't known that he was a man to actually get his hands dirty. All she'd ever heard of Sam Hale was that he designed luxury cars that his company built for the bored rich. "You work on them yourself?"

"I do. Got my start that way," he said with a sigh of satisfaction. "I was a mechanic," he told her, shaking his head in memory. "A damn good one. Worked night and day when my folks died to make sure Garret could go to college and have a good shot at life."

"What about your shot?" she asked, surprising herself as much as him.

He shrugged. "I did the college thing, but it was cars that drew me in. I built my reputation slowly, growing my business and then I built a custom car for a Hollywood producer. He liked what I did so much that he recommended me to his friends. And before I knew it, I was running Hale Custom Autos. But I still like to work on cars myself, get my hands on a flatlined engine and make it purr again. Guess you don't understand that, huh?"

"Actually, I do," she mused and found herself looking

at him in a whole new light. She'd assumed he was simply another wealthy man, locked in his office, running his own little world from the top of a pedestal. It seemed there was more to Sam Hale than she had thought. "Trompe l'oeil painters can use computer programs to design and detail out every move. But I'd rather get my own hands on a blank wall and make it something amazing."

"So," he said with that half smile she found so dangerously compelling, "you're telling me we have something in common after all?"

She looked at him, standing there all tall and dark and gorgeous. Seriously, he had enough charisma and magnetic attraction about him for two healthy men. She knew that for her own well-being, what she should do was say screw the job and the money and get back into her car. But she wasn't going to do that and she knew it.

"Yes," she admitted. "I guess I am."

For a brief moment, their eyes locked and the air between them practically sizzled. There was something here, she thought as her heart pounded and her mouth went dry. Something that was as exciting as it was dangerous. And she had zero business feeling this way about him. There was no way anything was going to happen between them.

He didn't trust her. He thought she was after his money. Well, to be honest, she was. At least what he was going to pay her for this job. And as far as Anna was concerned, Sam Hale was an overbearing, arrogant boob—except he apparently had unexpected depths.

With those thoughts ringing loudly in her head, she took a breath and shifted the subject to safer ground. "So, what exactly did you have in mind for your mural?"

"Business it is, then," he said, still studying her. "For now."

He walked to the small office area, separated from the garage by a half wall. There was a desk, two chairs, a single filing cabinet and a half-dead fern in a blue pot inside. The walls were white and blank. There was a skylight overhead, providing plenty of natural light, but there were no windows, which struck Anna as odd.

"I don't have a lot of windows in here," he said as if he knew exactly what she was thinking. "When I'm working on the cars, I like to keep the area as clean as possible. Don't want dust and dirt blowing in, but it gets claustrophobic in here after awhile."

"I can see why," she said, already studying the pristine white wall, letting her imagination kick in. "Can't you put in windows that don't open?"

He shook his head. "Dust can still get in with a loose seal or whatever. The skylights are double-sealed. Until I get down to serious work I can open the garage bay doors for air. But once the detail work starts, I'll be keeping the place shut up tight."

"Okay, do you want anything in particular?"

Another slow smile curved his mouth. "I can think of a couple of things."

"I'll bet," she said, taking a step back from him just for good measure. "But I was talking about the mural."

He shook his head. "I'll leave that to you. I just want to be able to look at something that makes me feel less closed in. Can you do it?"

"I can." She walked to her supplies and pulled out pencils, a yardstick and blue painter's tape.

"Do you need anything from me?"

"Just for you to go away," she said, knowing she'd

never be able to concentrate if he was in the room watching her.

"You got it." He started out of the office. "I'll be working in the garage. If you need anything, let me know."

"You're working *here?*"

He smiled again and Anna felt that rush of something hot and wicked sweep through her one more time. She hadn't counted on having him underfoot all day. She'd expected him to leave her alone. The claustrophobic feel of the massive garage instantly notched up a level or two.

"I can run my company from here with a laptop and a phone," he was saying. "So until you're finished, I'll be right here. Every minute."

"Great."

He grinned and she knew he was enjoying her discomfort. Deliberately, she turned her back on him and went to work. If she could keep busy enough, she told herself firmly, she'd forget he was near.

Sadly, even Anna didn't believe that.

SHE SANG when she worked.

Sam groaned and banged his head on the uplifted hood when he straightened abruptly. Rubbing the aching spot on his skull, he shot a glare toward the woman taking up far too many of his thoughts. He'd thought having her here would be a good idea. He could watch her. Find out who she really was.

Sam had thought about calling his brother to let him know that Anna actually *did* have a price. But he decided against it. He knew Garret was over her, but Sam didn't want hard feelings between him and his brother. If Garret brought up her name again, Sam was simply going to point out to his younger brother that Anna had said flat-out that even though she hated him personally, she was going to take his money.

Wouldn't that prove once and for all that the gorgeous Anna was as mercenary as she was beautiful?

Wouldn't that prove to his brother that Sam had been right all along?

Only problem?

Sam wanted her.

Bad.

When his cell phone rang, he lunged for it, eager for a distraction. "Hale."

"You sound like you want to hit somebody."

Sam scowled at his brother's cheerful tone. It was Garret's fault that Sam was, at the moment, tied into knots. "You volunteering?"

"Hell, no," Garret said, laughing. "Just wanted to tell you I'm leaving town for a while."

"What?" Irritated, Sam wondered when the hell his younger brother was going to grow up. "You can't leave town. You've got a job."

"Oh, that didn't work out," Garret dismissed it easily.

"Damn it, Garret—"

"I didn't call for a lecture," his brother interrupted. "I'm heading to Aspen for a few days. Just wanted you to know, is all."

"Great," he muttered. "Thanks."

Garret sighed, clearly as irritated as Sam felt. "I don't want to fight with you, Sam. I just need some time, okay? That job you got me at the advertising firm was making me nuts."

Sam thought about the favor he'd called in with a friend in San Jose and realized he'd have to make another call to his old friend. To apologize for his brother. "Garret, you said you wanted that job."

"It just wasn't me."

"What *is?*" Sam asked, unable to understand his younger brother's inability to find something he had a passion for. So far, all the younger Hale had been really good at was women and snowboarding. "What're you going to do for a living, Garret?"

His brother laughed shortly. "Don't worry," he said. "I'll think of something."

That was what worried him, Sam told himself silently.

"Look, I'll be back for Christmas. Promise."

"All right," Sam said, lifting his gaze toward the office where Anna's singing had quieted. "I'll see you when you get back."

Anna stepped out of the office. When he hung up, she asked, "Problem?"

"No," he said flatly. He wasn't going to discuss his brother with the very woman he'd forced Garret to stop dating. "How's it coming?"

She watched him for a second or two, then said, "Great. Want a look?"

He walked to the office, brushed past her and stared at the wall where blue painter's tape was applied in a series of arches and straight lines. Sam couldn't see where she was going with this, but she seemed happy enough with it. "That's good?"

"It is," she said, coming up beside him. "I'm almost ready to start laying down some background color along with the outside detail lines."

"What is it?" he asked, watching her face rather than trying to make sense of the taped wall.

She looked up at him. "A surprise."

She was too close and smelled too good. Her dark red hair pulled back in a ponytail at the base of her neck, her bright green eyes glittered with excitement. Her blue denim jeans and oversize blue work shirt over a paint-stained black T-shirt somehow looked…perfect.

Sam had never seen a more beautiful woman. He was in deep trouble here and he knew it.

He just didn't care.

Before he could think better of it, he reached out, took her arm and dragged her close.

"Sam…" Her voice was a whisper.

"Don't talk, Anna," he told her and slowly bent his head to hers. He had to see if everything he'd felt when he first kissed her was still there.

She lifted one hand to his chest and he could have sworn he felt the heat of her palm slide down inside him, easing away the chill. "This isn't a good idea," she told him.

"You're still talking," he said.

"Right," she agreed, lifting her face to his. "Shutting up now."

Then he took her mouth with his, felt the hard punch of desire and knew that Anna Cameron was going to be way more trouble than he'd first believed.

6
_____

THE NEXT FEW DAYS settled into a routine. Anna worked in the office, Sam worked on his cars and they met in the middle for lunch provided by his housekeeper. By silent agreement, neither of them referred to the blisteringly hot kiss they'd shared in his office.

But the memory was there. Haunting them. Keeping each of them so tightly wound that just being close to each other sent up sparks.

Anna didn't know what to do. She hadn't wanted or expected to like Sam, but he was getting to her. Slipping beneath her radar, worming his way into her thoughts. Heaven knew he had already breached her body's defenses. Anytime he came near, her heartbeat sped up and every square inch of her jolted into electric life.

But it wasn't just the desire, the passion; it was more. Over the last few days, they'd talked and even laughed. He'd told her about some of his more "eccentric" customers and she'd shared a few of the truly hideous murals some of her clients had asked for. She actually liked working in the office, listening to the sound of power tools as he refurbished one of his cars.

At the bottom of it, though, she had to keep in mind that he didn't trust her. He thought she'd been willing to seduce his brother to save her father's company and what did that say about him? But he'd also given her free rein to paint whatever she wanted in his office. That was trust of a sort, wasn't it?

Yet, she remembered all the things Garret had told her the night he broke things off with her. Along with the whole out-to-get-my-money speech, Sam had also told Garret that he considered artists to be flaky and emotionally unstable. So what was she supposed to make of that?

"None of this makes sense," she told herself, glad that the day was almost over. Sam had gone up to the main house half an hour ago and she'd heard Mrs. Soren leave shortly after. As soon as Anna finished this one section of the mural, she'd be leaving, too. Christmas was getting closer and she still had shopping to do. Besides, one of her own traditions was to wander through Crystal Bay at night to enjoy all of the Christmas decorations. She hadn't had a chance to do that yet and she figured tonight was as good a time as any.

She reached up and with her fingertips, quickly brushed the line of paint she'd just laid down, softening the edge and blending the paint into the other background colors so that it became a pale wash of blue and gray that would, eventually, be the sky in her mural. Stepping back, she nodded to herself, and wiped her fingers on the rag stuffed into her pocket. Then she stretched her aching shoulder muscles and swiveled her neck, trying to ease the tension there as well.

Satisfied she'd done all she could, she quickly cleaned her brushes and closed up her paints. The sudden roar of a powerful engine splintered the quiet and Anna stepped outside to follow the sound.

A cold wind slapped at her as she spotted Sam, astride a huge, gleaming black motorcycle. He grinned at her approach and revved the engine again, making the bike sound like a hungry lion.

He wore a battered, brown leather jacket and balanced two helmets and another leather jacket across his lap. He looked way too good, Anna thought, feeling that rush of heat swamp her again. There might as well have been a *Danger* sign flashing over his head. But she still couldn't seem to stop herself from walking toward him, like a moth headed directly for the tantalizing flame.

She shouted over the rumble of the engine, "What's going on?"

"We need a break," he said, his voice deep and loud enough to carry. "Put this on."

He held out the leather jacket and Anna knew she should say no and head back inside. Sunset was already staining the sky and she should be headed home. Back, she thought, to her empty apartment, a hot shower and a cold glass of wine. Then she looked into his blue eyes and knew that she wasn't going anywhere but with him.

She slipped the jacket on and zipped it up. Then she accepted the helmet he offered her and tugged it on as well. He grinned at her and her stomach did a slow bump and roll. He pulled on his helmet, flipped the visor down and indicated that she do the same. Then he shouted, "Hop on!"

Knowing it was most definitely a mistake, Anna did just that. She climbed aboard the motorcycle, her thighs spread wide, aligning along his. She leaned into him and he turned his head to say, "Wrap your arms around me and hold on, Anna."

"Where are we going?"

"It's a surprise," he called back.

He'd already surprised her, she thought, feeling the rumble of the engine rippling throughout her body. She'd never been on a motorcycle before and she had a feeling that this trip, wherever he was taking her, was going to be memorable. She wrapped her arms tightly around his middle and inhaled sharply as he roared down the length of the driveway and out onto the road.

SAM DROVE ALONG THE COAST road for miles, and Anna watched as night claimed the sky. Trees lined one side of the wildly twisted road and the ocean, dazzled by moonlight, lay on the other.

She'd never experienced such a thrilling sense of freedom before. Fear rode just below the surface of her excitement, but she refused to acknowledge it. Instead, she focused solely on the incredible sense of being as one with Sam and the machine carrying them both through the darkness.

He doubled back after a long while and she realized they were headed back to Crystal Bay. Disappointment rose up in her as she realized she wasn't ready for the ride to end. For the magic to be finished. Lifting one hand from the handlebars, Sam pointed into the distance and she shifted her gaze to follow the motion. Her breath caught as she saw the town of Crystal Bay, sitting on a crescent-shaped harbor, spreading back through the trees. In the surrounding darkness, the town's Christmas lights shone from a distance like jewels strewn across the ground. She smiled and felt a stirring of something magical rise up around her.

Soon, they were roaring down Main Street and Anna wondered if everyone they passed was speculating. Sam's motorcycle was well known and she was guessing that her long, red hair hanging out from beneath her helmet would be enough for most people to identify her. The question was, did she care?

No. At the moment, no, she didn't care. She loved the feel of being on the powerful Harley with Sam. It was a moment snatched out of time. They couldn't speak, so they couldn't argue. They were wrapped so tightly together, each of them could feel the heat of the other's body.

Her own heartbeat was hammering in her chest and she thought she felt a matching rhythm coming from Sam's body. Anna swallowed hard and rested her head against his broad back. Her grip on him tightened as the rumbling of the engine vibrated her body and jolted every already-sensitive nerve ending.

Christmas lights blurred into a stream of color as they whizzed past. Shoppers hurried along crowded sidewalks. Pine garlands were strung across the street from lamppost to lamppost. Carols pumped from one of the stores they passed and she smiled behind her helmet. The giant Christmas tree in the town square glittered, while overhead, stars slipped in and out from behind clouds.

She didn't know why he'd taken her on this ride, but she was so glad he had. Anna felt *alive* in a way she had never known before. She wanted this night to never end, but of course, it did.

He slowed the motorcycle down as they pulled into the driveway of his home. Light spilled from the windows onto the lawn in golden patches and Mrs. Soren's car was gone from its usual parking space.

They were alone and instantly, Anna felt tense. It had been so liberating, riding behind Sam, tearing along the coast. But now they were back and nothing had really changed between them. There was that amazing sense of chemistry that burst into life whenever they were together. But at the heart of things, they were on opposite sides of a figurative wall.

He hit a button on the handlebars and as one of the garage doors opened, he steered the bike inside. An overhead light came on with the opening of the door and when he shut off the engine, the silence was deafening.

Reluctantly, she released her death grip around his waist, ignoring the empty feel of her arms. She reached up to pull off her helmet and shook her hair back. Her voice was soft and nearly breathless as she said, "That was amazing, Sam. Thanks."

"You're welcome." He climbed off the bike, then took both helmets and set them on a nearby bench.

She was still sitting on the black leather seat, afraid to stand up for fear her legs wouldn't support her. The engine was off, but her body was still vibrating. In fact, it felt as though every cell she possessed was electrified. Her gaze locked with his and she took a long, slow breath.

In the pale light, his blue eyes looked gray and stormy. She was willing to bet that the same wild passions were shining in her own eyes.

"Sam—"

"Anna—"

They spoke together and then closed their mouths in sync. Anna was edgy and she knew it. There were too many thoughts running through her mind. Too many emotions clamoring to be noticed and acknowledged. Carefully, she swung her leg over the back of the bike and stepped down onto the gleaming garage floor.

She swallowed hard. "You know, maybe I should just go now."

"Don't."

Her gaze snapped to his. Every breath was a challenge. Her heartbeat was so frantic that she could hear the roaring pound of it in her own ears. A damp, hot ache settled between her thighs at the same time tension gathered in her chest. She wanted to whimper with the force of the want nearly choking her. But acting on what she—*they*—were feeling wouldn't solve anything. Wouldn't change anything. It would only make things worse.

"Sam, you know as well as I do that I should leave."

He shook his head. "I don't want you to and I don't think you do either."

"It's not about want." *Unfortunately,* she added silently.

"It's all about want," he answered, walking toward her with slow, deliberate steps.

Every step that brought him closer to her sounded like a gunshot in the quiet. Anna's pulse was racing and her breath was now chugging in and out of her lungs. When he was close enough to touch her, Anna instinctively leaned in toward him. Her better judgment was being tossed aside. While a still-rational corner of her mind warned her that she was making a mistake, a much more powerful voice within told her to take what he offered. She knew then she wouldn't be leaving. Not until the desperate ache inside had been eased.

He scooped both hands into her hair, cupping her head in his hands, then he drew her closer, lowered his head and kissed her. Anna was done for.

Plain and simple, Sam Hale swept all common sense right out of her mind. He silenced that warning shriek inside her and awakened the part of her that wanted. Needed.

She was blistered by the heat racing through her. She welcomed it, moved into him and wrapped her arms around him. Nestling as close to him as she could, Anna gave him everything she had.

Their tongues tangled in a fierce dance of desire. Breathing became secondary to the rising tide of passion erupting between them. Hands moved, explored, claimed. Bodies melded and whispered words of hunger rattled through the silence.

Finally, he tore his mouth from hers, stared down into her eyes and demanded, "Come with me."

She met his gaze, saw exactly what she needed to see and knew that denying him wasn't an option. Because she didn't want to leave. She wanted to feel as alive as she had on the back of that motorcycle—alone in the dark with *him*.

"Yes," she said softly. "Now."

Hand in hand, they raced across the yard, Sam's longer strides forcing Anna to run at his side. She laughed shortly, the sound escaping into the night and dissolving like soap bubbles.

He opened the back door, drew her inside and closed the door behind them. Swinging her up against him, he held her so tightly she could hardly breathe. Yet she didn't care. All she cared about was his mouth on hers, his hands stroking up and down her back in a proprietary manner that absolutely thrilled her.

"You taste so damn good," he murmured, breaking away to nibble at the base of her throat.

She sighed because she didn't need words to tell him what she was thinking, feeling. He just knew.

He slid his hands up under her shirt, skimming his fingertips across her skin until she was shivering in his arms. Then he smiled down at her and said, "Not in the kitchen, damn it. Upstairs. In my bed."

Here was her last chance, that tiny voice in the back of her mind whispered. Last chance to back out before she made what could be an incredible mistake. She stared up into those amazingly blue eyes of his and nodded. "Yes, Sam."

He grinned, swept her up into his arms and headed for the hallway.

"I can walk," she said on a laugh.

"Your legs are too short," he countered. "I'm faster."

"Good point." She snuggled into him, kissing his neck, the underside of his jaw. Her hands slid across his chest and she felt the pounding of his heart beneath her palms.

He took the stairs at a dead run and rushed her down a dimly lit hall so quickly that she noticed nothing. Then he was stalking into his bedroom and Anna took a quick look around.

Boldly masculine, the furniture was big, dark and heavy. Deep blue drapes were pulled back, allowing the moonlight to pour through the wide windows to lay across a bed big enough for four people to sleep comfortably.

But sleeping wasn't on her mind.

He set her on her feet and instantly reached to pull off his shirt. Anna watched and took a short, sharp breath at the first sight of his broad, bare chest. Muscular and tanned, he actually rippled when he moved and she wanted nothing more than to be held against that expanse of warm, golden skin.

In seconds, they were naked. Sam tugged the navy blue duvet off the mattress and then they were tumbling onto the cool, crisp sheets. He seemed to be touching her everywhere at once. Her body was humming with sensation and her mind fogged over as he dipped one hand to her core and cupped her heat.

"Sam…" She lifted her hips into his touch, seeking more, needing more.

He leaned on one elbow, looking down at her, watching her eyes as she twisted and writhed beneath his touch. She read a desperate craving in his eyes and that only served to inflame her own desires.

He dipped one finger into her warmth and she groaned, lifting into his touch. Her hands moved up and down his arms, nails scraping along his skin. His thumb caressed that one small nub of sensation until Anna felt as though she were about to splinter into a million jagged pieces.

Her breath was strangled as she fought to reach the pinnacle that was waiting for her. She needed it. Needed him. "Sam, please. Now. Inside me."

He dipped his head and took one of her nipples into his mouth, licking and nibbling, before suckling at her until she felt the draw of his mouth all the way to her toes. She grabbed at his shoulders, then stabbed her fingers through his thick, dark hair. Holding his head, she drew his gaze to hers and whispered, "I need you, Sam."

"I've got to have you, Anna. All of you." He shifted then, moving over to kneel between her parted thighs. Scooping his hands beneath her bottom, he lifted her off the mattress and as she fumbled for something to hold on to, he covered her aching heat with his mouth.

Anna hissed in a breath and closed her eyes only to open them again an instant later. She wanted to watch him. Wanted to see as well as feel what he was doing to her. His lips and tongue moved over her flesh with a deliberation that pushed her higher and higher. He tasted her, licked her and took her to the very peak of that release she knew was waiting for her.

Then he pulled back and left her dangling over the precipice.

"Sam!" She called his name in a broken voice and heard the desperate need in her tone. "Don't you dare stop now," she warned.

That smile of his curved his mouth as he shook his head. "Not stopping, Anna, just shifting gears."

He laid her down on the mattress, caught her gaze with his and entered her body in one long, smooth stroke. She gasped, arching into him. He filled her completely and as her body stretched to accommodate him, she lifted her hips into him to take him deeper.

"Easy…" He whispered it, the word almost strangled. "You start moving and this is going to be over way too fast."

She smiled up at him, and pulled his face to hers for a kiss. "I'll take my chances."

"My kind of woman." He kissed her back as his body moved into hers, setting a fast rhythm that she eagerly matched.

He pushed her higher and higher and Anna felt herself spinning completely out of control. She'd never known anything like this. This was so much more than she'd expected. So much more than anything she'd ever experienced.

It was magic, she thought wildly. The very magic she'd dreamed of finding one day. And it was more than the incredible chemistry they shared, Anna thought with a start. She was falling for Sam Hale—and there was no way that this would end in anything but misery.

Sam had already told his brother that she wasn't, in effect, "good enough" for him. So why would she be good enough for Sam himself?

Heart suddenly aching, she looked up into his eyes and was held, spellbound as she shattered. Her body clenched around his and she held him tightly to her as he followed her into the sensation-filled abyss.

7

"YOU SLEPT WITH HIM."

Anna hadn't expected the truth to be quite so obvious, but she shouldn't have been surprised. Tula had gotten home from visiting her cousin and had come straight over to talk, bringing a bottle of wine with her. Now that they had the wine poured and were settling in for a good talk, Tula had taken about five seconds to blurt out her suspicions.

Anna blinked at her friend but didn't bother to deny the obvious. "How could you tell?"

"You're practically radioactive you're glowing so brightly," Tula said as she plopped down on Anna's living room couch. "Man, go away for a few days and the whole world tips on its axis. I thought you hated Sam."

"I thought so, too," Anna muttered and dropped onto the other end of the sofa. Shoving both hands through her hair, she shook her head. "Honestly, I don't know how this happened. He made me so mad at first and then, we started talking and he's really funny and nicer than I thought and he kisses so well and before you know it, we were on his motorcycle looking at Christmas lights and then we were at his house and in his bed and *boom*."

Tula stared at her for a long moment before whispering, "Wow."

"Yeah, wow." Anna shifted her gaze to the Christmas tree, where a few packages lay in a bright carpet of color. Shaking her head, she idly said, "I don't know what I'm going to do."

"You're in love with him, aren't you?"

"I don't know—" She said it automatically, then stopped herself. "That's a lie. Yeah, I am. For all the good it'll do me."

"Oh, Anna, it could work out."

She smiled, in spite of the growing sense of dread inside. "I don't think so. He didn't think I was good enough for his brother, remember?"

Tula waved that off with a sniff. "Please, you were way too good for Garret."

Anna laughed. She'd always been able to count on her best friend. Still, she couldn't shake the feeling she'd had since leaving Sam's bed the night before. That she was on borrowed time and that she was feeling a lot more for him than he was for her. There was simply no way this was going to end well.

"Thanks for that," she said, reaching out to squeeze Tula's hand. "But I'm tired of thinking about me. Tell me why your cousin Sherry wanted to see you so badly."

Tula sighed and reached to the coffee table for her glass of white wine. "You're not going to believe this, but Sherry's pregnant."

"Really? Who's the father?"

"I don't know," Tula said and took a sip of her wine.

"She refused to tell me. But what's worse, she hasn't even told the guy he's going to be a father."

Anna couldn't imagine keeping something like that to herself. "Why would she do that?"

"I don't know." Tula frowned. "I told her that if the guy was worth sleeping with, he's worth telling him the truth, but she wouldn't listen."

"So why'd she want to see you?"

Tula leaned back into the couch. "She wanted to name me the legal guardian of the baby just in case something happens to her."

"But she hasn't even had it yet."

"You know Sherry. Afraid of everything. Although," Tula said, "she's not scared of raising a baby alone, which would absolutely terrify me."

"Did you agree to be the baby's guardian?"

"Sure I did," she said. "We're family."

"So," Anna told her, picking up her own wine, "we've each had a busy few days, huh?"

"Guess so," Tula agreed. "Though yours, I'm thinking, was way more fun."

THE NEXT FEW DAYS were a blur of stolen moments and passion hot enough to burn a man to a cinder. Sam dreamed of Anna at night and thought of nothing but her during the day. Every time he was with her, he wanted her more.

Scrubbing one hand across the back of his neck, he kicked the wall behind his desk and hardly felt the pain. He'd come into the office to avoid Anna at home. He couldn't see her without wanting his hands on her and he couldn't think when he was touching her.

How the hell could Sam lay claim to Anna when he

had practically forced his brother to walk away from her? Would his brother ever forgive him? Could he risk losing his only family on the chance that what he and Anna had was lasting?

"Mr. Hale?"

He looked up as his assistant opened the door. "What is it, Kathy?"

"A Mr. Cameron here to see you."

Shock had him speechless for a second or two, but he recovered quickly. "Send him in."

Sam stood up to greet Anna's father and the older man shook his hand with a wary look. Suddenly, Sam felt a little uneasy. After all, he was sleeping with the man's daughter. "Good to see you, Dave."

"Sam." The man glanced around the spacious office before settling his gaze on Sam's again. "I won't take up much of your time. Just thought we should have a little talk."

"About what?" Oh, he *knew* what.

"Anna."

"Ah."

"Crystal Bay's a small town," Dave was saying. "Secrets are impossible to keep. So I figure we both know what's going on."

"Meaning?" Sam asked, unwilling to give any information on the off chance that Dave was still in the dark.

The older man frowned at him. "*Meaning,* I know you've been seeing my daughter just as you know my company's in trouble."

"Dave…" What the hell was he supposed to say? He knew Dave Cameron was a proud man.

He lifted one hand in a bid for silence. "Whatever's between you and Anna is your business. You're both adults.

What I'm here to tell you is, contrary to what everyone in town is thinking, I won't use my daughter as a bargaining chip for business."

Scowling himself now, Sam took a deep breath. "And I wouldn't use her either."

Dave studied him for a long minute. "Then we understand each other?"

"I think so," Sam said, bristling a little under the man's close scrutiny.

"Fine, then. I'll wish you a good day and be on my way." Dave started for the door, then stopped and looked back. "One more thing. You hurt my little girl and we'll be having another talk."

The man was gone before Sam could respond. But then, what could he possibly have said? He felt like a damn teenager after a dressing-down. The hell of it was, he had the feeling he'd deserved it.

CHRISTMAS WAS JUST a few days away when Anna finally finished the mural in Sam's home office. She could admit to herself that when she'd begun this job, she'd actually considered giving him some ghastly painting. A horrific view out an artificial window. But that idea hadn't lasted more than a moment or two. Her own professionalism prevented her doing anything less than her absolute best.

And now that she stood back to get the full effect of her work, she had to admit that she'd really outdone herself this time.

She was glad of it, too. Now every time Sam looked at this wall, he would think of her. It was the perfect goodbye. Because she'd come to the conclusion only the night before that what was between them had to end. There was no future in it. And she was only hurting herself. Falling for Sam Hale had been inevitable. But she wouldn't stay with him, knowing what she did about how he really felt about her.

Sex between them was incredible. She knew he felt the same way. But desire was a long way from any kind of *real* feeling. She'd been deluding herself into thinking that something could come of this, when the truth was, he would never allow himself to care for her because when it came right down to it, he didn't trust her.

Well, she couldn't keep fooling herself. It was better to get out now, while the pain was still livable. If she waited any longer, she knew the loss of him would kill her.

Pasting a bright smile on her face, she closed up the last of her paint jars, tucked them away in the carrier, then took a breath. Steadied as much as she was going to be, she opened the office door and called out, "Sam? I'm finished. You can see it now."

He looked up from the car he was bent over and smiled at her. Anna's heart jolted and she knew she would miss that smile of his.

"The big secret revealed, huh?" He wiped his hands on a towel, tossed it across the car fender and headed her way. "Can't wait."

She stepped back so he could enter and shifted her gaze to his face as he saw the finished painting for the first time. His eyes widened and his jaw dropped. He couldn't have had a more perfect reaction.

"That's incredible," he said, walking closer to it.

"The ocean's still wet, so don't touch," she warned.

"The ocean's always wet, babe."

"Very funny."

Still shaking his head, he leaned in closer to the wall.

"That's really amazing, Anna." He shot her a look over his shoulder. "I'm impressed."

"Thanks."

It had turned out well, she thought, studying her own work objectively. A gracefully arched window, shadowed from an unseen sun, opened up to a seascape that looked as vivid as life. Blue-gray sky, storm clouds on the horizon. Waves crashing against rocks, sending spray so high that it dotted the painted-on glass of the open window. A tumble of flowers and vines spread across the window sill, dripping color and motion onto a still life that made it seem all the more alive and real.

"What's this?"

"Hmm?" She glanced to where he was pointing. With a shrug and a smile, she admitted, "I was a little angry with you when I painted that part."

"Yeah, I can see that."

He grinned anyway, though, so Anna was glad she'd left in the snake with Sam Hale's features peeping out from the vines on the windowsill.

"You," he said as he walked toward her with a familiar glint in his eyes, "are a very talented woman."

"Thank you," she answered, her voice hardly more than a whisper.

He pulled her into his arms, dipped his head to kiss her and then seemed to notice her hesitation. "What is it?"

She should tell him now, Anna thought. Tell him that whatever was between them was over. But damn it, she wanted one more time in his arms. One more glimpse of the magic before she turned her back on it forever.

"Nothing," she said and reached up to wrap her arms around his neck. "It's nothing."

Then he kissed her and she forgot everything but what he made her feel.

HER BODY BLISSFULLY humming with remnants of pleasure, Anna turned her head on the pillow and looked at
the man beside her. How had she come to feel so much for
him in such a short amount of time? And did that really
matter? The simple truth was, she loved him and every
moment she spent with him was only setting herself up
for disaster and pain.

She had to end this while she still could.

"Sam," she said abruptly into the quiet, "this isn't
going to work out."

He grinned, rolled to his side and slid one hand down
the length of her naked body, making her shiver even as
new fires erupted inside.

"Seems to be working just fine."

"No," she insisted, rolling out from under his touch. If
she didn't say something now, she never would. Scram-
bling off the bed, she stood up and reached for her clothes.
"It's really not."

"What are you talking about?"

She had his attention now, she thought, looking down
into beautiful blue eyes that were narrowed in suspicion.

"Just that we can't do this anymore," she blurted.

"Why the hell not?"

She tugged her shirt over her head and shook back her
hair. "I can't keep being with you when I know exactly
what you really think of me."

He pushed off the bed and stood naked, facing her.
He was amazing-looking and Anna had to fight hard
not to be distracted. "What? What do you mean what I
think of you?"

This was harder than she had expected it to be, but
Anna kept going. She told herself that pain now would

save her misery later, so it was best to just get this done so they could both move on with their lives.

"I *mean*," she told him, "Garret told me exactly what you said about me. Not only do you think I'm after him for money, but that you consider me flaky and immature and—why are you *laughing?*"

He shook his head, grabbed up his jeans and tugged them on. "Because this is so stupid."

"Oh, thanks very much."

"I didn't say *you* were stupid," he muttered, then spoke up more loudly. "Why is arguing with women so frustrating? The flaky and immature thing? That's not what I think of you. It's what I think of Garret. He refuses to grow up and I'm starting to wonder if he's even capable of it."

Only slightly mollified, Anna said, "But you did think I was after your money."

He didn't deny it. What would be the point? They both knew the truth. After a second or two, he said, "Okay, yeah. I did. Why the hell else would a woman like you be dating Garret?"

"You really believe I could do something like that? Use someone? Barter myself?"

He scowled and folded his arms over the chest she'd been draped across only moments ago. "I don't have to remind you that your father's company is failing—or that I've got more than enough money to save it."

"No," she assured him haughtily, "you really don't."

"Stop being so damn insulted. You wouldn't have been the first woman to use sex to get what you wanted."

She fisted her hands at her hips. "And is that what I'm doing now? With you?"

He glared at her. "How the hell am I supposed to know? You tell me."

Stung to the heart of her, Anna's unshed tears nearly blinded her. She stepped into her shoes and lifted her chin to match him glare for glare. "If you really do think so little of me, then I was wrong about you from the beginning."

He didn't say a word, just stood there, watching her. With every pulse beat, another tiny piece of Anna's heart broke away and shattered. Gathering up what dignity she had left, she said quietly, "I never want to see you again. You can mail me a check for my work."

"Fine," he answered quietly.

Before she left, she took one last jab. "When you're in your office, I hope you look at the snake often and remember why it has your features."

8

CHRISTMAS DAY was just awful.

The Cameron family holiday breakfast was strained as Anna watched her father strive to remain cheerful despite the deepening worry lines at the corners of his eyes. Clarissa made a big show of a supposed "cold" that kept her constantly sniffing and wiping her eyes with her handkerchief.

And Anna missed Sam desperately.

She hadn't spoken to him in days, which only told her that she'd made the right decision. Sam had no doubt realized that they were better off apart. Truth didn't make the pain any easier to live with, though.

Yet, watching her father go through the motions on a holiday he loved was unsettling. She was worried enough about him that her own pain was taking a backseat.

After an exchange of presents, Anna joined her father in his study for a cup of coffee. Clarissa excused herself to take some cold medication.

"Dad," Anna said, sitting beside him on the brown leather sofa, "is it really so bad?"

Her father frowned and Anna knew she was crossing

into unexplored territory. Ordinarily, her dad preferred that she and Clarissa be happy and completely ignorant of his business dealings. But after a moment or two, he gave a resigned sigh.

Patting her hand, he admitted, "It's not looking good right now, honey."

"Is there anything I can do?"

"I don't want you worried about this, understand?" He gave her tight smile. "Things will work out as they're supposed to. I'm sure the new year will bring plenty of opportunities."

Her heart already aching from the loss of Sam, Anna felt another wrench. Her father had worked hard his entire life to build a company he was proud of. Was he really going to lose it? And if he did, what would it do to him?

"No sad faces," he chided, leaning in to kiss her forehead. "We've got some Christmas cakes to eat, re-member?"

Another family tradition. Decadent cupcakes covered in Christmassy icing were always eaten after breakfast in the Cameron house. She watched her father fight past his own disappointments and worries and knew she could do no less.

"Yes, we do, Dad. Want me to go get them from the kitchen?"

"Please. Take them into the living room by the tree." He stood up, still smiling tightly. "I'll just give Clarissa a hand finding her cold medication and we'll join you."

"Okay." There was a knot in her throat but she wouldn't let her father down. If he wanted to have a normal Christmas morning, then that's exactly what they would do. As he started walking away, though, she said, "I love you, Dad."

His smile was warm and real as he answered, "I love you, too, Anna. Now don't worry, all right?"

She nodded, though her concerns were still there. But she wouldn't contribute to her father's worries, so she silently vowed to keep her anxiety well-hidden.

"HAVE YOU HEARD FROM HIM?" Tula asked later that night over a Christmas dinner of takeout tacos.

Because Tula had no family, the two of them always had Christmas dinner together—with only one rule. Nobody cooked. So every year, they looked around for any restaurant that happened to be open. This year, it was Garcia's Familia. The food was terrific, but Anna wasn't enjoying it anyway.

Hard to eat when it felt as though there was a ball of lead in the pit of your stomach.

"Sam?" Anna shook her head and took a sip of wine. She pushed the tines of her fork through the Mexican rice as if drawing a picture. "No. And it's better that way. Really."

"Yeah," Tula told her. "I can see that. This is working out great for you."

Sighing, Anna set her plate on the coffee table and sat back on her couch. Her gaze fixed blankly on the brightly lit Christmas tree, she wondered what Sam was doing. If he missed her as much as she missed him. And she wondered how he had become so important to her in such a short length of time.

"Anna, you're miserable. Why don't you call him?"

She glanced at her friend and ruefully shook her head. "What would be the point? Nothing's changed. Even if it's not a conscious notion, he still thinks I'm after him for his money."

"That's crazy," Tula said with a snort of derision. Picking up her wine, she took a drink and said, "You had a fight. People always say things they don't mean in a fight."

"Or the truth comes out," Anna suggested. She'd already had this same conversation with herself a dozen times. She'd thought about that last fight from every angle and each time she came to one conclusion. "Either way, it's just over."

The phone rang, but she didn't move to pick it up. She didn't feel like talking to anyone anyway. Her heart hurt, not just for what she'd lost in Sam, but for her father. And there was nothing she could do about either situation.

"You're not going to get that?" Tula asked.

She shook her head. "Let the machine pick it up."

Which it did a moment later. She listened to her outgoing message and then her heart jolted at the sound of Sam's voice.

"Anna?" His deep voice sounded commanding. "If you're there, pick up."

Tula waved at her frantically, but Anna shook her head again. She had to curl her fingers into fists to keep from reaching for the stupid phone, but she did it. She couldn't talk to him. Not now. Maybe not ever again. It was hard, but it would be even more difficult if she didn't stay strong.

Sam sighed into the phone, then said, "Listen, I, uh, wanted to say merry Christmas—"

Anna's heart tugged a little at that and the twisting pain made her close her eyes. If things had been different, Sam might have been here right now, with her and Tula, having dinner and laughing. But things weren't different and they weren't going to be.

"Talk to me, Anna. Don't let it end like this."

"Oh, God," she whispered.

When she still didn't pick up, he muttered something unintelligible and hung up.

"Yeah," Tula said, every word coated in sarcasm, "I can see why you don't want to talk to *him*. Sounds like a heartless bastard."

"You're not helping," Anna told her.

"This time," her friend said sagely, "I think you're going to have to help yourself."

SAM GLARED at the damn phone as if Anna not speaking to him were its fault instead of his own.

"*Idiot,*" he muttered thickly, shoving one hand through his hair. He'd done nothing but think about Anna for the last few days. Their last argument was on constant replay in his thoughts. And every time he relived it, he saw the shock on her face and the hurt in her eyes. He still wasn't sure how the damn argument had erupted and he'd like nothing better than to step back in time and bite back the words that had hurt her so badly.

Why the hell had he said something so stupid? He knew damn well that she wasn't after his money. He had been convinced of that as soon as he saw how much time and effort and artistry she'd poured into the mural she had painted for him. No mercenary woman would have cared so much about doing a good job. She would have come in, slapped some color on a wall and cashed his check.

But Anna had pride. Integrity.

And *his* heart, damn it.

He poured a Scotch and took a seat on the sofa. The Christmas tree was lit up and soft jazz pumped through the stereo. It would have been perfect, he thought. If Anna were there.

Instead, there was a hollow spot in his chest that he couldn't see being filled anytime soon. God, if he had to live the rest of his life with this emptiness inside…

"Sitting alone in the dark?" Garret said when he came into the room. "Not a good sign, Sam."

"It's not dark," he protested lamely. "The tree lights are on."

"Yeah." Garret grabbed a beer from the wet bar, then sat down in a chair close to his brother. He took a long drink and said, "So, you want to tell me what's eating you?"

"What?" Sam shot his brother a look.

"I was gone like a week or so, not years. You're…" he tipped his head to one side and studied Sam "…different, somehow. Still mean as hell, of course, but there's something else, too."

This was a rare moment, Sam thought. His younger brother was noticing something outside himself. And maybe it was a sign that the younger Hale brother was finally taking a step toward maturity. God, he hoped so. Because Sam knew what he had to do.

He'd missed Anna like he would have an arm or a leg. Somehow, in the last couple of weeks, she had become as necessary to him as breathing. And he couldn't live without her. So he had to tell his brother that not only wasn't Garret going to get Anna back, but also that Sam was in love with her himself.

Love.

Wasn't the first time he'd thought that word over the last few days. But it was the first time he'd welcomed it. And admitting the truth, if only to himself, made him feel…good. He looked at his brother and knew that what he was about to say could cost him the relationship. But he had no choice. He had to try to make things right with Anna.

"Actually," Sam said, setting his glass of Scotch aside. He sat up, and braced his forearms on his thighs. Looking directly into his brother's eyes he said, "There is something else."

Garret paled at the suddenly serious tone. "Are you okay? You're not sick are you?"

"No." Sam laughed shortly and realized it was the first time he'd even smiled since losing Anna. That thought steeled him for what came next. "Nothing like that. But you remember when I told you to break up with Anna Cameron?"

Garret rolled his eyes. "You mean when you ordered me to stop seeing the man-hunting gold digger? Yeah, Sam. I remember."

Sam bristled, hearing his own words tossed at him. God, he'd been an idiot. "She's not, you know. A gold digger."

One of Garret's eyebrows lifted and he took a swig of his beer. "Interesting. I seem to recall trying to convince you of that."

"Yeah, well. Things have changed."

"I'm getting that. So let's hear it." He sat back, kicked his legs out in front of him and crossed his feet.

Sam couldn't sit still. He jumped up and paced to the wide front window where the Christmas tree lights were reflected on the glass. Staring out at the night, he started talking.

"I was going to get her back for you," he admitted.

"What?" Garret jolted upright. "Just a minute—"

"*Was*," Sam repeated, turning now to look at his brother. "Look, I didn't mean for this to happen, to go around you like this, but the truth is, I'm in love with Anna."

He waited, letting his words sink in. Watching his brother's face, Sam didn't miss the wide smile or the relieved sigh.

"Thank God."

"Excuse me?" Sam said.

"I don't want Anna back, Sam." Garret blew out a breath.

Now Sam was confused. He'd thought his brother had real feelings for Anna. "But I thought—"

"Is this what's been bugging you since I got home?" Garret asked, standing up to walk to his brother's side.

"Well, yeah." Sam hadn't expected their little chat to go so well and damned if he could figure out why it was. But he was grateful, as well as surprised.

"Then relax, brother," Garret said and clapped him on the shoulder. "I'm *entirely* over Anna. I mean, I knew she wasn't after the family money, but she wasn't for me anyway. That's the only reason I went along with you telling me what to do. I mean, come on, what am I? Twelve?"

Sam scowled at him, but realized he should have considered that before. Garret never had done anything he didn't want to.

"I'm glad for you, Sam. You're a way better fit with her than I ever could have been. She's nice and everything, but she's too traditional for me."

"Traditional." Sam laughed, still stunned by his brother's reaction. "And you told her I thought she was flaky and immature."

Garret laughed, too, then shrugged. "Well, I wasn't going to tell her that you had called *me* that."

Sam looked at his younger brother and felt a rush of love for him. Didn't matter if Garret hadn't found his way yet, Sam was suddenly sure that he would. Now all that was left was for Sam himself to find a way back to Anna.

"Is it just me?" Garret wondered aloud. "I thought love was supposed to make you feel good and you still look crappy. What's going on?"

He scrubbed one hand across the back of his neck and stared out at the night again. "Anna's not real happy with me right now."

"Ah, that explains it."

Sam shot a look at his brother. "What?"

Garret grinned. "Why the snake Anna painted on your wall has *your* face."

"Yeah, that's a long story."

"Why don't you tell me about it?" Garret said. "We'll have another drink. And then I'll tell you all about the professional snowboarder I met in Aspen."

Sam shook his head and smiled. "What's her name?"

Garret winked. "Shania. She's gorgeous. And amazing—brilliant, talented. She's really something special. And in two days, we're flying to Geneva for a couple of weeks to do some serious boarding."

Sam pulled his brother in for a brief, hard hug, then let him go again. "I'm not gonna worry about you anymore, Garret," he said with a smile. "I think you're going to do just fine."

Garret's features sobered and he nodded as if accepting an award. "Thanks for that, Sam," he said. "I really will be all right, you know. So now that I'm off your worry

list, why don't you tell me all about Anna and we can figure out a way to get her back in your life?"

"I'll tell you," Sam said, draping one arm over his
brother's shoulders to steer him over to the chairs. "Then
you can tell me all about Shania. As for me, I'm doing
whatever I have to to get Anna back."

9

CHRISTMAS WAS OVER and New Year's Eve was just a day away. Anna had buried herself in work, wishing away the holidays, wanting to get lost in the dark, gray days of January. A storm was settling in over Crystal Bay and the cold damp suited Anna's mood perfectly.

Maybe her father was right. Maybe the new year would be filled with lots of opportunities. But at the very least, time would be passing. And the more time passed, the easier it would become to get over Sam.

At least, that's what Anna fervently hoped.

"For now, though," she told herself firmly, "I'm going to concentrate on work and try to put everything else out of my mind."

Sounded good in theory, but Sam's image would never completely leave her thoughts. He was with her, sleeping and waking. He was always there, just behind the mental door she tried repeatedly to close.

"How's it coming, Anna?"

"What?" She jolted and her grip on the paintbrush in her hand tightened. Whipping around, she looked at Mateo Corzino as he walked toward her. The owner of

Corzino's, home of the best lasagna on the California coast, Mateo had hired her to do a mural on the wall of his restaurant.

It was a big job that could keep her busy for a couple of weeks. He wanted a view of a Sicilian harbor, fishing boats tied up at a dock, complete with cliffs and sand-colored buildings in the background. And he wanted it to look as though the view was seen through a crumbling wall. She was eager to dig in, loving the challenge and a crumbling wall was one of her favorite effects. If only she could fully concentrate instead of having her heart and mind torn in two.

"Jeez," he said with a grin, "didn't mean to scare you."

"Sorry." She shook her head and laughed a little. "I guess I was just thinking so hard I didn't hear you come up."

He glanced at the wall where she'd just begun laying down the dark brown tracer lines that would eventually look like cracks in old plaster.

"It already looks real," he said, a touch of awe in his voice. "I don't know how you do it."

Pleased, Anna smiled and wiped her fingers on a paint rag. "Well, I don't know how you make that amazing sauce of yours either, so we're even."

"Speaking of that, I'd better get back to the kitchen. My wife's minding the stove *and* the baby." He looked at the wall again and nodded in appreciation. "You need anything, you give a shout. The restaurant won't be open until dinner, so no one will bother you."

"Thanks, Mateo," she said, but he was already gone, hurrying back to his family. She heard a deep baby giggle coming from the kitchen and then Mateo's wife laughed along.

Anna sighed and turned back to her paints. Emptiness filled her as she reached up to paint another jagged line on the wall. As she did, she felt as though she were capturing in paint the cracks in her own broken heart.

She worked for another hour or two uninterrupted. Then she heard a frantic knocking on the glass door behind her. Anna ignored it, figuring that Mateo would be rushing out to take care of an overeager customer. But when the knocking continued, Anna sighed, and stepped out from behind a tall, potted ficus tree.

Clarissa was standing outside the restaurant, leaning up against the glass, shading her eyes so that she could look inside. A second later, that frantic knocking started up again.

Mateo finally headed out of the kitchen and Anna stopped him. "I'll take care of it, Mateo. Sorry."

"Oh, sure," he said, recognizing Anna's stepmother. "No problem."

Anna hurried to the door, turned the lock and opened it. "Clarissa, what is it? What's happened?" Then she saw her stepmother's eyes were red and swollen, tears streaming down her face. Grabbing hold of the woman, Anna demanded, "Is it Dad? Is he okay?"

Clarissa nodded, gulped audibly and lunged for her. Hugging Anna tightly, she tried to talk around her own tears, but the words were garbled.

Relieved that her father was all right, Anna patted the woman's back until she calmed down, then pulled away and said, "What's going on, Clarissa? Why are you crying?"

"Oh," the woman said, rummaging in her black bag for a handkerchief, "it's just so wonderful…"

Anna's heart picked up a normal rhythm. Not bad

news, then. She waited impatiently for her stepmother to wipe her eyes and blow her nose. Then, at last, Clarissa spoke again.

"I had to find you, Anna," she said. "Tell you right away. I know how worried you've been for your father and you just had to know the good news."

Patience, Anna reminded herself, though the opposite feeling was pumping through her fast and hard. You needed patience with Clarissa.

"If it's good news," Anna said softly, steering Clarissa to a chair, "then I definitely want to hear it."

But Clarissa didn't want to sit down. She stopped suddenly, gave Anna another hard, tight hug and stepped back, giving her a brilliant smile. "Thank you, Anna. I don't know how you did it, but thank you."

"I don't understand," she said, feeling that hard-won patience begin to dissolve. "What are you thanking me for?"

Clarissa's eyes widened and her smile got even brighter.

"You don't know? I can't believe you don't know," she said. "I thought for sure you were behind this somehow, but now…"

Anna took a breath and blew it out again. "Honestly, Clarissa, I do love you, but if you don't tell me what's going on soon—"

"Of course, of course." Clarissa grabbed hold of Anna's paint-stained hands and said, "It's Sam Hale. He contacted your father yesterday…Hale Luxury Autos has signed an exclusive contract with Cameron Leather." Her tears started again in earnest, but her brilliant smile never wavered. "Your father's company is safe, Anna. He's so relieved. So happy. I thought you had talked to Sam about this. Somehow arranged it all and I had to come and thank you for whatever you'd done."

"Sam called Dad?" she echoed, her heart jumping into an accelerated beat. She hadn't talked to Sam in days, but he'd called her father. Done this to help her father.

Hope leaped to life in her chest and she silently prayed that this meant what she thought it might. Dazzled, confused, Anna realized that Clarissa was talking again and forced herself to pay attention.

"He did. They met this morning with Sam's and your father's lawyers and settled it all in an hour. Everything's taken care of and, oh, Anna, it's so wonderful to see your father really happy again." Clarissa reached out and hugged Anna tightly before letting her go. "It's as if a boulder had been rolled off his shoulders."

"Why would Sam do this?" Anna wondered aloud, not really expecting an answer. Was it possible that he did feel more for her than want?

"I don't know, dear," Clarissa said softly. "I thought he'd done it for you."

Why would he, though? she asked herself. Why, when she'd broken it off with him, refused to take his calls? Why would he do something so wonderful?

Anna tore off the oversize apron she normally wore when she was working. Bunching it together, she passed it off to Clarissa and said, "I have to go. Will you tell Mateo I'll be back?"

"Going to Sam?" Clarissa asked softly.

"Yes," she said, frantic now to see him. She had to know why he'd done this. Had to know if he felt even half as much for her as she did for him.

"Good for you, honey," her stepmother told her, reaching out to pat her cheek. "You go on. I'll tell Mateo. But come to the house for dinner tonight, all right? I know your father will want to share this with you. We can celebrate."

"I will, Clarissa," Anna said and impulsively kissed the woman's cheek.

Hopefully, she thought as she ran out the door, there would be a *lot* to celebrate.

10

SAM CURSED as he jammed his thumb on the undercarriage of the Bentley. Should have known better than to be out here working, he told himself as his thumb throbbed in time to his heartbeat. His mind wasn't on the work and that was a recipe for danger.

But as he'd given his staff two weeks off, he hadn't been able to face going into an empty building. Instead, he turned and went into the small office off the garage. He stood in the doorway, staring at the painting Anna had completed what now seemed like a lifetime ago.

The illusion of the ocean view was so clear, so real, he half expected to feel a breeze sliding through that painted-on window. Then his gaze dropped to the hidden snake peeking out of the flower vine. He scowled as he realized that he'd deserved to have her immortalize him like that. Damn it, he cared for her and he hadn't told her. He'd let his own suspicions drive her away when all he really wanted was her. Here. Now.

"This isn't helping," he muttered, trying to find something to do. Something to occupy his mind so it wouldn't automatically turn to—

"I thought I'd find you here."

He went still as a post. Her voice came from behind him and he'd hungered to hear it for so many days, he wanted to just take a second to enjoy it. But when she didn't speak again, he turned around to face her.

Her long, auburn hair was pulled into a ponytail and she was wearing paint-stained jeans and a black sweatshirt, also decorated with splotches of paint. Her eyes were locked on his and Sam thought he'd never seen anything more beautiful.

Behind her, he could see that the promised rain had finally arrived. The sky was gray and trees were bending in the wet wind.

"I went to your office first," she said.

He just looked at her. He couldn't seem to get his fill. "I closed it until after the holidays."

"Yeah, I saw the sign." She walked closer, the heels of her boots tapping in tandem with the rain.

It took everything Sam had not to go to her, wrap his arms around her and hold on. He wanted her with an ache that had only gotten more overpowering over the last few days. And he knew unless he had her in his life, he was doomed to misery.

"You've got paint on your cheek," he said.

She shrugged. "I'm working at Corzino's."

He nodded and wondered why they were suddenly being so damn polite.

"I know what you did," she said and walked close enough that he could smell her. The scent of her shampoo mingled with the sharp scent of paint and he almost smiled. Because to him, that was the essence of Anna.

"And?" he asked, staring down into her emerald green eyes.

"And, I want to know why," she told him softly.

"You know why," he admitted, his blood stirring, his body quickening. She was so close and he'd missed her so much.

After his meeting with Dave Cameron, he'd known that he'd have to face Anna. But he hadn't been sure what her reaction would be. Hell, she was a hard woman to predict, which was only one of the reasons he was crazy about her.

She watched him through guarded eyes. "I hope I do. Why don't you tell me?"

Grumbling now, he admitted, "I did it because I love you, okay? You wouldn't answer the damn phone and I knew you wouldn't see me. So this was the only way I had to tell you."

"Sam…"

"It's not the only reason," he told her, talking fast now that he had her here and it was so important to make her see what he was feeling. "Your dad's a good man and it's a good business decision for both of us, but you're the main reason I did it, Anna. I did it because of you. *For* you."

When she didn't say anything, he added, "I don't expect anything from you. You don't have to do anything. Hell, I don't even expect you to believe that I love you, but I do."

She still wasn't talking, and Sam suddenly couldn't stand still under her gaze. He grabbed her, giving into the instinctive urge clawing at him. He pulled her close, stared down into those green eyes of hers and said, "I'd do anything for you, Anna."

He loved her.

Anna sighed, grinned up at him and threw her arms

around his neck, holding on for all she was worth. "Oh, Sam, I love you, too. I love you so much."

"God." He buried his face in the curve of her neck and swept his big hands up and down her spine, as if reassuring him that she was once again in his arms.

He kissed her, long and deep, and Anna felt her world right itself again. Fires burned inside her and she knew that with him in her life, she would never again be cold.

"You could have said something," he accused, when he finally broke the kiss long enough to look down at her. "Did you have to let me keep babbling?"

She grinned and leaned into him, arching her body into his. "Sorry. But after you said you loved me, I sort of zoned out."

"Is that right?" His voice was low and almost seemed to rumble along her nerve endings.

"Yeah, it is. I do love you, Sam," she said, staring into his eyes and letting him see everything she was feeling. "And what you did for my dad—you didn't have to."

"I know that," he said, and bent to kiss her again. Once. Twice. "I wanted to do it, not because I had to but because I knew it would make you happy."

"You make me happy, Sam. Just you."

"I'm making that my mission in life," he told her. "Because I never want to be without you again, Anna."

"Never," she whispered and sighed as he kissed her again and again.

At last, though, he pulled back and pointed at the mural. "This is the first time I've come in here since you left," he admitted. "I couldn't look at that painting without thinking of you. Couldn't look at that snake without remembering that I'd let you go."

She laid her head on his broad chest and smiled at the

steady beat of his heart. "I'll paint over that snake," she promised.

"No," he told her. "Leave it. It's a good reminder to me."

"Of what?"

"Everytime I see it, I'll remember how close I came to losing you, and that'll make me appreciate what we've got together even more."

Tears filled her eyes as she smiled at him. "Tell me what we've got, Sam."

"Everything, Anna," he said. "Marry me and we'll have everything."

"Yes." She didn't have to think about it. Didn't have to wonder. Didn't have to ask herself if she was sure. It didn't matter if she'd met him two weeks ago or two years ago. This was the one man for her. The man she would love for the rest of her life. "Yes, I'll marry you."

One corner of his mouth tipped into that delicious half smile she loved so much. "Just what I wanted to hear."

His hands swept under the hem of her sweatshirt to cup her breasts and she groaned at the contact. He tweaked her nipples through the lace of her bra and Anna sighed in pleasure.

"I know a great way to spend a rainy day," he said.

She sighed, and almost surrendered before she remembered, "Oh, I can't! I have to work. I told Mateo and—"

Sam kissed her again until she couldn't think, let alone speak. When he lifted his head, he smiled down at her. "It's okay," he said. "We've got tonight to celebrate."

She winced and groaned aloud as she remembered she'd already made a promise to her stepmother. "I promised Clarissa I'd go to the house for dinner. To celebrate.

You have to come, too, so we can tell them our news together."

He laughed and rested his forehead against hers. "Dinner with the family. Agreed. And I should probably have a talk with your dad about us anyway. But *after,* it's just you and me."

"Absolutely." She couldn't wait to get him alone. To feel his body sliding into hers. To hear him say he loved her again and to know that she would be with him forever.

"Since we missed our first Christmas together," Sam was saying, "we've got some catching up to do."

"What did you have in mind?" she asked a little breathlessly.

"Well," Sam said, "I'm thinking we'll have some wine, sit in front of the Christmas tree and open our presents."

"Presents?" she asked, confused.

He dropped his fingers to the snap of her jeans and flicked it open. Anna gasped as he undid her zipper and slid one hand across her abdomen. Then she understood.

"Ah. *Open* our presents," she said, moving into his touch. "Yep, that's a great idea. We could even call it our first tradition."

"You really are my kind of woman," he mused, zipping up her jeans and snapping them closed again.

"And don't you forget it," Anna told him, her insides melting at the wild, wicked look in his eyes.

"Not a chance, babe." Taking her hand in his, he kissed her knuckles, then said, "Come on, I'll drive you to Mateo's. I don't want you taking chances in this rain."

Anna hugged him and whispered, "Rain? What rain? All I can see is sunshine and rainbows."

While the rain pelted down from a steel-gray sky,

inside the garage there was warmth and love and the promise of tomorrow.

Sam held on to her for another long minute, giving each of them a chance to settle. To relish the realization that they were together now and everything was going to be just as it should be.

"Happy New Year, Anna."

"Happy New Year, Sam."

* * * * *

MISTLETOE MAGIC

SANDRA HYATT

After completing a business degree, travelling and then settling into a career in marketing, **Sandra Hyatt** was relieved to experience one of life's *eureka!* moments while on maternity leave—she discovered that writing books, although a lot slower, was just as much fun as reading them.

She knows life doesn't always hand out happy endings and figures that's why books ought to. She loves being along for the journey with her characters as they work around, over and through the obstacles standing in their way.

Sandra has lived in both the US and England and currently lives near the coast in New Zealand with her school sweetheart and their two children.

You can visit her at www.sandrahyatt.com.

1

THE BABBLE of chatter and laughter ceased.

The only sounds left in the sudden hush of the living room were the rich baritone of Bing Crosby crooning "I'll Be Home for Christmas," and the crackle of the fire in the stone fireplace.

Perplexed, Meg Elliot turned, careful not to spill the pyramid of Christmas tarts from the silver tray in her hands.

And came face-to-face with a stranger.

Face-to-chest, actually. She had to look up from the navy polo shirt stretched across his shoulders to see his face. Dark, wavy hair, in need of a cut, brushed his forehead. He was clean-shaven and tanned. Too tanned for this time of year at Lake Tahoe, and not a skier's tan. But it was the silver eyes boring into her with unreadable intent that stilled her.

She knew those eyes.

But she didn't know this man.

She'd met so many people in the last few months, it was no surprise that she might forget a face. Except for the fact that this man was not the forgettable type—imposing, disconcerting and way too handsome.

How had he even gotten in? Caesar, guard dog extraordinaire, invariably created an unholy ruckus when anyone, even her friends, approached the house. It had taken him all of the three months she'd lived here to get used to her. And the stranger standing in front of her, silent and watchful, most definitely did not fall into the category of friend. He dropped a leather overnight bag to the carpet with a quiet thud.

There was something so expectant in the way he and, she realized, her guests, watched her. And waited.

The seconds ticked by. Who was he? She needed the answer to that single, simple question before she knew how to react.

He glanced up. Above her hung a chandelier, and incongruous among the glinting crystal dangled a sprig of mistletoe.

Surely not?

Meg looked back at him, looked again into those eyes. Eyes she'd only ever seen the likes of once before.

She felt the color drain from her face. He eased the tray from her hands, placed it on the table behind her. "Luke?" His name left her lips on a whisper.

He watched her struggle for calm, and his mouth stretched into a smile that held little humor. He slid large hands over her jaw to cup her face. "Hi, honey, I'm home," he said softly as he lowered his head.

Too stunned to react, Meg stood rooted to the spot. Warm lips collided with hers. There was hunger in his kiss, hunger and a quest for control.

She wouldn't react. Wouldn't *let* herself react.

His fingers threaded into her hair as he claimed her mouth in a blatant attempt to dominate her, and then he gentled his kiss. That surprising gentling melted her defenses and dissolved rational thought.

He was alive. He was home. He was kissing her again.

He'd kissed her only once before. She'd thought her memories had been colored by the circumstances of the time.

Apparently not.

This kiss was every bit as beguiling and as latent with promise as that first one.

But the moment she found herself kissing him back, reaching for him, he lifted his head and then set her away from him as though it was she who had initiated the kiss and he needed to put distance between them to prevent her from doing it again.

Dimly, she heard a burst of applause.

Her awareness returned. Her guests—the organizing committee for tomorrow night's charity dinner—were witnessing this scene play out. She felt the color rush back to her cheeks.

Luke's gaze didn't leave her face. "Aren't you going to introduce me, darling? I saw only a few familiar faces."

Not daring to look away, she said, "Everyone," and the word came out a hoarse whisper that made him grin a shark's grin. She cleared her throat. "This is Luke Maitland. My husband."

Then it all happened in a blur: hugs, congratulations, assurances that they knew she'd want to be alone with her husband after his unexpected return. Within minutes she and the stranger she'd married stood together at his front door as the quiet purr of the last departing vehicle faded into the night.

Meg stepped out and away from the arm he had draped possessively and firmly—as though he knew she wanted to bolt after that final car—over her shoulder. Frigid air wrapped itself around her in its stead.

He followed close as she led the way back to the high-ceilinged living room. His living room. Platters of nibbles still sat on the coffee table, Bing still sang, but everything had changed.

Those eyes. How could she not have known him instantly?

Finally, when the silence had stretched way beyond comfortable, Meg spoke. "You're looking…better." The last time she'd seen him he'd been lying, pale and unshaven, on a makeshift hospital bed on an Indonesian island. And taller. In the few days she'd spent with him, he'd invariably been lying down, or bent with pain when he'd tried to stand. Illness had a way of diminishing people. There was nothing diminished about him now. Upright and strong, he comfortably cleared six foot.

"Disappointed?" he asked quietly.

The question stunned her. "No! How can you ask that? I thought you might die."

"So did I. But that wouldn't necessarily have worked out badly for you." He glanced around the sumptuous living room.

They'd spent only a few days together, but she'd thought she'd had a bond with the observant, insightful man in her care. A man who, despite his pain, had made her laugh. The man she remembered had been nothing like this—cool and distant. Suspicious. Then again, the man she remembered had been close to death. "No, it would have worked out terribly."

His gaze never wavered. "You got my house. It could have been permanent. And you'll have realized by now that there's much more than the house."

Back then, he'd talked only of the beauty and magic of the area, of how he'd wanted someone who could appreciate it to have it, someone who understood him. She'd had no idea when she'd married him just how wealthy he was, that when he'd said house he meant mansion on the shore of Lake Tahoe, complete with private jetty, indoor pool, game room, boardroom and a library stocked floor to ceiling with books. She could have lived happily for years in the library alone.

Meg crossed to the fireplace and positioned herself behind an armchair, her fingers pressing into the padding of its high leather back. "You have no right to just walk in here—"

"To my own house?"

"To just walk in," she continued, "and start accusing me of...what exactly is it you're accusing me of?"

He paused and she held her breath, waiting, uncertain. "Nothing," he said on a rough sigh, dragging a hand across the back of his neck, and some of the accusation leached from his eyes.

"Luke, it was all your idea. You practically demanded I marry you."

He strolled closer, picked up one of the Christmas cards from the mantelpiece and glanced at the inside before replacing it. "I don't remember much more than a token resistance from you."

"You were sick, so let me help you remember. As I recall it, you were desperate. You even invoked the memory of your mother."

She'd met his mother only once. Meg had gone with a friend to hear her speak at a lunchtime fundraiser in L.A. and had been so impressed that she'd introduced herself to her afterward. They'd ended up having coffee together and talking for hours. It was as a result of that one fateful meeting that when things had ended between Meg and her then-boyfriend she'd thought of doing something completely different. Had thought of Indonesia and the Maitland Foundation. A path that had led her to here and now. "You asked me to do it for her—because of how much I'd respected her and because I knew how revered she'd been on the island. And you even threatened that if I didn't accept you were going to propose to the very next woman who walked into the room." She'd believed him to be serious and in an uncharacteristic fit of possessiveness Meg hadn't wanted anyone else to have "her" patient, the man she'd spent so many hours talking to. "You said I was doing you a favor."

Hard to imagine how that could be true now, how plain Meg Elliot, with little to call her own, could have done a handsome millionaire a favor by marrying him.

He rested an arm on the mantel and stared at the fire. A smile touched his lips and then vanished. Uncomfortable in the same room as the stranger who was her husband, Meg edged around the chair and toward the door. She needed space, needed to get to her own room and process what was happening, figure out what she did next. His return changed everything.

"You must be tired." She had no idea where he'd come from or how far he'd traveled today. But it was late and deep lines creased the skin around his eyes, so she assumed her guess had some foundation. "We can talk all this through in the morning."

Luke straightened and strode to the door, cutting off her exit. "You're right. I am tired." He looked down at her, then lifted his hand to twist a lock of her hair around his finger. "I take it our bed's in the master bedroom."

Meg swallowed. "Our?" He was joking. Testing her. She was sure of it. Almost one-hundred-percent sure. Ninety-eight at least. Even if she had been the type of woman someone like him would be attracted to, theirs had been an arrangement of practicality and desperation. An arrangement that they'd agreed would end when he returned home.

"You got the benefits of being my wife. Surely I get some benefit in being your husband?"

She pushed his hand away and squared off to him. "You got benefits. Because of me, your brother hasn't moved into this house already."

"Half brother," he corrected her. "And that wasn't the benefit I was thinking of."

"It was when you married me. Or maybe you didn't care about there being any benefit to you, but you most definitely cared about making sure Jason didn't benefit. Cared enough to marry a stranger."

"A stranger with the gentlest hands."

Meg stilled.

"I thought about those hands as I was recuperating."

His sudden change of tone and topic disconcerted her and she took a step back. He was still trying to dominate her, unsettle her, this time with words. That was all it was. She couldn't let him know the effectiveness of his strategy, how very unsettled she was. She, too, had thought about her hands on him.

"You have a lot to explain to me. Where have you been? Why haven't you been in touch before now?"

He watched her steadily. "Nagging me already?"

"Legitimate questions."

"I have several of my own."

"Understandably. So I suggest we both get a good

night's sleep and deal with them in the morning. The guest wing is that way." She pointed down the hallway.

"The guest wing? In my own house?"

"My things are in your room. I'll shift them out tomorrow. But for tonight, yes, you can have the guest room." Over the lonely months Meg had imagined many possible scenarios for Luke's homecoming—they had varied from tender to joyful to passionate.

This tension-laden standoff certainly hadn't been one of them.

LUKE WATCHED HIS wife's pretty blue eyes as he searched for the familiar in her face, searched for the differences. Time was, women jumped at the chance of going to bed with him. Although admittedly he was a little out of practice. Still, appalled horror was definitely a first for him.

He'd dreamed of this woman. And granted, many of those dreams had been the product of delirium. Many, but not all. The others had been the product of good old-fashioned desire. He hadn't known whether that attraction was merely the product of time and circumstance.

And he still couldn't answer that question for sure. Different time, different circumstance and he could still feel the pull of the woman standing in front of him.

Who was this woman he'd married?

He recognized the irony in his situation. Most of his life he'd kept people at a distance and now he had a wife he scarcely knew.

He reached for the tendril of golden-brown hair that curled against her pale throat. She blocked his hand, wrapping slender fingers around his wrist. "Afraid of me, Meg?" Her scent was something floral. Innocent. And distracting.

She dropped his wrist, lifted her chin and her wide clear eyes searched his face. Defiance overlaid a glimmer of wariness. "Should I be?"

He could still feel the imprint of her fingers, her skin against his. It had been like that whenever she'd touched him. "What do you think?" He didn't know why he was goading her. He'd had scarcely more than a few hours' sleep in the last forty-eight hours. All he really wanted was to lie down somewhere, he didn't care where, and close his eyes. He'd come home, not knowing what to expect, but knowing she couldn't have been as simultaneously wholesome and desirable as his memory wanted to paint her. Besides, he'd never really been into wholesome.

"I think, no."

He hadn't even known if he'd be able to find her. He certainly hadn't expected her to be hosting a party in his own house. It tarnished the wholesome image, made him doubt his judgment and his memories. "You're sure?"

"I think, for some perverse reason, you'd like me to be afraid of you. But the man I remember was decent and kind."

He watched her lips, a soft coral pink. He hadn't intended on kissing her. But her lack of recognition of him had galled. And besides, she had been standing under the mistletoe. What was a husband supposed to do? "I was sick. I wasn't entirely myself."

"Some things don't change."

Another first, someone defending him to himself. "And some things change completely, Mrs. Maitland." For instance, he now had the wife he'd sworn he'd never burden his life with.

"I'm not Mrs. Maitland. I never took your name. It didn't seem right."

He didn't know whether he was relieved or affronted. "Just my house. My money. My life." He curled his hand around the newel at the base of the stairs.

Her eyes narrowed and her hands went to her hips. "You're swaying, and talking almost as much gibberish as you were that last day on the island. Go to bed."

"Come with me." He was in no state to do anything other than sleep. But she didn't know that. "I've been sleeping alone for so long."

"Luke." She said his name with such frustrated impatience, and none of her earlier trepidation, that maybe she did know.

"That wasn't how you used to say my name." He'd heard her the times when she'd thought he was sleeping. And even when she'd known him to be awake, there had been such tenderness in her voice. "And not how I dreamed of hearing you say it."

"First my hands, now my voice. Any other parts of me you dreamed of?"

Luke smiled. "I don't think you want to know." Color climbed her cheeks.

2

LUKE WOKE ALONE in a broad, soft bed. Nothing unusual about the alone part, but the bed was a different story altogether. The snow-white sheets smelled fresh and clean and felt crisp against his skin. A feather pillow cushioned his head. Opening his eyes, he scanned the room. A miniature Christmas tree stood on the dresser. Christmas?

Then he remembered last night. Though he'd been so exhausted, it was all a little vague. Coming home. Finding Meg, the woman he'd married out of desperation and anger, here. And he remembered the mistletoe. *That* memory was crystal clear. He also recalled his last sight of her hurrying up the stairs away from him.

Throwing back the covers, he strode to the window and pushed the curtains wide, needing to orient himself to the time and the season. Outside, ponderosa pines framed a panoramic view of Lake Tahoe. A leaden sky hung low and oppressive with the threat of snow but gave no real clue as to the time of morning.

He stretched, easing his shoulder through a full range of movement. It was his shoulder that had started it all. A gash from a handsaw dropped from the roof of the almost-completed school building. In the heat and humidity the cut became infected. The infection steadily worsened. And the remote Indonesian island's depleted medical supplies hadn't run to the antibiotics he'd needed.

He'd only gone to the island to fulfill a long overdue promise to his mother to take a closer look at the Maitland Foundation's work there. She'd headed up that office until her death a year ago. But while seeing the foundation's work, he'd discovered his half brother's duplicity. And the visit had nearly ended up costing his life.

He'd also discovered Meg.

And got himself a wife.

A wife he now had to un-get.

A movement on the path leading up from the lake toward his house caught his eye. His wife. Meg. Not Meg Maitland. But Meg…he couldn't even remember her surname. Wearing sweats and a form-fitting, long-sleeved top, with her hair tied into a high, swinging ponytail, she jogged along the path toward him, her breath making small puffs of mist in the air. Caesar trotted at her side, a stick in his mouth. His dog at least had known him last night, even if he now seemed more than happy with his allegiance to her.

She glanced up, saw him, then averted her gaze. Was he—? Luke looked down. He wore boxers—one of his few purchases on the way home. So, what was her problem? Whatever it was, she definitely wasn't looking back his way. She tossed the stick for Caesar and when he returned with it, she bent over and fussed with him for a while before disappearing round the side of the house.

Fifteen minutes later, Luke, showered and fully dressed, rummaged through his kitchen cupboards looking for something to eat. The pantry was better stocked than he ever remembered it being.

At the sound of footsteps, he turned. She, too, had showered and now wore appealingly snug jeans and a red-and-white sweater. She looked fresh and innocent, like she ought to still believe in Santa Claus. But looks could be deceiving. He had a lot of questions for her. Questions he intended to get answers to today.

He hadn't exactly behaved with his trademark calm detachment last night. A fact he regretted. But he couldn't quite bring himself to regret kissing her. It might have been his only opportunity. Soon she would be out of his house and out of his life. That's what they'd agreed should happen if—when, she'd insisted—he came back. Though they hadn't discussed time frames.

"Do you want me to make you lunch?" she asked.

"Lunch? I usually start with breakfast."

A smile twitched at her lips. "After midday, I usually call it lunch."

He remembered that smile, how easily and often it played about her mouth, how it made her blue eyes sparkle like sunlight on water, reminding him of the lake he loved. Making her smile had been one of his few pleasures when he'd been laid low. "You're kidding me." He knew he'd been tired, but…he searched the kitchen. The clock on the microwave read one-forty. And he knew that wasn't a.m.

"You must have been exhausted." She watched him warily.

He nodded.

"Sit down. I'll make you a sandwich."

Was she was trying to soften him up, being all sweet and obliging, this woman installed in his house, his life?

Did she want something from him? Of late, it seemed everyone—friends, enemies, officials—wanted something.

His cynicism must have shown because her hands went to her hips. "Oh, for goodness' sake, sit down." She pointed, straight-armed, at one of the bar stools behind the breakfast bar. "I'm not going to try and poison you and I don't want anything from you. I'm offering—and it's a one-time-only offer—to make you lunch. While you look infinitely better than you did back on the island and much better than you did last night even, to be honest, you still don't look great. And as from now, I'm going to refuse to care."

Luke smiled as he strolled to take the seat he'd been ordered to. So, his Florence Nightingale wasn't all sweetness and light. He liked her better for it. It made her more real. He watched her moving about his kitchen, opening and shutting cupboards and the fridge with what he deemed unnecessary force. She didn't bother asking him what he did or didn't want on his sandwich, which didn't bother him, because he was so ravenous he didn't care.

He'd never sat here and watched a woman in his own kitchen before. He wasn't sure he liked it.

Gradually, her movements slowed and gentled to something practiced and efficient as she set about putting the sandwich together for him. He watched her deft hands with their delicate fingers, watched the sway of her hips and the curve of her rear as she crossed the kitchen for this or that, and decided that a woman in his kitchen wasn't entirely a bad thing. A few minutes later, she slid the plate across the breakfast bar toward him.

"Thank you."

The simple courtesy seemed to surprise her, which

shouldn't surprise him. He hadn't exactly been Mr. Charming last night. Or this morning.

Luke turned his attention to the sandwich. He was halfway through it when a cup of coffee materialized beside his plate. He looked up and met her gaze. Her earlier stony expression had softened. "Thank you," he said again.

And was rewarded with a soft smile and felt again a glimmer of the brief connection they'd once shared. "You're welcome. You still drink it black?"

He nodded. Not that there'd been the option of having it any other way of late. She turned her back on him and adjusted the radio till she found a station playing Christmas carols. She wore her hair out and the soft curls brushed just past her shoulders. He'd never seen it out before. On the island, for practicality's sake, it had always been tied up. And last night, apart from that single tendril she'd allowed to curl beside her throat, it had been twisted into something fancy at the back of her head. He hadn't realized that it was quite so long or silky and his fingers itched to touch it, to know the feel of it. He clenched his fists and his jaw. Hair was hair. He did *not* want to know how hers felt. What he wanted was to get his life back to normal.

And that did not include having a wife in it.

She'd made herself a coffee, too, and picked up her cup, cradling it with two hands as she leaned back against the counter on the far side of the kitchen.

Luke returned his attention to his sandwich and didn't look at her again until he was finished. But when he did he found her gaze still steady on him.

"You were hungry?"

"Apparently."

"I can make you another one. Or get you some fruit."

"It's my house, Meg. I can look after myself."

She bit her bottom lip.

"So, tell me—" They both spoke at once.

"You first," she said.

"Tell me about the last three months."

She shrugged. "I left the island, came back here. It took a while to convince Mark of the truth of my story and that your letter to him hadn't been signed under duress. Putting in the tree house incident was what clinched it. He figured you wouldn't have told that story to anyone you didn't trust. Even at gunpoint." Her eyes danced.

"And you're now the only person in the world apart from Mark and me who knows."

"My lips are sealed." She pressed the lips in question together.

But they hadn't always been sealed like that. They'd parted for him last night. Let him into her warmth.

"Mark was great. He went along with everything, helping explain my presence to your friends. Apparently, you're so deeply private that no one was surprised they hadn't heard of me. Only pleased to meet me. And Mark helped me look for you."

How hard had they looked and how much had Mark—his attorney and his friend—helped her?

Kind, intelligent Mark. In those moments Luke had tried to be altruistic, he'd thought that if he didn't make it back, Meg and Mark might be good for each other. He wasn't feeling altruistic now. Far from it.

A too-familiar tension started to build. It was getting old, the second-guessing, the not knowing who to trust. "Do you want to walk?" He needed to get outside, to get moving.

And he needed to remember who his friends were. They weren't many but they were true. And Mark was one of them. Luke had no need or right to doubt him.

As for Meg, he wanted to trust her, but the jury was still out on that one. In reality, he'd known her only a few days in Indonesia and he'd been perilously ill most of that time. His judgment couldn't possibly have been sound. He'd been betrayed before by people he'd thought he knew. And he didn't truly know why she'd agreed to marry him.

"Sure." Gentle, trusting. She gathered up their few dishes, put them in the dishwasher, then followed him to the front door.

He opened the closet wondering whether his jacket would still be there. It was. On the same peg he always hung it on. The first one. So, she hadn't got rid of his stuff or even moved it for her own convenience. He'd wondered how much of his presence she'd expunged from the house when she'd kept him from his bedroom last night.

A red jacket hung beside his. He reached for it and the scarf hanging with it, passed them to her, then held open the front door.

As she walked past him, he caught the scent of her hair, green apples, and he had to fight an urge to stop her so that he could lower his head and inhale that freshness, inhale some of her seeming innocence. The sort of innocence a man could want to take advantage of.

"Jason hasn't bothered you?" Because Jason, his half brother, was exactly the type of man who would take a perverse pleasure in abusing innocence.

She hesitated. "Depends on what you mean by bothered?"

He pulled the door shut behind them. "Care to explain?"

They walked down the stairs together. "He comes around a lot. At first he was suspicious, a little bit antagonistic even. He had a lot more questions than anyone else about our relationship and our…marriage. And he seems to come round only when no one else is here."

At the foot of the stairs, she bent to pat Caesar, who'd bounded up, joyous at the prospect of another outing. Luke was sure his dog—part Alsatian, part something that really, really liked to fetch sticks—used to have more dignity, but he'd dropped to the ground and rolled over for Meg to scratch his belly. She had nice hands, delicate and gentle. And soothing. And he would not think about her hands. Specifically, he would not think about her hands on him. She straightened. "I gather I'm not the type of woman you usually dated."

"I guess not. You're definitely shorter." Meg barely came up to his chin. Her eyes narrowed suspiciously but she didn't say anything and he fathomed the reason for her skepticism. The last woman he'd dated was Melinda, an ex-model, willowy and glamorous. Who wouldn't in a million years have even contemplated a six-month stint of voluntary work in third world conditions. That was, in essence, the biggest difference.

"I met your last girlfriend."

"You did?" He couldn't imagine the two of them having anything in common. He started for the path and she walked at his side.

"She called around one day and Jason arrived just a few minutes after. He told her I was your wife, although I suspect she'd heard something to that effect already. And then he told me she was your ex-girlfriend."

And wouldn't Jason have enjoyed that spot of stirring. "How did she take it?"

"She smiled."

"That's good," he said hopefully. Melinda had broken it off with him several months before he'd gone to Indonesia. She had no cause to be upset.

"It wasn't a happy smile."

"Oh."

"I know it's none of my business, but why did you and her break up?"

Maybe she had a little cause. He cleared his throat. "Because I didn't want to get married."

"Which kind of explains the not-so-happy smile."

"I guess."

"She was very beautiful." She said it with a kind of awe. But as beautiful as Melinda had looked, she had nothing on Meg, whose source of beauty had nothing to do with the clothes she wore and everything to do with what shone from within.

"Perhaps you should explain to her why you married me," she said quietly.

"I'll think about it." He couldn't see that it would achieve anything, but Meg seemed to want it. Maybe to ease her own conscience. She seemed so earnest. So innocent. "How old are you?"

A grin tilted her lips and coaxed one from him in return. Admittedly, it was an odd question to ask his wife. "Twenty-eight," she said. Nearly ten years younger than him. A world of difference in age and cynicism. Maybe it was that openness to her that made her look so young, so appealing.

Meg broke their tenuous connection as she turned

away and continued walking toward the lake. "I learned your age from our marriage certificate."

That piece of paper legally binding them. He'd need to set about *un*binding them as soon as possible, because despite their verbal agreement that she'd leave when he got back, she was legally his wife. She'd have rights if she chose to exercise them.

She'd helped him, he owed her something. Certainly more than mere gratitude. How much more would be the pivotal question. And Mark would no doubt have an opinion on that as well as the most efficient and effective way to undo what he'd done. Set them both free. "What day is it?"

"Saturday."

He'd call Mark on his personal line later, set up a meeting for first thing Monday morning. The sooner that was sorted, the better. Regardless of how much she was likely to cost him. In the meantime, he'd be friendly but distant. He didn't want to alienate her. But on the other hand, he didn't want to encourage her to think there was anything more to their marriage than her having the use of his house until his return. He also needed to talk to Mark about Jason.

At the water's edge, they negotiated age-old granite boulders. As she clambered between two rocks, he offered his hand. Her glance flicked to his face, she took his hand—hers cool and fragile in his—and then eased it free as soon as the need passed, sliding it into her jacket pocket. He could almost want it back. He shoved his own hands into his pockets. "You were telling me about Jason. That at first he was suspicious…" Jason was an unscrupulous slimeball with a talent for ferreting out people's weaknesses. But he hid that side of his nature well and knew how to ingratiate himself with people.

"Then something changed. Once he accepted our… marriage," she glanced away as she said the word, "…he got a whole lot nicer, started offering to help me with things. But he had a lot of questions about where you were, why you weren't home with me. I'd told him, like you suggested, that you'd stayed on to straighten out things with the charity on the island and that you'd be home in a couple of months."

The track along the shore narrowed, forcing them to walk close, down-padded shoulders occasionally brushing. "Did you accept his help?" he asked.

"What do you mean?"

"A simple question."

"But there was something weird in the way you asked it, like you were accusing me of something."

"I wasn't accusing you of anything. Jason's offers of help have been known to take many forms."

"I don't really understand why you hate him so much. He can be a bit creepy, but he's had a tough life."

Not like you. The implication was clear. That was how Jason had got to Luke, too, playing the sympathy card, explaining how hard done by he'd been because of Luke's dead father, *their* father, a man who'd never acknowledged him, playing on Luke's feelings of guilt. So he'd given him a house, a job, money. And then Jason had betrayed him by blackmailing his mother. A fact he hadn't discovered till he was in Indonesia going through some of her possessions. He'd threatened to very publicly expose her dead husband's indiscretions, which according to Jason, were many and damning. In doing so, he'd not only stain the memory and reputation of their father, but more importantly, would harm the image of the charity he'd founded. A charity that meant the world to Luke's mother.

Luke had told Meg none of the details. Maybe he should have because it sounded as though Jason had been playing on Meg's sympathies, too. All Luke had shared with her, when his death was looking like a distinct possibility, was that he didn't want to die knowing Jason, as his closest living relative, might benefit in any way. "So how much help did you accept from him, and what did you mean by creepy?" The very thought of Jason anywhere near Meg was creepy. The man had the moral code of a hyena.

She shoved her hands deeper into her pockets. "He has an...unusual way about him. But he tried to be helpful. He gave me names of people and professionals for if I needed any work done, told me which restaurants were good. Things like that. But it was Mark who suggested the private investigator I used to try to track you down."

"You looked?"

"Of course I looked. But the investigator didn't turn up anything. So I went back there as soon as I got my visa renewed."

"To the island?"

"Yes." Sorrow clouded her eyes. "Where did you go? Where did everyone go?"

He hated the thought of her going back there. That it was for him made it even worse.

She'd left because the situation on the island had deteriorated rapidly into one of chaos and violence. She'd actually argued that she should stay with him, but the local staff had convinced her that they could care for him until the plane arrived to airlift him and a wounded islander to the nearest hospital for treatment.

"I don't know what happened to it, but the plane never arrived. We gave it a day, but after fresh fighting broke out, we fled the village and then the island."

She nodded. "No one I spoke to had heard of you or any of the villagers we knew. At least they said they didn't. There was nothing left of the village itself. Or the school."

He heard the bleakness in her voice. It had made her sad, and it had made him angry. But there was nothing either of them could do about it now. The village had been caught in the middle of an escalating dispute linked to a decades-old conflict. "I know some of them got away. Were able to start afresh." That small truth was the best he could offer her.

She walked on, visibly subdued. Despite his earlier resolve to keep his distance, Luke slipped his arm around her shoulders and pulled her closer to him. The future would separate them, but they shared a past that no one else would understand. And he would offer her what comfort he could—the comfort of a friend—inadequate as it might be.

He still had questions, but now no longer seemed the time to ask them. They walked the rest of the loop in silence. His arm still about her shoulders. Her leaning subtly into him. He should let her go, but something about walking like this, with her, was deeply peaceful. He remembered that about her, a feeling of stillness and calm when she'd been the one nursing him.

The house, festooned with Christmassy boughs of greenery, came into view. In the eight years he'd lived here he'd never once decorated for Christmas.

He'd thought about putting up a tree one year, but if he put a tree up, then he'd have to buy ornaments. And, well, it just never happened. There was no point for a man living on his own. But this morning he'd noticed festive touches everywhere. Red bows on the uprights of the stairs, Christmas towels in the guest bathroom, a Christmas tree decorated in only white bows and white lights, simple but effective. "Where will you go?"

She stiffened. "That's not your problem or your concern. But," she drew in a deep breath that lifted her shoulders, "can I stay till Monday? Till my car's ready. It's at the mechanic's. That's why the committee meeting was here last night."

He stopped, forcing her to stop with him and looked at her. "Of course you can stay." He should be grateful. He'd been thinking two or three weeks, maybe a month, would be reasonable. But the thought of her leaving Monday was like having the rug pulled out from under his feet. Now that she wanted to go, he wanted to keep her near. Surely he ought to at least know his wife a little, if only so that he knew how she was likely to play it during their divorce.

Plus it would look strange to both his friends and hers if his wife left so soon. Ultimately, of course, they'd have to deal with it. But there was no hurry. "Stay as long as you need."

"Thank you," she said softly. "But Monday will be good." She gently turned down his offer. He'd wanted her gone, so he had no call to feel rebuffed. It had been like that back on the island. The conflicting feelings she evoked. The desire to have her near, the resenting of that desire and then the desire to have her back when she left. Turns out it wasn't contrariness caused by being bedridden.

She smiled at some hidden thought. She had the sweet-est-looking lips. Eminently kissable. For all the admonishments he'd delivered to himself, he couldn't help wondering what she'd do if he kissed her again. No mistletoe, no audience.

She'd kissed him once. Back at the camp. The minister had left his bedside after marrying them. Darkness had fallen and Meg sat quietly by his side. She used to sometimes sit there and talk to him as he dozed, telling him stories from her childhood, as outside, unseen night insects sang.

The evening after their marriage she'd kept his hand in hers and Luke had lain there, eyes closed, trying to listen to what she said, but mainly just listening to the sound of her voice, the sound of home.

When he'd asked, after realizing it was something he should have asked first, she had talked about the boyfriend whose desertion had precipitated her trip to work with the foundation. About how she specialized in finding men who needed her for a time, emotionally, financially or physically, but then dumped her when the need had passed. Initially, she laughed at her own stories, but then, as she talked about her dreams of a family of her own, her voice changed, there was a catch to it, and then she stopped talking altogether. He opened his eyes to see a tear rolling down her cheek.

She tried for a smile. "Some wedding night, huh."

"Come here."

And she did. She moved from her chair to sit on the side of his bed.

"Closer."

She leaned down.

He brushed the tear away with his thumb and then slid his hand round to the back of her head, pulled her closer still and kissed her, slow and sweet, and he forgot about the pain and thought maybe he'd died and already gone to heaven.

She sat back up looking as shaken as he knew he'd feel if he wasn't so damn sick. Instead, he felt…a little better.

"Not bad for someone on death's doorstep." She tried to make light of what had just passed between them.

"Wait till I'm better." He winked. "I could make you forget all your sorrows."

"Is that a promise?"

"If you want it to be."

"Then get better. And I'll hold you to it."

"Now that's what I call an incentive."

It was the last time he'd been alone with her. The next day, she'd left on the boat that was to bring back supplies to replenish those raided from the island's medical facility.

But he wasn't sick now. He stopped walking and pulled her closer, let her see his intent. He read trepidation mixed with a little curiosity, a little anticipation in her gaze.

Beside them, Caesar growled deep and low. Meg stiffened and looked away. "Someone's here."

They rounded the side of the house to see a red Corvette driving away. Luke watched till Jason's car disappeared from sight before dropping his arm from Meg's shoulders and heading into the house. He hated what Jason had done to his mother, and hated the thought of him anywhere near Meg. He wanted the man out of his life for good.

The homemade wreath adorning his front door swung

as he pulled the door open. Controlling his breathing, he stepped inside and held the door for Meg. She stood on the path at the base of the stairs watching him, her expression unreadable, her nose and cheeks pink from the cold.

Finally, looking straight past him, she climbed the stairs. He shut the door behind them and watched as she unwound her scarf. The peace and connection he'd found in her presence only minutes ago had vanished. She'd shut herself off from him.

He stood between her and the closet and took her scarf from her hands. "You don't understand."

"And I don't need to. Families are complicated. It's your business. It's nothing to do with me." She unzipped her jacket.

"You're my wife."

She stilled for a second, looking at her hands. "In name only."

"But still my wife." He didn't know why he was invoking the "wife" clause; he should be the last one reinforcing it. But he wanted her to understand.

"Don't tell me you aren't thinking about how soon you can divorce me, if you haven't started proceedings already."

"I haven't started proceedings."

"Yet. But you'll be at Mark's office first thing Monday morning?"

Luke said nothing. Meg looked up, met his gaze and nodded her understanding.

As she shrugged off her jacket, he moved to stand behind her, helped ease it from her shoulders and down her arms. He caught the scent of green apples but couldn't afford to be distracted by it. "You can't tell me you don't want to get divorced, too?" She turned, they were so close that he could encircle her with his arms. Hold her. Tell her everything. His wife in name only. Or they could not talk at all. He could taste her lips. Touch her skin. Feel her heat.

"Of course I want it, too."

Divorce, they were talking about divorcing.

"That's why I don't need to get involved in your personal life. Any more than I already am."

He hung up her jacket. "Any more than you are?"

She swallowed. "I'm living in your house. And I've made friends with some of your friends and their partners. I couldn't help it. When they learned about me, they wanted to meet me, to get to know me. They've been kind. I like them."

He nodded, gave her time to go on.

"Julie finally left her husband. She stayed here for a week when she first left. And Sally and Kurt are expecting their second child. She's due in three months. I said I'd help with babysitting when she went into hospital. And when she came out. You know how organized she is. Of course that might not be so easy now." She was talking fast, not meeting his gaze. "And I'm sorry. It just sort of happened." She looked up at him, apology in her eyes.

Just like he used to when he'd been sick, he'd gotten distracted by the soft cadence of her voice rather than focusing on the specifics of her words. The details of her supposed crime had washed over him. And today there had been the added distraction of his very real ability to do something about it. He could reach out, trail a finger down the softness of her cheek, touch it to those lips.

Desire stirred.

3

MEG STEPPED back from Luke, the husband she didn't know, away from the warmth in his eyes. Warmth that had her thinking things she had no business thinking. She blamed the window. She'd come back from her walk with Caesar and looked up to see him standing at the wide picture window, wearing only boxers, his torso lean and sculpted, and a purely feminine thrill of appreciation had swept through her.

"I'm glad you found friends here, that you weren't alone," he said after a pause so long that she'd thought he hadn't been going to answer.

His softly spoken words disconcerted her. She didn't want to like him. At least not in the softening, melting way she could feel herself liking him. That was far more dangerous than the physical pull of attraction that she— and most likely the majority of the female population who came within his sphere—felt for him.

She'd agreed to marry him because he'd believed— rightly—that his death was a real possibility and it had seemed imperative to him that Jason not be able to inherit. She'd been prepared to do anything to ease his agitation.

But he hadn't died.

He was very much alive.

And watching her.

"But hopefully they have the good sense to stay away now that I'm back. All I want is peace and quiet."

Meg remembered the dinner. He might want peace and quiet but he wasn't going to get it. Not tonight, which was probably a good thing because Meg wasn't so sure she wanted to be alone with him.

"Show me round the house."

"I haven't changed anything. You don't need me to show you round it." Regardless of what he did or didn't need, *she* needed to put a little space between them. And she would—as soon as she'd told him about the dinner. Because the way they'd walked, with his arm around her, had felt so natural, and when he'd looked at her, he'd thought about kissing her and she'd wanted him to. It would feel so good, which would be all bad.

She was lonely. That was all. Her life had been on hold these last few months, but she was picking up the pieces again. She didn't need to lean on Luke.

Her work with the Maitland Foundation since she'd been back had been a welcome distraction.

"You've been having parties. That's a change."

"Do you mean last night? That was a final committee meeting."

"You put up Christmas decorations." He continued, not taking her opening to ask what the committee meeting was for. "That's a change. A bigger one than you know." He flicked one of the red bows tied to the stair uprights. "I don't usually do Christmas."

It seemed a sad thing to say. She couldn't imagine not marking Christmas in some way. "That's not changing as much as adding something temporary." She was going to have to tell him about tonight.

The bow slipped and they both reached to catch it, hands tangling as they trapped the red velvet against the smooth wood of the post, halting its downward slide. For a second they stilled. His warm hand covered hers, pinning it with the bow beneath it.

He was close again. And again his proximity, his warmth and scent had her resolutions slipping. Meg slid her hand from beneath his, bringing the broad ribbon with it, and took a step back. With nerveless fingers she smoothed out the loops of the bow. From the kitchen she heard the strains of "All I Want for Christmas is You."

"Do you remember our promise?"

She glanced up to see him watching her closely, desire kindling in the depths of his eyes. He couldn't mean the promise her thoughts had leaped to. He must have meant their vows. "To love and honor? And only those vows because there was no time to write our own. 'In sickness and in health and to disinherit your brother and give me somewhere to live when I got back here.'"

A smile flickered and vanished. "That wasn't the promise I was talking about."

Oh. That promise. The one she'd secretly cherished in her darkest hours, something full of the possibility of tenderness and passion and the affirmation of life, and the one she'd now hoped he'd forgotten. "I don't think anything we said or did back then applies to the here and now."

"Some things transcend time and place," he said evenly. "And a promise is a promise."

Meg swallowed and tugged a little more at the bow.

"I sometimes think that promise was what I lived for,"

he said, almost to himself, "what kept me hanging on when I should have died waiting for the antibiotics to reach me."

She took another step back. His smile returned, knowing and tempting. "If it helped, then I'm glad of it." The bow came completely undone in her unsteady fingers.

He reached for the loose end, so that it became a connection between the two of them. "Did you ever think of it? Or did you forget about me altogether?"

She avoided the first of his two questions. "I didn't forget about you."

He pulled his end of the ribbon closer to him, bringing her hand with it. Then he lifted her hand, supported it with his own and with a sudden frown studied the ring that adorned her ring finger. "Our wedding ring?"

Meg shrugged, though with him cradling her fisted hand in his palm, nonchalance was the last thing she felt. "I had to have something. People were asking. I bought it over the internet so nobody would see me going to a jeweler's to get it."

"And this convinced them?" With the forefinger of his free hand he touched the simple thin gold band. "I would have chosen something a little more…expensive."

"Its importance is in what it symbolizes, not what it's worth. As I told your friends, this was all I wanted. Its simplicity and purity were the perfect representation of our relationship. Besides, I didn't want to spend a lot."

He straightened her fingers and the velvet ribbon whispered to the floor between them. "You paid for it yourself?"

"Of course." She tried to ease her hand free, but he held firm. "It wasn't much."

"I can tell. And our engagement ring?" He looked from her hand to her face. "Where's that?"

She shook her head. "We weren't able to get a suitable engagement ring. It was hard enough getting the wedding band, which we had brought over from another island." She filled him in on the details of the story she'd concocted for his friends. "You wanted us to choose the engagement ring once you came home, but I was going to argue against that. I like the band on its own."

"What else were we going to do once I came home?"

She swallowed. "Well, there was…our honeymoon. People asked about that." Which now that his return was real would be a divorce instead. Meg tugged at her hand and he allowed it to slide free.

Luke folded his arms across his chest and she could read nothing of his thoughts, how he felt about the stories she'd had to make up because she hadn't been able to tell people he married her out of desperation. It had seemed important that nobody, and especially the half brother he was so keen to disinherit, knew the true circumstances. "Do we know where we're going for that?"

"You wanted St. Moritz or Paris, but I wanted Easter Island."

"So we compromised?"

Meg allowed a small smile. "Um…no. We settled on Easter Island because you've been to St. Moritz and Paris before, but neither of us has been to Easter Island. And besides, we both wanted to see the statues." They had talked about the statues in one of their bedside conversations.

"I agreed they'd be amazing to see. Doesn't mean that's where I'd take my bride. I'd definitely go for a little more luxury. A little more hotel time, something a little more romantic."

"That's how people know how smitten you are with me."

"Smitten?"

"Hey." She smiled at his indignant expression. "It was my fantasy."

"Was it not supposed to be reality-based?"

"You're saying it's beyond the realms of possibility?" Her smile faded. Of course someone like him, a multi-millionaire, consistently named in most-eligible-bachelor lists, wouldn't really ever be interested in her, Meg Elliot, nurse. "Your friends believed it," she said in her defense, then frowned. "At least they said they did. They thought I was good for you."

"That's not what I meant. I was talking about realistic honeymoon destinations, not the reality of you and me together."

But Meg was on a roll. "They said I'm not like the women you've dated in the past—ones who don't challenge you emotionally, who let you shut yourself off from them. You must have finally realized what's important in life, must have trusted your ability to give and receive love."

"All my friends said that, or just Sally, who thinks one psych paper in college makes her Carl Jung?"

Meg hesitated, then sighed. "Mainly Sally," she finally admitted. But she'd so wanted to believe her, wife of one of Luke's friends, that she'd bought into her assessment.

Luke's sudden burst of laughter was the last thing she expected. "So, Easter Island, I can't wait to see those statues."

"It's not funny." He was still laughing at her. "I didn't

realize when I agreed to this pretence how complicated it would get. I thought I'd come here and, well…I guess I didn't really think about it at all. But there were people with questions and expectations and I had to tell them something."

"I'm sure you did the best you could."

"But you would have handled it better? What would you have told them?"

"To mind their own damn business."

"You can't say that to people. And certainly not to your friends."

"I can and I do. And friends are the ones who take it the best."

"That's not my style."

"I guess I might have told them we were going somewhere private where I could keep the island promise I made to my wife. That would have been almost as effective at getting them to stop asking questions. They know I don't make promises lightly."

And just like that any trace of levity left his face, but he had to be joking still. Regardless, the sudden change threw her off balance, swept away any sense she'd had that she might be in control of their conversation.

To avoid the questioning intensity in his gaze and the confusion it stirred, she stooped and picked up the ribbon and began rolling it up. "That promise…" she said lightly, trying to inject a touch of dismissive humor into her voice "…it seems like it was a lifetime ago. Like we're not those same two people." She had the ribbon half rolled up when he caught the end. She studied their hands, joined by a strip of red velvet. His large and tanned, hers smaller and pale but thankfully steady.

"Look at me, Meg. And let me look at you." He still

sounded far too serious for her peace of mind. She could almost imagine a trace of need in his voice. "I held your face in my mind for so long. I can't quite get enough of the real thing."

Which seemed the oddest thing to say about her. She had a talent for blending in and going unnoticed. She was the type of person people often forgot having met. Slowly, she looked up. He kept perfectly still as her gaze tracked over his torso, settling inevitably on his face, on the eyes that showed his wanting.

"I'm going to kiss you."

An even bigger surprise. She swallowed and shook her head. "That would be a bad idea." Because if he kissed her, she'd kiss him back, and then he'd know she wanted him. But while she knew she should just turn and walk away, she didn't. Her feet wouldn't listen to her head. He lifted the red velvet, drawing her hand up with it, and then he captured her wrist, raising her hand farther till he touched her fingertips to his jaw. A shiver passed through her and the velvet dropped again to the floor.

She used to touch his jaw like that when he was sick and weakened and feverish. But he was far from sick or weak now, and if anyone was feverish, it was her.

He turned his head and pressed a kiss to her palm. Warmth, heat, liquefied her bones. "I remembered your touch."

She couldn't stop herself, she cupped her palm around his jaw. So smooth now, so strong. He framed her face with his hands and lowered his head toward hers.

She had time to back away.

She stayed precisely where he was.

He kissed with exquisite gentleness. His lips were soft and seeking as though he was savoring the taste of her in the same way she savored the taste and feel of him. He kissed, drew back a fraction, kissed again, brushing his lips over hers. He angled his head, deepened the kiss, teased her teeth and tongue. Her mouth parted beneath his. His kiss was…beautiful. It was perfection. The way they fit so naturally together held an aching rightness. Made her feel that she'd been missing this, him, for so long.

She slid her arms around his waist and stepped into him. And still he kissed her, his fingers threading deeper into her hair.

Meg forgot all the reasons why this was a bad idea and lost herself in his kiss, in the simple joining. He gave of himself, made no demands, and because of that swept her away, a leaf delighting in the wind, flying for that brief time between tree and ground.

And for that brief time it was just him, just her, no past or future, just the now and this kiss, his lips against hers.

Too soon, but what had to be minutes later, he lifted his head, his hands still framed her face, his thumbs lazily stroked her cheeks.

"Remind me in what possible way that could have been a bad idea. I'm thinking it was one of the best, if not *the* best idea I've ever had."

She opened her mouth to speak and waited for her brain to provide the words.

He slid his hands over her shoulders, down her arms, till he held both her hands in his. And Meg knew she was in deep, deep trouble because all she could think was that she wanted him to kiss her again and then she wanted more. Much, much more.

The chiming of the doorbell broke through the sensory spell he wove. Her first reaction was disappointment. Her second, as sanity returned, was relief. That kiss could only have led to places they couldn't go, not without horribly complicating what was already a far-too-complicated situation, and not without threatening the safe cocoon she'd spun around her heart.

She started for the door.

"Leave it," he said.

But she'd remembered who it likely was. "Um… No. We can't." *We can't leave it and we can't go where you're thinking. Where I was thinking. Wanting.*

Luke looked from the broad cedar door to Meg. "You know who that is?"

Meg glanced at her watch. "Maybe." They were punctual, a little early even, which normally she'd rate as a good quality.

"So it's someone for you?"

"Not exactly."

"Whoever it is, send them away. I don't feel like company today."

"I can't do that."

"Because?"

The chimes rang softly through the house again. "Because I think it's the caterers."

His eyes narrowed on her. "Why are there caterers ringing my doorbell?"

"Because they'd like to come in?" She kept her tone hopeful and innocent.

"Meg?" His tone was anything but hopeful or innocent. She'd have said more suspicious and accusing.

"They have some setting up to do. For the dinner tonight." The doorbell rang again and was followed by an insistent knock.

"Open it. And then I think you better tell me what dinner they're setting up for."

Meg let the small army of caterers in, guided them through to the kitchen and took as long as she could showing them anything and everything she thought they might need to know. She didn't leave till it became obvious she was only getting in their way.

She went back to the entranceway where she'd left Luke, where he'd kissed her, but he wasn't there. The red bow was back in place on the post. She could look for him, but she'd doubtless see him soon enough. In the meantime, she had things she needed to do. Like run away before she started acting on three months' worth of daydreams.

In her—Luke's—bedroom she pulled a plain black suitcase from the wardrobe and dropped it onto her—his—bed and unzipped the lid. From the top dresser drawer she gathered her underwear and put it into the case. The second drawer contained Luke's clothes. She opened the third drawer and pulled out her T-shirts.

"What are you doing?"

She tensed at the sound of his voice and spun, her T-shirts clasped to her chest, to see him standing in the doorway. "Packing."

"You do have a knack for stating the obvious."

"We agreed I'd go as soon as you got back."

"And then we agreed Monday, because your car is at the mechanic's." Luke strolled across the room and positioned himself in front of the wide window that most days allowed forever views out over the lake. Today, ominous clouds hid the far, snow-capped mountains, restricting the view instead to the lake's edge. "What is it you're frightened of?"

"Nothing." And even though he wasn't looking at her,

she clutched the T-shirts a little tighter, a flimsy barrier against his questions, his insight.

"Now, me, I'm frightened of you."

A ludicrous notion. "I don't think so. You hold all the power here. Your house, your territory." Not to mention his looks, his wealth, her weakness for him.

"What scares me, Meg," he said to the window, "is the way I feel when I look at you. And the way those feelings intensify when you look back at me."

His words stilled her, made her want to hope. She covered the foolish, unlikely hope with glibness. "And I'll just bet you're a 'feel the fear and do it anyway' kind of guy."

"Sometimes," he said quietly. "Not always. Sometimes the fear is to protect us."

Meg placed the T-shirts on top of her underwear, spreading them so they hid the scraps of lace that were her secret indulgence. Plain, practical Meg liked pretty, sometimes even sexy, lingerie.

Luke crossed to the dresser. She'd divided the space on top in half. One-third, two-thirds, actually. A third for his things, a watch and a framed photo of his mother only needed so much space. The two-thirds on the right was littered with her things. Perfume, a pair of earrings, a scented candle and… "Don't touch that."

He turned with a curling photo in his hand. "This?"

"Yes," she sighed, "that."

"Why not?"

"I didn't mean don't touch it. You can have it. Throw it out if you like."

He lifted a questioning eyebrow.

"I needed something to show people when I went back to try to find you. Clearly, I don't need it anymore." The photo showed the two of them, Luke sitting up in bed, looking ill but still with a certain intensity to his gaze, and Meg perched beside him looking worried and pointing to something off camera. Their wedding photo. She didn't even know why she'd left it out and on the dresser.

He was about to place the photo back where it had stood leaning against her perfume, when instead, he picked up the small crystal bottle and brought it to his nose. He closed his eyes and nodded. "Very Meg." Opening his eyes, he studied her. "Flowers and sweetness." Meg adjusted her T-shirts in the case.

"Tell me about this dinner the caterers in my kitchen are setting up for."

She opened her mouth to speak.

He held up a warning finger. "I just want the facts. No evasive answers. What party do you have planned for tonight?" He frowned. "And if you're planning a party, why are you packing as though you can't get out of here fast enough."

"There's a Christmas dinner for the Maitland Foundation here tonight. Most of the really big donors will be here. I haven't had all that much to do with the organization. I just agreed with Sally when she suggested that this house would be the perfect place for the dinner. And agreed with her that there was no reason it couldn't be here."

"She didn't tell you that she asks every year if she could have it here, and that every year I tell her no?"

Meg swallowed. Sally had told her she'd bear the blame if Luke got back before Christmas, but it didn't seem fair. "Actually, she did. But I couldn't see any reason not to have it here. You have a beautiful home. And it's so much more personal to have a dinner in a home than at a restaurant."

Luke blew out a heavy sigh. The hands at his sides had curled into fists. And for a few brief seconds he shut his eyes. Meg contemplated sneaking out. Too soon he opened them again, the silver sharp and intent. "So why are you packing now?"

"Now that you're back, I don't need to be here for it."

He crossed to the bed. Took everything out of her suitcase, dropped it onto the bedcover, then zipped the case shut. "Think again. If I have to be here for this dinner, then you most definitely do."

She unzipped the case and gathered up the pile of clothes. "No, I don't."

"These donors who are coming, they know I have a wife?"

"Yes, most of them," she said slowly, holding her clothes to her chest and hoping fervently that she'd covered her underwear with her T-shirts.

"Then they'll expect you to be here. The Maitland Foundation and its donors espouse strong family values. You could cost it thousands if you don't show, *Mrs.* Maitland."

"That's not fair."

"You're right, it's not." He smiled, devious and victorious. "I'll leave you to start getting ready." He stopped at the door and nodded at the clothes in her arms. "I'm sure the red will look fetching on you."

Meg glanced down. There were only two red items in her arms and neither of them was a T-shirt.

4

MEG PAUSED and wrapped her fingers around the polished wood of the banister. She'd made a point of staying out of the caterers'—and Luke's—way while she showered and dressed and put up her hair. But now she barely recognized the entranceway that she'd last seen just a few hours ago. Her homemade decorations were gone. The stairs were twined with ivy, among which nestled hundreds of glinting fairy lights. Below her, an enormous Christmas tree, topped with a star, glittered and sparkled in silver and gold in the entranceway, scenting the air with the fragrance of pine. Tall candelabra stood either side of the front door. The house was filled with the delicate notes of a string quartet playing Christmas music. It was as though someone had waved a wand and transformed the already graceful foyer into something magical.

Luke strode through the doors thrown wide from the next room and had a foot on the bottom step before he looked up and stilled. A slow, knowing smile spread across his face. "I was just coming to get you. Our guests are starting to arrive, darling."

The wand must have touched Luke as well. Before

now, she'd only ever seen him dressed casually. Even then, and even when ill, he'd looked striking, had an undeniable charisma. But now, in an elegant tuxedo, its cut and custom tailoring accentuating the breadth of his shoulders and his lean strength, he looked devastating. A surge of possessiveness and pride swept through her. This man was her husband.

She quashed both the possessiveness and the pride. She had no right to feel possessive of a man who wasn't in any way hers. And she had no right to the pride. He'd had to believe he was dying to offer marriage. Even so, he waited expectantly for her. And she couldn't quite calm the leap of her pulse.

Part of his attraction was the way when he looked at her she felt like he only saw her, only thought of her, as though she fascinated him every bit as much as he fascinated her.

Meg held a little tighter to the banister. She had only one dress suitable for a dinner like this. And it was red. Now Luke would think, and he'd be right, that she wore the red lace beneath it. Or worse, and he'd be wrong, that she wore it for him.

She descended the stairs. Wearing the demure but fitted dress and too-high heels, she was well out of her comfort zone. Or maybe it was his silver gaze steady on her that made her hyperaware of her every movement.

Tonight. She just had to get through tonight without succumbing to his pull. When she was away from him again she'd be fine, but when he was near, he scrambled her thought processes till she didn't know what she wanted, or till she wanted things she knew she oughtn't.

She stopped a step above him and finally, defiantly,

met his gaze. And looked quickly away, her defiance doused. Heat. She'd read heat in his eyes. For her.

It was insane.

As insane as the heat of the response deep within her that his gaze had ignited.

He needed to get back out into the real world, remember the type of woman he was attracted to, the type of woman who belonged in his world, and stop playing games with her.

Except it didn't feel like a game.

She looked back at him, he waited, his hand extended. Trapped by his gaze, Meg swallowed and put her hand in his, felt his fingers fold around hers. And at that touch, that gentle, unerring connection, something shifted and changed, including Meg in this evening's magic.

Hope flickered. Might she be entitled to one enchanted evening?

She did her best to quash the thoughts. A childhood spent lost in books and fairy tales was now having the unwanted repercussions her grandmother had warned of.

Luke smiled, that same smile he had back up in her—his—bedroom as his fingers tightened around hers. "Let's go, Mrs. Maitland, we're having a party." His tone was light, teasing. Maybe she'd imagined the heat.

The living room was now decorated in silver and gold, with enough candles to keep them going for months if the power ever went out. Luke paused in the doorway and glanced up. Mistletoe hung from the door frame. In full view of those guests who'd already arrived, he planted a quick, hard kiss on her lips. Then he put his mouth close to her ear and whispered, "I knew you'd look good in red." His words and his warm breath on the bare skin of her neck sent a shiver through her.

Pretending she hadn't heard, hadn't been affected by his words or his kiss, Meg dredged up a bright, but possibly vacant, smile as guests approached.

"Wyatt, Martha, good to see you. You've met my wife, Meg?" Luke released her hand but rested it instead at the curve of her waist. She wasn't sure which disturbed her composure more.

He stayed by her side almost all evening as he worked the room with skill and ease. As head of Maitland Corporation, he left the running of the foundation to Blake, the director, but he spoke with knowledge and passion about the foundation's work. He talked to almost everyone, smiling and magnanimous, while at the same time ensuring Meg was included in conversations, asking her opinion on whatever topic came up. But he also took advantage of every opportunity, and created more than a few of his own, to touch her: to take her hand, or touch her arm, to curve his palm around her waist, to cup her shoulder. Once, claiming she had a crumb of pastry from a canapé on her cheek, he'd turned to her and brushed his thumb across her face, letting her see the heat in his eyes, making her want him.

And if he wasn't at her side, he was watching her, making her think about him, about their promise. The evening became an exquisite torture.

A bejeweled woman, who'd just promised the foundation a hefty donation, turned away, her parting words *See you both at the New Year's Eve cocktail party,* ringing in Meg's ears and Luke's gaze pinning her. He lifted two champagne flutes from the tray of a circulating waiter and passed one to Meg. He led her to a somewhat quiet corner of the room and she took a sip of the sparkling liquid.

"I was going to tell you about the cocktail party."

"Clearly I need to take a look at *our* social calendar and see what's expected of me. It's not in my house, is it?"

"No."

"Then I'll deal."

They watched the mingling crush. By then she'd be long gone. "I didn't realize you were such a people person."

"I'm not," he said softly. "But I know how to play the game." He turned his back on the room so that only she could see his face and hear his words. "The only person I'm thinking about is you and how good you look in red. And how good you'll look out of it."

His words, blatant and seductive, shocked her. How had they got to this point and, more importantly, how did she stop it? Because while she was certain it was all just a part of the "game" to him, if affected her differently, more deeply than he could know. "Don't do that."

"Do what?"

"What you've been doing all evening. I'm trying to concentrate, to listen to what people are saying and you're making me think…"

"Think what, Meg?" His low voice seemed to sink through her to her core. "About the things I might like to do with you? Because I've been thinking about my husbandly privileges."

She backed a little farther into the corner. "You're not really my husband." But he'd caught what she'd been thinking and she hated that he knew it. That she was that transparent. Because being married to someone carried connotations regardless of the reasons for the marriage.

He leaned closer. "That's the thing, Meg, I really am your husband. And you know it. And you think about it."

"Stop it, Luke. Please."

Something in her tone or her words stilled him. He backed off a little, easing her need to either reach for him or run from him. "If you want me to."

She nodded. "I do. Thank you." She was Meg. She wasn't allowed to want him. Not in the real world. She looked past him to see Sally approaching, glowing with the success of the evening so far.

"You two make a gorgeous couple." Sally kissed both Meg and Luke. "I'm so pleased you finally found a good woman, Luke, and had the sense to marry her. I foresee a long and happy union."

If only in my dreams. The line from the Christmas song popped into Meg's head. Now clearly wasn't the time to tell Sally that she was leaving and that Luke would be starting divorce proceedings as soon as possible.

Luke smiled and raised his glass to Sally, which could look like he was agreeing with her. It could, if you were Meg, also look like he was avoiding commenting on what she'd said.

She sat beside Luke for the dinner, ignoring the occasional press of his thigh against hers. He kept their topics of conversation neutral, his tone and his glances warm, only a degree or two more than friendly. For all of his subtle teasing foreplay earlier, he seemed, from the time of her request, to have switched off, or at least turned down the wattage on the sensual messages.

Whereas Meg had to fight to hide her feelings, and fight to conceal the slow burning fuse of desire he'd lit and that now refused to be extinguished.

When the dinner was all but over, he sat back with his arm behind her and his hand curled around her arm, his thumb tracing lazy circles that sent heat spiraling through her. It was just a thumb. It shouldn't be able to do that.

She waited till he was deep in conversation with the man across the table before easing her chair back. Not deep enough, apparently. He dropped a firm hand to her thigh, anchoring her to her chair and looked at her, a knowing smile glinting in his eyes and touching his lips. "Oh, no, you don't. You're not running away now."

"I was just…" she could see him waiting for her excuse "…I'm not needed here," was the best she could come up with.

"I need you here."

She could almost wish that was true. He'd needed her once and married her because of it. That need had passed. He was back in his life, he was strong and healthy. His hand gentled on her thigh, but the heat of his palm burned through the silk of her dress, sizzled along her skin.

"I'm tired." She tried again, which was also true, although she didn't expect to sleep any more tonight than she had last night. Last night she'd been dealing mainly with the surprise of his sudden return. Tonight she'd be battling the strength of a desire that seemed to have flamed from nothing. Even though she realized now that the seeds had been sown and taken root back on the island. Then, she'd been able to ignore it, pretend it was something else. But she'd built fantasies around Luke. Fantasies she'd scarcely acknowledged.

She needed to leave. And not just this party. She needed to leave this house, break the spell she was falling under. Already she was way too close to the precipice of stupidity.

"You can't leave," he said quietly, "because I have plans for you, Meg. Slow, sensuous plans." Holding her gaze, his hand inched farther up her thigh.

Lost. She was lost. The precipice rushed closer.

He wanted her and he knew she wanted him, knew what his touch was doing to her, how it heated her, and he knew she wanted more of it.

Luke pushed his chair back. Claiming jet lag, he excused them both.

In the entranceway, he shut the double doors behind them, muting the sounds of music and conversation. Illuminated only by flickering candles and fairy lights, he murmured, "Mistletoe," and then pulled her to him and kissed her. Meg welcomed the press of his hard body against hers, reveled in the taste of him. The man she'd married. His mouth and lips and tongue teased and explored and seduced. Already, she knew the way their mouths fit together, knew the scent of him. He gripped her waist, slid his hands to cup her behind, she answered his pull with an involuntary rocking of her hips.

He shuddered in her arms and broke the kiss to rest his forehead against hers, breathing as heavily as she was. "I made you a promise, Meg. Will you let me keep it?"

5

MEG NODDED her agreement, the small movement moving both their heads. Reaching up, Luke pulled the mistletoe free, then led her past the Christmas tree slowing only enough to brush his lips across hers. Once, and then again. Light and shadows danced across his face.

They entered a hallway and he shut the door behind them, once again turning her, pressing her up against it as he kissed her, one hand holding the mistletoe above them, the other sliding up beneath her dress over nylon, encountering bare skin at the top of her thigh.

The hand stilled, the kiss stopped and the mistletoe dropped to the floor.

Luke drew back. "Stockings?" he asked, his voice hoarse but his fingers still burning against her skin.

Meg shrugged, her throat suddenly too dry for words. She hadn't meant the stockings for him; she preferred them to pantyhose, but she also liked their risqué-ness, as she liked her lacy lingerie. It was supposed to be her *secret* weakness.

"Pretty, quiet, Nurse Meg. I knew there was more to you than met the eye. Be very, very grateful I didn't know that till now." He took a step back from her. "Show me."

She hesitated. She was no lingerie model.

"Show me," he insisted again, his voice a command as though she were a siren, as though she, Meg Elliot, tempted him to danger.

"I can't." Shyness warred with a budding sense of power. "Not here. Someone could come this way."

Luke grasped her hand and tugged her down the hallway and into the first door they came to, shutting it behind them. Meg took a few steps into the library with its walls of books and its two-seater couch. She turned back to see Luke leaning against the door, watching her. "Show me."

Somewhere in the last hour she'd stopped pretending to herself that she didn't desire him, hadn't always recognized that something in him called to her. One night with her husband. She was entitled to that much, wasn't she?

Slowly, her hands against her thighs, she walked her fingers to gather up the fabric of her dress, lifting it higher till the tops of her stockings were just visible, a stark line against her pale skin. She opened her hands and let the fabric fall back into place.

Luke stood utterly still. Never had she seen such naked desire in a man's eyes. And it was all for her.

He closed the gap between them and holding her gaze ran both hands beneath her dress and up the outside of her thighs till his palms cupped the strip of skin between black nylon and red lace. His eyelids dropped lower and he drew in a deep, shuddering breath as his hands slid farther around, cupping and pulling her against him.

And then he kissed her, the way only he ever had, fitting his mouth perfectly to hers, slowly, sweetly, joining them seamlessly and with just his kiss transporting her, promising her pleasure. Heat and urgency and need that inflamed her with reciprocal need. Hooking his thumbs over the edge of her panties, he slid them down her legs and she stepped out of them—a scrap of lace on the dark wood flooring.

Large, warm hands skimmed back up her thighs, passing the tops of her stockings till they rested on bare skin.

She'd drunk only a few sips of champagne throughout the evening; the intoxication that governed her now was fueled by desire. Meg tugged the hem of his shirt free, sliding her own hands against the heat of him. She pulled his bow tie undone, and with frantic fingers worked at the buttons of his finely pleated shirt till she could push apart the sides and touch her palms, her fingers, to the strength and contours of his torso. She eased his shirt back from his shoulders. A raised scar ran across his right shoulder. The gash that had started the chain of events that led to now. She touched her lips to his shoulder, grateful for the first time for that injury.

Beneath her fingertips lay the heated silk of skin over hard, contoured muscle, the light abrasion of hair, she felt his deeply indrawn breath and the rapid beat of his heart, knew it matched her own.

He cupped his hand between her legs, slid a finger through her folds, found her wet for him. Silver eyes darkened to pewter. "Tell me what you want, Meg."

No one had ever asked her that. And the answer was both complicated and blindingly simple. "I want you. Now."

He led her to the couch, sat and pulled her down on top of him, her knees straddling his thighs, she pressed her center against the hardness of him. Luke kissed her lips, her throat, her shoulder. He pushed the skirt of her dress up so he could freely touch the skin that seemed to so delight him. Enthralling her in the process.

He slipped the clips from her hair so that it tumbled loose around her shoulders. Finding the zipper at the back of her dress, he slid it down, peeled the dress from her so that it was now no more than a silken red pool of fabric around her waist.

"Show me how you like to be touched. I want to give you pleasure."

Already he was. So much more pleasure than she'd ever known. Warm hands and warmer lips skimmed over every inch, every curve and dip of bare and lace-covered skin, caressing and teasing, adding fuel to the already-burning flames, till she writhed with need. She covered his hands with hers as he cupped her breasts and her head fell back.

For now, he was her husband. And she wanted him. Needed him. Hard and deep within her.

For now.

"Condom?" Please, please let him have one because heaven knew what she'd do if he didn't.

He nodded, pulling a foil square from his pocket as she reached for his zipper and freed the straining length of him. Waiting just long enough for him to cover himself, she slid down onto the length of him, bringing him home, shuddering with pleasure as he stretched and filled her.

His gaze locked with hers, intent and powerful, as she rocked against him, with him, over him. Passion turned his eyes storm-dark. Her fingers dug into his shoulders as his hands gripped her hips and they found a building rhythm of their own. Clamoring need and desperate desire drove them higher and faster till sensation, the effervescence of champagne bubbles, filled and overwhelmed her. She cried her arching completion moments before he drove his release home.

Meg fell forward, resting her head on the top of his and he snaked his arms around her waist and held her to him, his ear to her thudding heart. When he'd promised to make her forget her sorrows, she hadn't realized he'd make her forget her very self. That in his arms she would forget her inhibitions and become the woman she imagined she saw in his eyes.

The silence and stillness of the room stole over them as her heartbeat slowed and her gasping breath eased.

What now? Too soon the taunting inner voice asked. What now, indeed. She had no idea, no answer. Her mind still reeled from the power and passion of their lovemaking. She pulled away from Luke, and his clasp loosened. She slipped her arms back into the sleeves of her dress. He helped ease the fabric up over her shoulders, planting a kiss between her breasts the moment before the spot was covered. She eased out of his lap and Luke stood, too.

Not meeting his gaze, she turned and searched for her panties. She bent to pick them up, but they were snatched out of her reach before she touched them. He slipped them into his pocket.

Wordlessly, they walked to the library door. She reached for the handle, but he covered her hand with his. And when she looked at him, he kissed her, gentle and lingering. They turned the handle together and stepped out into the hallway. When she would have headed the way they had come he shook his head, and with a firm grip on her hand led her farther down the hallway. He stopped at the third door. The guest room. His room.

His seeking gaze searched her face. "This time I want you naked and beneath me."

Meg caught her bottom lip with her teeth. Apparently finding what he sought, Luke opened the door and pulled her with him into the darkened room, whispering, "Never let it be said that I didn't utterly satisfy my wife."

MEG WOKE IN her husband's bed, her head resting in the hollow of his shoulder, her arm draped over his chest, her legs entwined with his.

He'd kept his promise and given her so much more.

Slowly, carefully, she disentangled herself and eased from the bed. He didn't so much as stir.

As she slipped back into her dress and gathered up her discarded stockings and shoes, she paused by the wide window. They'd slept with the curtains open and overnight a light snow had fallen, dusting the trees and boulders on the lake shore. The sight was so beautiful that it made her heart ache. Soon she'd be gone from here. She'd stepped onto a stage and played her part. But the time for her exit was drawing inexorably closer.

Feeling like an intruder, she slunk back through the still house. Bundling up against the cold, she took Caesar for his morning walk along the shore, tossing his stick repeatedly. Tempted by beauty's promise of stillness and serenity, she walked out to the end of the jetty and looked over the lake. The mountains on the far side were still obscured by heavy cloud.

At the sound of footsteps, she turned, a leap in her pulse. Not Luke but Jason. Her heart sank and she realized she'd hoped, wanted, it to be Luke. Wanted to see the man she'd made love to last night. Wanted to see his face and at the same time was afraid to. In the light of day would there be any of last night's tenderness and connection, or would it be regret and distance she saw there?

"I thought I saw someone down here." Jason smiled, warmth in his voice. He looked a little like Luke. Similar build and coloring but his watery-blue eyes were always moving, scanning the surroundings.

Meg smiled back, but doubts gnawed at her. What had Jason done to cause Luke to dislike him so intensely? Intensely enough that he would rather marry her than have his half brother inherit from him.

"So are the rumors true? Has my brother come home?"

Half brother. Meg nearly said that out loud. Luke was always careful to draw the distinction. "Yes."

Jason's smile wavered and he glanced over his shoulder at the house. Was that anxiety in his question? Jason had always seemed eager for Luke's return.

"I was just going back inside. Come in. He's probably up by now." Meg walked back along the jetty. Jason fell into step beside her.

"I'm on my way to meet someone and I want to go before there's any more snow. I haven't got time to stop. I'll call in later."

She shrugged. "I'll let him know to expect you."

"And let him know…"

She waited for him to finish.

"Nothing," he finally said. "Just…put in a good word for me, will you?" She walked round to the front of the house with him. As he drove away, she climbed the stairs.

The front door swung open. Luke, in jeans and bare feet, pulled an olive-green T-shirt over his head. He tugged the hem of the shirt over the plane of his stomach and looked past Meg. Jason's red Corvette disappeared around a bend in the road, leaving it empty and still. "Damn." Luke's gaze came back to her. "How long was he here and what did he want?"

"Not long and to know if you were home." Meg stepped past Luke and into the house. The Christmas tree dominated the entranceway. They'd kissed here last night. Her face heated with the recollections of where that had led to.

Luke's hand wrapped around her wrist, stopping her when she would have walked away, turning her back to face him. "What did you tell him?"

"I told him that yes, you were home."

"What else?"

Meg tugged her hand free. "Ask him yourself. I don't want to be a pawn in your petty squabbles."

"They're not petty."

"No, I suppose not." For all that she hadn't known Luke long, she knew him well enough to be certain of that. "But I still don't want to be caught in the middle of whatever it is. I think Jason really did try to help me while you were gone."

"If he did, it was for his own reasons." The creases in his brow deepened. "He blackmailed my mother."

A woman who'd devoted her life to others. A year after her death, the villagers still spoke of her with love, talked about her compassion and understanding and her ability to get things done. They'd probably still be talking about her a decade from now. And Jason had blackmailed her? "No." He wouldn't have, would he?

"Right up until her death. I didn't find out till I went through her papers in Indonesia."

"I remember your saying you'd discovered something about him. You were so angry."

"Still am."

As Meg repositioned a gold bauble on the tree, she

could just make out his distorted reflection in its surface. "What are you going to do about it?"

"I haven't made a final decision. I want to talk to him first. Confront him with it."

"Will you bring charges?" She turned back to him.

Grimness tightened his mouth. A mouth that could give such pleasure. "Most likely. After I strip him of the car, the house and the job I gave him."

"Oh."

"Don't play the disappointed-in-me card, Meg. The man was blackmailing my mother. I owe it to her."

"You're right, and I'm not disappointed."

"But?"

"I just wondered if that was your only option."

"Unless you can suggest a better one, one that does justice to my mother?"

As Meg shook her head, he slid his phone from the pocket of his jeans, punched in a number. "Jason. You should have stuck around." Did Jason hear the command in the quietly spoken sentence? Meg tuned out the short conversation as she walked away. Luke caught up with her in the kitchen as she was pouring two coffees. "He'll be back later today."

She passed him a mug. As she lifted hers to her nose to inhale the fragrance, the ring on her finger caught her eye. The dinner was over, there was no need for her to wear it any longer. Putting down her coffee, she twisted the simple gold band from her finger and held it out to him.

He looked at her hand but didn't reach for the ring and a glimmer of a smile touched his lips. "You can't give it back to me. I never gave it to you in the first place."

Oh. Right. So much for that gesture. Feeling like a fool, she went to slip the ring into her pocket. He did reach for her then. He picked up her left hand and slid the ring back into place. "But leave it there for now. I didn't want to make you a pawn, Meg. I wanted to give you something."

"And to stop Jason getting anything."

"Mainly that," he agreed. "And you know what else?"

"What?"

"This isn't how I planned on starting this morning."

She didn't want to think about what he might mean by that. There were a number of possibilities. All of the ones that sprang to her mind were unwise.

He tugged her closer, pressed a soft, beguiling kiss to her lips. Very unwise.

"Good morning," he said with a smile once he'd pulled away, his gaze locking on to hers.

All of her tension had melted with just that one kiss. It was a masterful tactic, a potent secret weapon in his arsenal. "Good morning." *Kiss me again.*

But he didn't. "Have you had breakfast? Or is it lunchtime already again?"

"Breakfast, and no, I haven't eaten. But Luke, I think I should go."

She watched his face, his eyes, but couldn't read his reaction. "Eat first," he finally said.

Not, *No, don't go, Meg,* which she would have been foolish to expect. Sometimes, though, she was foolish. Last night being the most recent example. Making love to a man she had no future with. Letting herself love him, even just a little.

In the kitchen, he had her sit on a stool at the breakfast bar while he got out a pan and bacon and eggs. "How did you learn to cook?" No man had ever cooked for her.

He passed her a mug of coffee. "Mom got heavily into her charity work from an early age. She wasn't always around a lot. And when I was a teenager I went through several years of being constantly hungry. Appetite's a great motivator. It's not like I can produce a gourmet meal or anything, but I can do the basics. You want a filling, sustaining meal after or before a day's snow skiing or water skiing? I'm your man."

I'm your man? The expression was depressingly appealing. As was the man himself.

Within a few minutes he'd carried two plates of eggs and crispy bacon to the small oak table in the breakfast nook. He sat at a right angle to her and they ate in a silence that would have been restful were it not for Meg's regret and quiet despair about how soon this was ending.

Beyond the window, snow flakes began to drift and swirl.

She hadn't heard a weather report in days, but Jason had spoken as though more snow was expected. "Thank you." She stood from the table. "Now I should go." She had to end it. The sooner the better. Drawn-out goodbyes were too hard, too painful.

"I thought your car was at the mechanic's till tomorrow."

That was her problem. "It is." She caught her bottom lip in her teeth. "You could take me to Sally's?"

Silver eyes assessed her. "Is that what you want?"

No, I want you to ask me to stay. To see where this thing we have leads. Unless this thing we have is all in my head. "Yes, it's what I want."

"Because from what I know of you, the things you've told me, the things I've seen, you don't always consult your own needs."

Meg said nothing. Was she that transparent? She did put other people's needs ahead of her own. That was how she'd been brought up. That was what she was supposed to do, wasn't it?

"You've called her?" he asked after a pause.

"Not yet." But she would, and could only hope that Sally kept her questions to herself. For her months here she'd pretended she'd had a real marriage. Now, two days after her husband's return, she was seeking sanctuary at her friend's place. But fortunately, in those two months, Sally truly had become a friend.

"What does staying at Sally's achieve?"

Couldn't he just let it go? She sighed and tried to keep her voice neutral. "Distance. Perspective. It gives you your home and your life back." But mainly, it would stop her doing dumb things like watching his hands as he held his fork or his cup and remembering the feel of those hands on her.

Luke looked toward the window but said nothing.

Meg paused at the doorway. "I'll need an hour to gather up all my things from around the house and finish packing."

He gave a single abrupt nod and she left the room. It was easy enough to pack up her clothes and belongings from the master bedroom, but she took her time, folding slowly, uncharacteristically uncertain about how best to pack her bags. In the wardrobe, she let herself touch Luke's suits, his sweaters. Beside the bed, she straightened the fishing magazine and the book that she'd left all this time on the bedside table. She'd read the book— a thriller—her first month here. Imagining a connection with him as she did so. Her fingers turning the same pages his had.

She lingered in front of the wide window. Its view over

the lake had always brought her a measure of serenity. It didn't today. Today, the dark turbulent sky matched the oppression she felt.

She finished in the bedroom but needed to check the rest of the rooms. Over the months she'd lived here, she'd managed to spread herself and her bits and pieces throughout the house. She'd have to do a room-by-room search.

At the door to the library, she paused, not sure she wanted to face the scene of last night's…encounter. She toyed with the idea of just buying a new book to replace the half read one she'd left in there, then decided she was being ridiculous. She was a grown woman, for goodness' sake. She pushed open the door and stepped inside.

Luke sat on the couch, a sheaf of hand-written papers on his lap, his long denim-clad legs stretched out and crossed at the ankles. He looked up as she entered and the memories came flooding back.

Memories of sights; shadows and contours, and scents; his shampoo, his sweat, the essence of Luke himself and sensation; frantic hands, warm lips on skin, desperate longing and utter completion filled her mind. Images of her own reckless abandon.

"I just," she cleared her throat, "came to get my book." She pointed at the book on the small table beside him. He watched her silently as she dashed forward to snatch it up and backed out of the room.

As she shut the door behind her again, she thought she heard him speak. A short phrase, too indistinct for her to make out. *Show me*. She was imagining things. Nothing to show. No stockings today, no red lace. White and a little lacy, with a small bow between her breasts.

But mainly plain. That's who she really was. But for a few forbidden seconds she imagined the things she could wear for him if— She cut off her own thoughts. No ifs. No maybes. They'd had an agreement. She'd lived up to her part of it. And now she was going. Last night was…a bonus. Such an inadequate word. A night's insight into a world of possibilities, of pleasure and promise and wholeness.

Ten minutes later he found her on the stairway, strode up to meet her and took her case from her hand. He carried it down, set it by the Christmas tree in the entrance. "There's more?"

"One."

She followed him up to the bedroom. Her second case, bulging and heavy, sat at the base of the bed. He looked about the room, his gaze sweeping from the bed to her face. "I'll think of you when I'm sleeping in here."

"Don't, Luke."

"Don't think of you when I'm sleeping in here? Or don't tell you that I will?"

"Don't…tell me." It was only fair that he think of her; she'd thought of him often enough as she'd lain there, and knew she would think of him still wherever she went next. For a time at least. But time healed all, dulled memories and yearnings. Eventually she'd forget him. Forget last night. Move on. She had to.

"I spoke to Mark this morning."

The simple statement doused the recollections. Mark was his attorney as well as his friend. "And?"

"And he's coming round tomorrow morning. But he said, whatever we do, we shouldn't sleep together." His lips twitched.

How could he think this was funny? But his amusement called a response from her, a spark of un-Meg-like mischief. Mark would surely be appalled at how incautious their actions had been. "Did you tell him?"

Luke shook his head. "Didn't want to spoil his weekend. I'll tell him tomorrow."

"It won't make a difference, you know." She wanted Luke to know that. "I don't want anything from you. I never did. The fact that we slept together doesn't change that."

"Nothing, Meg?" He picked up her case as though it was weightless. "When you have money, it seems everyone wants something from you. It's hard to believe that there are people who really don't."

Maybe he wouldn't truly believe that till she walked away from him.

"Even my mother. She only approved of me and what I did because it meant I could donate money to her causes. And maybe she was right."

"That wasn't the only reason she approved of you. She loved you."

"I'm sure she did." He spoke without conviction.

"She couldn't not have." Meg spoke with more vehemence than she'd meant to. She half loved him herself and she'd known him only a whisper of time.

Luke's eyebrows lifted. And Meg regretted the intensity of her words. Did they reveal too much? Too much of what? She couldn't even say herself. Her feelings, her heart, were galloping ahead to places her mind knew they shouldn't. They'd passed like, and attraction, passed fascination and warmth, were mired in enthrallment, a deep drugging spell of connection and wanting and rightness.

But she wouldn't let it be anything more than that. It was a spell that could, and would have to, be broken. Because she was leaving.

That was what they'd agreed.

6

Luke carried Meg's suitcase downstairs, set it beside the first and said what he'd known for the last hour. "We're going to have to wait till the snow stops and the roads are cleared." She followed his gaze through the panes of glass bordering the door. Snow had blanketed the pines and the ground outside in white and was still falling.

He didn't know what to expect. Frustration that she couldn't get away, as she so clearly wanted to, or resignation that she was stuck here with him for longer still? He didn't expect her to step toward the door and place her fingertips on the glass, soft wonderment in her expression. "I grew up in southern California. It never snowed." She glanced at him. "It's so beautiful," she said, turning back to the window.

As she was, beautiful and serene and unspoiled, like the snow outside.

And always able to find a silver lining.

"It might be. But it's no good for driving in." He was deliberately brusque because it beat the hell out of getting sappy, of letting the way she affected him on so many levels show. They'd made love last night, but she was going this morning. It was for the best. Too much time with her was blurring the lines between what he ought to do, send her off so that she could find someone less jaded, someone who shared her optimism and her dreams, and what he wanted to do, take her back upstairs to his bed, make her his, hope a winter-long blizzard moved in.

He needed to find some kind of middle ground. "Let's go for a walk."

Her slow smile of pleasure and approval warmed him. Or maybe all she felt was relief at not being trapped indoors with him. He handed her her coat from the closet. "There are so many things we'll never do together. But we've got this day, whether we like it or not."

She'd be gone soon enough. A walk in the snow couldn't hurt. Layers and layers of clothing. And it was surely better than being inside with her with little to do except be ambushed by thoughts of making love to her again, sinking into her heat, of watching a different kind of wonderment on her face, of seeing her ecstasy. Which was how he'd spent the morning. Staying out of her way but acutely aware of her.

She was her own kind of delirium. He could no longer pretend his reaction to her was a product of fever, and honesty compelled him to admit that something about her had called to him well before his infection had become serious. The attraction of innocence, of her optimism? Wanting to drench himself in her aura. *Snap out of it.* He shoved his arms into his coat, hands into gloves and his feet into snow boots and stood apart from her, not so much as looking at her, while he listened to her movements, the rustle of clothing, the zipper on her jacket sliding up, a soft stomp as she pushed her feet into boots.

He opened the door and stepped outside, breathed

deeply of the Meg-free air. The door closed behind him. Her shoulder nestled against his. Her scent assailed him. The scent he'd reveled in last night.

She walked ahead, tripping lightly down the steps, her footsteps crunching through snow as she skipped ahead, her brightly colored Sherpa hat bobbing with her footsteps, the tassels by her ears swinging like braids. Already she was committed to an idea that was nothing more than an off-the-cuff suggestion to find a way through the situation. Luke followed, gloved hands in his pockets, his step measured and slow. She stopped, flung her arms wide, tipped her face skyward and spun in a slow circle, embracing the day. Already her nose and cheeks were pink. He wanted to kiss her. Heaven help him. He wanted to kiss those cheeks, those eyes, those lips. "Help me make a snowman." She crouched down, gathered a ball of snow and began rolling it.

She'd make a great mother. Not something he'd ever thought before about the women he'd been involved with. She had so much of the carefree spirit of a child within her. And yet she'd seen hardship, she'd been confronted with it daily in Indonesia. Seen it and chosen to keep the flame of optimism alight within her. He crouched, too, began rolling a second snowball. He couldn't remember the last time he'd done this, certainly not since he was a child. He stacked his snowball on top of the larger one she'd rolled and began rolling a third for the head.

"Carrot," she announced, "for the nose. And I don't suppose you have buttons?"

He shook his head.

She headed back to the house. "I'll find something."

Luke was settling the head in place when Meg came hurrying back with a carrot and two plums. She pressed the carrot and fruit into place, one of the plums shedding a single purple tear. Then she wrapped her scarf around the snowman's neck and pulled a camera from her pocket. "Stand by Frosty."

"Frosty?"

"It's almost Christmas. What else are we supposed to call him?"

He reached for the camera. "You stand by...Frosty. I'll take your picture."

She shook her head and the light in her eyes dimmed just a little. "I'd like one of you."

To remember him by? "For that matter, I'd like one of you." To remember her by. Even though he had the feeling his problem was going to be in trying to forget her.

She shrugged and stood by the snowman. "Come stand with us. My arm is just long enough to take a picture of us both."

He stood at her side and taking a glove off, eased the camera from her hand. "My arm's longer." She pressed up against him and without thinking, he slid his free arm around her shoulders, pulled her closer. The thinking occurred too late, when he inhaled the fragrance of her shampoo. "On three. One. Two. Three." The shutter clicked.

"One more," she said. "Just in case."

"On three again." This time on three, as the shutter clicked she wriggled in his hold and planted a quick kiss on his cheek.

"Let me see it," she said as though she hadn't just done that—kissed him as though it was a perfectly ordinary thing to do. Which, perhaps with someone else it would be, but from Meg it hadn't felt ordinary. It had felt like a gift.

Refusing to be distracted, he adjusted the setting to replay and, not looking at the picture, passed her the camera. What he did look at was her. Her breath coming in small misty puffs. Her cheeks and nose getting redder still with the cold. The lips that had moments ago touched his face. So much for not getting distracted.

He dropped all pretence of resolution and cupped a hand to one rosy cheek. Meg looked up, a smile playing about her lips. The smile dimmed and her lips parted as she read his intent. Using his teeth he pulled his other glove off, let it fall to the snow so that he could frame her face with both his hands. Skin against skin.

Slowly, he lowered his head and kissed her.

Properly.

If they only had this day left, if he only had a finite and too-limited number of kisses left, then he wasn't going to let her waste them on his cheek.

The warmth of her mouth was an erotic contrast to the chill of her lips. Her heat, as his tongue teased and tasted, swamped him. She wrapped her arms around his waist and kissed him back, softened against him. Pure Meg. Laughter and depth, temptation and innocence. His past, his present and his— Just his past and his present. That's all it would be.

He kissed her still, widening his stance so that he could fit her more closely against him. Kissing her out here was safe. Layers of clothing and a bitter chill to prevent his taking any of them off. But the temptation was so great that he'd likely stay out till they both froze just for the pleasure of feeling her pliant mouth beneath his, her warmth and sweetness, her eagerness.

It was Meg who broke the kiss, leaning back, her arms

looped around his waist so that her hips pressed a little
more firmly against his. "I don't think we should."

He'd think a little more clearly if it wasn't for those
hips. He knew all the reasons why she was right. This
was ending. And it needed to end cleanly. As cleanly
as was possible given what had already passed between
them. He didn't want to hurt her. "You're right. But just
one more." He waited for her smile, waited till the in-
decision in her eyes was swept away by agreement and
the flare of hunger as she abandoned reason and caution
and lifted her face to his. Meg. His wife. So quick to respond to him. Something primal stirred. More than lust.
He chose not to examine it, let desire and pure pleasure
take the upper hand.

They were both breathing heavily, their breaths mingling in the air, by the time she again pulled away. And
this time she broke all contact, stepping away from his
touch, turning to adjust the snowman's carrot nose. "We
should go in."

And this time he knew better than to disagree. Because
despite what he'd thought, kissing her out here wasn't
safe. Far from it. Kissing the way they had been spoke
too openly of more, of picking up where they'd left off
last night. Of his falling into her heat. Of staying there.

"Besides, I'm cold." Her cheeks were flushed.

Luke lifted her hand, pulled a glove off and enclosed
her fingers in his. He tucked her hand against his side as
he led her back to the house.

Inside again, he hung up their coats. He didn't look
at her cases by the front door as he led her toward the
living room, knew a moment's hesitation as they passed
the Christmas tree, he wouldn't kiss her inside, knew
another moment as they passed the stairs, the stairs he

wouldn't lead her up to his bedroom. Finally in the relative sanctuary of the living room, he lit the fire. "Stand here. Warm yourself."

Unquestioning and not meeting his gaze, she held her hands out to the flames.

Luke left the room, returned in five minutes carrying two cups of cocoa. He didn't know why looking after her gave him such pleasure and satisfaction, but it did. She stood exactly where he'd left her, staring into the flames.

"You're warm enough?" He handed her a cup of cocoa and she nodded as she took it, seemingly intrigued by the marshmallows floating on the top.

"What now?" she asked.

Almost all of the ideas that sprang to mind were unwise. "I have a suggestion."

Her gaze lifted and narrowed on him.

"Not that." He laughed. Because if he didn't laugh he'd take the assumption as an invitation. "Not that the idea doesn't have merit." A slow blush crept up her face. "I'm suggesting a movie." She quickly covered the flash of disappointment in her gaze. But the flash had pleased the unwise part of him. Like her, he covered the reaction. He slid a movie into the player, picked up the remote. "The snow's stopped. Soon enough the roads will be cleared and you'll leave." He led her to the couch and sat close beside her, pulling the broad coffee table closer so that he could rest his feet on it. She watched him, waiting for him to continue. He settled into the soft black leather of the couch, pulled her back with him and tried to explain his reasoning. "I never intended to marry. Never thought I would. I don't need other people the way some do. I'm content on my own." He slipped an arm around her shoulders. "So this might be it. My only chance to spend time with my wife. To experience married life. We can be like an old couple who have comfortable routines they've settled into over a lifetime of being together. Cocoa and a movie on a snowy afternoon. We'll argue over chick flick or action movie." He picked up the remote, pointed it at the TV and the screen flickered to life. "Action movie will win because we watched your chick flick last week."

As the opening credits rolled and on-screen a car wound its way up a rocky mountainside at night, she nestled a little closer and stretched her legs out alongside his, resting her small feet, in their red socks, beside his.

They were an hour into the movie which had managed to capture only a portion of his awareness away from her, when Caesar started barking. Moments later the doorbell chimed. Luke glanced at his watch, his mood darkening. He stood. "You keep watching. I just have to deal with this."

She reached for the remote, located the Pause button. "I'll wait."

"I'm not sure how long this will take. Depends on how much of a fuss he makes."

"He? Jason?"

Luke nodded, resenting this intrusion, the sullying of his afternoon with her. But he needed to deal with it. He'd been thinking about their earlier conversation, about finding a way to deal with Jason that did justice to his mother.

"I'll wait," she said, looking away from him as she settled back into the cushioning leather, looking small and stoic, expecting better of him than he was prepared to give. On-screen, the hero was frozen with a gun pressed to the villain's temple, his eyes bleak.

7

SECONDS AFTER Luke strode from the room, the sound of voices, muted but clipped, reached Meg, then faded as they headed to Luke's office along the hallway. She made a bowl of popcorn, set it on the coffee table and then crossed to the wide windows. Outside, Frosty stood a lonely sentinel on the lawn, Meg's scarf loose about his neck, his eyes dark and desolate. For a time she heard nothing. Then shouting. She crossed to the open living room door, her fingers gripping the door frame, hesitant.

Only one man was shouting. Jason. She couldn't hear Luke at all.

She was still standing there, distressed by the anger she heard and wondering whether there was anything she could do to help, when the voice quieted. A minute later, Jason stormed out of Luke's office, slamming the door behind him. He stalked along the hallway toward her.

"Will you be okay?"

Jason looked up, a dark dislike glittered in his eyes. "Don't pretend you care."

"I'm not pretending."

His step slowed. "Then call your husband off."

"It's not my place."

Jason shook his head, disbelieving. "Indonesia. What the hell am I supposed to do there?"

"Indonesia?" That was what Luke had decided?

"The precious Maitland Foundation. I'm supposed to spend the next two years in hell."

"Beats jail," she said quietly.

"He couldn't prove it."

Not, I didn't do it. "It's not so bad. You might even like it. It might even be good for you."

"That's what he said." Jason strode away cursing, and Meg went back into the living room, resumed her seat on the couch. Such a world of difference between the two men. Outside, an engine roared into life. Tires screeched. Several minutes later Luke eased himself down beside her, slipped his arm back around her shoulders. He tugged her in close.

"Good choice." She chanced a glance at him. He didn't look happy but wasn't quite as grim as when he'd left.

He leaned closer, kissed the top of her head and for a second rested his cheek there. "I guess so. Now start this movie up again or I'll have to assume control of the remote." No mention of the fact that the roads must now be drivable.

Meg relaxed against him, breathed in his nearness and pressed the button for play.

If only.

If only they were a married couple and this was their life. If only he wanted to spend all his snowy afternoons, and rainy and sunny and windy ones, with her. A good man sharing the moments as he held her. Not to mention his nights and mornings, too. Instead of a man who wanted to have this brief time with her and then send her on her way.

Too soon the movie ended. She should stand, move away from Luke, get him to take her to Sally's. But she didn't move.

"The sequel's even better," he said, his arm still draped over her shoulders, his body pressed against hers.

"I'd heard that it was. So often they're not." She was pathetic. Wanting this. Wanting the crumbs of his presence and affection. She was too scared to analyze what it was she felt for her husband, but it was powerful enough that she wanted to eke out every moment she had left with him.

"I have it. Do you want to watch it?"

More than anything, because it bought her another couple of hours with Luke. She made to stand because another couple of hours only prolonged the inevitable. He wanted hours; she wanted years, a lifetime even. He pulled her effortlessly back down. "I should get going to Sally's," she said. She'd always been the type to rip a bandage off and get the pain over with.

"Should or want to?" He searched her face.

"Should." It was the last thing she wanted.

"Then don't. Stay here. This is okay, isn't it?" As though that was the only thing stopping her from staying.

This was so much better than okay, which was precisely why she *should* go to Sally's.

"I make a mean spaghetti Bolognese."

"Wouldn't it be better for both of us if I left now?"

He contemplated her question, gave it more thought than she'd expected and she found herself on tenterhooks for his answer. Finally, he shook his head. "I like being near you, Meg. I don't know why. You ease something within me. I'm going to miss you when you go, so I'm in no hurry for that to happen."

He spoke an echo of her thoughts out loud.

Whatever time they had would be all that she would get. She wasn't going to curtail it. She sank back into the cushions of the couch, determined instead to make every minute, every second of these precious hours count, to store every moment in her memory.

As they watched the sequel, the afternoon bled into dusk which darkened quickly to night. They ate together, his spaghetti Bolognese as good as he'd claimed. And then they watched the third and final installment.

As the closing credits rolled, neither of them made any move to stand.

Far from it. "Lie down here with me," he said as though he knew that if she got up from the couch it would be to leave. It had to be. "It's wide enough."

So they lay down facing one another, heads on cushions. His hand resting at the curve of her waist.

"What will you do when you leave here?" he asked.

Meg chewed her lip. "Sally's offered me a job with the Maitland Foundation."

"You've accepted?"

She shook her head. "I wanted to see what you thought. Whether that might keep me too close?"

His hand curved more firmly around her. "The thought of having you close isn't such a terrible thing."

"But after people have thought we were married."

"We were married."

"Not properly."

He shifted his hand, found hers, touched a finger to the gold band adorning it. "Tell that to the minister."

"I just mean that it could be awkward."

"I do what I think is right. I thought, still do, that marrying you was the right thing to do at the time." He pulled her a little closer. "I've had no cause to regret that decision."

"You don't regret what we did last night?"

A smile spread across his face. "How could I possibly regret that? The very thought of it could sustain me for years to come."

"I can't help feeling that we're missing something. That we ought to be regretting it."

"In that case, you're thinking too much."

Maybe he was right. She was overthinking things. They'd had their night. She'd be able to take those memories and these with her, tucked up beside him, the scent of his cologne, the snow outside, the fire inside. He would be her benchmark, her standard. But he so far outshone anyone else she'd ever met that it was impossible to imagine that standard being reached again.

They lay on the couch talking for hours about everything and nothing. She'd never shared so much of herself with anyone or felt so honored and warmed by the trust he showed in sharing with her.

They changed positions so that he was spooned behind her, stroking her side. After a time his hand slowed and stopped. His breathing softened.

Meg still lay awake. "What if I loved you?" she whispered into the darkness.

She felt a deeper stillness steal over him.

He'd heard.

He said nothing.

And she knew there was no "what if" about it. Somewhere, somehow she'd fallen in love with him, with his quiet strength and his deep integrity, with his silver eyes and the way he kissed her, held her, and because he of all people seemed to see the person she was inside.

But he hadn't asked for that—her love.

"That wouldn't be a good idea," he said gently.

LUKE FELT MEG shrink a little away from him and against overriding impulse he didn't pull her back. She didn't really love him. She couldn't because he was all wrong for her. He was too old, too cynical about life and people and love. He was a loner. Wasn't he?

She deserved someone closer to her own age, someone closer to her in optimism and kindness. She imagined qualities in him he didn't have.

He would let her go. Set her free.

In the morning.

And the thought filled him with desolation. It was the thought of a Meg-less existence that broke his resolve, made him pull her in closer to him, made him try to absorb a little of her essence into himself. He wanted something from her that he'd never wanted from a woman before—just to be with her, to have her near. And the nearer the better. The feelings were so new that he didn't know what to do with them, how to deal with them.

She'd helped him so much. Helped him on the island when he'd first been injured, helped him by marrying him, and the very thought of her had sustained him when he'd been ill. Even now, lying here like this, her breathing soft and gentle, she soothed something within him, filled and completed him. In so many ways she was his better half. But she deserved more. She deserved to find her own better half.

So he would help her by letting her go.

THE DOORBELL CHIMED through the house. Meg and Luke struggled to sitting, his arm falling from her. Through the windows a clear, bright day showed snow-covered mountains on the far side of the crystalline lake. Meg had never been so disappointed to see a beautiful day.

Luke stood, running a hand through his hair as he looked down at her. "That'll be Mark."

His attorney. That announcement, more than the weather even, told her that her time with Luke was over. She'd served her purpose, and in return had found a deep, brief perfection. That would be enough. It had to be.

They walked to the front door together. He would take Mark to his office. "This shouldn't take too long."

She nodded. She'd be gone before then. It was the best, the only, way. She wasn't going to stay for the humiliation of the terms he wanted to end their connection with, no matter how gently he would do it.

He turned for his office. Mark looked at her, pity in his gaze. "He'll look after you," he murmured.

Great, even his attorney felt sorry for her.

Luke stopped at the office door. "Wait," he said as though he knew she'd already decided to go. He held her gaze until she nodded.

Unable to stay in the house where for such a brief time she'd found bliss, Meg took Caesar outside, striding unseeing along the path she'd walked so often, and tried to shut out her awareness of the ticking time bomb that was Luke's meeting with Mark.

Caesar found and then dropped a stick in the center of the path. "Not today, buddy." She strode past it, but when he next overtook her, it was back in his mouth.

It was over. Her fantasy. And she knew the answer to the question she'd posed to Luke—would her working close by be a problem. It might not be for him, but it would be for her. Seeing him and having to not let him see she loved him. Hearing people talk about him. Seeing him dating other women. No, it definitely wasn't going to work for her. She wasn't that reasonable. She wasn't that thick-skinned.

She stopped at the base of a dead and blackened pine that alone had at some point been struck by lightning. Caesar dropped his stick and sniffed, his nose tracking to the body of a small bird, a mountain chickadee, lying still and stiff. Meg stared at the little corpse, her heart breaking at the sight.

She had to leave.

Despite tacitly agreeing to wait, she couldn't. She would get her car and go. She would do it before the meeting was even over, before Luke and Mark gently, kindly explained the details of how her happiness was to end. Because she knew she couldn't take their explanations with anything like the dignity they deserved. She considered her options. Sally would come if she called. Her friend would take her to collect her car. And then she could go. Somewhere. Anywhere. Away.

Pulling her phone from her pocket, she hurried back along the path. She caught sight of the lake and the snow-capped mountains through the screen of pine trees and stopped. It was a sight that had always filled her with peace and given her strength. She took a moment to absorb the view for the last time.

Caesar dropped his stick onto her foot.

She shook her head at him. "You don't give up, do you, buddy?" She bent to pick up the stick and stilled with her fingers wrapped around its roughened bark.

He didn't give up. He *never* gave up. Not when it came

to something he wanted. Even now he watched her, tail wagging, willing her to throw the stick.

Crystal-clear understanding and resolution welled within her.

Meg straightened and threw the stick. She wasn't running away. Not this time. She wasn't subjugating her needs. She wasn't going to go without telling Luke that she loved him. Without asking him to at least try to love her back. To give her, them, a chance.

Something had begun between them back on the island and that something had blossomed and grown into so much more.

He'd said himself that she should give her needs priority, ask more for the things she wanted. And the only thing, the only one, she wanted and needed was him.

He could grow to love her back. She knew it. He just had to let himself. Because not only was he necessary to her, she was, if not necessary, then at least good, for him. She believed that much with all her heavy heart. A heart that nurtured an insistent flicker of hope.

All she had to lose was her pride. And it was worth the sacrifice to know that she wasn't going to turn tail. She ran. Not away from him but toward him, toward their home, up the steps pausing briefly at the Christmas tree to make her wish on the single bright star at its top and burst into his office.

Conversation stopped as Luke and Mark looked up at her from the leather armchairs in front of Luke's desk, surprise in two pairs of eyes. They both stood. Meg's gaze went briefly to the single thin stack of papers neatly aligned on Luke's desk. Divorce papers? Her heart hammered in her chest.

She walked up to Luke, lifted the mistletoe she'd

pulled from the Christmas tree and held it above his head. Stretching up onto her tiptoes, she kissed him, joining her mouth to his, trying to put a forewarning of her love into the tenderness of her kiss.

His arms slid obligingly around her waist, he angled his head to deepen the kiss. She could almost give in to the temptation of just this, being held in his arms. But she needed more. She broke the kiss, stepped back and out of his hold. "Mark, I want to talk to my husband. Alone." She kept her gaze on Luke, he met it steadily, emotions in his eyes she didn't dare interpret and a glimmer of wry amusement at her demand.

"I was just going. I'll see myself out." Mark's voice reached her seconds before he shut the office door quietly behind him. Leaving her alone with Luke.

For the longest time she stared at him, he was everything to her; he was the man she loved. She just had to tell him that.

She took a deep breath and pointed to his desk. "I won't sign those papers."

He frowned and his gaze flicked to the desk.

"I don't care what you're offering. I want more. I want you. I'm not going to let you shut me out of your life because you don't want to need anyone. It doesn't work that way. You need me. You just don't know it. And I…I need you. I love you. You might not be ready for that yet, but you have to give it, me, a chance."

Luke closed the distance she'd tried to establish and pressed a finger to her lips, silencing her. He eased the mistletoe from her fingers, held it above her head and sliding his finger from her lips, replaced it with his mouth, looped his arms once more around her.

Too soon he broke the kiss. "I don't want you to sign those papers."

"You don't?"

"No." He shook his head and a smile touched his lips. "They're to do with Jason. Not you. Not us."

"But I thought…Mark…he wasn't here because of me, because of you wanting a divorce?"

"We did discuss you."

"And?"

"I told him we'd slept together."

"And?"

"And I told him I love you, which was wrong of me."

Because it wasn't the truth? Her jaw clenched with the force of suppressed emotion.

He stroked his thumbs over her cheeks. "Because you should have been the first one I told." He brushed a kiss across her lips. "It wasn't until Mark walked in that I was forced to contemplate a Meg-less existence. The prospect was dreadful. From the first moment I saw you, I knew you were somehow necessary to me. I didn't realize how or why, but I do now. I want you in my life, my home, my heart. Always. If you'll have me."

Meg nodded, her throat too clogged to speak.

"Is that a yes?"

She nodded again.

He lifted his hands to her face, his silver eyes glittering with emotion. "Hi, honey, we're home," he said. And then, finally, he kissed her.

* * * * *

IT'S CHRISTMAS, COWBOY!

VICKI LEWIS THOMPSON

For Jen and Rhonda—I'm honoured to be in an anthology with both of you. Merry Christmas! (Does this count as a card?)

New York Times bestselling author **Vicki Lewis Thompson**'s love affair with cowboys started with the Lone Ranger, continued through Maverick and took a turn south of the border with Zorro. She views cowboys as the Western version of knights in shining armour—rugged men who value honour, honesty and hard work. Fortunately for her, she lives in the Arizona desert, where broad-shouldered, lean-hipped cowboys abound. Blessed with such an abundance of inspiration, she only hopes that she can do them justice. Visit her website at www.vickilewisthompson.com.

1

A RUNAWAY HORSE AND AN approaching blizzard made for a bad combo, especially the afternoon before Christmas. Tucker Rankin's eyes watered as he gunned the snow-mobile in an effort to catch Houdini, a black-and-white stallion with a taste for freedom. The roar of the snow-mobile and the white rooster tail it created shattered the peace and quiet of a Wyoming landscape blanketed by last week's storm.

About two hours of daylight remained, and the bliz-zard could hit anytime. The black-and-white paint might survive out here alone tonight, but then again, he might not. Meanwhile everyone at the Last Chance Ranch was gearing up for a festive holiday. Tucker knew all about ruined Christmas celebrations and was determined to save both the stallion and the day.

As a recent hire who didn't much care about Christ-mas, Tucker had volunteered to get all the Last Chance horses, including Houdini, into their stalls around noon in anticipation of the blizzard. He'd gone back to check on them at about 3:00 p.m. and had come nose-to-nose with Houdini, who'd let himself out of his stall.

Tucker had grabbed for the horse's halter and missed as Houdini bolted through the open barn door. After making a quick call on his cell to the main house, Tucker had stuffed a sack of oats and a lead rope in the saddlebag of one of the ranch snowmobiles and headed off in pursuit of the stallion.

He cussed out the horse, but mostly he blamed himself. He should have anticipated the jail break, considering the stallion had done it before. Thank God he hadn't unlatched any of the other stalls, which was another one of his tricks.

Houdini could potentially earn thousands in stud fees for the Last Chance provided he didn't freeze his ass out here tonight. Jack Chance, who—along with his two brothers, Nick and Gabe, and his widowed mother, Sarah—owned the Jackson Hole area ranch, had bought the two-year-old for a song because Houdini was untrained and rambunctious. The horse's previous owner had meant to school him, but those plans had been sidetracked by various personal issues.

In the few weeks Houdini had spent at the Last Chance, he'd learned to tolerate a halter and a lead rope, but he had a long way to go before he could be used as a stud, let alone for cutting-horse competitions. His natural curiosity and inventiveness made him a royal pain to deal with.

Tucker felt a certain kinship with the rowdy horse. He hadn't exactly been a model of responsible behavior, either. He'd partied all through high school and had seen no reason to stop doing that after graduation ten years ago. He'd worked just enough to stay solvent.

It was a dead-end street, and when Jack Chance had hired him back in September, they'd discussed Tucker's lack of focus. Tucker had promised he was ready to buckle down and make something of himself. Accidentally allowing Houdini to escape might be a forgivable offense, but Tucker didn't feel that he had room to make mistakes. Retrieving the horse was his job.

Because he'd grown up in the area, he knew that the Last Chance prided itself on offering people and animals a fresh start. He and Houdini had come to the right place. Tucker appreciated that fact, but obviously the horse, after being allowed to do as he pleased for two years, did not.

At least his trail was easy to follow in the fallen snow. That wouldn't be true in a blizzard, however, and flakes had begun swirling through the frigid air. Tucker's sheepskin coat wasn't enough protection from this kind of weather, even with the collar turned up.

He crammed his Stetson on tight and reached up to anchor it with a gloved hand whenever it threatened to blow off. He wished he'd picked up some goggles, but he'd been too intent on rescuing the horse to think of his own comfort. The moisture from his eyes turned his lashes to icicles, but that couldn't be helped.

Thank God the horse had stayed out in the open instead of running into the trees. Tucker needed to catch him before he changed his mind about that, because the snowmobile would be no use in the forested part of Chance land.

Pointing the snowmobile toward a small rise, Tucker hoped to get a glimpse of the horse. Sure enough, the paint galloped merrily through the meadow about two hundred yards ahead of him. The snow was deep enough to spray in all directions, but not deep enough to be dangerous and cause injuries. Houdini seemed to be having the time of his life.

Tucker stopped the snowmobile and gave a sharp whistle, knowing that was probably a waste of breath. True to form, Houdini didn't break stride. Fogging the air with some choice words, Tucker took off after him.

If the stakes hadn't been so high, Tucker would have enjoyed this chase. Houdini was the picture of carefree pleasure, his tail a white flag signaling his delight at escaping the barn. Tucker understood the urge to throw off the traces. He'd done it often enough.

But reckless behavior had consequences. After one too many drinks last summer, he'd ended up wrecking his truck. Only dumb luck had kept him from injuring or killing someone, and that wreck and subsequent DUI had been a wake-up call.

He'd always admired the Chance brothers—going to work for them represented progress in his mind. He wanted their respect, and letting a valuable stallion escape was a step in the wrong direction. Recapturing Houdini was critical for the horse, but also for Tucker's self-confidence.

Now that he had the stallion in his sights, he felt better about the likelihood of catching him. Getting back might be a little tricky, though. Snow fell more rapidly with every second. It blocked most of the light and at times obscured his view of the racing horse.

Once he had the horse, he'd call the ranch and let them know his status. Ahead of them, a barbed-wire fence came into view, which meant they'd traveled farther than he'd thought and were at the boundary of Chance land. He'd never ridden in this direction before.

That fence could be a huge problem. Houdini could jump it if he took a notion, and the snowmobile...couldn't. "Don't jump the damn fence," Tucker muttered under his breath. "Please."

Houdini galloped toward it as if he had every intention of doing that. Beyond the fence stood a small log cabin with lights on and a ribbon of smoke rising from the chimney. If they had a snowmobile parked in the outbuilding, he'd ask to borrow it if he had to.

But he'd rather capture the horse on this side of the fence and be done with it. He pushed the snowmobile faster, determined to reach Houdini before the horse made it to the fence. He concentrated so hard on that goal that he didn't notice a large rock jutting out of the snow until the snowmobile's runner found it.

Next thing he knew, he lay flat on his back in the snow, the wind knocked clean out of him. The blood roared in his ears as he struggled to breathe. What a fine mess. Houdini was probably over the fence and half a mile away by now. The snowmobile was silent, probably wrecked.

Then a black-and-white muzzle appeared above him. A blast of steamy air hit his face as Houdini snorted.

Relief flooded through Tucker as he grabbed the horse's halter. "Gotcha."

LACEY EVANS HAD HEARD the approaching snowmobile and hoped it wouldn't be anyone coming to check on her. She was doing fine out here by herself, thank you very much. The cabin was filled with the aroma of stew simmering, bread baking and a fire crackling.

The cabin's owner had seemed nervous about renting to her after she'd explained that her male companion wouldn't be joining her as planned. She'd finally convinced the owner that her Forest Service job made her more qualified than most men to spend a few days alone in an isolated cabin. And that definitely included her piece-of-crap ex-boyfriend Lenny.

Going to the window, she peered through the falling

snow and figured out that a cowboy on a snowmobile was
chasing a horse on the far side of the barbed-wire fence.
One of the Chance boys' paints had apparently escaped.
She watched the chase with interest.

But when the snowmobile flipped, she shoved her feet
into her boots, pulled a stocking cap over her head and
snatched up her coat. That cowboy could be in trouble.

Thank goodness he didn't seem to be badly hurt. By
the time she reached the fence, he was on his feet and had
somehow captured the horse. The snowmobile didn't look
particularly good, though. It had landed upside down, and
one runner was bent all to hell.

She took the time to put on her insulated gloves. "Are
you okay?" she called out.

"I'm fine." His voice was tight with strain. "I…whoa,
boy. Whoa!" The horse whinnied and tried to rear, but
the cowboy hung on with both gloved hands and brought
the horse's head back down.

She admired his determination to keep a grip on the
horse, which looked like the devil's own mount as it blew
steam from its nostrils and pawed at the ground. "Should
I call somebody?"

"That's okay. I have my cell." He looked from the horse
to the snowmobile and back at her. "But he's a handful.
It'd be a help if you could fetch the lead rope out of the
snowmobile's saddlebag. He usually settles down once
he's on the lead."

"I can do that." She'd also pick up his hat, which was
lying in the snow. She knew how cowboys felt about
their hats.

Parting the barbed wire carefully, she leaned down and
stepped between the strands. "Will he try to kick me?"

"No." The cowboy gulped in air. "He's not mean. Just

likes to be in control. I'll feel better once I have a lead rope on him."

Lacey retrieved the fallen hat before crouching down and pulling the rope out of the saddlebag. "And then what?"

"I...don't know." The snow fell faster and he muttered under his breath.

She could guess the nature of those mutterings as she handed him the rope and his hat. Anyone from this area knew that Wyoming blizzards could be deadly.

She thought he was local because he looked vaguely familiar. He wasn't a Chance, though. She'd grown up here and knew what each of the Chance men looked like. Still, something about this cowboy was familiar. She'd seen those green eyes and dark hair before.

"Thanks." He put on his hat and clipped the rope to the horse's halter as the snow swirled and gusted around them.

"I hope you're not thinking of riding back."

He greeted that with a short laugh. "He's never been ridden."

"You can wait it out in my cabin, but that doesn't solve the horse issue."

He glanced from the horse to her cabin. "What's in the outbuilding?"

"My Jeep." She raised her voice to be heard over the howl of the wind. "But we can't risk driving in this."

"I know." He secured his hat with one gloved hand when it started to blow off. "But can we stable him there for the night?"

"I guess." She considered the logistics of getting through the fence. "You got wire cutters?"

"Nope."

"Then I'll get mine."

"You have wire cutters?"

"I work for the Forest Service." She started to walk away and turned back as curiosity got the better of her. "Do I know you from somewhere?"

"I grew up here. The name's Tucker Rankin."

"Tucker?" Her eyes widened. "I'm Lacey. Lacey Evans. Jackson Hole High School."

"I'll be damned."

"Small world. I'll be back as quick as I can." She hurried toward the fence and ducked through the strands of barbed wire.

Tucker Rankin. She hadn't thought about him in years. Hurrying toward the cabin's outbuilding, she sorted through her recollections of Tucker. He'd been a bad boy back then, too wild for her, although she'd secretly found him very sexy.

But one vivid memory surfaced. She'd gone to the Christmas formal their senior year against her better judgment. But a sweet, nerdy boy had asked her and she hadn't had the heart to turn him down.

Normally she just didn't do Christmas. Her mother had died when she was fifteen, and her mom had been the person who'd made the holiday special. After that it had been less painful to ignore Christmas completely.

Her dad had remarried when she was seventeen, and although Lacey had tried valiantly to appreciate her stepmother's efforts, the lady wasn't the most sensitive person in the world. She'd crudely trampled on all Lacey's mother's traditions.

A pre-lit artificial tree and battery-operated candles appeared. Cranberry and popcorn garlands were proclaimed too messy. Gifts were opened Christmas Eve instead of Christmas morning. Any reference to Santa was labeled a childish fantasy.

Lacey's sister and brother had adapted, but Lacey, being the oldest, had the strongest memories of pine-scented boughs, flickering beeswax candles, hand-strung garlands and wrapped packages under the tree on Christmas morning. She'd never made the adjustment. Still, she'd agreed to be Arnold's date for the Christmas formal.

Just her luck, the dance committee had decorated a huge evergreen that filled the gym with its fragrance, and they'd continued the torture by placing beeswax votives around the room. When Lacey had slipped outside, tearful with nostalgia, Tucker had been there, too, enjoying a forbidden cigarette.

He'd offered her his coat, and they'd exchanged views on Christmas. She'd found out that his mom had died on Christmas Eve when he was twelve, which was a way worse situation than hers. He didn't celebrate the holiday anymore, either, but a girl had asked him to the formal.

Turned out she'd done it to make another guy jealous, and her ex had arrived to claim her five minutes ago. Tucker wasn't having a particularly good time at this Christmas event, either. They'd shared their holiday angst, both past and present, that night.

They'd also shared a heated kiss that had scared the living daylights out of her. Rattled by the lust he'd inspired with one kiss, she'd returned his coat and dashed back inside. They'd never talked again.

After taking her wire cutters out of the Jeep, she quickly assessed the interior of the outbuilding that doubled as a garage. A horse would fit in there next to her Jeep, which was old and beat up. A few kicks from a horse's hooves wouldn't be noticed.

Inviting Tucker into her cabin to spend the night wasn't quite so convenient. She'd planned to spend three days there with Lenny. Until a week ago, BTB (Before The Bimbo), she and Lenny had been practically engaged, and she'd intended to take a stab at celebrating Christmas on a small scale.

A one-bedroom hideaway had seemed adequate for a couple. But she and Tucker were not a couple, and there was only one bed. He was too tall to fit comfortably on the couch, and she hated to make him sleep on the floor when she had no sleeping bag or air mattress.

But the blizzard was upon them and he had to get in out of it. They'd work out the details later. She lowered her head and leaned into the wind as she returned to the fence. Tucker stood like a marble statue beside the horse, and Lacey wondered if he held himself rigid so he wouldn't betray any weakness with an unmanly shiver.

"I called the ranch." His lips looked a little blue and his eyelashes and eyebrows were crusted with snow. "I said I'd wait out the storm here. I explained you were an old high school friend."

"Perfect." She had a little trouble manipulating the wire cutters with her thick gloves on, but she managed to cut both strands and pull them back, creating a decent-size opening. "Let's get going. It's cold out here."

His chuckle became a cough. "I noticed. Oh, wait. There's a sack of oats in the saddlebag. I'll lead Houdini if you'll grab the oats. He'll need something to eat."

"Right." She moved quickly through the opening in the fence and over to the snowmobile, which, at the rate it was snowing, would soon be covered. Oats in hand, she followed Tucker through the fence and across what had been a defined road an hour ago. Soon it would be obliterated, too.

She dashed around both horse and man to open the double doors into the outbuilding. The cold must have had a calming effect on the paint, because he walked into the shelter without protest. Maybe he had realized that it wasn't so much fun being outside in a blizzard.

Lacey gestured to the heater designed to prevent engines from freezing. "This should help keep him warmer, too."

"He'll appreciate that." Tucker brushed the snow from Houdini's back before glancing around the makeshift garage. "Do you think I could use that bucket in the corner to feed him some oats?"

"Don't see why not." She retrieved the bucket and handed it to him, along with the small sack of oats. "Will this be enough?"

"I'll only give him half for now, in case I need to ration it." He opened the sack and poured some into the bucket while managing to hold it away from Houdini. Once he set it down, the horse shoved his nose deep into the bucket and began munching. The bucket rattled against the outbuilding's cement floor.

Lacey couldn't imagine that little bit of oats would satisfy an animal of Houdini's size. "I brought apples, and I have some carrots left over from the stew I made, if you want to give him those later on."

"Stew?" Tucker was so obviously trying to control his shivers as he smiled at her. "God, that s-sounds wonderful."

"You're frozen, aren't you?"

"Pretty much."

"Then let's get inside and warm you up." She'd thought

it was an innocent remark, but as they closed the horse inside the outbuilding and she led the way into the cabin, she thought about how she could warm him up, and it had nothing to do with stew.

That kiss had replayed itself in her mind quite a few times since she'd found out who he was. He'd had a reputation in high school as a skilled lover, and if that kiss had been a sample, his reputation had been well deserved. For several months after the kiss, she'd had potent dreams involving naked bodies writhing on soft sheets.

And here she was, snowbound with the object of her teenage fantasies. She blew out an impatient breath. What nonsense. For all she knew Tucker was married and had a couple of kids.

Once they were inside the warm cabin and had started divesting themselves of their jackets and gloves, she glanced at him. "I suppose someone will be really disappointed if you don't show up for Christmas Eve."

He hooked his coat on a peg by the door and followed it with his hat. "Can't say that they will." He turned to gaze at her. "Are you out here by yourself?"

"Yes." So he was single, apparently. "It just turned out that way." She tried not to gawk, but damn, he was even better looking now than he had been in high school. His features were more chiseled, and the hint of a beard gave him a rugged look that stirred up butterflies in her stomach.

His glance swept the cabin's living room and open kitchen. "No holiday decorations, I see."

"Nope." And he smelled good, too—the musky scent of a man who worked with animals. She hadn't realized how much she liked that earthy aroma on a man.

"I'm going to take a wild guess that you're not into this

holiday any more than you were years ago when we had that conversation outside the school gym."

"So you remember that." She met his gaze. It wasn't the conversation she was focusing on, but what had followed. The mouth she'd kissed long ago looked much the same except for some added smile lines bracketing his firm lips.

"Yeah, I do remember, in fact." A telltale flicker in his green eyes contradicted his casual tone.

Her heart rate increased another notch. She'd bet money he was thinking about that kiss, too. "Well, you're right. I still don't much like Christmas. How about you?"

"Can't say it's my favorite time of year."

She kept her attention on his face, but she was very aware of the snug fit of his Western shirt. The soft blue plaid revealed muscles honed by ranch work. "I'll bet the Last Chance goes all out."

He rolled his eyes. "You have no idea. Fifteen-foot tree in the living room, holly and pine boughs on the banister going upstairs, red velvet bows on everything that doesn't move. They've even decorated the damned barn."

She ignored a sharp pang of longing. Being surrounded by that kind of festive atmosphere would only make her sad. "You won't find that here."

"Good. Maybe it's just as well we ended up together tonight." He smiled. "We're birds of a feather."

Oh, yeah. She remembered that smile—the one that went from boyish to seductive in zero-point-five seconds. Heat spiraled through her system. Ten years ago she hadn't allowed herself to be swept away by his animal magnetism. But tonight, after being dumped last week by the man she'd thought she'd eventually marry, all bets were off.

2

LACEY EVANS. WHENEVER he'd thought of her in the years since high school, which had been more times than he cared to admit, he'd pictured her with a stodgy but successful husband and a couple of cute kids. Once again she'd be totally out of reach, as she had been when they were in high school.

Instead, against all odds, he was standing in this cozy cabin with her. She didn't seem to be attached to a guy, let alone have any kids. She hadn't known he would show up, so the setting she'd created had nothing to do with him.

But she couldn't have planned a more tempting scenario than a welcoming fire, a home-cooked meal and the prospect of spending time with a woman he'd wanted desperately when he was eighteen. Who needed Christmas?

The years had been good to her. Her honey-colored hair was slightly darker now, and she wore it shorter, too, an easy-care mop of caramel curls. Those curls were tousled by the stocking cap she'd pulled off, and he had the urge to comb her hair into place with his fingers.

Her blue eyes were no longer so wide and endearingly innocent. After she'd run from his kiss that night, her cheeks bright pink, he'd decided that he'd been French-kissing a virgin. But there was nothing virginal in her frank appraisal of him now. The glow in those amazing eyes told him that if he kissed her again, she wouldn't run.

The possibility heated his blood, and suddenly, he wasn't the least bit cold. She'd had that effect on him from the first day he'd glimpsed her walking down the hall at Jackson Hole High, her snug sweater and jeans showing off a sweetly curved figure. He'd thought he'd died and gone to heaven the one and only time he'd held her in his arms.

When she'd ended that unforgettable kiss, she'd returned his coat. He'd left it off in hopes cold air would deflate his penis enough for him to walk to his truck and drive home. The wait had seemed like hours.

He liked to think he had more control these days, but apparently not when it came to Lacey. She still favored snug jeans and close-fitting sweaters. Today's sweater was green, which signaled full speed ahead to his eager package.

Tucker decided, in the name of his own self-respect, to show some restraint. Although he wasn't proud of it, he'd engaged in some meaningless sex over the years. When life was one big party, a guy didn't much care who he slept with if the woman was willing and warm.

But Lacey was different. She wasn't just some girl he'd met in a cowboy bar. Yeah, he wanted her, but he didn't have to act on that urge. Instead, he could distract himself by concentrating on a different kind of hunger.

He glanced over at the stove, the source of mouth-watering aromas. "I don't know much about cooking, but is there any chance that stew is ready to eat?"

She smiled. "Yep. Your timing is excellent."

"Dumb luck." But he'd had quite a bit of luck lately, especially landing the job at the Last Chance. He was beginning to wonder if Houdini's escape had been an example of good luck disguised as potential disaster. "What can I do to help?"

"Not a thing. If you want to wash up, there's soap and towels in the bathroom." She gestured toward a short hall. "First door on your left."

"Thanks. Good plan." He probably smelled of horse. Some women liked that, but he didn't know if Lacey did or not. He headed down the hall, his boots clicking on the hardwood floor of the cabin.

The bathroom was plain—white fixtures and a tub with a white shower curtain. Tucker caught a glimpse of himself in the medicine cabinet mirror and winced. Hat hair, red nose, five-o'clock shadow. He must have imagined that glint of interest in her eyes. What woman would be attracted to *that?*

Rolling back his sleeves, he turned on the water and picked up the soap. He couldn't do anything about the five-o'clock shadow, but soap and warm water would make him feel more presentable. Then he noticed that the soap was embedded with an image of Santa Claus.

The cabin's owners might have left it, but the lack of frills everywhere else made that unlikely. Probably somebody had given it to Lacey and she was practical enough to make use of it. He could help her with that.

He lathered up, scrubbing his face and hands until they tingled. The soap smelled like candy canes. He hadn't thought of those in a while. His mom used to buy a lot of them to decorate the tree because they were affordable.

His dad had thought the whole tree thing was a waste of money, but his mom had insisted on having one every year. She and Tucker had strung popcorn and made chains of construction paper. That had all ended when she died.

No point in dredging up those memories, though, especially when he was with a woman who also ignored the holiday except for some soap she was trying to use up. He splashed cold water on his face, grabbed a towel and dried off. Then he finger-combed his hair as best he could.

He walked back into the kitchen, where a loaf of what looked like homemade bread sat on a cutting board in the middle of the table. Lacey was dishing stew into a couple of generously sized bowls. The light caught in her caramel curls as she glanced up and smiled at him.

His breath stalled at the beauty of the scene, at the beauty of her, all flushed from the heat of the stove. Or maybe her extra color had something to do with him being there. That was a happy prospect.

"This looks wonderful. Thank you." Then he had a thought. "Listen, if you feed me now, are you going to have enough supplies for your stay?"

"Oh, yeah." She laughed as she opened the refrigerator, which was stuffed. "I read the weather reports and decided to be prepared for anything. As I said, I can probably help feed your horse if it comes to that."

"He's not exactly my horse. I just work there. But I'm relieved to know you stocked up."

"The good news is I'm loaded with provisions. The bad news is the provisions are everything I like, but you may not like the same things."

"Beggars can't be choosers. I'm grateful for whatever you're willing to share."

Her quick glance in his direction told him that she'd taken that in a way he hadn't meant. God, he hoped he hadn't offended her. "Sorry. That didn't come out right."

She became very busy ladling out the stew. "Don't worry about it. I mean, we had that one silly moment together after the winter formal, but I'm not at all your type."

"Why do you say that?"

"It's obvious." She set the bowls down on the table with brisk efficiency. "You went out with the party girls, whereas I was—"

"Too good for me."

"What?" She looked up in obvious surprise.

"You heard me. I was the bad boy with the souped-up truck and mediocre grades. You were an honor student with goals and a curfew."

"Okay, so we were different, but I never thought I was too good for you, Tucker."

"No, you wouldn't think that, because you're a nice person. But I knew it. It didn't stop me from kissing you, though. I saw my opportunity and took advantage of you being sad and vulnerable." He rubbed the back of his neck, where tension had gathered. He hadn't meant to start confessing his sins, but now that he had… "I shouldn't have kissed you that night."

"So you regret it?"

He met her gaze and something in the depths of those blue eyes demanded complete honesty. "No," he said softly. "I'm not that noble."

"Well, that's a relief." The corners of her mouth turned up in a saucy smile.

He stared at her. He still hadn't quite made the adjustment from the virginal Lacey to the more self-assured woman standing in front of him. Once he did, he'd have a helluva time keeping his hands to himself.

She gestured toward the table as if ready to change the

subject. "As I was saying, the supplies are all things I like. That means your choice of beverage is coffee, water, or wine. Most cowboys I know prefer beer."

He was more than ready to change the subject. Although he did prefer beer, he'd been known to drink wine. But he wasn't going to use up whatever she'd brought for herself. That would be rude. "I'll just drink water."

"You're sure? I'm having wine and unless you hate it, you're welcome to have some with me."

"I don't hate it, but I wouldn't feel right using up your—"

"Oh, for heaven's sake." She pulled two goblets out of the cupboard and set one by each plate. "Besides, I think we need to toast."

"To Christmas?" He had a tough time believing she'd want to do that.

"No, to meeting again after all these years."

"Oh." He was flattered that she'd count it a toasting occasion. "I guess we could toast to that."

"It's quite a coincidence, don't you think?"

"I do. It took a runaway horse and a wrecked snowmobile to accomplish it."

She opened the wine and poured each of them a glass. "And a slimeball. Let's not forget my worthless ex."

"Husband?" His high spirits plummeted. He should have known she hadn't intended to be out here all by herself, that a man had originally been part of the deal.

"Boyfriend." She picked up her wineglass and handed one to him. "Fortunately that's all he ever was."

Tucker understood now why she'd looked at him with interest. With his playboy reputation, he had a history of attracting women on the rebound. That kind of relationship wasn't built to last. Either the woman moved on after she felt better about herself or she went back to her ex.

Usually that was fine with him, because he was careful not to get invested. But he didn't feel like being Lacey's rebound guy. She held a special place in his heart, and he didn't want to tarnish that memory.

Still, he knew his lines in situations like this. "Your ex is obviously a loser if he let you go."

"Thank you. I agree." She lifted her glass. "To old friends."

"To old friends." He touched his glass to hers and drank. But as he lowered the glass, honesty made him speak up. "We weren't really friends in high school, Lacey."

"Depends on how you define it. I thought we became friends that night outside the gym."

"I guess." If she hadn't run away, they would have become more than friends. He was glad they hadn't. He'd have enough trouble keeping this night from veering toward sex when all he'd done was kiss her. If she hadn't left, he would have continued the seduction he'd begun with that kiss. He'd been eighteen and flooded with hormones.

Now he was twenty-eight, and still somewhat hormone driven, but not to the exclusion of all reason. When necessary he could summon a little common sense. Lacey was a woman he could fall for, and yet she'd been recently dumped. That combo meant she was off limits.

She waved a hand at the table. "Let's eat."

"Good idea." Tucker hadn't been particularly polished when he'd arrived at the Last Chance, but Sarah Chance was a stickler for good manners. He'd learned that any cowboy who worked at the ranch had better know the fundamentals or risk losing his job.

Setting down his wineglass, he rounded the table to pull out Lacey's chair.

"How gallant." She accepted the gesture with a smile and slipped gracefully into the chair.

As he scooted it forward, he breathed in the scent of candy canes and woman. Obviously she'd used that soap, too. He wanted to bury his nose in the curve of her neck and nibble on her earlobe. But that wouldn't be wise.

He took a seat opposite her, unfolded the paper napkin she'd provided and settled it on his lap. Outside, the wind rattled the windowpanes, which made their dinner seem all the more cozy in comparison. The food smelled delicious, but hungry as he was, he waited for Lacey to start eating.

She began by picking up a serrated knife and slicing off a couple pieces of bread. The scent of it burst forth, beckoning him with an aroma that reminded him of good sex. He'd always thought food and lovemaking went together.

He set that notion firmly aside. "I didn't know you could cook."

"You still don't." She held out the breadboard. "For all you know, this tastes like Styrofoam."

He picked up the heel, bit into its soft center, and closed his eyes. Heaven.

"It must be all right."

"Mmm." He glanced at her and nodded enthusiastically as he chewed.

"Fortunately my mom taught me to bake when I was a kid. I picked up basic cooking skills when I realized my dad was hopeless in the kitchen. Of course, now he has Helen."

Grasping at a subject that didn't involve naked bodies, he asked about her family as they both dug into the beef stew.

She chose to ignore her dad and Helen and talk about her siblings, instead. Kathy, four years younger than she was, had married and moved to Ohio. Steven was finishing a degree in engineering at the University of Wyoming. Even given Lacey's reluctance to celebrate Christmas, Tucker was surprised she wasn't with her family right now, and he said as much.

"I know it's not very evolved of me, but I grit my teeth whenever I have to watch the way Helen celebrates Christmas," she said. "So I keep my participation to a minimum. This year I used Lenny as an excuse. I told them he was likely to propose over the holiday, and that I thought the two of us should create our own special memories by renting this cute little cabin for a week during Christmas."

"Do they know Lenny's not here with you?"

"No. I decided when he bailed that I'd keep that info to myself and come out here alone. The irony is that I really had planned to have a semi-normal Christmas with him. He likes the holiday, so I was going to make an effort for his sake, sort of to prove I could."

Tucker put down his spoon. "What happened with Lenny?" He cared about her broken heart and was willing to let her talk it out. That didn't mean he had to make it all better with some good sex, though. There was such a thing as self-preservation.

"Two weeks ago he met somebody he liked better,

somebody who didn't have—to use his phrase—my baggage."

Tucker had the immediate urge to clean the guy's clock. "Hell, everyone has baggage."

"I know." She sliced off two more pieces of bread and gestured for him to take one. "Maybe Lenny and his girl-friend, Suzanne, have matching luggage tags."

"Could be, but I'll bet they're attached to the most bor-ing suitcases in the world, that black nylon kind a million other people have."

She smiled at him. "I like to think so."

"Whereas yours has style. It might even be purple."

That made her laugh. "Okay, that's my new slogan. *I may have baggage, but I carry it with style.*"

"You do, Lacey." He picked up his wineglass and lifted it in her direction. The sparkle was back in her blue eyes, and he liked seeing that. "You definitely do."

"Thanks, Tucker." She lifted her glass, too. "So do you."

She wouldn't think so if she knew what a screwup he'd been recently. He wished now that he'd made more of himself in the years since they'd last met. She'd probably earned a degree before landing her Forest Service job.

Then something occurred to him. "Did you go into forestry because of the trees?" Once the words were out of his mouth, he realized how stupid that sounded. Didn't everybody who majored in forestry love trees? "I mean, because you used to love the evergreens at Christmas time."

She paused, a spoonful of stew halfway to her mouth, and stared at him. "You are the only person who's made that connection. I didn't realize it myself until recently, when I started thinking about celebrating a real Christmas here with Lenny and knew I'd want a real tree."

"But you gave up the idea when he…" He wasn't sure what term to use that wouldn't be insulting.

"When he dumped me. You can say it. It's the truth, after all. And a girl who's been dumped right before Christmas usually isn't ready to deck the halls with boughs of holly, if you get my drift." She continued eating her stew.

"Maybe that's exactly the time to do it."

She stopped eating and gazed at him. "How so?"

"You were going to celebrate Christmas for Lenny's sake, right?"

"Yeah, but obviously I picked the wrong guy to jump-start my Christmas spirit. He's pushed me right back into bah-humbug territory."

Tucker recognized that kind of thinking. For years he'd seen himself as a victim of circumstance. Hearing it coming from Lacey was unsettling. Funny how much easier it was to figure out what other people should do to make themselves happy.

"Tucker, why are you looking at me like that?"

"I'm just wondering why you'd break out the decorations for a guy, but not for yourself. Why let his dumb decisions keep you from celebrating if you have the urge to do it?"

She frowned. "I'm not saying I wanted to, but I thought it was time to see if I could, because depriving him of the holiday wasn't fair."

"Is it fair to deprive yourself? When we talked outside the gym, I got the impression that you used to love Christmas, especially the way your mother celebrated it." And so had he. His words were as much directed at himself as at her.

Her expression softened. "I did love it back then, but I can't re-create that kind of Christmas because my mom was such a huge part of it, and she's gone. I thought maybe I'd try for some new traditions with Lenny, but bravely forging my own rituals without anyone to share them seems a little desperate and pathetic."

"I get that. I've thought exactly the same thing, so in the past I've spent Christmas Eve in a bar, which is desperate and pathetic in its own way."

"I usually plan a trip somewhere tropical." She shrugged. "It sort of works."

He had a sudden image of Lacey in a bikini sipping an umbrella drink. He shoved that image away immediately. "That's classier than my option."

"Last Christmas I talked Lenny into flying to Bermuda, but he hated that it didn't feel like Christmas. I still wasn't ready to spend the holiday at his family's house or mine, so this was the compromise."

Tucker blew out a breath. "I'm sorry it all fell apart, Lacey. He's an impatient creep who doesn't know what he's lost."

"To be honest, I was having doubts about the relationship. We weren't clicking the way I thought a committed couple should. Spending Christmas here was going to be a kind of test." She grimaced. "Guess it was, at that."

"You're way better off. You deserve somebody special." Any guy who rejected such a wonderful woman was terminally stupid.

"Thanks." Once again her eyes took on a happy gleam.

He hoped his next suggestion wouldn't bring back the shadows that had lurked in her gaze earlier. He cleared his throat. "Anyway, we're stuck together for at least to-night, and we understand each other's take on Christmas. I'm thinking it's the perfect chance to get over ourselves and celebrate the damned holiday."

3

"CELEBRATE CHRISTMAS?" Lacey couldn't believe he'd said that. Of all the people in the world, Tucker seemed the least likely to suggest such a thing. "We can't."

"Why not?"

"I didn't bring any decorations, for one thing. I had planned to, but when Lenny bailed, I donated all the stuff I'd bought to the Salvation Army."

"Except the soap."

She rolled her eyes. "Ah, yes, the soap. It was a secret Santa thing at work, and I happened to be out of soap, so I brought it on this trip instead of throwing it in the Salvation Army donation bag. Are you suggesting we prop the soap on the mantel and call it good?"

He grinned at her. "It's a start."

That grin was lethal. She didn't really want to decorate for Christmas, but if he did, she was willing to go along just on the basis of that killer smile. He also had a point about celebrating with someone who understood the issues. She wouldn't have to fake anything with Tucker.

"I have some emergency candles in case the power

goes out," she said. "We could put one on each side of the soap."

He nodded. "See how this plan is taking shape already?"

"Oh, yeah. We'll rival Rockefeller Center in no time."

"Don't make fun. Santa soap and candles could look really nice on the mantel, even if the candles aren't beeswax, which I'm guessing they're not."

"Nope. Just those cheap white paraffin kind." She gazed at him, marveling that he'd remembered a detail like beeswax candles. "So you really were listening when we had that conversation."

"Of course. Got any popcorn?"

"A couple of bags of the microwave kind, but—"

"Needle and thread?"

"Some. I carry a little sewing kit in my cosmetic bag, but—"

He pushed back his chair. "Then let's get popping. It needs to cool before we string it."

"Tucker, we don't have a tree."

"Don't worry." His green gaze found hers. "We will." Then he walked over and took his coat and hat off the peg where it was hanging by the front door.

"Wait a minute." She stood and followed him. "You can't go out there and cut down a tree. I'm renting this place. The landlord would have a fit."

"I'm not going to cut it down." He settled his hat on his head. "I'll dig it up. Then we can put it back in the ground later. No one has to know."

"The ground's frozen."

"Most places, yes, but on the sunny side of the cabin, it might not be as hard." He shoved his arms into the sleeves of his sheepskin coat.

"But there's a blizzard going on!" As if to emphasize the fact, the wind howled down the chimney and made the fire gyrate wildly.

"That makes it more exciting." He dazzled her with another smile. That, combined with the shadow of a beard, made him look rakish and slightly dangerous.

"You're crazy." Breathing quickly, both from the zing of attraction and her determination to stop him, she backed against the door, arms spread. "I won't let you go out there."

He winked, the picture of male assurance. "Yeah, you will. We're going to do this."

"No, we aren't. People get lost and die in snowstorms, sometimes when they're within a few feet of shelter because they get lost in all that whiteness."

He buttoned up his coat. "I know that. I promise to stay close enough to the cabin and the outbuilding that I can still see them."

"You could get distracted looking for a tree to dig up."

"I could, but I won't. By the way, do you have a shovel in your Jeep?"

"I'm not going to tell you."

"Which means yes."

"Doesn't matter." She remained planted firmly in front of the door. "I'm not moving."

His gaze reflected amusement as it swept over her. "I should warn you that once I get an idea in my head, I can't let it go."

"You'll have to let this one go." She lifted her chin in defiance. "I've been involved in too many search and rescue missions to allow you to take the chance of freezing to death out there. I'd given you more credit for good sense."

"There's your first mistake." And without warning, he leaned in and kissed her.

Her gasp of surprise allowed him to deepen the kiss, which quickly evolved into something spectacular. Bracing both hands against the door beside her head, he angled his mouth over hers and pressed in deep. The sweet invasion made her forget whatever silly argument they'd been having.

As his lips moved against hers in slow seduction, as his tongue explored with lazy intent, her senses rocketed back to the night of the Christmas formal. Yes, this was how she remembered his kiss—a take-no-prisoners assault that reduced her to a ragdoll willing to surrender to whatever he wanted.

She clutched his shoulders as the room seemed to spin. When he lifted his head to smile down at her, she realized the room hadn't been spinning, but she had. He'd circled her waist with both hands and turned her around so that she no longer blocked the door. She'd been so immersed in his kiss that she hadn't noticed.

"I promise not to get lost in the snow," he said. Then he released her and was out the door before she could frame a response.

"You don't fight fair!" she called after him when she managed to catch her breath.

The door opened a crack. "Nuke the popcorn!" Then he closed the door and was gone.

Grabbing the doorknob, she pulled the door open. A blast of frigid air filled with wet snow hit her in the face. "Use the rope!" She hurled the command out into the bitter cold where she could barely see him, head down, burrowing into the storm like a linebacker. "There's a long rope in the Jeep!"

"Thanks!" His answer was faint, but at least he'd heard and acknowledged her order.

She closed the door and stood there shivering, her arms wrapped protectively around her body. He was nuts, crazy as a loon. What kind of man risked his safety to bring a Christmas tree to a woman who didn't want to celebrate in the first place?

Yet she sensed that this wasn't all about her. In helping to slay her demons, he was also facing down his own. She couldn't very well deny him the chance to do that, and if he used the rope, tying it to the latch on the outbuilding and then around his waist, he would have a lifeline back to safety.

The rope was part of her search and rescue gear, but it would serve the purpose of orienting Tucker while he tried to locate a tree. People who lived in this part of the country often tied rope lines between the house and the barn so they'd have something to guide them when they checked on the animals during a snowstorm. Knowing Tucker would use that rope made her feel marginally better about him taking on this job.

He'd been a reckless kid in high school, and so far he'd confirmed that he still possessed that trait. Taking a snowmobile into the teeth of a storm to chase a runaway horse might be brave, but it was also foolish. If the horse had run in a different direction, away from all habitation… She didn't like to think how that might have turned out.

And yet, his reckless nature was part of what made him so sexy. When he'd impulsively kissed her, mostly to get his own way about the tree, she'd tasted a kind of thrilling abandon that didn't come her way often. In fact, she hadn't encountered it since the night of the Christmas formal.

Was that kiss simply a means to an end, getting past her objections to his plan? Or would he take it a step further when he returned? Then again, maybe he'd wait for her to make the next move.

Now that he was outside, she had a chance to think more clearly about what might or might not happen between them tonight. She should decide what she wanted now instead of making that decision in the heat of the moment. As she'd just discovered, a moment with Tucker could get very hot very fast.

Oh, who was she kidding? There was no decision to be made here. Her fantasy man had appeared on her doorstep when neither of them was committed to someone else. If she ever intended to discover what making love to Tucker was all about, now was the time.

And that prospect set her panties on fire. She hurried into the bathroom and rummaged through her cosmetic case to see if…yes! She still had the box of condoms she'd become accustomed to taking along on trips with Lenny. He never seemed to remember, which should have been another sign that he was the wrong guy. The right guy wouldn't leave that responsibility up to the woman in his life.

She tucked the box back into the case and closed the lid. Her heart was beating so fast she pressed a hand to her chest and took a shaky breath. She had the man, and she had the condoms. This could be the best Christmas Eve of her entire life.

AS NEEDLES OF SNOW hit his cheeks and the wind threatened to blow him over on his way to the outbuilding,

Tucker considered the fact that Lacey might be right. He very well could be crazy for coming out here to dig up a tree. Back in the cabin he'd pictured himself as a valiant hero who braved the storm to bring her an evergreen on Christmas Eve.

But when a guy made a boast like that, he had to produce or come off as a braggart who couldn't follow through. The possibility of staggering back into the cabin, treeless and frozen, hadn't occurred to him when he'd left. It sure as hell occurred to him now that he was in a pitched battle with the wind and snow.

Adding to his idiocy was his most recent move—kissing Lacey. He really shouldn't have done that, but kissing her had seemed like a better option than standing there arguing with her. He'd known it would distract her.

Maybe, somewhere in his pea brain, he'd hoped she wouldn't kiss the way he remembered, which would help him put the brakes on his lust. But no. If anything, his memory hadn't done justice to the experience of going mouth-to-mouth with Lacey.

He thought again of Lenny and couldn't imagine how anyone could give up kisses like that. Maybe she didn't kiss Lenny the same way. Maybe Tucker brought out her inner wild woman.

Yeah, right. That kind of thinking was exactly what got him into trouble every damned time. He'd decide that the woman in question had never had someone love her right, and it was up to him, Supercock, to give her the kind of pleasure she deserved. He needed to forget that crap.

At the moment, he had one heroic job, and that involved digging up a Christmas tree. That should cool his jets for the time being. The storm was a humdinger.

Luckily he was moving into the wind, which pushed

his hat onto his head. But on the way back he'd be in danger of losing it, especially if and when he dug up a tree and had to wrangle that back to the cabin. He was definitely nuts for doing this.

Well, maybe not entirely. He and Lacey really did need to get over their holiday issues. Speaking for himself, the idea of making Christmas happen for the first time since his mom died held a certain appeal. He'd never been moved to do it for anyone else, but he was obviously a sucker for Lacey. Sharing a Christmas celebration with her seemed like the right thing to do on many counts.

But first he had to come up with the tree. And get into the damned outbuilding when snow had piled up against a door that was probably frozen shut by now. He kicked most of the snow away and pried open the latch.

This had sounded so easy when he'd described it to Lacey. Putting his whole weight behind the effort, he finally wrenched open the door with a loud crack. Instantly he positioned himself in the opening in case Houdini stood right there, ready to make a run for it. When no Houdini nose shoved against his chest, he slipped inside quickly and reached for the light switch as he pulled the door closed.

Houdini dozed peacefully in his allotted space next to the Jeep. Apparently the horse had worn himself out running through the snow earlier. Bonus. The Jeep looked okay, but some fresh chew marks on a two-by-four stud were probably Houdini's handiwork. Tucker decided not to worry about that now. He'd assess the damage after the storm ended.

Relieved that Houdini seemed to be settled into his temporary quarters just fine, Tucker rummaged in the back of the Jeep and located both a shovel and the hefty coil of rope. He also needed something for the tree's root ball, but the only bucket turned out to be the one he'd used for Houdini's oats. He'd need that again.

On a shelf near the door, he found an empty burlap sack and took that, instead. The outbuilding felt cozy, but Tucker didn't linger. He had a tree to dig up.

Once he was back outside in the bone-chilling cold, he secured the outbuilding's double doors and tied one end of the rope to the latch. He wrapped the other end around his waist and knotted it, although his dexterity was hampered by the freezing temperature and the shovel and sack he held.

Finally he was armed and ready to bag himself a tree. Failure was not an option.

He took a moment to orient himself and walked around to the back side of the cabin, which faced south and was the most likely to have unfrozen ground. He trailed Lacey's rope behind him. Although he'd initially imagined hauling in a man-size blue spruce, he'd scaled back his expectations to a child-size pine. In some things, size mattered. In this case, it was the thought that counted.

But he didn't have a lot of choices. Exactly one tree grew next to the cabin in what might be unfrozen ground. The tree had a nice shape, but it stood at least seven feet tall. Tucker surveyed the situation, took note of the condition of his fingers, toes and nose, and decided digging up this very tree was the best he could hope for.

Some time later—could have been thirty minutes, could have been an hour, could have been two hours— he enclosed the tree's roots in the burlap sack and half carried, half dragged the tree around to the front of the cabin and up the steps to the small porch. She'd better love it, that was all he could say. He would have thought all that effort would warm him up, but instead he was one gigantic icicle.

As if she'd been listening for his approach, she threw open the door. "At last! I was ready to send out the St. Bernard with a keg of whiskey!"

"Took longer than I thought."

Her attention strayed to the tree lying on the porch. "Oh, Tucker. It's perfect." She stepped back so he could wrestle the tree inside. "Plus it smells *wonderful*."

He'd have to take her word for it. His nostrils were frozen shut. He'd been mouth-breathing for what seemed like hours.

"I cleared a place for it in the corner."

Branches scraped along the hardwood floor and he hoped the tree wasn't leaking sap. Then he realized that nothing would be leaking sap, including him, when the outside temperature was this cold. All gelatinous substances would be solids by now.

He'd dug up as much of the root system as he had the energy for. Consequently, the tree had a solid base of roots and soil inside the burlap. Once he tipped the tree upright, it stood straight and looked magnificent, exactly as he'd pictured it would.

"Tucker, that's amazing."

He glanced over and discovered her gratitude and awe was directed at him, not the tree. He'd impressed her, and suddenly the ordeal was worth every finger-numbing, toe-numbing second he'd endured.

Feeling like Paul Bunyan, he stood back and admired his work. "Now *that's* a Christmas tree."

"Yes, it most definitely is."

Next he tried to unbutton his coat, which was a chore

because he couldn't feel his fingers and had forgotten he was still wearing gloves.

"Here, let me help you with that." Moving in front of him, she gently pulled off his gloves and dropped them to the floor.

His fingers began to tingle as the numbness disappeared. He flexed them and decided he'd been through worse.

Then she began unfastening the buttons on his coat, which were covered with snow.

He let his arms drop to his sides and watched her intently pursuing her goal. If he wasn't so damned cold, this would be erotic. Good thing he was frozen, because now that he'd brought home the trophy tree, he had the unwise urge to claim his reward.

Fortunately his penis wouldn't be up to claiming anything until he'd thawed out some. Even then, he had another sizable issue that would keep his bad boy in check. Thank God he was totally condomless. The heady feeling of being admired and fussed over for his tree-bagging abilities was making mincemeat of his vow not to get physical with her.

"You're really shaking, Tucker. I'm worried that you're suffering from mild hypothermia." She peeled off his coat and dropped it on the floor.

He doubted that. He'd been dealing with this kind of weather all his life, and he'd never had a problem with it. But he was human, and having her fret over his well-being felt nice, so he kept his mouth shut.

"Sit down on the couch. I'll take off your boots."

He complied.

She pulled off his boots with brisk efficiency and then removed his wool socks. "God, your feet are like ice."

He didn't know if they were or not. He couldn't feel them yet.

"Come with me." She grasped his hand, which was still prickling, and urged him to his feet. "What you need is to get out of these clothes and into a warm bed."

He couldn't recall ever refusing a beautiful woman's invitation to get into her bed, but he had to refuse this time. "That's okay. I'll be fine here by the fire."

"Look, this isn't up for debate. I'm not about to have you put your health at risk because of this daring tree project. It was a wonderful gesture, and I want you to be well enough to enjoy it." She tugged harder. "Now, come on. Don't make me get nasty."

He had to admit that crawling into a warm bed sounded terrific, at least until he warmed up. She hadn't said she'd get in there with him, so maybe it would be okay. Once he wasn't shivering so much, he'd get dressed again and they'd decorate the tree together.

"Okay. Just for a few minutes." He allowed himself to be led into the bedroom. Nothing would happen there. Without condoms, nothing *could* happen there. End of story.

4

LACEY WASN'T ABOUT to let Tucker's heroic Christmas tree project put him at risk. The fact that he was shaking was a good sign and meant his body was still trying to warm itself. But he'd been out there nearly an hour, and she wasn't taking any chances considering how isolated they were.

She'd put him to bed and brew him some tea. Anyone who'd dealt with hypothermia would do the same. The fact that he was six-foot-plus of dark-haired, green-eyed yumminess wasn't the dominant factor, here.

But it was *a* factor. She threw back the covers on the cabin's queen-size bed before turning to him. Her gaze traveled from his broad shoulders to his narrow hips, and she swallowed. Taking off his gloves and coat were one thing. Removing the rest of his clothes was quite another.

She glanced into his eyes, which seemed somewhat unfocused. "Do you think you can undress yourself?"

His teeth chattered as he continued to shiver. "Sure. Go on back by the f-fire. I'll b-be fine." He fumbled with the snaps on his shirt.

"Never mind." She nudged his hands away. "It'll go

faster if I do it." Taking a deep breath, she tackled the snaps. The material was cold, but she was encouraged by the warmth of his body underneath. He was still quivering, but at least his skin wasn't clammy. "I think you're going to be okay. This is just a precaution."

He nodded as he stood meekly letting her unfasten the snaps at his wrists and pull the shirt from his waistband. Once she'd tossed the shirt on the floor, she worked his T-shirt off. He leaned down slightly so she could pull it over his head.

At that point her objectivity began to slip. She forced herself to ignore the breadth of his chest, the dark hair sprinkled over it, and the intoxicating scent of his skin. She reminded herself that hypothermia was serious, a condition not to be messed with.

Keeping that thought foremost in her mind, she reached for his belt buckle. But as she did, his hand closed over hers.

"That's good enough," he said. "You can stop, now."

She glanced up and met a gaze so hot she nearly went up in flames.

"I don't need to crawl into that bed, after all." His voice was husky. "If you'll just go on out to the living room and wait for me, I'll be there in a few minutes."

Her heart raced and moisture gathered between her thighs. It didn't take a genius to figure out that she'd aroused him with the undressing routine. Standing here by the bed presented the ideal opportunity to do something about that. She admitted the possibility of sex with him had been in the back of her mind, assuming he really didn't have hypothermia.

And yet Tucker acted as if he didn't intend to take advantage of the situation she'd created for them. Given his reputation and his obvious attraction to her, she had to believe he wanted to. Lack of birth control had to be the thing stopping him.

So now what? Should she announce that she had a box of condoms? That seemed sort of…tacky. But if she didn't let him know about them, he would continue to avoid any possibility of having sex with her tonight. That would be a waste for both of them.

"I mean it, Lacey. You need to leave."

She kept looking into his eyes because they were begging her to stay even though his words told her to go. She swallowed. "What—what if I don't want to leave?"

He groaned. "It's best if you do."

"What would you say if I told you I have…condoms?"

His eyes widened.

"I was always in charge of bringing them, and I forgot to take them out of my travel case for this trip."

"You were always in charge of condoms? What kind of man expects that of a woman?"

"The same kind who dumps her right before Christmas, I guess. Anyway, I have them."

He blew out a breath. "Right."

Oh, God. The issue wasn't condoms. Or if it was, he was put off by the idea of using some bought for another man. What she'd thought was a happy accident might be a colossal insult.

How awkward was this? Her face hot with embarrassment, she looked away. "Never mind," she murmured. "Forget I said anything. I'll see you in the living room." She started to leave.

"Wait." He caught her arm.

"Listen, Tucker, I'm sure your instincts are on target." She still didn't look at him.

"Or maybe yours are." He pulled her gently back until she was facing him. "Just so you know, I want you desperately."

"Yes, but you have misgivings."

His smile was soft. "Not anymore." And then he kissed her with such thoroughness that she believed him.

He continued to kiss her until her resistance disappeared and her body grew molten with desire. Soon nothing was more important than making love with Tucker. And even though he had a reputation for making any woman he touched feel that way, she knew that for this moment, she was the only one who mattered to him. That was enough.

At last he released her and brushed his thumb slowly over her well-kissed mouth. "The condoms are where?"

"Finish getting out of your clothes." She moved reluctantly from the warmth of his arms and headed for the door. "I'll get the box."

Once she was in the bathroom, she told herself not to look in the mirror, but of course she did, and groaned in dismay. Hair going every which way, no makeup, and worst of all, her pink cheeks and sparkling eyes made her look *wholesome*. Tucker had never dated wholesome girls in high school, and she'd bet good money he didn't date wholesome girls now, either.

But then she remembered the way he'd kissed her just now, and there was nothing wholesome about the way she'd kissed him back. She wasn't the shy virgin he'd met outside the school gym that night. She shouldn't be worrying about whether she'd measure up to the other women he'd had.

"Lacey?" he called out from the bedroom. "Is everything okay?"

"Yes," she called back. Grabbing the box of condoms, she walked across the hall and into the bedroom.

Tucker sat up in bed, the covers pulled to his waist. He was leaning casually against a pillow he'd placed between his back and the headboard, but there was nothing casual about the way he looked at her. His gaze was intense, and the hint of a frown creased the spot between his dark eyebrows.

He took a deep breath, and his magnificent chest heaved. "I wondered if you'd changed your mind."

"I haven't changed my mind, but…I'll admit to being a little intimidated by you."

His frown deepened. "Intimidated?"

"You had quite a reputation in high school."

He grimaced. "Don't believe everything you hear."

"Even if I didn't believe all of it, I'm pretty sure that you're more skilled and experienced at this than I am. So…" She paused, her pulse racing out of control. "What if I'm a big disappointment?"

He met her gaze. "I guess it's always possible."

"You think so?" She really hadn't expected him to agree with her. Most men she knew, when presented with a willing woman holding a box of condoms, would brush aside any concerns and get to the action.

"But then, I could be a big disappointment to you, too."

"I seriously doubt that, Tucker."

"After listening to all the gossip, you're probably expecting me to be the best you've ever had."

She couldn't deny it so she said nothing.

"That's a lot of pressure."

She felt ashamed of herself. "You're right. I'm sorry, Tucker. I didn't really think about—"

"On the other hand, it's possible I will be the best

you've ever had." His wicked grin flashed. "Why don't you take off those clothes so you can find out?"

She nearly passed out from excitement. She couldn't breathe from the force of it. Now that was the kind of comment she would have expected from him. Heart pounding wildly, she tossed him the box of condoms.

He caught them in one hand without taking his gaze from hers. "For all you know," he said quietly, "I'm expecting you to be the best I've ever had."

Her reply was breathless. "Please don't get your hopes up." With trembling hands, she started removing her clothes.

"Sex is like dancing." Still looking into her eyes, he opened the box of condoms, reached over and upended it on the nightstand. "You're only as good as your partner."

She'd never seen a man empty a box of condoms like that, as if he might need the entire contents eventually and wanted them all available. "That could work both ways," she said. "I could cramp your style." She'd peeled off everything but her bra and panties. If only they were black silk instead of white cotton.

"No, you won't."

She reached behind her back, unfastened her bra and let it slide down her arms to the floor.

He groaned softly. "You *seriously* won't. Look at you."

Her body grew several degrees hotter. "I'm nothing special."

"That's where you're wrong. You're perfect."

No man had ever called her perfect before, and it must have gone to her head, because as she slipped off her panties, she added a little shimmy to the move.

"You're killing me, Lacey. I need you over here ASAP."

"You do?" She wasn't sure where the temptress voice had come from, either. "Why is that?"

He threw back the covers to reveal his gloriously erect penis. "Does that answer your question?"

She thought she could be forgiven for staring. A girl wasn't treated to something that beautiful every day. In fact, this particular girl had never seen equipment quite so gorgeous.

It summoned an ache from deep inside her, an ache demanding to be assuaged. For the first time in her life she understood the concept of penis envy. If she could have that particular penis available to her on a regular basis, she would be the envy of every woman in the state of Wyoming.

She sashayed slowly over to the bed. She'd never sashayed before, but she was inspired to do it now. "You need to put on its party outfit."

In one smooth movement, he picked up a condom packet from the nightstand and handed it to her. "You can do the honors."

"I'd be delighted." She quivered with eagerness, and even though she'd never been called upon to do this before, she vowed to be cool about it. She ripped open the package. "I've heard moistening it helps."

"You might not like the taste."

"Oh, I bet I will." Heart hammering, she sat on the edge of the bed, wrapped her fingers around his penis and lowered her mouth to the glistening tip.

"I meant the taste of the con—ahhhh…never mind."

She raised her head. "Did I do something wrong?"

"Nope." His eyes had glazed over. "That's great. More of that."

"Okay." Sucking gently, she took him in all the way to

the back of her throat and heard him mutter a soft curse. She lifted her head again. "Problem?"

"Uh-huh." His voice sounded strained. "You're very good."

"And that's bad?" He was so velvety soft, yet so deliciously firm that she couldn't resist stroking him.

"It can be." His jaw tightened. "If you keep that up, the party will be over before you know it."

She stopped stroking immediately. "I don't want that."

"Neither do I."

"I thought, with all your experience, you'd be able to—"

"You'd think so, wouldn't you? But watching that curly mop of yours sliding up and down while you... I can't take it."

She touched her hair, suddenly self-conscious. "I know my hair's a mess."

"A wonderful mess." He shoved his fingers into her hair and cradled her head in both hands. "Your hair is perfect for making love all night long." Then he kissed her with such enthusiasm that she forgot all about the state of her hair.

She had to believe that she was perfect, and her hair was perfect, and something about her was so potent that he lost all the sexual control he'd developed over the years. He finally stopped kissing her long enough for her to put the condom on him.

Earlier he must have thought she was going to put the condom in her mouth before rolling it over his penis. She hadn't thought of that, but he'd given her another idea. She was moist in other places, too, and a devilish urge made her put the condom down there to gather up some extra lubrication.

He watched her in rapt fascination. "I'm in serious trouble with you, lady."

"Then let's get into trouble together." She rolled on the condom. By the time she'd finished, he was breathing like a long-distance runner nearing the finish line. "I'm usually a lot calmer about this, Lacey, but…"

"But I get you really, really, hot."

"That's an understatement. Crude as this might sound, you'd better climb on before the train leaves the station."

If she'd been expecting a long, slow seduction where he aroused her to a fever pitch by kissing her all over, she wasn't going to get it, at least not this time. Truthfully, long and slow would have frustrated the hell out of her. She'd gone way past simmer to a full boil, and she wanted him to do her *now*. He could take his sweet time later.

Bracing her hands on his shoulders, she straddled his hips.

"I love your breasts." He cupped them in his large hands. "I haven't paid enough attention to them."

"Don't worry about it." Centering herself over the object of her desire, she wiggled a little to make sure she had him where she wanted him.

He made a strangled sound deep in his throat and his fingers flexed, lightly squeezing her breasts. "Don't wait."

"I won't." And with that, she lowered herself with deliberation, taking him up to the hilt, closing her eyes and moaning as he stretched and filled her. Ecstasy.

He gulped for air and brushed his thumbs over her taut nipples. Tilting her head back, she reveled in the erotic friction and instinctively responded by starting to lift her hips in preparation for another downward stroke.

Suddenly his hands were there, gripping her tight,

holding her down. "Be still for a second. Let me...get my bearings."

She opened her eyes and looked into his. The wild hunger she saw in those green depths made her womb contract.

He gasped. "Lacey..."

"Didn't mean to. I just—"

"I know. Me, too. We might have to go for it."

"I'm in."

His grip tightened on her hips as he held her gaze. "Then ride me, Lacey. Give me all you've got."

Clutching his shoulders and looking into his eyes, she rose up and came down, rose up again and came down faster.

"Yeah." He urged her on, guiding the motion of her hips. "Like that. Like *that*."

Her orgasm thundered closer with every wild thrust. Her bottom smacked against his thighs, and she began to utter little cries that grew louder, and louder yet. She realized that they were utterly and completely alone. No one could hear, and she could let go as she'd never let go before.

His jaw flexed. "Come for me, Lacey. Come for me!"

She couldn't have stopped her climax if she'd tried. It engulfed her, making her abandon all modesty as she pressed down on that glorious cock and arched into a mindless spiral of sensation. Holding her tight, he drove upward with a bellow of satisfaction, finding the open gate to nirvana and joining her there.

For those few moments, they seemed inseparable. She'd never felt that intensity of emotion, that unique oneness with anyone else. She'd expected polished technique from a man like Tucker. She'd expected pleasure and sinful delight. But she'd never, in her wildest dreams, expected…transcendence.

She wanted to believe she was special, and that the connection had been as unique for him as it had been for her. But that was probably a foolish hope. He was an accomplished lover, the kind of guy who could have almost any woman he wanted.

In a twist of fate, a blizzard had trapped him with her for the night. He'd gallantly made her feel like the only woman in the world for him. He probably did that no matter who he took to bed, and she'd do well to remember that.

5

TUCKER REALIZED SOON after the most profound climax of his life that he was screwed. He'd allowed his hero complex to take over again, and he would pay dearly for that. But hell, she'd been almost engaged to a guy who made *her* buy the condoms.

That had been bad enough, but when he saw the look on her face when she'd thought he was rejecting her hesitant offer to have sex, he hadn't been able to stand it. She deserved so much more than the jerk she'd been going with. Tucker didn't consider himself in the *so much more* category, but he could at least make her feel good on Christmas Eve.

Well, now, he had. From her wild response and the way her body had clenched his during her orgasm, he was certain he'd given her a happy time. And because no good deed went unpunished, he'd just had the most soul-shattering sexual experience of his life.

If history repeated itself, and it usually did, Lacey would either move on or go back to her ex. Either way he was hosed, and this time he wasn't sure how well he'd handle it. True, the rebound guy didn't always get kicked to the curb. He shouldn't automatically assume that Lacey would do that.

He'd love some reassurance that she wouldn't, but how did you ask a woman if she'd felt reality shift in the past few minutes? For all he knew, she always responded with that kind of enthusiasm. He rather doubted it, but trying to find out would be awkward, to say the least. He'd sound like a loser lacking all self-confidence.

She slumped against him, her forehead resting on his shoulder, her breathing slowly returning to normal.

He rubbed her back, marveling at the silky texture of her skin. He'd always imagined that she'd feel like this, but imagining and knowing were such different things. Now he'd never forget the softness under his fingertips. And he'd want to experience it again and again. That might not be in the cards for him.

As he thought about that, he decided on his plan of action. He'd suggested that they celebrate Christmas with a tree, candles, a popcorn garland and a bar of Santa soap. They should follow through on that, and maybe when they weren't in this bed, he'd get an inkling of her true attitude toward him and toward a potential continuation of this relationship.

For years he'd regretted not following up on that kiss. He'd sometimes thought that she couldn't possibly be as perfect for him as he'd imagined. As it turned out, she was even more perfect.

He finger-combed her butterscotch curls. "If we don't get that tree decorated soon, Santa won't leave you any presents."

She stirred and lifted her head to smile lazily at him. "Who needs presents?"

He considered that a promising statement. "Good

point, but after all I went through to bring a tree inside, I think we should put some kind of decorations on it."

She laughed softly. "Nag, nag, nag."

"Did you nuke the popcorn?"

"I did."

"Then let's go string it."

She gazed into his eyes. "You're really serious about this, aren't you?"

"Crazy as it seems, I am. This is the most traction I've ever gotten on the Christmas thing since my mom passed away. I feel a breakthrough coming on."

She nodded. "Then we should honor that."

"Thank you." He was reminded that she was a truly nice person who, if she let him down, would let him down easy.

About twenty minutes later, they'd dressed and laid out their supplies on the kitchen table. She'd volunteered to string popcorn, and he was making a chain of aluminum foil, twisting the foil into links. In his opinion it was an improvement over construction paper and paste, which he didn't have on hand, anyway.

She poked a sewing needle carefully through a piece of popcorn, her head bent and her expression focused. "I'd forgotten how much I like doing this."

He thought about mentioning that she looked adorable stringing popcorn, her rosy lips pursed and her brow puckered in concentration. He decided against saying anything. Too many comments like that and he might scare her off.

Glancing up, she noticed his chain. "That's awesome. I never would have thought of that, but it'll reflect the light."

"We used to cut strips of foil and hang it as icicles, but this is better."

"We need something to give the tree a little color, though." Lost in thought, she continued to string popcorn. Then she glanced up, her eyes alight. "Hershey's Kisses! I just remembered I have a bag of them I brought for snacks. Naturally this time of year they're wrapped in red, green and silver. We can tie threads on them and hang them from the branches!"

"Ingenious." She didn't need Hershey's Kisses when he was prepared to shower her with the real kind. In fact, he already missed touching her, and they'd only been working on this project for ten minutes. At least they'd agreed to only decorate the front of the tree.

A foil chain could be created much faster than a popcorn garland, and soon he had one about twelve feet long. Standing, he draped it on the tree in a zig-zag pattern.

"Very pretty." Her eyes sparkled in that happy way that made his heart swell with satisfaction. "I'm going to remember that trick," she said. "It's really effective."

"Are you saying you might decorate a tree again next year?" God, he wanted to be there if she did.

Her smile dimmed a little. "I don't know."

"I'd help you." He held his breath.

"That would be nice. I mean, if you're available."

"It shouldn't be a problem." He could tell she was hedging her bets, but then, so was he. She hadn't rejected his offer to help her with a tree next year.

He'd take that as a reasonable beginning. "I'll start on the kisses if you want."

She lifted her face to his, her lips curved in a tempting smile. "Which kind?"

Lust slammed into him, but he held himself in check,

not wanting her to know just how much he craved her. Not yet, anyway. Bracing his hands on the table, he leaned in close. "You tell me."

Heat smoldered in her eyes, but then she grinned. "Hershey's, I guess. If you start on the other kind, we'll never finish decorating this tree, and you did haul it in here at great personal sacrifice."

"Now that you mention it, shouldn't you give me at least one kiss in honor of that great personal sacrifice?"

"All right. Just one." She closed her eyes.

He could have moved a few inches and touched his lips to hers, but he didn't.

She opened her eyes again. "I thought you wanted a kiss?"

"I do. I thought you were going to give me one."

"I am. Go ahead."

"Nope. This is my reward, which means you're supposed to kiss *me*."

"Oh. I see the distinction." Putting down her popcorn garland, she reached up with both hands, took him by the ears and pulled him forcefully down to connect with her laughing mouth.

He was laughing, too, but about three seconds into the kiss, the mood shifted. With a soft moan, she let go of his ears, tunneled her fingers through his hair and thrust her tongue in deep. Desperate to feel her against him, he dragged her out of the chair and heard it clatter to the floor.

No matter. Keeping his mouth firmly on hers, he scooped her up, kicked the chair out of the way and carried her into the bedroom. Laying her crossways on the bed, he followed her down as he fumbled with her clothes and she wrenched his shirt open, the snaps popping like gunfire.

He hadn't paid nearly enough attention to her breasts the first time, but he'd make up for it now. After he yanked her sweater over her head, she arched her back so he could unhook her bra. Soon that joined the sweater on the far side of the bed.

If he'd been hot before, the tactile pleasure of her breasts beneath his hands and mouth turned him into an inferno. He stroked, nipped and tasted until he was wild from wanting her. But he couldn't have her until they'd both rid themselves of their jeans.

Gasping, he pushed himself away from her rosy nipples and stood at the side of the bed so he could shuck his pants. She took her cue from him and wiggled out of hers. That wiggle temporarily mesmerized him as a surge of desire took his breath away.

She wasn't practiced at being seductive, yet somehow she'd turned out to be the sexiest woman he'd ever taken to bed. Every move she made turned him on. He was fascinated by her.

Once she was naked, she scooted around so she was lying lengthwise on the bed. Then she reached for one of the packets on the nightstand, and he realized he was just standing there gaping at her when he should be moving this process along.

Taking the packet from her outstretched hand, he put on the condom. If he only had this glorious opportunity to be with her for one night, he was still one lucky cowboy, and he needed to let her know that.

He could do it by slowing the pace and loving her the way she deserved to be loved, instead of behaving like a rutting bull elk. He moved over her carefully, dropping soft kisses on her cheeks, her eyelids, and finally, on her mouth. "Thank you," he murmured.

Breathing fast, she slid her hands up his chest. "For the condom?"

"That, too." He nuzzled the tender spot behind her ear. "But mostly for allowing me stay with you tonight."

"I couldn't very well let you freeze to death." Her hands roamed around to his back, stroking, kneading, caressing.

"No, but you didn't have to let me do this." He ran his tongue along her collarbone and felt her shiver beneath him. "Or this." Leaning down, he placed a ring of kisses around her nipple.

"Which I hope is leading to this." She grasped his cock and gave it a quick squeeze.

"Lacey!" Lifting his head, he looked into eyes bright with a combination of lust and laughter. "Damn it, I'm trying to be romantic."

She resumed massaging his chest. "I appreciate that, Tucker, but you had the RPMs way up there a few seconds ago, and as a consequence I'm still operating full throttle. How about you drop the clutch and peel out?"

"But I want you to know that I cherish this—"

"I know you do. You nearly froze to death digging up a Christmas tree so I could have a real one to decorate. Then you carried me into the bedroom. No man's ever done that, bodily picked me up and taken me to bed."

"They haven't?" He felt good about that.

"Nope. And let me tell you, it makes a girl feel special to be carried into the bedroom like Scarlett O'Hara."

"Good. I want you to feel special."

"You know what else makes a girl feel special?"

"What?"

"When a guy is so desperate to have her, he can't wait another second. She can see that he has this intense need to thrust deep inside her, to join with her in the most basic way that a man and a woman—"

"Got it." Holding her gaze, he drew back and swiftly buried his cock up to the hilt. The sensation of being inside her while he looked into her eyes made him dizzy with joy. He took a shaky breath. "Like that?"

"Exactly like that." Her blue eyes seemed to mirror the intensity he felt. As she cupped his face in both hands, her words came out in a breathless rush. "If you ask me, this is pretty romantic."

"Glad you think so." He drew back and rocked forward again, moving in tight, locking them together. "How about that?"

"Even more romantic."

"Then, lady, get ready to be romanced out of your mind." He began a steady, insistent rhythm, thrusting deep each time. He felt triumphant as her eyes darkened and her skin flushed pink. Her hands fluttered from his face to his shoulders, and then to his hips. Her fingers dug in as she rose to meet him and began to whimper with need.

As her cries increased in urgency, he bore down, seeking her climax, but also seeking something more, something elusive. He longed to reach the essence of her, to touch that part of her that no other man had ever touched.

Her body moved in perfect time with his as they joined in a race to ecstasy. And then, as if she'd flung open a door, he felt it—her complete and utter surrender. He abandoned the last of his restraint, giving to her as she'd given to him, holding nothing back, driving into her again and again, his cries echoing hers.

Her spasms began a breath before his, and he shouted with the joy of it as they came and came and came...together.

For long moments his body shook as he stayed braced above her. He'd closed his eyes at the very last, the better to focus on the rolling splendor of climaxing when she did. But now he opened his eyes and looked down at her.

She gasped for breath, obviously unable to speak yet. But her luminous gaze told him more than words that he hadn't been wrong. Something magical had happened between them.

As her breathing slowed, she reached up and stroked his cheek. "I love how you make me feel," she murmured.

"That's good." He cleared sudden emotion from his throat. "Because I love how you make me feel, too." He had no idea if this magic between them would last for an hour or a lifetime, but he vowed to be grateful for the gift and not worry about its duration.

He leaned down and kissed her. "Come on," he murmured. "We need to finish decorating the tree."

"Slave driver."

He lifted his head to smile at her. "You know you want to."

"I do, actually. I want to see how that popcorn garland looks once it's done."

"See, I knew it. Besides, I think we have a good system going."

"Oh? What's that?"

"Make love, decorate the tree, make love, decorate the tree." He punctuated his sentence with more kisses. "That's working for me."

"Yeah, but eventually we'll have the tree all decorated. Then what?"

He gave her a stricken look. "I guess we'll just have to make love nonstop after that."

"Wow, that sounds drastic."

"I know." He shrugged. "But that's all we'll have left. We'll have to make the best of it."

6

THE SYSTEM WORKED to perfection, and as Lacey had predicted, they ran out of decorations and ended up back in bed for the rest of the night. Eventually they even went to sleep in that bed, with Lacey nestled inside the curve of Tucker's body.

She woke up in the gray light of dawn with a sense of safety, peace and happiness she hadn't felt in years. Tucker was already up, and the sound of a crackling fire and the scent of evergreen and coffee brewing filled her with memories of waking up as a child on Christmas morning.

Throwing back the covers she shivered in the chilly bedroom as she pulled her blue terry bathrobe and fuzzy blue slippers out of the closet. Of course there would be no presents under the tree, but anticipation bubbled through her anyway. It was Christmas morning and she had someone special to spend it with.

He sat on the couch in front of the fire drinking a mug of coffee, but he put the mug on the end table immediately and stood when she came in the room. His smile flashed. "Merry Christmas."

He'd lit the emergency candles sitting on the mantel, and light from the fire reflected off the aluminum foil chain and Hershey's Kisses. Her snowy-white popcorn garland was the perfect touch against the dark green branches. As if that weren't enough, a foil-wrapped box lay at the base of the tree. It even had a fluffy white bow.

She glanced at Tucker. "A present?"

"It's not much."

She approached the tree, marveling at how he could have come up with anything at all under the circumstances. No matter what he'd put in that box, she was touched to the point of feeling her throat close up. It was Christmas morning, and a wonderful man had somehow created a present for her to open.

Sitting on the floor beside the tree, exactly as she used to when she was little, she picked up the box, her eyes moist. Then she laughed softly. The ribbon was toilet paper.

She cleared her throat. "You're very clever."

"I used more than I wanted to, because it kept tearing."

"You did all this while I was asleep?"

He nodded and walked over, mug in hand. "It's funny, but I never used to be able to sleep on Christmas Eve. I was always too excited. It's like that feeling sort of came back."

She gazed up at him. "I know what you mean. When I woke up and smelled the tree and heard the fire, it made me all cozy and warm inside, like I used to feel on Christmas morning. Then I walked in here and discovered a present." She patted the floor beside her. "Come and sit with me while I open it."

"Okay, but I hope you're not expecting too much." He

leaned down and set his coffee mug on the floor before sitting cross-legged beside her.

"The fact that this present even exists is a miracle. I didn't think about dreaming up a gift for you."

He shrugged. "Like I said, I was too excited to sleep."

"Well, I'm very impressed that you did this." She tried to get the bow off without tearing it, but it came apart despite her careful effort. "Sorry."

"Hey, it's just toilet paper. Don't worry about it."

"Yes, but you worked so hard to make the bow. I wanted to save it." She tucked the wad of toilet paper in her bathrobe pocket and took off the aluminum foil wrapper. Underneath was a box of graham crackers, except it felt too light to still have crackers in it.

"I put the packets of crackers in the cupboard so I could use the box."

"I am amazed at your ingenuity."

He leaned closer. "Be careful when you open it."

"It's not alive, is it?"

"No, but it's kind of delicate."

She glanced over at him and her heart squeezed. He'd made her something and now he was almost breathless as he waited to find out what she thought of it. Her world shifted in that moment as she fell helplessly, hopelessly in love.

Opening the top of the cracker box, she reached gently inside and pulled out…a foil angel.

"It's for the top of the tree," he said.

"It's beautiful."

"Hey, are you crying?"

"No." She sniffed and wiped her eyes. "Yes. Oh, Tucker." Laying the angel carefully on the floor next to the tree, she turned to him and climbed into his lap.

He wrapped his arms around her and held her close. "I didn't mean to make you cry."

"They're good tears." She nestled against his warm body and sighed. "Tucker, it feels like Christmas."

"Yes." He stroked her hair. "Yes, it does."

THE MORNING FELT SO RIGHT that Tucker hated to think about leaving. But the storm had ended and he needed to contact the ranch. After attaching the angel to the top of the tree, he shoveled a path to the outbuilding and gave Houdini the rest of the oats and some of the carrots Lacey had left over. Then he texted Jack, who responded that someone would be over with a snowmobile within the next two hours.

Tucker relayed that information to Lacey over breakfast. She'd served him scrambled eggs, bacon and the best cinnamon toast he'd ever eaten. He wanted to stay and spend the day with her, but that wouldn't be happening for several reasons.

First of all, he had to help get Houdini back home. And although Lacey was on vacation, he wasn't. The ranch was short-staffed over the holidays, and he was needed there. He'd made a point of saying he would cover for the hands who'd gone home to their families over Christmas.

He gazed at her sitting across the table from him. She still wore her bathrobe. Without makeup and with her hair still tousled, she looked like a teenager. He thought how wonderful life would be if he could spend every morning across the breakfast table with her.

He put down his coffee mug with a sigh. "I hate to go."

"Couldn't you come back later? Borrow a different snowmobile?"

He shook his head. "Not really. They need me at the

ranch." Then he had an idea. "Would you like to come over there for Christmas dinner? I'm sure they'll want to show their appreciation for what you've done, and at least that way we could spend some time together."

She regarded him steadily. "I would love that."

"Great! Dinner's around four. I'll come over with a snowmobile and get you about three, and then bring you back here after dinner. I won't be able to stay all night, but I could stay for…a little while."

"Okay." Her smile told him she knew exactly how they'd spend that *little while*. "That sounds very nice."

It sounded more than nice to him. It sounded promising.

"And by the way, I'm looking forward to seeing all the decorations at the ranch." She swept a hand around the room. "All this has changed my attitude. You were smart to insist on creating our own celebration."

"It worked for me, too. I—" He heard a cell phone, but it wasn't his. "I think you have a call."

"Yeah." She looked disconcerted. "Excuse me." She picked up her phone from the kitchen counter and walked into the bedroom with it.

Tucker wasn't sure how he knew who had called, but he knew, all the same. He'd bet his last dollar Lenny was on the phone. His stomach felt queasy and he stood up, unable to sit any longer. Coffee mug in hand, he paced the living room.

He couldn't hear what Lacey said, but from the low pitch of her voice, he knew the conversation was serious. Maybe something had come up regarding a member of her family. He tried to convince himself this was a family matter, but he didn't believe it. The way things worked in his world, the minute he started getting invested in a woman, something like this happened.

After what seemed like an eternity, she walked out of the bedroom. "That was Lenny."

His stomach pitched. "Oh?"

"He misses me." She looked slightly dazed. "He said he made a terrible mistake by breaking up with me and he wants to get back together. He said he'd find a way to get out here today, so we could spend the holiday the way we'd planned."

He wanted to yell at her that Lenny couldn't come to this cabin and enjoy the tree he'd dug up, or the decorations he'd made, or the woman he'd fallen in love with. Because he was in love with Lacey, probably had been a little bit in love with her for years.

Cruelly, he'd had these few hours to fall completely head-over-heels, and now she would go back to Lenny because that's what women did. They had a great time with Tucker and then went back to their regularly scheduled lives.

He swallowed. "So I guess you won't be coming over to the Last Chance, after all."

"I didn't say that." There was an edge to her voice.

He started the painful process of putting blockades around his heart. "No, but you won't, will you?"

"I don't know, Tucker." She sounded almost angry. "Do you want me to?"

"That's entirely up to you, Lacey." He might have said more, but the roar of a snowmobile cut off their conversation. It was too soon for Lenny to be arriving, so it had to be someone from the Last Chance. Tucker grabbed his hat and coat from the peg by the door. "I need to get going."

"I'm sure you do."

He paused by the door. "Give the ranch a call if you decide you want to come for dinner." He'd deliberately said *the ranch* because he'd never given her his cell phone number and he wasn't going to stop and do it now. He had to get the hell out of there before the pain overwhelmed him. She was going back to Lenny. Goddammit, she was going back to that idiot Lenny!

LACEY STOOD WITHOUT MOVING, her cell phone clutched in her hand. Tucker hadn't been able to get out of there fast enough, and her head was still spinning from his dash to freedom. She could hear him outside laughing and joking with whoever had come to pick him up. It seemed as if he'd already put her out of his mind.

Heartbreaking though it might be, she had to face the possibility that she was simply a bright spot in his life, a person he'd remember fondly but not someone he'd keep around for the long haul. Years ago Tucker had dated lots of girls, but he'd never stuck with one for very long. Maybe he was built that way.

When she'd told him about Lenny, he'd leaped to the conclusion that she was going back to him. Maybe he'd been relieved about that. He'd left the Christmas dinner invitation up to her instead of saying that he really wanted her there. In actuality, she had no idea how much she meant to Tucker. She only knew how much he meant to her.

He'd left before she could tell him what she'd said to Lenny. *What we had wasn't love. I know that, now, because I've truly fallen in love, maybe for the first time in my life.*

How odd that she'd told Lenny, but Tucker was oblivious. If she had any pride at all, he would remain oblivious. Then she looked at the tree in the corner with the angel on top and decided that pride was overrated.

Tucker might not know it, but he had a lot of love to give and she was just the person who could bring it out in him. She wasn't going to abandon her feelings for him because he was too dense to realize he needed her. They needed each other. They'd proved that last night and this morning.

Loving him seemed right, and even if he didn't totally love her back, he had some affection for her. After all, he'd dug up the tree for her, and he'd made an angel to go on top of it. Those two things meant more, in her estimation, than the great sex they'd shared, although that was a bonus. It was good to be turned on by the man you loved.

The sound of the snowmobile starting up prompted her to walk over to the window. They'd tied Houdini's lead rope to the back of the snowmobile and Tucker was just now climbing on behind whoever had driven over to get him. He turned and glanced back at the cabin.

She raised a hand in farewell, even though she didn't think he could see her. But she counted it as a good sign that he'd looked back. He might not be as ready to write her off as he'd seemed. She wondered if pride had kept him from telling her that she meant something to him.

Glancing at the cell phone in her hand, she took note of the time. She'd give him a couple of hours to get situated before she called and asked for a ride to the ranch. She had no intention of waiting until three.

She wasn't nearly through with him, and he wasn't through with her, either, not if she could help it. If nothing else, she could use some help replanting the tree he'd dug up.

TUCKER WAS GETTING DRESSED after a long-overdue shave and shower when the bunkhouse phone rang. He was the only person down there, so he hurried over to the wall phone while he fastened the snaps on his dark green Western shirt. He picked up the phone. "This is Tucker."

"Hey, Tuck." Jack's voice boomed over the phone and raucous noise in the background indicated the Christmas party was starting a little earlier than planned.

Tucker decided from Jack's cheerful tone that he was already into the eggnog. The guy had seemed damned happy to get Houdini back in one piece, and Tucker had now become *Tuck,* which he took as a sign of Jack's goodwill. "What's up?"

"That woman you stayed with last night called here asking if you'd come over and pick her up. She said you invited her for dinner. Did you?"

"Uh…" Tucker's heart lurched into high gear. He'd been so sure he'd never hear from Lacey again, and he had trouble wrapping his mind around this new development. "Yeah, I did. I hope that's okay."

"It's more than okay. Mom's been chewing my ass about why I didn't invite her when I went over there to get you. I wish I'd known you invited her. I could've saved myself some grief. Oh, and tell her to bring an overnight case. Mom won't hear of you taking her back tonight. Too cold."

"She might not go for that."

"Then you'll have to use your manly charm to convince her. Since the fence is still down, you can take the shortcut. I expect to see you both back here ASAP."

"You want me to go now?" Tucker glanced at the bunkhouse clock. "It's only one. I thought dinner wasn't until four."

"That's the official time the food will be on the table, but…hang on." Jack lowered the phone and called out to someone that he had the situation in hand. Then he was back. "Did you hear that? They're bugging me about this lady. What's her name again?"

"Lacey Evans."

"Yeah, Lacey. Gabe and Nick think they remember her from school. Anyway, you need to produce this woman before I end up in some serious shit for lacking good manners. Take one of the snowmobiles. But don't wreck it, okay?"

"I won't. And I'll pay for fixing—"

"Ah, hell, don't worry about it. I just can't afford to lose another one of those machines in the middle of snow season. See you soon, buddy. With the girl," Jack said, ending the call.

Tucker hung up the phone, but he was so distracted that he walked out of the bunkhouse minus his hat and coat. The freezing weather sent him right back in to retrieve them. He'd have to snap out of it or he really would wreck another snowmobile.

Forcing himself to concentrate on one thing at a time, he eventually headed across the snowy meadow in the same direction he'd gone the day before when he'd chased Houdini. He and Jack had retraced this route going back to the ranch, so by now the snowmobile had created a recognizable path in the snow.

That was fortunate for Tucker, who thought far more about Lacey than he thought about driving the snowmobile. He'd worked so hard to banish her from his mind earlier today because he'd been convinced she was reuniting with Lenny. Apparently not. And that meant…

He didn't know what that meant, or rather, he was afraid to speculate for fear he'd be slammed again.

No smoke came from the chimney as he approached the cabin, which was a good thing. She couldn't go off and leave a fire burning. But then, she'd know that, being a Forest Service employee.

His chest tightened as he parked the snowmobile near the porch. She'd shoveled most of the snow from the steps and he wished he'd been here to help her. He wished he could walk through that door, close it and stay right here instead of carting her back across the snow to the ranch house where he'd have to share her with a whole lot of people.

As he mounted the steps, the blood rushed in his ears. He hadn't been this nervous about seeing a woman in… he'd never been this nervous, come to think of it.

Lacey opened the door. "Thanks for coming to get me." She stood there looking ready to party in a bright red sweater and crisp jeans. She even had on makeup and gold hoop earrings.

"What happened to Lenny?" He hadn't meant to blurt it out like that, but it was uppermost on his mind and apparently he'd lost control of his tongue. "I thought he was coming out here."

"You thought wrong." She stepped back from the door. "Come in for a minute, Tucker. I have something to say."

He struggled to breathe normally, and when he finally dragged in some air, he got a whiff of the peppermint-soap scent clinging to her. He wanted to gobble her up. He took off his hat, mostly so he'd have something to do with his hands.

She closed the door and turned to him. "Tucker, about Lenny. I—"

"Sarah Chance wants you to bring an overnight bag," he said, deliberately interrupting her. He didn't want to hear about Lenny. Maybe Lenny had been delayed and was coming tomorrow, so Lacey had decided to accept the dinner invitation, after all. "Sarah thinks it's too cold for you to come home tonight, so she's inviting you to stay at the ranch house."

"That sounds great. Now, let me tell you about Lenny."

"I don't want to hear about Lenny, okay? If you've decided to go back to him, that's your business. It has nothing to do with me, so—"

"Tucker, shut up." Walking over to him, she grabbed his face in both hands, pulled his head down and kissed him, hard. The kiss was over in a second and she backed away again. Her eyes glittered as she looked up at him. "Get this straight, cowboy. I don't want Lenny."

"You don't?" An avalanche of relief made him dizzy.

"No. I want you."

He stared at her, not quite willing to trust what he thought he'd just heard.

"I'm taking a chance that you like me enough to give us a shot," she continued. "I realize you're not normally a one-woman man, or at least you didn't used to be when I knew you before, but I'd like you to consider—"

"Yes." He tossed his hat across the room where it landed, he hoped, somewhere in the vicinity of the couch. Then he wrapped both arms around her.

"Yes, what?"

"Yes to being a one-woman man, if you're the woman."

Her beautiful mouth curved in a soft smile. "That's pretty much what I had in mind. I…seem to be falling in love with you."

"Dear God, if this is a dream, I don't want to wake up."

She reached up and pinched his earlobe.

"Ow! What was that for?"

"You're not dreaming."

Still doubting his senses, he gazed down at her. "I must be. The woman I'm falling in love with just said she's falling in love with me."

She went very still. "You're falling in love with me?"

"Yeah." He combed his fingers through her glossy curls. "It's been going on for years, and after the time we've shared in this cabin, it's officially a full-blown case. But I was so sure when Lenny called that you—"

"Why? After our special Christmas, how could you think that I'd go running back to a jerk like Lenny?"

"Because it's happened…a few times before. It seems that I'm generally viewed as a short-term kind of guy."

Her blue gaze grew soft. "Like the girl at the formal, who used you to make her boyfriend jealous?"

"Yeah, or the woman who needed some hot sex to feel better about herself, or the woman who decided that I was fun, but her ex had better career prospects. I could give you more examples, but you get the idea."

"Oh, Tucker." She stroked his cheeks with her thumbs. "No wonder you didn't believe in me. But you will. I promise you will."

He looked into her eyes and saw the love shining there. Only a fool would doubt it. Leaning down, he feathered a gentle kiss over her lips. "I already do believe in you, Lacey." And he kissed her again.

She drew back and placed her finger against his mouth. "Don't we have a party to go to?"

"Good point." Reluctantly he released her, pulled his cell phone out of his coat pocket and hit the speed dial number for the ranch. He wasn't sure who answered because the noise level was so high. "This is Tucker." He winked at Lacey. "We'll be a little late for the party. Something came up." He disconnected really fast because Lacey had started laughing.

"What?" Dropping the phone back in his coat pocket, he grinned at her as he began unbuttoning his coat.

"You don't think that was too broad a hint?"

"I don't care if it was." He hung his coat on a peg by the door. "It's Christmas and everyone should be allowed to celebrate however they choose." He pulled her close. "Merry Christmas, Lacey."

She smiled up at him. "Merry Christmas, Tucker."

And as he kissed her, he thought about the many Christmas holidays they would celebrate together. They would all be special, because they'd rediscovered the magic of Christmas. But this day, the day they discovered the magic of their love, would always be the most special of all.

* * * * *

NORTHERN FANTASY

JENNIFER LaBRECQUE

To Vicki and Rhonda—
anthology buds extraordinaire.
Happy Holidays!

After a varied career path that included barbecue-joint waitress, corporate numbers-cruncher and bug-business maven, **Jennifer LaBrecque** has found her true calling writing contemporary romance. Named 2001 Notable New Author of the Year and 2002 winner of the prestigious Maggie Award for Excellence, she is also a two-time RITA® Award finalist. Jennifer lives in suburban Atlanta with a chihuahua who runs the whole show.

1

JARED MARTIN loosened his tie and collar and ordered a bourbon and ginger ale from the flight attendant, more than ready to trade Manhattan's hustle and bustle for some Alaskan wilderness for a few days. Next to him, Nick Hudson ordered a drink as well.

A light snow fell outside the jet's windows on the first leg of their transcontinental flight from New York's La-Guardia to Good Riddance, Alaska. They'd finish the trip via bush plane from Anchorage to the little town.

"Thanks for traveling across the country during the holidays to be in my wedding," Nick said.

"Anytime." Jared grinned. "Not that I'd recommend you make getting married a reoccurring event." Jared was looking forward to it—the trip, that was. He wasn't big on weddings, especially these days, but he and Nick had been tight since middle school. So when Nick invited Jared to be one of his groomsmen, he'd said yes without hesitation.

"I hear you. I plan to make this a once-in-a-lifetime event, because Gus is a once-in-a-lifetime kind of woman. Damn, I don't know how I got so lucky."

"That's for sure. What she sees in you… Some guys get all the breaks."

Jared had initially thought" Nick had lost his mind when he'd turned up for a Saturday afternoon game of hoops eleven months ago and mentioned he was marrying a woman, Augustina "Gus" Tippens, he'd only just met while traveling. That was nuts in Jared's book. And then he'd really thought it was crazy when Gus, a chef, had given up her restaurant in Alaska to move back to New York to work.

However, after actually seeing Gus and Nick together, Jared got it. He was a guy and admittedly not the most "tuned in" or romantic male out there, but even he saw how right and close Gus and Nick were together. They seemed to have a connection Jared and his ex-wife had never had. Jared wondered if he'd ever have something like that.

"Oh, crap. I didn't think before I said that…you know, what with…damn, I'm just stepping in deeper and deeper."

Jared cracked up. Nick didn't fumble often but when he did… "Keep wading, buddy. It's okay. I got a divorce. No biggie."

"Yeah, well, I didn't mean—"

"Nick, it's cool."

The flight attendant dropped off their drinks, one of the benefits of flying first class—first on, first off, and first served.

Nick shook his head. "Trish lost her mind."

Trish. Jared's ex-wife. Funny how quickly he'd learned to think of her that way when for three years he'd thought of her as his wife. Had it really only been nine months ago that she'd announced she was leaving him for her hairdresser? WTF? Who got left for a guy who did hair? Apparently Jared did.

Yep, she'd waltzed in and announced all he ever wanted to do was make money, packed her shit and left. Funny, but Trish had always been more than willing to spend the money he made. He had not, however, bothered to point that out.

True enough he put in a lot of hours, but as a Wall Street trader, staying on top of the game meant staying one step ahead. Trish's leaving had just given him more time to work harder.

He shrugged. "Trish did what she had to do." He'd been surprised at first but then he'd realized the signs had been there—he'd just been too busy to see them. And he'd be damned if he'd ever tell her, but the truth of the matter was he hadn't put much effort—okay, really none—into making their marriage work. He'd taken Trish and their relationship for granted. Now that some time had passed, he could see that.

"Gus has been worried about you."

He and Trish had gone to dinner with Gus and Nick a couple of times. After Trish had bailed…well, Jared had done the only thing he knew, which was immerse himself in work. Gus and Nick had invited him out numerous times after the split but work had just been easier.

"Gus is a sweetheart, but she doesn't need to worry about me," Jared said. He rubbed his hand over his head and tossed out something he'd been considering for a couple of weeks now. "I've been thinking about leaving the city anyway."

"What the hell?" Nick looked genuinely surprised.

"You've been thinking about leaving? To go where and do what? You're as New York as they come."

There was a restlessness, a discontent that had been eating at him, that he couldn't seem to shake. "I'm burned out." He'd thought it but it was the first time he'd actually spoken the words aloud to anyone.

"You're serious? Where would you go? What would you do?"

Jared didn't have a clue as to an alternate career and location, he just knew something was missing from his life…and it wasn't his ex-wife. "I don't know yet, I just know I'm ready for a change."

Nick sent him a searching glance, wearing his journalist-on-a-story face. "Are you having a midlife crisis at thirty-one?"

Jared took a healthy swallow of his bourbon and ginger ale. "Possibly." He'd been fast-tracking ever since graduating from Wharton with an MBA and signing on with a prestigious Wall Street firm. He'd met Trish in a martini bar one evening when he was hanging out with some guys from the office after work. A year and a half later, they were tying the knot with a wedding extravaganza followed by a honeymoon in the Seychelles. And the bitch of it was she might say he worked too much, but she wouldn't have given him the time of day if he hadn't been a hotshot Wall Streeter.

And now he was just sick of the whole damned thing. He'd never anticipated being at this place where he was tired of the game. For the first time in his life he no longer knew what he wanted—he simply knew something was missing. "A new career and a new start somewhere sounds better and better. I'd be more than happy to toss in the towel on the condo and the job and try a little dose of being commitment free."

Nick followed another searching gaze with a shrug. "Then you're heading to the right place. Good Riddance is where you get to leave behind what ails you."

Jared had heard all about Good Riddance from both Gus and Nick. Gus's mother's best friend, Merrilee Danville Weatherspoon, had founded the town twenty-something years ago, when she'd loaded up her RV, left her husband behind in Georgia and drove until she turned up in the spot that felt right. She'd called it Good Riddance. To Jared it sounded as unique and unorthodox, in its own way, as parts of New York.

Jared had read Nick's travel blog with great interest last December, when he'd covered the little Alaskan town's Chrismoose celebration—a week-long holiday festival of arts and crafts, sporting competitions, a Ms. Chrismoose pageant, and a parade. The event was based on a hermit who lived in the wilderness and would ride his pet moose into Good Riddance two days before Christmas.

Jared and Nick were arriving at the tail end of Chrismoose. Traveling any closer to Christmas Eve was too crazy and uncertain, especially when they needed to get to Good Riddance for Nick's wedding.

"It sounds like just where I want to be."

"Well, if you want something different, you damn sure aren't going to be in Kansas anymore, Toto."

It sounded good to him. No New York and no commitments—that just what he wanted in his foreseeable future.

THEODORA "TEDDY" MONROE stood as still as possible while Ellie Lightfoot pinned the bridesmaid dress into place, the fabric a sensual slide against Teddy's skin. Standing still was an unnatural state of being for her. That is, unless she was playing a role which required her to be dead or sedentary.

Not that those roles came her way very often, which was a direct reflection of living in Good Riddance, Alaska, the middle of nowhere in a state that was about as far as possible from where she longed to be—New York, the place where roles abounded.

One more month and she'd be moving to the Big Apple. Just the thought made it even harder to stand still—she wanted to dance with sheer excitement. She felt as if her whole life was on the verge of blooming wide open— like a caterpillar transformed from the chrysalis stage into a butterfly. This was what she'd wanted for as long as she could remember—to study acting and pursue a career onstage.

Gus and Nick had found Teddy a waitressing gig and a studio apartment in Brooklyn—Manhattan was far too pricey for her budget—right around the corner from Nick's cousin Angela. Gus had sent pictures, warning her the apartment was small. It simply looked marvelous to Teddy, but then again she'd willingly live in a closet as long as that closet was part of the bustle and opportunity of New York.

"Okay, turn around slowly," Ellie said, her dark eyes scanning the fit of the dress. Ellie's glossy black braid, which bespoke her Native heritage, hung over one shoulder. Teddy's dress had been made in New York but shipped to Good Riddance for the final fitting. Ellie was a genius with a needle and thread.

"Don't you just love weddings?" Merrilee said, clapping her hands together. She and Gus sat on the bed. Eartha Kitt's rendition of "Santa Baby," one of Teddy's all-time faves, drifted in through the open bedroom door from the CD player in the next room, adding to the fun atmosphere. Gus had whipped up a gingerbread cake and popped it in the oven. The aroma, maddeningly mouth-watering, permeated the air.

"Any news on your wedding front, Ellie?" Gus asked.

Ellie's quiet smile wreathed her face. "Not yet. We are still waiting on the sign." The entire town had been shocked when Nelson and Ellie had announced their pending marriage and Nelson's plans to pursue medical school. Nelson, who had been training as a shaman, still followed the ways of waiting on answers through signs. Their wedding sign had yet to appear.

Merrilee was obviously delighted by all the wedding trappings strewn about in the bedroom of the apartment above the restaurant Gus used to run. "That crimson velvet is beautiful on you, Teddy. It really brings out your creamy skin and your blond hair."

She'd been a little nervous the color might wash her out, but it worked.

"I do like the rich color." She looked at Gus, the bride-to-be who was also her former employer and friend, who'd flown in from New York two days ago, and smiled. "You did a good job picking out the dresses."

Gus nodded a happy acknowledgment. "I did, didn't I? And they look good on both of Nick's sisters."

Ellie tucked and pinned one more time. "Okay, now let me unzip you and we're done." She tilted her head to one side. "It's beautiful on you."

"Thanks."

It had been a challenge with Gus, Teddy and Merrilee, the matron of honor, in Good Riddance and Nick's sisters in New York. Plus there was an age range from fifty-nine to twenty-four. Teddy had yet to meet Nick's family— they'd be flying in later—but she'd seen pictures. Like him, Nick's sisters had dark hair and startling blue eyes. The dark red would look great on them.

Gus shook her head, looking slightly shell shocked. "I'm not quite sure how it happened but this wedding has escalated to huge."

Teddy stepped out of the dress, taking care to avoid the straight pins, and reached for her jeans.

"It's because you've got a whole new family to embrace you now, honey," Merrilee said with an indulgent smile.

Gus leaving Good Riddance had been hard for Merrilee who loved her like a daughter. But plain and simple, Gus had never belonged in Good Riddance.

Teddy might have been raised in Good Riddance but she no longer belonged here, either. She'd lost her own mother at fourteen, and her father had long before left for parts unknown. But she'd been fortunate enough to have her older sister Marcia, who'd provided a loving, stable home environment.

When she was alive, Teddy's mother had encouraged and nourished Teddy's dream of being a stage actress. After her mother's death, Teddy had found a collection of journals her mother had kept. They'd broken her heart.

Cassandra Monroe had forsaken following her dream of being a classical concert pianist to follow Bill Monroe hither and yon only to have him abandon her and their two daughters in Alaska.

After reading her mother's journals Teddy had grown more determined than ever to make a go of acting, not just for herself but for her mother as well. Teddy had read in the journals that her mother had never wanted Teddy and Marcia to feel as if they were a burden, and it had also just been too painful for Cassandra to talk about the dreams she'd relinquished. So instead of telling her daughters, she'd confined her thoughts to paper and ink.

Working in the restaurant downstairs with Gus for two and a half years, Teddy had set aside every spare penny. Discovering her former fiancé was dead had freed Gus to return to New York.

Lucky, Gus's former short-order cook, had taken over the running of the restaurant in Good Riddance. But it had been critical Teddy stay for at least a couple of months to smooth the transition and to allow Lucky to find and train someone to take Teddy's place, as well. She was helping out during Chrismoose but tonight was her final night at the restaurant.

She'd moved into Gus's apartment above the restaurant to try to get her sister, Marcia, used to the idea of her leaving. Incredibly overprotective of her little sister, Marcia had finally given her blessing on Teddy moving to New York.

She'd begun to wonder if she'd ever leave Good Riddance. Good Riddance was a wonderful place, but it simply wasn't where she'd fulfill her purpose.

Finally, *finally*, everything was in place and in a short period of time she'd be gone.

"I can't wait for everyone to meet Nick's family," Gus said. "You guys are going to love them and they're going to adore everyone here."

Teddy zipped her jeans and tugged her sweater on over her head.

"I'm looking forward to seeing them again," Merrilee said. She and her husband, Bull, had flown to New York in early spring to meet Nick's family.

Ellie carried the dress and they all moved into the open den and kitchen.

"I can't wait to meet them," Teddy said. She was thrilled Nick's family had more than embraced Gus. And once Teddy moved to New York…well, she'd been reassured the Hudsons would take her under their wing, as well.

Merrilee and Ellie settled on the couch while Teddy and Gus moved into the kitchen.

Gus, pulling the gingerbread out of the oven, slanted Teddy an arch glance. "Yeah, well, wait until Nick gets here with his buddy Jared. You'll be glad to meet him, too."

Teddy measured out coffee. She'd kept her love life on hold for several years. Her mother was definitely a cautionary tale. It would've been far too easy to get caught up in a guy and trade in her dreams and aspirations of being an actress for a ring on her finger and settling in Good Riddance, so she'd simply steered clear of any romantic entanglements. "I'm always up for eye candy. And this guy's from New York, so…"

"He's hot. Not as hot as Nick, mind you, but a looker nonetheless." So she'd said earlier when she was giving them the rundown on Nick's best friend. Teddy knew he was a recently divorced stockbroker and a workaholic. She also knew his parents were, according to Nick, pretty awful. He'd categorized them as social climbers who found Jared always just short of the mark. Apparently Jared had spent a lot of time at Nick's house as a teen-ager. And she knew Nick and Jared met for racquetball once a week.

Teddy added water and turned on the coffeemaker. She was all for checking him out, but she'd draw the line there.

She wasn't about to be sidetracked by a man at this stage in her life.

2

"WELCOME TO GOOD RIDDANCE, where you can leave behind what troubles you," the venerated Merrilee Danville Weatherspoon greeted Jared when he entered the tiny air terminal that doubled as a bed-and-breakfast and shared space with the town's only restaurant. Clad in a pink-and-gray flannel shirt trimmed in lace, she looked younger than he'd expected.

"I'm happy to be here," Jared said, most sincerely. He'd wanted a change and, by God, this place seemed about as far removed from New York's relentless hustle and bustle as you could get. Even before Nick had pointed it out on the puddle-jumper flight from Anchorage, Jared had already noted the absence of street lights.

However, even in the surreal twilight that enveloped the land, he could clearly see Good Riddance had only one central street and not a single traffic light. One end of town held a plethora of travel trailers, RVs and even a couple of tents for what must truly be the hardy—or rather fool-hardy—souls, all in town for the Chrismoose festival.

Outside it was cold and rather dark, with a fairly heavy snow falling at four in the afternoon, but inside the "terminal" was reminiscent of some Norman Rockwell wilderness rendering.

A gray-bearded man resided in a rocking chair flanking a chess table next to a pot-bellied stove, apparently engaged in the game by himself. He reminded Jared of some of the old men who hung out in some of the smaller neighborhood parks off the beaten path.

Photos—a haphazard amalgamation of black-and-whites and full-colors, some framed, some not, of people, places and things—covered the timbered walls. Next to the Christmas tree, a full-size plush moose wore a Santa costume. The scents of coffee, hot cocoa, gingerbread and wood smoke hung in the air.

It was a marked contrast to the towering silver tinsel tree outfitted in oversize red ornaments that stood in the lobby of the glass-and-chrome building that housed his office. The homespun charm he found here was a welcome change.

This year he'd elected to forego the tired office winter-holiday party—it was now politically incorrect to refer to it as a Christmas party—where there were actually pools going beforehand as to who would overindulge and make asses of themselves and who would wind up with who in the coat closet, restroom or breakroom. He really didn't care whether he'd looked like he wasn't a team player when he'd passed on the party. He no longer gave a flying flip.

Miracle on 34th Street was playing on the TV in the corner. If there were any miracles to be found on 34th Street he'd missed them thus far. Across the room, a man of Native heritage demonstrated flute-carving to a small but rapt group. Being ensconced in so much hominess *almost* checked Jared's urge to get a final reading on the Dow via his BlackBerry. Good Riddance was just what the doctor ordered. Nonetheless he went on-line and pulled up the day's final figures. A couple of clicks and he had checked individual stocks. Overall, not a bad closing.

He looked up from his BlackBerry to find Merrilee watching him with raised eyebrows. "Are you back with us now?" she asked.

Going online using a mobile device was *de rigueur* where he came from. Nobody even blinked at it. In fact, it was likely the other person was checking email or texting at the same time as well. However, he suddenly felt as if he'd crossed some line of good manners and tucked his BlackBerry into its case. "Sorry, just needed to check on a few things."

"No problem," Merrilee said. She turned to Nick with a smile. "Gus is holding court next door." *Next door* was the restaurant attached to the terminal and still went by the name of Gus's. "You know how busy it is during Chrismoose, and then word got around Gus was back in town and they're really packing folks in." A door about midway across the room boasted a sign above it, Welcome To Gus's. Even with the television in this room and the small group chatting up front, the muted noise from Gus's was apparent. Merrilee eyed their suitcases. "You probably don't want to work your way through the crowd with that. You can leave them here for now or take the outside entrance."

Gus's living quarters had been above the restaurant. The two-bedroom suite was accessible both from inside the restaurant and from the exterior stairs Nick had pointed out when they landed. Someone else had moved in since Gus left but Gus and Nick were going to share one bedroom and Jared got the couch. Apparently quarters were hard to come by during the Chrismoose festival in Good Riddance. Sleeping on a couch for a few nights wouldn't kill him.

"How about we just leave them here for now?" Nick said.

"No problem." Merrilee waved them to a corner on the other side of her desk. Jared and Nick deposited their luggage before Merrilee hustled them toward the connecting door. "Now get. Go introduce Jared to everyone and I'm sure you're both starving since we're four hours behind New York."

Now that she mentioned it, Jared hadn't really eaten anything all day other than a bagel he'd grabbed on the way to the train this morning. "I could eat a horse," he said.

Merrilee laughed. "You won't find horse but moose and caribou for sure." She shooed them forward. "Bull's bartending. He'll want to meet Jared for sure."

Nick grinned and gave her a quick hug. "We'll see Bull first and then I'll introduce Jared to everyone."

It was good to see the obvious affection between them. Merrilee was as close to a mother-in-law as Nick was going to have. According to Nick, Merrilee had resented the hell out of him when he'd first shown up last year. Obviously she'd gotten over it.

A couple came down the stairs to the left of the front

door. Upstairs must be the bed portion of the bed-and-breakfast.

As the couple beelined for Merrilee, Nick and Jared crossed the worn wood floor. Nick opened the door to the restaurant, and as the sound had indicated beforehand, it was mayhem on the other side. Actually, it reminded Jared of a Manhattan happy hour on a Friday evening. To the left of the door the bar area was packed, all the seats taken and several people standing and talking.

Booths lined one wall beyond the bar, and another to the right of the front door, with tables filling in the floor space. To the far right a group was throwing darts, and both pool tables were also seeing action. Jared spotted Gus, with her dark hair—a single swath of signature white in the front—at a large table in the corner.

He nudged Nick. "Gus is over there."

Nick nodded. "Let's meet Bull and grab a drink, then we'll head over."

Working their way to the bar wasn't nearly as quick or easy as he'd thought it'd be. Unlike during a Manhattan happy hour, damn near everyone recognized Nick and stopped him to welcome him back and offer congratulations on the impending wedding. A few of the men jokingly offered condolences. However, everyone they encountered was warm and friendly.

They finally gained the polished bar with the brass foot rail running its length. A stuffed moose head with a Santa hat jauntily angled over one eye reigned amongst the shelved bottles of liquor and glasses on the wall behind the bar. A thickset man sporting a gray ponytail and a full beard was working a draft beer pull. He looked like a Vietnam vet who'd be known as Bull.

He was. Bull and Nick clapped one another on the back and Nick followed up with introductions.

"How was the flight in?" Bull asked.

"Long, but uneventful."

Bull grinned. "Uneventful's always a good thing when you're in the air."

"You bet your sweet ass."

The bar was as busy as the rest of the place. Nick and Jared each snagged a drink and made their way across the room to Gus. After a quick welcoming hug, Gus started the introductions. There were the Sisnukets, a delicate blonde named Tessa and her husband, Clint, reputedly the best Native guide in this area of Alaska. The local doctor, a striking redhead named Skye Shannihan, and her fiancé, Dalton Summers, one of the bush pilots operating out of Good Riddance. According to Nick, the couple was leaving tomorrow to spend Christmas with Skye's family in Atlanta. Nick's crew, his parents, sisters and their families were staying in Summers's two cabins at a place called Shadow Lake. Jared was particularly intrigued when he met a guy named Logan, who had recently moved his corporate job as CFO for a mining operation to Good Riddance so he could marry Jenna, a perky blonde building a spa facility. He hadn't expected to find the CFO of an international enterprise hanging out in this remote town. Jared thought it was cool that with a little help from technology, Logan had managed to pull himself out of the rat race yet still stay in the game.

A Native guy with a long dark ponytail was Clint's cousin Nelson Sisnuket, who worked as a doctor's assistant. The dark-haired woman next to him was his fiancée,

Ellie Lightfoot, a school teacher. Across the table, Sven Sorenson could've played the lead in a Viking flick, but was actually a builder.

Jared shook hands with everyone. "Okay, I can't swear I'll remember everyone's name but I'll try."

Across the table, Jenna smiled. "Just blame it on jet lag if you run into one of us and go blank."

Jared was laughing when suddenly the fine hairs on the back of his neck and along his arms stood up.

Gus smiled at someone past his shoulder. "And now you get to meet Teddy."

Jared turned and found himself looking into the prettiest light brown eyes he'd ever seen. Something hot and wild seemed to course through him. He could've sworn the floor literally shifted beneath his feet.

And then he crashed to his knees in front of her.

TEDDY OPENED HER MOUTH but no sound came out. One minute she was face-to-face with a gorgeous guy and the next minute he was on the floor at her feet. She'd never had anything like that happen to her. How did a woman react to that? And well, what did it mean?

The man at her feet had to be Jared Martin. Despite how busy they were, she'd seen him the moment he walked in with Nick. When Gus had deemed him hot… well, that was an understatement. Teddy had written him off earlier as probably too…something. Uh-uh. He was all "just right." Tall and lean with a sculpted face, he looked smart, sophisticated and expensive.

For a moment she would've been hard pressed to even know her own name. It was as if something she'd been waiting on had just walked through the door, but she hadn't been waiting on anything, except the opportunity to get to New York.

Lust was the first thing that had registered in her brain. That he was out of her small-town league had been the immediate chaser thought that followed. And now...what?

Little John, a regular who stood at least six-foot-seven, bent down. "Sorry, dude. I lost my footing and didn't mean to bump into you that way."

Ah, that made sense. He'd been caught off guard and felled by Little John.

Jared regained his feet, brushing at the knees of his pants. "No harm done," he said to Little John. "A little humiliation is good for the soul now and then."

Good-looking and a sense of humor...and a voice that did all kinds of funny things to her insides.

Little John smiled, nodded and turned back around to his pals. Jared looked at Teddy with a smile that quirked up the right side of his mouth slightly higher than the left. And those eyes...a pale blue that was in marked contrast to his dark lashes. She was, quite uncharacteristically, at a loss for words, her heart thumping like mad against her ribs.

"And now that I've made a stellar impression by literally falling at your feet, it's nice to meet you."

Teddy smiled at his self-deprecating aplomb. She held out her hand, managing to dredge up some semblance of composure. "There's something terribly satisfying in having a man kneel at your feet."

He wrapped his hand around hers. Teddy felt the impact of his touch all the way to her toes. "Does it happen often?" he said.

She was all squirrel-headed from his touch and looked at him blankly. "What?"

"Men falling at your feet?"

He released her hand and she smiled at him. "Absolutely, it happens all the time. I've almost gotten used to it."

"Ah, so I'm just one of many," he said.

With a start, Teddy realized everyone at the table was watching them with avid interest. Gus wore a knowing smirk. For the span of a few seconds Teddy had totally lost track of being in a crowded restaurant. Shaking hands with Jared had been that potent.

Work, Teddy, work, she reminded herself. She needed to focus on work rather than the heat Jared Martin had unleashed in her. This time she made sure her smile included Nick, as well.

"The specials tonight are caribou stew, moose stroganoff and elk lasagna. What can I get everyone?"

The large group had been having drinks, eating chips and salsa and waiting on Nick and Jared to arrive. It felt so strange to have Gus sitting at the table as a patron rather than being behind the counter running the kitchen. Teddy had missed Gus.

Self-consciousness washed over Teddy. She was altogether too aware of Jared's eyes on her as she took the orders around the table. Of course, she'd had men flirt with her—not only was she a passably attractive female in a state where the men vastly outnumbered the women, she also worked in a bar. She'd selectively dated a few guys, but no one had ever affected her this way. And this man was going to be sleeping on her sofa tonight...and tomorrow night, as well. Of course, she might spend a little time with him and discover he was a jerk. But she didn't think so. She had a feeling her ship was sunk.

3

JARED HAD TO CONFESS he wasn't fully paying attention to the conversation flowing around him. He couldn't seem to stop watching Teddy as she moved about the restaurant. Her energy and enthusiasm captivated him. Her blond hair was up in a ponytail and the way it bobbed and swung as she worked was straight-up sexy. There was nothing overtly enticing about the way she was dressed. She wore jeans tucked into flat, animal-skin boots and a red Christmas sweater with a moose on the front. Jingle bell earrings dangled from her ears. However, there was an inherent sensuality to the way she moved, as if she was extremely comfortable in her own skin. He noticed her in a way he hadn't noticed a woman in a long time, perhaps ever—as if he was seeing nuances and layers he'd never noticed before in other women, his ex-wife included.

More than once their glances had caught and held across the crowded room. As the evening wore on, Jared was increasingly aware he'd buried himself in work for the past nine months with no female companionship since Trish had moved out and they'd divorced.

Next to him, Nick said, "Want to get our luggage upstairs and settle in a bit, and then if you're still alert and alive we can come back downstairs?"

Jared should've been exhausted given the jet lag and the fact he'd crammed a full day's work into a couple of hours before catching the shuttle to the airport and hooking up with Nick there, but he felt energized in a way he hadn't in a long time. "Sure."

They made their way back through the room, stopping by the bar area to settle their bill. The food had been good, the company great, and watching Teddy Monroe better still. Nick caught her eye and she walked over. "Jared and I are going to take our luggage upstairs. We'll come back down if we're both still alive. Jared's on the sofa, right?"

"Yep. There's a pillow and a couple of blankets." She looked at Jared, the impact of her brown eyes twisting his gut into a knot of hot want. "Make yourself at home. If you find you forgot something you need such as a toothbrush or razor, Merrilee keeps extras next door for the bed-and-breakfast."

"What time do you finish up here?" he asked, getting straight to the point. There'd been any number of interesting conversations going on at the table over dinner, but she was the person in the room he couldn't stop looking at and thinking about.

Teddy's smile left him feeling…he didn't exactly know, but God, she was sexy. "We close at ten and then it's about forty-five minutes to get everything cleaned and ready for the next day."

Nick chimed in. "Don't even bother to offer to help. Trust me, I've seen it firsthand. They have this down to a science."

"Don't let him fool you." Her smile encompassed Nick as well as Jared. "Nick was pretty good at stepping in and taking over when I came down with the flu last year."

Jared remembered the story from when he and Trish had first gone to dinner with Nick and Gus.

Nick shrugged. "We managed. But thank goodness there's no flu outbreak this Chrismoose season."

Teddy nodded. "Yeah, knock on wood." She rapped lightly against the bar's surface for good measure. "I've never been so sick in all of my life. Last year it was a mess with the flu going around."

Jared liked how genuine she was. "That's what I heard."

Lucky called out another order up and Teddy was back in work mode. "Okay, I'll see you guys later."

Jared stood rooted to the spot and watched her walk away, her ponytail swinging and her neat tush swaying.

Nick laughed and elbowed him as they closed the distance to the connecting door between the restaurant and the terminal. "Easy there. You're about one step away from drooling."

Jared shook his head slightly, trying to clear it. They walked into the deserted terminal. A sled dog curled next to the stove raised his head long enough to look at them then lowered it and closed his eyes again. Jared heard someone moving around upstairs.

Leave it to Nick to have summed it up so neatly— Jared wasn't even going to try denying being damn close to drooling over Teddy Monroe. "Hey, she's pretty. Very pretty. What can I say?"

Nick grinned. "It's good to see you back in the land of the living."

"She have a boyfriend?" Not that it would particularly make a difference. Competition was healthy and if she had a boyfriend, Jared would give him a run for his money—he was that damned attracted to Teddy.

"Not as far as I know." Good answer. "In fact, not only does she not have a boyfriend, she's moving to New York next month."

"Are you serious?" Jared grabbed his suitcase. What the hell was wrong with Nick that he hadn't mentioned any of this? Jared immediately felt sheepish. Uh, maybe it was because Nick was getting freaking married.

Nick nodded. "Yep. She wants to go to acting school. She stayed here to help Lucky get on his feet and sock away some extra cash. Gus is going to hook her up with a restaurant job while she's in school. And we found her an apartment just around the corner from my cousin Angela. Remember Angela?" Jared nodded. Of course he did. Angela and her brother Mark had spent nearly as much time at Nick's house as Jared had.

Dammit. Wouldn't you know it? He was ready to check out of the city and a woman who totally blew him away appeared on his horizon? "That's cool. I may not be there by then, but good for her."

"You're really serious about leaving New York?" Nick opened the door leading outside and even though Jared was accustomed to New York winters, the cold hit him like a slap in the face. Snow drifted down in a desultory fashion.

"Yeah, I'm serious." The snow crunched beneath their feet as they walked the length of the building, crossing to a set of stairs on the far rear corner of the building. Small planes sat in the dark on the other side of the small runway to the right.

The muted activity from the restaurant and bar was

audible but out here the evening was cold and calm. In the distance a wolf howled. Within seconds the call was answered. Jared looked up. Without the city lights, the sky seemed vast but at the same time close enough that he could touch the velvet darkness.

"This is the other entrance to Gus's...I mean, Teddy's apartment," Nick said.

They climbed the stairs and entered the apartment. Jared stopped in surprise. An open floor plan, sleek furniture, and the odd touch of whimsy here and there reminded him of a Soho loft. This was a definite departure from the frontier décor in the terminal and bar below. A four-foot tree sat on one end table next to the sofa, winking and blinking Christmas cheer from its colored lights.

"Wow, this is definitely not what I expected here." Jared closed the door behind him, shutting out the cold and lightly falling snow.

"That's the same reaction I had the first time I saw it." Nick looked around. "Gus left the big furniture here because it was damn expensive to ship it. She just took photos and artwork. Teddy's brought in her own stuff." The artwork on the wall was all black-and-white prints of theaters and stages and a couple of playbills. Jared itched to pick up and examine more closely a framed photograph on the other end table of three females, one of which looked like a very young version of Teddy. "She's a little more free-spirited than Gus. I love my woman but she can be uptight."

"Gus is good for you," Jared said with a smile but he meant it. Nick's family had always kept him rooted and he needed a woman who did the same. And there was a huge difference in being rooted and being tied down.

"Yeah, she is good for me, isn't she?" Something about Nick's goofy expression touched Jared. He was damn glad his buddy had found Gus. "Well, ace, this is where you're bunking for the next couple of nights. Gus and I are in here," Nick said, walking into a bedroom to the right. "This was Gus's room all along so when Teddy moved in she just took over what had been the guest room." The other bedroom was to the left, with a bathroom in between the two.

Jared sat down on the couch and asked the question he'd wanted to ask since meeting Teddy. "So what's the deal with Teddy? What's her story?"

Nick gave him a quick rundown, bullet-pointing in journalistic fashion. Her father had abandoned the family and then the mother had died. Teddy's older sister had raised her. The sister made a living raising and training sled dogs on the outskirts of town. From what Nick knew from Gus, Teddy hadn't dated much, focusing instead on her family and friends and saving her money for the move.

"So, she not only looks good but she has integrity, too," Jared said.

"And she's a damn nice girl to boot," Nick said on a teasing note. "So, what do you want to do? Shower? Crash? Check out the tube? They have satellite. Or head back downstairs?"

That was a no-brainer. He wanted to check out Teddy Monroe some more. "Definitely head back downstairs."

"OKAY, DONE, AND THANKS so much you guys," Teddy said at ten-twenty. Instead of the customary forty-five-minute cleanup, it'd been done in twenty. Gus, as she had the last several nights, had insisted on helping for old times' sake. Nick had laughed and said he wasn't about to be left out of the party and Jared had good-naturedly claimed he didn't know what he was doing but he could follow directions as well as the next Joe. Not only had it gone fast, but it had been fun.

Teddy admitted it. She was smitten. Jared Martin was the total package. From his sophisticated, but casual good looks, to his sense of humor, to his crisp accent, he was like a Christmas package that had shown up early, wrapped in charm and sexiness. She'd been almost painfully aware of everything about him during their cleanup—where he was, what he was doing, the fit of his shirt over his broad shoulders, the crisp cadence of his voice, the faint whiff of expensive, sophisticated aftershave, and the heat of his gaze. More than once she'd felt him looking at her. It was enough to weaken a woman's knees—well, this woman's anyway.

And while Teddy didn't have a ton of experience, she had enough sense to know when a man was flirting with her and Jared had been flirting all during the cleanup operation.

Gus and Nick stood in the restaurant, holding hands. "If you guys don't mind, we're going to stay down here for a bit. We've got a date," Nick said.

Teddy smiled and sighed inside at how romantic it was. Because there wasn't anywhere to go in Good Riddance on a date in the winter other than Gus's, Nick and Gus had "dated" after hours in the restaurant when Nick had first arrived.

Teddy's heart beat a little faster and harder at the thought of having time alone with this handsome man.

"No problem," Teddy said.

Together she and Jared crossed to the door at the back of the restaurant that opened to the interior stairwell leading to her apartment.

"Don't wait up for us," Gus said with a smile.

"You kids don't do anything we wouldn't do," Nick tacked on, smirking.

On any other given day Teddy might've been embarrassed by Nick's comment but she and Jared had shared one too many heated glances throughout the night. She'd been about five degrees warmer simply with him in the room tonight. And face it, men like Jared Martin didn't come her way every day—well, basically never before.

Teddy closed the door behind them, shutting out the restaurant, plunging them in close-quartered intimacy in the stairwell. Her heart thudded against her ribs and her breath caught in her throat as Jared's arm brushed her waist in the dark, his breath stirring against her hair. The air between them seemed to pulse with awareness.

Teddy flipped on the light switch in the hallway. Laughing at Nick's comment, they climbed the stairs to the apartment.

When they got upstairs, she ushered Jared inside. The lamp was on at one end of the sofa and the Christmas tree lights twinkled in the other end, but other than that the room was cast in shadows.

The air seemed to shift around them and cocoon them the same as it had in the stairwell. "Thanks for pitching in tonight," Teddy said, suddenly at a bit of a loss now that it was just the two of them. She had the totally alien notion she didn't want to sit about making small talk. She wanted to do what she'd longed to do since her first glimpse of him—she wanted to kiss him and be kissed by him.

"It was no problem," Jared said.

It felt different in the apartment with him there. It wasn't as if he was a piece of furniture but it was as if she'd just discovered what had been missing. He should've seemed as out of place as a guy from New York City could seem in an Alaskan village. But, instead, he fit right in with the apartment.

"Are you ready to drop?" she said.

"Actually, I've caught a second wind and I'm wide awake. What do you usually do after you wrap up work? I don't want to interrupt your schedule."

Teddy usually showered when she finished up for the evening but she simply couldn't bring herself to do that now—no way she could strip naked in the bathroom, knowing Jared was one closed door away. The mere notion sent a shiver through her. That felt far too suggestive and intimate and she just couldn't do it, not until Nick and Gus were up here with them.

So, she skipped the showering part and fast-forwarded to the next thing. "I usually have a glass of wine and just sort of decompress," she said, moving toward the dark kitchen. "Would you care for a glass of wine?"

She didn't keep anything stronger in her apartment. She'd noticed he drank bourbon and ginger ale earlier. She'd also noted he'd cut himself off after one pre-dinner drink. She was always aware of stuff like that. Her few memories of her father invariably involved too much alcohol and the unpleasant aftermath. That particular situation had never ended well regardless of what was going on. It had actually been a relief when he'd taken off one day and never come back. How much a man drank and how he handled himself was an issue for Teddy.

Jared stepped into the dark kitchen and seemed to fill it with his presence. "Sure, I'll join you in a glass of wine. And either red or white is fine as long as it's not real sweet."

Teddy laughed breathlessly. "Okay, no Moscato for you."

She poured each of them a glass of shiraz and turned on the iPod docking station. Bing Crosby crooned about a white Christmas. Teddy loved classic Christmas tunes by Bing, Nat King Cole and Perry Como.

"Here you go," she said, handing Jared his glass. Her fingers brushed his and the air seemed to sizzle between them. She settled on one end of the sofa, leaving him the option of the other end or one of the two armchairs. She found it somewhat gratifying he chose the other end of the sofa.

Teddy tucked one leg beneath her, angling in his direction and settled back against the couch's arm.

"So, you're a stockbroker," she said.

"So, you want to be an actress," he said at the same time.

They both laughed.

"You first."

"You first."

"How about ladies first?" he said with a smile that fanned the heat inside her.

That helped to break the ice a little and Teddy found it was easy to talk to him, despite the sexual awareness that seemed to dance through her. She gave him the abbreviated version of her upcoming plans. She was surprised, however, when he knew the school she wanted to attend. It wasn't as if she'd selected the Julliard of acting schools. "You've actually heard of it?"

"I have. It's a great school. My cousin studied there. He's doing some off-Broadway stuff now. When you get to the city I'll introduce you to Gaylord."

"Gaylord?" she parroted without thinking.

Jared grimaced. "I know. Aunt Claudine named him after her favorite grandfather but could she have possibly hung a worse name on him, especially for a theater actor? And by the way, he's not. And there's no good way to shorten his name. He doesn't want to be called Gay and Lord doesn't work either. When he was a kid Aunt Claudine insisted on him going by Gaylord. He goes by Chuck today."

Teddy laughed. "I can see why. And I'd love to meet him this spring." But it wasn't springtime she was thinking about now.

He shrugged, his shoulders appearing all the more broad in his button-down shirt with the Christmas tree lights behind him. For one insane moment, with the tree behind him, it looked as if he were under the tree. And to further her crazy train of thought, Teddy knew without a doubt that Jared Martin was just what she'd like to find under her tree this Christmas. Well, more specifically, she'd prefer to find him in her bed…preferably without all of those troublesome clothes he was currently wearing.

She smiled privately. She'd had the flu last Christmas and it seemed as if she had a fever again now. However, this was a different kind of fever altogether. And she knew precisely what she needed for a cure.

Him.

4

WHAT THE HELL was he thinking? He was alone with a woman he hadn't been able to take his eyes off of all night and he'd brought up his *cousin*? Not only had he mentioned Gaylord, who would have lots in common with Teddy, but then he'd gone out of his way to reassure her Gaylord was straight and offered to introduce them.

"I'm open to meeting as many people as possible," she said, her smile rocking him.

He smiled back. She'd just told him she wasn't caught up in meeting Gaylord because he was a straight guy.

She held her wineglass in one hand and the other arm she stretched along the back of the couch. She rubbed small circles with her finger. Her hands were elegant with short, functional nails. There it was again. It was subtle but she had an energy about her that drew him.

Jared sipped at his wine and copied her, stretching his arm along the back of the sofa, as well. He lightly traced his finger along the back of her hand, leaving her every opportunity to pull her hand away. She didn't. She simply smiled at him over the rim of her wineglass, her brown eyes taking on a smoky quality.

Her skin was soft and smooth like warm velvet beneath his fingertip. Tension wound between them, beckoned them.

"We just met," he said, leaning in closer.

"I know." Her husky tone stroked through him.

"This is crazy."

"Insane," she agreed. "And I bet you never opt for insanity."

"I never have before."

They both placed their wineglasses on the coffee table and moved toward one another on the couch. Jared leaned in and her breath fanned against his face. There was something almost miraculous about Teddy Monroe, something that got next to him, that tugged at him.

"Would you take your hair down? I've wondered all night what it would feel like."

"You have?"

"I have."

She reached behind her head, her movements sensual and languid, and pulled the elastic out of her hair. With a slow shake of her head, her hair tumbled about her shoulders. She threaded her fingers through it, as if combing it. "Better?"

"Much." He fingered one of the blond swaths. In the lamp light it looked like molten honey and felt like silk. "You have beautiful hair," he said.

"Thank you." She leaned in closer.

He buried his hand in her hair and his fingertips brushed against the back of her neck. She shivered faintly beneath his touch.

And it should feel kind of crazy considering he'd just met her but the strong urge to kiss her simply felt right.

He pulled her to him. Her lips were warm, soft…and potent. Even though she tasted faintly of red wine, the effect was like a shot of smooth, aged whiskey going down. Heat spiraled through him and went straight to his head… both of them.

Teddy deepened the kiss and Jared ran with it. Her mouth opened beneath his and he swept the moist recesses with his tongue. He explored the soft, wet heat of the inside of her cheeks, the velvet length of her tongue. She moaned into his mouth and he swallowed her sound, absorbing it.

Her sweet, hot mouth wasn't enough and he slaked kisses against the line of her jaw, down the column of her neck to the area just below and slightly behind her ear. "Oh, oh, oh," she said, half gasp, half actual words.

Her neck was incredibly sensitive. He teased his tongue against the soft skin and she arched her back and canted her head to one side, allowing him greater access. She grabbed his shoulders and held on to him, her fingers digging into his muscles. Her impassioned response turned him on all the more. Jared felt more alive, more in tune with her than he'd ever felt with anyone before.

He nuzzled at her neck, kissed, and then sucked at the tender spot. It was as if he couldn't get enough of her. He lapped at the delicate shell of her ear, then traced the line with the tip of his tongue.

Meanwhile her touch was warm and arousing as she kneaded the muscles in his shoulders, down to his chest. She found his male nipples through his shirt and teased her fingers against them, the sensation arrowing straight to his penis.

And then they were kissing again. Teddy wrapped her

arms around his waist, her hands smoothing along his back. Her kiss was intense, deep, hot. He cupped one of her breasts in his hand and she moaned, pushing harder into his palm. She was just the right size and she felt so good he thought he might explode. Even through the layers of her bra and sweater her nipple thrust against his palm.

His dick was throbbing like nobody's business, straining against the zipper of his pants. He cupped both of her breasts in his hands, massaging and kneading. Her ragged breath matched his.

He'd only just met her, she was a virtual stranger, and he wanted to strip her naked and plunge into her. He wanted to feel the heat of her skin against his own without sweaters or jeans or underwear.

Jared pulled her onto his lap. Linking her arms around his neck, she settled against him.

TEDDY WAS ON FIRE. No man had ever kissed her or touched her like Jared, where she felt as if she were beyond the point of reason. She had never, ever known this frantic need—to have him closer, to feel his hands and mouth against her breasts, to experience the smooth, hot thrust of him inside her. She ached for him. She felt as if every desire she'd ever known was concentrated in her breasts and between her thighs.

Seize the day, the moment, the opportunity urged a part of her she hadn't even known existed. She reached between them and grasped the hem of her sweater in both of her hands. She was on the upward pull when somewhere in the still-functioning part of her brain, she realized something was wrong. Not wrong per se, just different. She heard footsteps climbing the stairs and voices in the stairwell.

Gus. Nick. On their way here. Like a shot she tugged her sweater back down while scooting back to one end of the couch. She snagged her wine with her right hand and attempted to straighten her hair with her left.

Meanwhile, Jared shifted back to the opposite end and picked up his glass of wine, as well. Teddy glanced point-edly at his crotch where his erection was making itself known by tenting the front of his trousers impressively. He crossed his ankle over his knee which helped. She supposed there wasn't much to be done outside of that.

His voice wasn't quite steady when he said what she guessed was the first thing that popped into his head by way of making conversation other than *I'd really like to sleep with you* which was doubtless his primary thought. "Thanks again for letting me stay here."

"No prob—" Her voice sounded as if it had been dipped in rust. She cleared her throat and tried again, "No problem."

The door opened and Gus and Nick stepped into the room. They both looked startled. "Oh," Nick said, "we thought you'd be in bed by now."

Teddy felt herself blush to the roots of her hair. Hope-fully some of it was masked by the room's dim lighting. She hoisted her glass. "We were just getting there. I mean after, you know, we had a glass of wine."

Somehow that didn't make it any better. And she was doubly sure that between Gus's sharp eyes and Nick's nose for ferreting out details and news, they both knew Teddy and Jared had been getting hot and heavy on the couch.

"What he means," Gus said, mercifully, "is he thought Jared would've hit the wall by now."

Teddy stood. "I kept him up talking." He was up all right, but it wasn't because of talking. She didn't dare glance Jared's way. Now that the heat had gone out of the moment, she was moderately mortified.

Jared spoke up, "I got a second wind so I'm wide awake. Teddy was gracious enough to keep me company." He hoisted his glass in her direction. "By the way, the wine is excellent, almost as good as the company."

"Is that a shiraz or a pinot?" Gus asked.

"It's a shiraz," Teddy said, already moving toward the kitchen. "Can I get you a glass?"

"Don't mind if I do," Nick said.

Gus nodded. "Sure, I'll try it."

Her mind whirling, Teddy poured two more glasses of wine. She'd only just met Jared and within no time she'd been on his lap. Another minute and Nick and Gus would've walked in to find her sweaterless. Actually, given the momentum and the heat behind their encounter, she was certain one more minute beyond losing her sweater and she'd have been without her bra as well.

And God knows what Jared must think of her. This was so not her modus operandi. She did not jump on the laps of men like some sex-starved chick—primarily because she wasn't. She wasn't fast and she wasn't easy but she'd just come across as both.

She handed Nick and Gus their wine and retrieved her own. However, she was too jangled to sit down with the three of them right now, which was altogether more disconcerting because she was supposed to be an actress dammit, and she should be able to act her way through this situation, but she simply couldn't.

"If you guys don't need the bathroom right away, I think I'll hop in the shower," Teddy said.

There was a general round of consensus that no one needed the facilities at the moment so Teddy took her glass of wine and fled to her room.

She was gathering up clean underwear and her pajamas and robe when a knock sounded on her door. She was so jumpy she nearly startled out of her skin. "Yes?"

"It's me," Gus said. Of course it was. Neither Nick nor Jared would knock on her bedroom door. "Can I come in for a second?"

"Sure. It's unlocked."

Gus stepped into the room, her wineglass in hand, and closed the door behind her.

"I told them I wanted to check a wedding detail with you before I forgot it," Gus said. And then in typical Gus fashion, she cut to the chase. "But I really wanted to make sure you were okay."

Teddy took a sip of her wine and nodded. "I'm fine but it was that obvious?" Okay, she was completely mortified. She sank to the mattress's edge.

"No," Gus said, shaking her head. Teddy shot her a disbelieving look. "Okay, it was obvious when we walked in we'd interrupted something but it wasn't a surprise. Jared couldn't keep his eyes off of you all night and you seemed pretty interested, too."

"He's a good-looking man and he's not your run-of-the-mill Alaskan bush male." *That* was a gross understatement. He was urbane and charming and sophisticated… all the things she longed for in a man.

"No, Jared is definitely not that." Gus propped against the door frame. "You look at him and you think East Coast. You look at him and you think The City."

"Right." She looked at him and her entire body broke into a hallelujah chorus of want.

"So, what's the problem? It's only because I've worked with you and I know you so well that I could tell you were upset, but you were definitely upset. What's going on?"

"What's going on is if you and Nick had been a few minutes later, things would've been downright embarrassing. I was about to take off my sweater, and not because he'd asked me to but because I wanted to. I finally meet a man like him and I practically throw myself at him. God knows what he must think of me. You know me, Gus. You know I'm not like that."

"Teddy, I don't believe for a minute Jared thinks anything bad about you. As I said before, he couldn't keep his eyes off of you tonight. When they brought up the luggage, he asked Nick if you had a boyfriend. Nick told him no. And tonight, what would he have seen when he saw you working? You weren't flirting with the customers. You were being you. I can't imagine he thinks you're anything other than what you are—a beautiful, outgoing woman who just met a man she clicks with. And he's a nice guy, Teddy. Trust me, I've seen the way women look at him when we've been out with him. He could've had any woman he wanted after he and Trish split. But as far as I know, and I'd know through Nick, he hasn't dated anyone and I don't think he's slept with anyone."

"Oh." That was good, make it great, to know. He wasn't a player and apparently it wasn't just a case of her being available and willing. If he were so inclined, she imagined he could have women lining up for him back in Manhattan.

"Yeah, *oh*. As far as I can see, you're two nice people who hit a real vein of attraction. Having been there and done that, my suggestion is go for it."

5

TEDDY ROLLED OUT of bed late the following morning. She had expected to toss and turn all night but oddly enough, after she'd showered and hit the bed, she'd been dead to the world.

Someone was in the shower—she heard the water running. Her bedroom was chilly so she made quick work of dressing. She slipped on jeans and another Christmas sweater, this one green with white snowflakes of varying size outlined in glitter all over it, and fastened snowflake earrings to her lobes. She pulled on thick socks, dragged a brush through her hair and made a quick job of eyeliner and mascara.

She stepped out of her bedroom, the aroma of fresh-brewed coffee greeting her from the kitchen. She usually prepared the coffee pot the night before, but she'd been so disconcerted last night, she'd totally forgotten.

Next to the door, Gus and Nick were putting on their coats. "Morning," they said in unison. Teddy smiled. They really were the perfect couple.

"Good morning," Teddy said. "Where are you two off to so early this morning?" Obviously it was Jared in the shower and obviously he and she were about to be alone again.

"Skye and Dalton left this morning for Atlanta," Gus said, "and we're going to get the cabins ready for the Hudson clan's arrival this afternoon. Skye offered but it hardly seemed fair considering she was working all day yesterday and I've just been doing nothing."

Teddy laughed. "Nothing except getting ready for a wedding." She nodded toward the kitchen. "Thanks for making the coffee."

"No problem. We'll be back in a couple of hours. Jared's planning on checking out the town."

Nick grinned. "At least he doesn't have to worry about getting lost."

Gus punched him in the shoulder and Teddy laughed. "That's for sure. See you guys later."

The door had just closed behind the couple when the water shut off in the bathroom. Teddy moved into the kitchen and poured herself a cup of coffee, but her mind was definitely on the man on the other side of the door—naked and wet. She'd had her hands on him last night, felt the play of muscle beneath her fingertips, and she had no problem picturing him just getting out of the shower.

She turned the radio on in the kitchen, catching the top-of-the-hour local news. Teddy didn't want Jared coming out of the bathroom and to find her just standing around in the kitchen. She needed to be doing something.

While she sipped her coffee, she unloaded the dishwasher. She'd thought when she moved in that she wouldn't really use the appliance since it was just her. Wrong. Every couple of days she had enough to run a load.

She was almost through when the bathroom door

opened and Jared emerged. Good grief but he looked good. He wore a pair of jeans with a long-sleeved polo shirt. His dark hair was darker still from being wet. Suddenly, breathing became a challenge.

Teddy aimed for what she hoped was a natural smile. "Good morning. I hope you slept well."

"Fine, thanks. The couch is actually pretty comfortable."

"Good." Okay, they'd exhausted that subject quickly enough. "How about a cup of coffee?"

"Thanks. It smells great." He walked toward the kitchen.

Teddy felt so awkward and it was all her, not him. He seemed fine, normal—well, not that she knew him well enough to gauge normal but he didn't seem uncomfortable at all. The discomfort was all hers and as embarrassing as it would be, she needed to clear the air.

She poured another cup of the fragrant brew and handed it to him. "Sugar's on the counter and there's half-and-half in the fridge. Anything fancier and you're out of luck."

"Straight up is what I prefer." A question glinted in his eyes.

The best thing to do was simply to get this over with. She'd thought that she knew what she wanted to say to him, but now that the time had come, she stumbled through it. "About last night... I don't usually... That's not how I normally—"

Jared shook his head. "Teddy, it's okay. At the risk of sounding as if I'm full of myself, I didn't think last night was your norm. It's not my norm, either, just for the record."

"It's not?" She'd heard it from Gus but she liked hearing it from him also.

He scrubbed his hand through his still-damp hair, leaving it sticking up at a few odd angles. "No. It's not." He reached out and ran his finger lightly down her arm, leaving a trail of heat in his wake.

What was it about him that seemed to reach inside her and touch a part that had never been touched before?

"I'm not sure whether I was relieved or frustrated when Nick and Gus came in," Teddy said, turning away to put the last of the silverware in the drawer.

"Honey, I can assure you I know exactly where I stand on that issue." Jared wrapped one arm around her waist from behind. He pushed aside her hair on the left side and then wrapped his other arm around her, as well. He kissed the side and back of her neck.

She closed her eyes, savoring the feel of his lips against that oh-so-sensitive area. How did he know just the place that did it for her? She wasn't sure if her knees could fully support her as he nuzzled and kissed her neck, taking her from zero to sixty quicker than an Indy car driver.

In his arms, beneath the ministrations of his mouth, her awkwardness vanished, her desire from last night returning in spades. She put her hands on top of his, loving the feel of his masculine, hair-sprinkled skin beneath hers.

She guided his hands up until they were cupping her breasts. "We have unfinished business from last night," she said.

"We do, don't we?" He weighed her breasts in his palms. While his mouth was busy on her neck, he stroked and squeezed. He teased his fingertips against her nipples.

"Why don't we go to your bedroom?" he said. "It might

be a little more comfortable than the kitchen, unless you just have a thing for the kitchen."

She laughed softly, turning in his arms. "No, I don't have a thing for the kitchen." Once again, she took his hand in hers and together they made their way to her bedroom. Jared closed the door behind him.

"Nick and Gus will be gone for a couple of hours," Teddy said.

"Good, but just in case…" His smile said he didn't want a repeat of last night. Neither did she.

Outside it was still dark. "Hold that thought." She wasn't sure if she'd ever have this opportunity with someone who turned her on the way Jared did and she wanted to do it right. She darted out of the room and gathered a couple of candles scattered around the den. She also snagged the lighter thingie. She returned, toe-ing the door closed behind her.

She lit the candles and killed the bedside lamp, casting the room in flickering light.

Jared pulled the edge of his shirt tails free of his jeans and up and over his head. He wore an undershirt beneath. "Layering," he said with a rakish grin. He left on the undershirt, reaching for his belt. Within seconds he'd unbuttoned and unzipped his jeans, as well. He pulled off his socks along with the jeans, leaving him standing before her in an undershirt and briefs.

His arms looked as good as they'd felt last night. There was no mistaking he managed to get in gym time. His quads and calves were muscular. Dark hair sexily sprinkled his forearms and legs. Teddy rather inanely noted he had nicely shaped feet.

She reached for the hem of her sweater and he shook his head, a slow sensual smile curving his lips. "Let me."

She dropped her arms to her sides. Jared grasped the bottom edge, one hand on each side of her, and tugged it up. His hiss of indrawn breath was extremely gratifying when he pulled it up past her bra. Then it was over her head and tossed aside. He moved with surety to the button of her jeans, the backs of his fingers brushing against the skin of her belly as he worked the button free and then slowly tugged down the zipper.

He squatted as he slid the denim over her hips and down her legs. She stepped out of the jeans and he worked her socks down and off as if they were the finest, sexiest silk hosiery rather than thick, practical wool.

"You're beautiful," he said, looking up at her from his position at her feet.

"You don't have to say that."

"I know I don't. I'm saying it because I mean it." He stood and faced her, hesitating. "I was married for three years. After my wife and I split I was tested because she'd been seeing someone else. I haven't been with anyone else. I'm clean."

That was blunt and frank, but Teddy appreciated him bringing the issue up and out. "I…uh…I'm fine, too." It had been over a year since she'd been intimate and she'd gotten a clean bill of health afterward. There was, however, another awkward issue. "I don't have any protection."

"Years ago, my father told me to never leave home without it." His smile held a hard edge. "It was probably the only good advice he ever gave me. I've made it a practice to always carry a spare."

Teddy figured it was a good thing she'd lit candles otherwise the mood might've been totally killed by the practicalities of modern sex.

Jared smoothed his hands over her shoulders. His touch ignited something sweet and hot inside her. Together they lay down on the rumpled, unmade bed. Jared kissed her, a mix of tenderness and eagerness. They were still both in their underwear and Teddy was thankful he seemed to have tuned in to the fact that once they'd trekked to the bedroom, they needed to rekindle the heat they'd found last night in the den and this morning in the kitchen.

It wasn't hard to do. They shared long hot kisses. His hair-roughened thighs pressed against her while he stroked her waist and the curve of her back. The feel of him beneath her fingertips and his scent—fresh and clean, with a hint of tangy aftershave—intoxicated her.

She worked his T-shirt up and over his head, dropping back to the mattress to fully appreciate his physique. He had a nicely muscled, hair-scattered chest. Jared wasn't beefy like some of the guys who worked out too much and he wasn't skinny—Jared's chest was just right, a mix of lean muscle with only a hint of bulk. The trail of hair leading down his belly and disappearing beneath the edge of his briefs added to his sexiness quotient.

"The briefs, too," she said, her voice low and husky, her mouth dry with anticipation while other parts of her were very much wet.

He stood by the side of the bed and did as she'd requested. Teddy didn't have much experience with naked men but what she saw, she liked. His equipment was definitely larger than any she'd seen before but it wasn't grotesquely or even intimidatingly big. Once again, she'd vote for just right.

He knelt on the edge of the bed and slid one bra strap, then the other down her shoulders. He reached beneath her and unhooked her bra. Slowly, as if he were unwrapping a present and wanted to savor the experience rather than ripping into it, he pulled her bra away. His eyes glittered in the candlelight.

He bent his head and languidly licked one nipple and then the other. Teddy felt as if she was coming undone at the stroke of his tongue against her tips. With a groan he took one pink nubbin into his mouth and sucked. Sweet, sweet heaven. He alternated from one breast to the other, leaving her writhing, the area between her thighs drenched, her breasts heavy with need.

Jared kissed his way down her chest and the slight rise of her belly to nuzzle at her panty-covered mound. He licked the inside of one thigh and then the other. Using his teeth, he tugged her panties down past her hips. He hooked his fingers in to finish the material's journey down her legs.

He bent his head, parting her thighs and did what no man had ever done before. He leaned in and kissed her intimately, his mouth and tongue warm and wet and she thought she might just expire on the spot at how good it felt. He kissed, licked and sucked over and over until she was nearly mindless. Finally, when she was clutching the sheets in her fists and thought she couldn't stand it any longer, he raised his head.

"So sweet," he murmured. He slowly slid up her body and kissed her. Teddy tasted herself on his lips. She found it intensely erotic.

He rolled on a condom and spooned behind her. She'd never had sex in this position but instinctively she raised her top leg to grant him access.

She gasped as he slowly entered her, filling her. He felt good. And then it just got better as he worked in and out. Teddy found her own rhythm, thrusting back against him. He reached around and caught her breast in his hand, squeezing, toying with her nipple.

"Oh, oh, oh," she said in sync with the rhythm they'd both set.

"Here, roll onto your back," he said. At this rate she'd do pretty much anything he requested if it all felt as good as what they'd done so far.

When she was on her back, he positioned himself between her knees and pulled her to him. There was something very arousing about the slide of sheets beneath her, and the strength in his hands and arms. He entered her again and once again she gasped at just how good he felt inside her. Leaning forward on his arms, he was deep into her, her face buried against his neck, even as he buried his face into her neck. His breath was warm and wonderful against her. And then he caught her sensitive skin between his lips and sucked as he ground into her and Teddy's world shattered into a million fragments of light.

6

JARED DIDN'T KNOW what had hit him. He'd never felt like this before. Sex had never been like this, not even with Trish. Not only had it been good, it had been somewhere beyond that. He couldn't even say exactly what it was, but it was out there. And then it struck him—he was content for the first time ever. It had taken him a moment to figure it out, to recognize the feeling, because it was foreign to him. And he'd never really been aware of his discontent before now.

He'd been sated before, sex was good for that. But there was a marked difference in satiation and contentment.

He pulled Teddy closer, her hair against his cheek, her buttocks nestled against his thigh and hip. "How are you?" he asked.

She practically purred. "I'm wonderful," she said, echoing his sentiments. She stretched, shifting against him, and smiled. "I guess we should get up. I'm supposed to be at Jenna's spa—" she glanced at the clock "—in half an hour."

Somehow he found that disappointing. She hadn't struck him as a spa kind of woman—not that there was anything wrong with women who went to the spa, it was just so common in Manhattan. It seemed so many of the women he knew prided themselves on having a high-maintenance reputation. "Got a spa appointment set up?"

She shot him a look that was part amusement and part disbelief. "I've been helping out part-time during Chrismoose when we're swamped with visitors. She was supposed to have her new spa open but a fire delayed that, so now she's working temporarily in part of the community center. She's booked up."

Jared noted Teddy's generosity. She'd signed on to help Lucky transition the restaurant, plus she'd pitched in to help during Chrismoose. And now she was giving Jenna a hand.

"What do you do there? Massage? You certainly have the touch. Not that I've ever had a massage, but if I was going to have one, well, I liked the way your hands felt on me."

She smiled, the smile that seemed to be hers alone, unlike any other. "Hmm, thanks. I like the way yours felt on me as well. But no, I'm not qualified as a massage therapist or any of the other high-brow positions there. I've been covering the reception area and cleaning and setting up the rooms afterward."

Okay, that fit more with the woman he'd just met but already felt as if he knew. She was a mix of earthiness, energy and a slight dreamer quality that showed in her acting aspirations.

Call him uncharitable, but he couldn't help but think that Trish would've been mortified to admit she worked in the capacity of cleaning or setting up anything. Hell, most of the women he knew inflated what they did to make themselves and their jobs sound more important than they were. Hyperbole came with the territory as far as he could tell.

"Do you like working at Jenna's?" he said.

She rolled out of bed, pulling on her underwear. "Sure. I really like Jenna and it's a good way to meet people. Otherwise I'd just be sitting around twiddling my thumbs. As you'll discover, there's not a whole lot to do in Good Riddance."

"How long have you lived here?"

"My family moved here when I was four. I don't remember much at all about where we were before. It's a great place in a lot of ways, but I can't pursue my career here and that's important to me. Everyone has a purpose in life and I think we're all unfulfilled until we discover our purpose and then live it."

It was uncanny how she'd just voiced what had been nagging at him for months now. "And you feel your purpose is acting?"

"No. I *know* my purpose is acting. I've known it from when I was a kid. And now it's time for me to get out there and do what I was meant to do."

He liked her surety and her determination. Far be it from him to ask her if she knew just how damn hard it was to earn a spot on a marquee. He had a feeling she did.

"What about you? You never did say last night. How did you get involved in stockbroking?" She smiled as she tugged on her socks. "It's sort of hard to imagine a kid sitting around thinking they want to run Wall Street."

"Not if you grew up in my house." Success and the world of finance had been part of his life for as long as he could remember. There had seemed to be no viable alternatives. Lately he was thinking it was time for him to review his options. If he left the firm now, he left on a high note, and that was always the best time to go.

"Oh. That doesn't sound like fun."

He grinned. "The fun was always over at Nick's house."

Teddy brushed her hair, static electricity leaving long strands sticking up. She merely grinned at him in the mirror and pulled it back, holding it in place at the nape of her neck with a long barrette. She turned and walked over to the bed and patted his hand. "Don't worry, I grew up in a sucky household, too. But the main thing is we make the best of the hand we're dealt. I'll be finished around one today. Want to meet up at Gus's for lunch afterward?"

"Are you asking me for a date?"

"Well, yes, I am, Mr. Martin."

"Then let's back things up a little because I fully intended to ask you for a date. Want to meet me for lunch today around one downstairs?"

"I'd love to. I'll be the one wearing the snowflake sweater."

"I think I can manage to pick you out of the crowd."

They were joking, but he realized as she closed the door behind her that he could easily pick her out of a crowd, because she was one of a kind.

"YOU'RE CERTAINLY glowing this morning," Jenna said with a broad smile as Teddy slipped on the black "lab coat" with Spa embroidered in gold across the left breast. Jenna had gone ahead and brought in the accessories for the new place even though it wouldn't be open now until spring.

Teddy did feel as if she was glowing…and floating on a cloud. "Uh-huh."

"I'm thinking this has a lot to do with a certain New Yorker who was at dinner last night."

"It might. It just might." Jared was wonderful. Teddy began folding the clean hand towels in the basket behind the makeshift front counter.

"It's about time," Jenna said, waggling her delicately arched eyebrows.

"I guess it is, isn't it?" She sighed. "It was just so quick."

"That's a shame," Jenna murmured, deliberately mis-understanding her.

Teddy laughed and rolled her eyes. "Not quick that way. I mean, I just met him. I don't really know him."

Jenna waved her hand in dismissal. "That's the way it happens sometimes. Look at me and Logan."

"Uh, you guys went to high school together, Jenna."

Another dismissing brush of her hand in the air pshawed Teddy's logic. "Whatever. I think it's when you least expect it, that it whacks you upside the head."

Teddy paused, but she and Jenna had grown close in the last year. Jenna was a good listener and gave great advice. Teddy could talk to her about things she couldn't talk to her older sister about sometimes. Now would be one of those times. "Jenna, the sex was great. It's never been like that before."

"Double good for you. Make hay while the sun shines. And just think, you'll have someone already in place when you move to New York."

"Well, if we're pulling out clichés, I'm not counting those chickens before they hatch. Good Riddance is one thing, Manhattan is another. I think the competition's a little stiffer there." The very idea made her stomach clench.

Jenna quirked one of her eyebrows. "He's been living in Manhattan and he hasn't been seeing anyone so apparently that competition's not as heavy-duty as you make it sound."

Teddy wasn't surprised Jenna knew all about Jared. For the most part, there were no secrets in Good Riddance. Except when the occasional secret surfaced it was a doozy, such as when everyone found out that Merrilee hadn't been divorced for the past twenty-five years and was still married to the man they'd thought was her ex-husband. Or when they'd discovered Gus had been engaged to a psychopath who'd stalked her, so she'd changed her name and gone into hiding in Good Riddance. But other than that, everyone seemed inclined to share everyone else's business without compunction, so it was no shock Jenna knew Jared was divorced and hadn't been seeing anyone since his divorce.

"Yeah, well, there's nothing like being in the right spot at the right time. And I believe we can safely assume I'm his post-divorce rebound."

"You never know. It could be more."

"Not on my part and I'm pretty sure Jared's feet are solidly on the ground." Teddy knew that sometimes people thought she was a dreamer because of her acting aspirations. Nothing was further from the truth. Her acting career was a goal. She'd very determinedly saved her money, always with that goal in mind. And most importantly, she'd guarded against getting involved too deeply with anyone, her mother being the proverbial caution-ary tale.

No, Teddy would never trade her goals and dreams for a man, any man. She knew firsthand the way that turned out. And the easiest way to do that was to simply have fun but not get too involved. Jared was here for three days. Sex or no sex, emotional involvement wouldn't be a problem. How attached could you get to a person in that time span?

JARED WAS ALREADY sitting at a table in the restaurant, nursing a cup of coffee, when Nick and Gus came in and spotted him.

"So," Nick said as he and Gus settled at the table. "How'd your morning go?"

Between his activities with Teddy and his subsequent walk through town, Jared couldn't remember a better time. "It's the best day I've had in recent memory. I think I'm in love."

"Say what?" Nick said and Gus did a double-take.

"With Good Riddance. I spent the morning walking around checking out the businesses, meeting people. It's the most laid-back place I've ever been. I really dig it here."

Nick looked at him as if he'd lost his mind. "You re-alize this is a busy time of year for the town. In fact it's buzzing. There's twice as many people as usual because of the Chrismoose festival."

"Yeah, I get it. It's great! No honking horns, no traf-fic jams, and you don't have to look past skyscrapers to see the sun. There's fresh snow and trees instead of dirty snow and concrete. The air smells amazing. And there's not a fake Santa on every street corner."

Nick looked at him and shook his head. "You'd go nuts within a month of living here. It's a nice, make that *great*, place to visit, but…"

Given their earlier conversation, he hadn't expected Nick to be so surprised.

Gus spoke up. "Nick's right, Jared. I lived here for four years. It was a haven and the people are wonderful, but it's not New York. I'm fairly certain you'd go stir-crazy."

"Maybe. But then again, maybe not. I think it might take a long time, or it might simply never happen. I like it here."

"Well, good, then we don't have to worry that you won't enjoy the next couple of days."

"Heck, no. You're going to have a hard time getting me on the plane to head back to New York."

Gus laughed. "I'll put Teddy in charge of making sure you make it back to New York. And speaking of the devil…"

Gus trailed off as Teddy arrived at the table. "Speaking of the devil? Me?" Teddy, her eyes sparkling and a smile curving her lips, settled into the empty chair next to Jared. Her arm brushed against his and just that brief touch coursed through him.

"We were just telling Jared we're putting you in charge of getting him back to New York," Gus said. "He's decided Good Riddance is the place to be."

Teddy laughed. "Yeah, right." She looked from Gus to Nick, her laughter dying. "Wait…you're serious?" She looked at Jared as if he'd manifested a third eye. "We have no—" she made a circle with her finger and thumb in case he was missing the point "—traffic lights."

"I noticed."

"Okay, if you say so." Teddy laughed again, shaking her head, but there was a hollow note to her laughter and a hint of a shadow in her eyes. "Are we still on for snowmobiling this afternoon?"

While they took all of this for granted, it was a whole new world to Jared. He'd never been snowmobiling before. He was seriously excited about it. When had his life gotten into such a rut? Hell, maybe he'd been born in a rut and never made a move to get out...before now. Perhaps that had been part of his marital woes. "I'm looking forward to it," he said.

But not as much as he was looking forward to some more alone time with Teddy because all too soon he'd be getting back on a plane for New York, if only to wrap up his affairs there. He was feeling more and more at home in Good Riddance.

7

THE MOMENT TEDDY closed the door, Jared slipped his arms around her from behind.

"I've been waiting all day to do this," he said, nuzzling her neck and pulling her against him.

"Mmm." Teddy offered up a sigh of contentment. "Alone at last."

"My sentiments exactly, but snowmobiling was fun."

"It was, wasn't it? Especially with you behind me."

"You don't know how many times I wanted to kiss you." He teased his lips against the nape of her neck, sending a shiver coursing through her.

She turned, linking her arms around his neck, her internal thermostat hitting a high note. "Gus is taking Nick's mother and sisters to Jenna's spa this afternoon."

"And Nick is taking his brother-in-laws and father ice fishing."

Which translated to alone time in her apartment for them. She teased him. "You didn't want to go ice fishing?"

"I had something else in mind that involved far fewer clothes...."

"Now that sounds like a good idea."

They went into Teddy's room and closed the door. Although Gus and Nick were supposed to be otherwise occupied, erring on the side of caution struck Teddy as a good thing.

"I like your town," Jared said.

"Good. I like your 'town' too."

"That's only because you haven't lived there all your life," he said.

"You might feel differently about Good Riddance if you'd been here since kindergarten, as well." He couldn't seriously be considering staying here. First, he was simply too New York and second, well, it was simply too unfair if he showed up just as she was leaving... And she *was* leaving.

"It's possible."

"Probable," she said. The thought crossed her mind that it was a good thing Jared hadn't turned up in Good Riddance any earlier in her life or she might've been sorely tempted to not leave. But she had a ticket now, and she'd bet after another day or two Good Riddance's rustic charm would wear thin and Jared would be ready to hot-foot it back to Manhattan.

He slid his hands beneath her sweater's hem and caressed her back. His touch, sure and warm, banished all thoughts except how good it felt and how much she wanted more.

They lay down on the bed and took their time undressing one another, exploring, savoring the experience. Everything about this man turned her on—the lean but defined muscles, the smattering of hair on his chest, the texture of his skin against hers, his scent, the way he smiled, one corner of his mouth quirking higher than the other, and the way he moved.

His mouth captured hers and she sighed her satisfaction into their kiss. She cupped his buttocks in her hands—she loved his ass. He had the perfect man-ass—tight, taut and well-shaped.

He was here for such a short time and who knew where things would be when they were both in New York.... She jumped out of bed. "Hold that thought."

She stepped into the walk-in closet and pulled the door closed behind her. She'd played in a production of a farce a couple of years ago in Anchorage. Anchorage was the only "real" theater in the state and that was a stretch. Plus she'd had to fly there and stay with a cast mate for the entire run. She'd played a buxom French maid in the production and she'd had to provide her own costume—nothing like theater on a shoestring budget.

She'd been waiting on this opportunity for a long time. If Jared thought she was weird, he was leaving in two days anyway, so no worries. If he liked it, they'd have a good time. She pulled on black hose with a garter belt, a black lace thong and a frilly white apron, leaving the rest of the costume on a hanger. Slipping on a pair of black heels, she cracked the closet door. Only one thing left. "Close your eyes," she said.

"They're closed."

"No peeking."

"No peeking."

She stepped out of the closet and hurried over to the dresser. She quickly twisted and pinned her hair up and brushed on some red lipstick. She pinned on the frilly little cap that completed the outfit.

She checked herself in the mirror—well, as much as she could see. If Jared wasn't turned on, she was going to look pretty stupid. And if he was…then they'd both reap the benefits.

"You can look now, monsieur," she said with the same accent she'd used in the play. "I am Celeste." The name she'd used before. "I am here to serve you."

"Wow." He propped up on one elbow to get a better look. "Double wow."

This had definitely been a good idea, judging from his reaction and the look in his eyes. She approached the bed. "What would you like, monsieur? I will do whatever you say."

He told her in a low, husky voice exactly what he'd like. Smiling, her heart racing in anticipation and excitement, she climbed up onto the bed and straddled him. His erection pressed against the crotch of her wet panties. "Like this?"

"Oh, yeah." He reached up and traced the edge of her nipple with his fingertip. Oh, yeah was right. He pulled her to him and licked the nipple he'd just outlined. She shuddered and grasped his shoulders. His mouth was warm and wet and just the right combination of gentle and rough as he sucked, licked and nipped her breasts.

"Oh, I like that," she said, careful to keep her voice in character. "That feels so good." Actually it felt better than good. She wasn't even sure what it meant but she threw out whatever came to her in French. "C'est vrai. Oui, oui, oui."

Meanwhile, she rubbed her satin-covered mound against the hard line of his penis, her excitement notching higher and higher. She liked having him naked beneath her while she had on the hose and heels and thong and the sheer apron.

He stroked his hands over her hips. Reaching behind her, he grabbed her thong in one hand and pulled gently, tugging it tight between her wet folds. She moaned. "Oui."

Teddy's excitement notched up to fever pitch when he told her what he wanted her to do next. Her hand not quite steady, she delved beneath the edge of her panties into her slick channel. Her fingers coated with her essence, she smeared it on his nipple. She repeated it on his other nipple. On instinct, she slowly, deliberately licked each of her fingers before she leaned forward to complete the rest of his request. She dragged her tongue over his eraser-head-hard tips, licking herself off him.

"Oh, baby. That's so, so hot."

She thought so, too.

He rolled on a condom and pulling her thong aside, he guided her up with his hands. Willingly she came down on him, taking all of him inside her at once. She paused for a second, settling on him, rocking against him, and then she rode him so hard and with such enthusiasm that her hair came down and she didn't care. All she cared about was how good it felt, how much they were both enjoying it.

His face tightened and she knew he was close to the edge. He reached between them and found her clit with his finger. Her orgasm exploded inside her and she felt him come right after her. As the last tremors shook her, she collapsed on top of him, incapable of anything more. She felt as if her entire body had become boneless. His breath gusted against her hair. "Thank you," he said.

"Mais, non," she murmured. "Merci."

TWO DAYS LATER, Jared stood in his tux behind Nick's best man as Nick and Gus exchanged vows at the Good Riddance community center. Having the ceremony at the community center was a little unorthodox, but it was the only building large enough to hold the crowd that had shown up for the wedding. And altogether Good Riddance was an unorthodox kind of place, so it fit. Gus's restaurant had been a gathering place for the town for several years and Gus was obviously held in high esteem.

Jared's mind wandered as the officiating minister droned on about the sanctity of marriage, his attention snagged by Teddy standing on the bride's side of the lineup. Good God but she was beautiful and sexy in that red velvet dress, her upswept hair leaving her sensitive neck bare. He had no idea how he'd gotten so lucky. Teddy was an incredible woman and not just in the sack, although that was off the charts, too. She was fun, but over the course of the last few days he'd discovered she had a serious side, as well.

Teddy glanced at him, obviously feeling him looking at her. She didn't exactly smile, but her eyes lit up. There was something about her, about them. They were good together in a way he'd never been with anyone else. Yesterday they'd made cookies in her kitchen. He'd never made cookies before in his life—it just wasn't his thing. And quite frankly, if anyone had ever asked him to he would have said thanks but no thanks. But he'd had a great time making gingerbread cookies and decorating them. If he hadn't met her, he would've never known how much fun it could be. What else would he miss out on without Teddy in his life?

Lots. Perhaps everything. As illogical as it seemed,

he was far more in love with her than he'd ever been with Trish. She suited him in a way Trish never had. He knew gut-deep that he'd found with her what Nick had with Gus.

He realized with a start that the wedding was over and Nick and Gus were now officially married, when the crowd broke into cheering and the newlyweds took off down the aisle. Within a minute he was holding out his arm to escort Teddy in the best man and matron of honor's wake. It felt very right and natural to have her walking down the aisle on his arm. The idea quickly followed that she belonged by his side.

They followed the other couples back to the dressing area. Teddy sighed. "Wasn't it beautiful?"

Jared wasn't about to disappoint her by admitting he'd zoned out during most of the ceremony. "Yes, it was, and so are you."

It was funny, he'd seen her naked at least twice a day—after that first night, he'd simply moved into her bedroom with no comment from either Gus or Nick—but now a soft blush suffused her neck and face at his compliment. "Thank you."

He ducked into one of the empty rooms, pulling her in with him and closing the door. He backed her up against the door and her arms were immediately around his neck. He kissed her, the need to have her a sudden ravenous hunger inside him. She kissed him back with an intensity that said she felt the same. Once again, that powerful connection flowing between them seemed deeper than mere lust.

"Here. Now. Take me," she said, already pulling up her skirt. One-handed he unzipped his trousers and pulled out his penis which was at full raging attention. While Teddy slid her panties down and stepped out of one leg of them, Jared rolled on a condom. That was good enough. He hooked her leg over his arm and slid into her. Hot, wet and tight she was ever so, so sweet. No other woman had ever felt as good as she did when he was inside her.

They were both excited and further aroused by making love against a door while the rest of Good Riddance milled about outside. All too soon he felt himself coming. He swallowed her cries as she spasmed around him.

Her breathing was ragged.

"I love you," he said against her forehead. They weren't words he'd intended to say, but nonetheless he didn't regret them.

He didn't know what exactly he expected—well, perhaps a reciprocated sentiment—but he sure as hell didn't expect what he got. Teddy had bent down and pulled her panties back up. Her hand already on the door knob she looked back over her shoulder at him. "We'll just both pretend you didn't say that, and I'm sure it's time we joined the others."

In a flash she had the door open and the opportunity to respond privately was gone.

What the hell? He'd just handed her his heart and she'd tossed it back at his feet. This was not the woman he thought he knew. They might have a reception to get through, but before the day was over he planned to find out just what was going on in her pretty head.

8

TEDDY MOVED THROUGH the reception with a smile on her face but inside her mind was whirling. He'd said he loved her. For one moment her heart had soared in recognition that she felt the same way. And then common sense had kicked in. It was too soon and too dangerous. That falling in love business could wreck her career plans, especially when he was so wrapped up in how great Good Riddance was.

Merrilee came up and put an arm around Teddy. "You sure do look beautiful today. You and Jared certainly make a nice-looking couple."

What was up with everyone today? "Um, thanks," Teddy said.

"Gus is getting ready to throw her bouquet. You need to go get in the group."

"That's okay. I think I'll leave the other ladies to it."

"Nonsense," Merrilee said. "Anyway, it's bad luck for the new bride and groom if all the single women don't join the group. You don't want bad luck for Gus and Nick on your head, do you? Go."

Teddy suspected Merrilee was bending the truth. She'd

never heard the part about it being bad luck if all the single women didn't try to catch the bouquet. But then again, there was a lot about weddings she didn't know. For the most part, weddings didn't interest her. While some of the other girls had sat around dreaming of their special day, Teddy had been dreaming of Broadway. Their starring roles had been to stroll down the aisle. Her starring role was to be onstage.

Heels and heart dragging, she joined the group of women ready to vie for the tossed flowers. She stood in the back. Jenna spotted her and cut through the group to tug her up to the front of the small crowd. "Oh, no, Teddy. No hiding in the back."

She didn't have to look to know Jared was watching her from across the room. She felt his eyes on her. "I don't even want to do this," she said to Jenna.

"Sure you do."

The group started a countdown, "Three…two…one…"

Gus tossed the flowers tied in crimson ribbon. It was like a bad dream in slow-mo. Teddy watched as the arrangement headed straight for her like a heat-seeking missile. In the end, she instinctively cradled her arms, unable to allow the bouquet to hit the ground.

Sweet, low-key Ellie stood next to her looking disappointed. Teddy offered her the flowers. "Here. Take them. I don't want them."

"I can't. It's not the same." Ellie smiled, catching Nelson's eye across the room. "I don't need them anyway."

Great! She had a bouquet she didn't want and Ellie had been disappointed. Things were going to hell in a handbasket and it had all started with Jared's declaration. She could kill him for saying he loved her. It had turned everything upside down. She didn't want to talk about or think about love—it complicated everything. Anyway, how could he love her and she'd had some sort of crazy mixed-up feelings for him but how could she love him? They didn't really know one another. People didn't fall in love in three days. That was the stuff of books and movies. And look where it had gotten her mother. Teddy wouldn't be so foolish.

"OBVIOUSLY I SAID the wrong thing earlier," Jared said. He knew he sounded stiff and awkward but she'd steadfastly ignored him all through the reception until he'd finally corralled her for a dance and she'd have looked bad to have turned him down.

She visibly drew a deep breath. "I just don't know why you said it. We've only known each other for three days."

"It's pretty hard for me to believe, too, but sometimes things happen."

"Yeah and I know firsthand how things can turn out. My mother married in haste and spent the rest of her life repenting at leisure. She gave up her career to follow my dad and he eventually deserted us."

"I'm not asking you to give up anything. I was just telling you how I felt. Have I asked for anything in return except maybe for you to give us a chance?"

"I don't know. I just… My career is important to me. You want to live in Good Riddance and I want to live in New York and that's a fair distance apart."

"I know it is. I would never ask you to give up acting. It's not a mutually exclusive situation. It doesn't have to be me or your career." He could tell by the closed look on her normally expressive face he'd have to pull out everything he had. "Look at Gus and Nick. What was it? Five, maybe seven days? When he first told me I thought he was insane, but once I saw them together I got it. And look, it's been a year and they're doing great." Damn, wasn't the woman usually the one to do this kind of convincing?

He ran his hand through his hair. He was a man who was used to taking risks. If ever there was a time to put himself on the line, it was now. "I've been doing a lot of thinking. I thought I was burned out at work, and maybe I am, but I can't just walk away from my career and New York. I initially fell in love with Good Riddance, but you're the real draw. You're the sparkle in my life, not the place."

"I have to think. I need a little space."

"Does that mean you want me to sleep on the couch tonight?" It was his last night here. Her answer would be very telling.

"I think that's a good idea."

Damn. That pretty much said it all.

TEDDY TOSSED restlessly in her bed, unable to sleep. She was doing the right thing wasn't she, staying focused on her career? Now that she was finally prepared to move forward with her dream, she didn't want to make a misstep. But what if she was turning her back on the best man she'd ever met? Was it just some crazy romantic notion that the two of them could have something special in such a short period of time?

She eventually drifted off to sleep. She was dreaming, she had to be, when her mother came to her—the dream was so real she could almost feel the mattress sinking as her mother sat on the bed beside her.

"Mom?"

Her mother didn't say anything but she reached out and smoothed the hair back from Teddy's forehead, a gesture so familiar Teddy's chest tightened with the cherished touch that had been absent from her life for the past nine years. Teddy realized, in her dream, that her mother's smile was different. It was still the same sweet curve of her generous mouth, but the tinge of sadness was gone.

Her mother's lips didn't move but Teddy clearly heard her speak. "Teddy, don't be afraid to love. Your life doesn't have to echo mine if you love. And, darling, my life wasn't a bad one. I had you girls, and I wouldn't trade my time with you and Marcia for any career."

In her dream Teddy could see the surprise on her own face. "You know I read your journals?"

Her mother smiled and continued to speak without actually speaking. "Of course I know, darling. Give him a chance. Give the two of you a chance. Falling in love doesn't mean you can't have a career, too."

Before Teddy could speak again she awoke and her mother vanished as quickly as she'd appeared. Teddy lay in bed, her heart pounding—not from fear but from the exhilaration of seeing her mother, even if it was in a dream. If it had been a dream. Teddy wasn't all too sure her mother hadn't actually appeared before her.

And suddenly the fear she'd felt when Jared told her he loved her disappeared. All her anxiety over her feelings for him dissipated. She realized with a start that things felt so right with Jared she'd been scared, she'd been on standby, waiting for something to go wrong. And it was still a possibility, but she no longer considered it a probability.

Teddy slipped out of bed and padded across the room, opening her door. The couch was empty. Entering the room, she found Jared at the window overlooking town. He had to have heard her but he didn't turn around. She knew she had hurt him. She approached him and slipped her arms around him from behind. Resting her cheek against his back, she said, "I'm sorry."

"Never apologize for being truthful."

"Okay. Then I'll tell you that I…well…I love you, too. I want to give us a chance to see where we go."

He turned, his face cautious, and she didn't blame him a bit given her earlier reaction. "You're sure?"

"I'm positive." She ran her fingers over his jaw. It was amazing how important he'd become to her in such a short period of time. But hadn't she sensed she was a goner from the moment he'd landed on his knees in front of her? "But I don't want you to stay in New York if that's not where you want to be." She'd never do that to another person and their relationship would never survive it.

He caught her hand in his and pressed his lips to her fingers. "Nick asked me on the way out here if I was having an early midlife crisis. All I knew was something was missing in my life. And I know now I've found what I was missing. You."

"Oh, Jared." She wasn't sure whether she wanted to cry or shout for joy, but instead she merely sighed and leaned her head against his chest.

"Teddy…"

"Yeah?"

"You think maybe we could go back to bed now?"

She laughed. Spoken like a true man. Her man.

* * * * *

HE'LL BE HOME
FOR CHRISTMAS

RHONDA NELSON

To Vicki and Jen, my novella mates, for making
this anthology such a joy to write.
Merry Christmas!

A Waldenbooks bestselling author, two-time
RITA® Award nominee, *RT Book Reviews*
Reviewers' Choice nominee and National
Readers' Choice Award winner, **Rhonda Nelson**
has more than twenty-five published books to
her credit and thoroughly enjoys dreaming up
her characters and manipulating the worlds they
live in. She and her family make their chaotic but
happy home in a small town in northern Alabama.
She loves to hear from her readers, so be sure to
check her out at www.readRhondaNelson.com.

1

Major Silas Davenport knew the instant he pulled into the pebbled driveway of his parents' beachside retirement cottage that something wasn't right.

For starters, they weren't there.

No cars in the driveway, no Christmas lights twinkling from the window, no tacky inflatable Santa Claus on the small landscaped yard. Hell, not even a wreath on the front door. His mother was one of those people who typically had her Christmas shopping done by mid-July, so the idea that they were merely out shopping wasn't likely. Dinner then? he wondered. Somehow he didn't think so. There were two newspapers on the front step and the mailbox had been rubber-banded shut, presumably to keep the mail from tumbling out.

His spidey senses started tingling.

He sighed heavily and let himself out of the car, thankful that he recognized the fake rock by the sidewalk that held the hide-a-key. It had been at their old house—the one he'd grown up in—as well.

Well, hell. So much for his surprise, Silas thought, deflated.

He'd just spent the better part of twenty-four hours in transit. The idea of his family's happy shock when he arrived unexpectedly on their doorstep for Christmas had kept him bolstered. His cheeks puffed as he exhaled mightily.

Instead, he was going to walk into an empty house, no warm greeting or hot meal, no smiling faces, no joyous reunion, no Christmas music playing in the background, no mulled cider warming on the stove.

In retrospect, rather than trying to surprise his family, he probably should have gone ahead and told them that he'd been granted leave. Silas imagined that every soldier in Uncle Sam's Army had applied for leave over the holidays and he'd been no exception. But actually *getting* it was rare, so he hadn't expected he'd have the opportunity to come home. He'd been prepared to spend another miserable Christmas in Iraq, surrounded by men he loved and admired, but who weren't actually his family.

This was the first time in two years he'd been stateside for the holiday and he'd been looking forward to his mother's orange rolls and his dad's homemade wine. To listening to his mother lament his little sister's newest boyfriend—she was currently backpacking across Europe with him, much to their horror—and catching up on all the family gossip. Who was pregnant? Who was engaged? Who was divorcing? The typical grist running through the family gossip mill. It was those little things that made him feel as though he still belonged with his people, was still a member of the tribe, so to speak.

Silas pulled his duffel bag from the backseat of the rental car, then quickly found the key and let himself into the house. It was quiet, as he'd expected, but a pair of women's shoes sat by the front door, as though they'd just been toed off, and he caught the faint sound of music and splashing water.

He frowned, intrigued. "Mom?" he called. "Dad?"

Nothing.

Silas set his bag aside, noting the faint scent of oranges and yeast, and started toward what was actually the key selling point to any beachfront property—the back porch. The house's layout was simple enough. A central set of shotgun rooms—living room, dining room, kitchen— with two master suites on either side of the kitchen, but accessed through short halls off the dining room. Another bedroom, his, was upstairs and had the best view of all. Between the crash of the surf and the scent of his mother's homemade Danishes rising over the kitchen, it was a little piece of heaven—one that he'd been particularly looking forward to.

For whatever reason, he got the grim premonition that he could forget about the orange rolls and usual holiday treats. The fudge, the breakfast casseroles, the ham. The house was chilly, which meant that whenever his parents had left they hadn't anticipated being back for a while and had turned the thermostat down. Secondly, things were too tidy, not lived-in and, though he hadn't seen Cletus—his parents' most recent rescued cat—yet, fresh food was in the bowl.

Were that not enough to clue him in, he'd identified the sound of splashing water coming from the screened-in front porch—the hot tub, specifically—and the music? Ray LaMontagne's "Trouble," accompanied, quite badly, by a woman singing along in a terribly off-key voice.

"Trouble..."

Silas grinned. He'd give her points for being heart-felt, even if he could skewer her performance for technical accuracy.

He carefully opened the back door, spied the clothes on the floor—sweater, jeans, red lacy panties and matching bra—and felt his previously low spirits rise accordingly.

So the mystery woman was naked. In his parents' hot tub.

If she was pretty, too, then maybe his Christmas wasn't going to suck so much after all.

He had a nanosecond to notice curly black hair, a pair of startled cornflower-blue eyes and lush raspberry-red lips…before her mouth opened in a bloodcurdling scream.

DELPHIE MOREAU'S FIRST instinct was to jump out of the hot tub and run for her life, but she was naked and evidently—she'd have to truly think about this later—saving face was more important than saving her life. Clearly something was wrong when a woman would rather *die* than die of embarrassment. She clasped her hands over her bare breasts and wailed for all she was worth.

Seeming startled, the extraordinarily good-looking potential murderer held up his hands in a peaceful gesture and, instead of attacking her, laughed softly. It was a low, intimate chuckle that made her middle go squishy and warm.

"I'm Silas Davenport," he said above her screams. "This is my parents' house."

Ah, Delphie thought, her eyes rounding, the terror dying swiftly in her throat. She paused to look at him and felt a chagrined blush flash across her cheeks. That explained the military garb and the strong resemblance to Charlie Davenport. This man was a taller, much more muscled version of her retired neighbor. Where Charlie's black hair had turned white, his son's was still inky and still very thick. If she hadn't been so startled she was sure that she would have recognized him from the photos in the living room.

So this was the legendary Silas. In the flesh. And what very nice flesh, indeed. Evidently his mother hadn't been exaggerating when she'd extolled the physical virtues of her son. Delphie had imagined that every mother thought her son was handsome and—though he'd certainly looked nice in the pictures she'd seen—occasionally photos could lie.

Clearly the ones she'd seen hadn't.

Furthermore, if everything else his mother had told her was true, then she was half in love with him already.

He grinned at her and wore an expression that brought her sanity into question.

Delphie slunk lower into the water, hoping that the bubbly surface would cover her bare body. She hadn't shaved her legs this morning, she thought dimly. As if it would matter. Sheesh. She was losing her mind. Her face was already flushed from the heat of the water and the two glasses of wine she'd consumed, but impossibly, embarrassment made her cheeks burn even hotter, making her acutely aware of her vulnerable state.

Silas rubbed his hand over the back of his neck. "Er… who are you?" he asked.

Well, yes, he'd want to know that, wouldn't he? Aside from being half-drunk and completely naked, what the hell was wrong with her? She dredged her soul for an ounce of dignity and lifted her chin.

"I'm Delphie Moreau, your parents' neighbor from across the street."

A flash of recognition lit his dark gaze and he inclined his head. "Mom's mentioned you. You're the decorator, right?"

"Interior designer," she clarified. Her skill set was a little more advanced. She didn't just pick out accessories, fabrics and paint swatches. She designed beautiful living spaces based on functionality and a client's needs. She was licensed, knew building code and specs and was handier with a tape measure than a lot of construction workers she knew.

His gaze drifted over her bare shoulders. "Use the hot tub a lot, do you?"

Despite the heat, she felt goose bumps skitter over her skin and her nipples pearl. "Only when I'm keeping an eye on things for them." A thought suddenly struck her foggy mind and she gasped. "You're not home for Christmas, are you?"

Another smile. *Mercy.* "I am, actually."

Oh, no, Delphie thought, wincing. Charlie and Helen were going to be so disappointed. Her gaze slid hesitantly to Silas. Eek! How to tell him?

He waited a beat, then blew out a breath and his eyes widened significantly. "But evidently my parents are not."

She bit her bottom lip and shook her head regretfully. "They left two days ago on a cruise to the Bahamas. With your sister in Europe and you in Iraq they didn't want to face the holiday here alone. They couldn't have possibly known you were coming, otherwise they—"

He shook his head, a silent indicator that she didn't have to finish. "I had the grand idea of surprising them," he admitted with a rueful grimace. "Definitely poor planning on my part. I just never expected them to be gone."

"I'm sorry," she told him. She knew from Helen that Silas hadn't been home for the past couple of years. She couldn't even begin to imagine his disappointment—or theirs, for that matter, when they found out that they'd missed him. They'd be crushed.

"Maybe you could call them," Delphie suggested, grasping at any idea to avoid this outcome. "If there's a way for them to come home, then I know they would."

He pulled a doubtful face. "If they've been gone two days, then they're in open sea," he said. "It would just make them miserable, knowing that I'm here and that they're unable to get to me."

He was right, she knew. Still…

His gaze swept the scene again, lingering on her clothes on the floor, the open wine bottle on the table next to the hot tub and the empty glass. "Sorry for interrupting your party," he said, a smile tugging at his especially sexy mouth. "A special occasion?"

"Not particularly," she said, once again aware of the fact that she was completely naked with a stranger in the room.

Actually, were she to label it, she'd have to say it was a pity party. Her younger stepsister, Lena, was getting married on Christmas Eve. Delphie was happy for her, of course. What kind of person would she be if she weren't? What kind of person begrudges another person happiness?

Unfortunately, while Delphie was genuinely pleased that Lena had found the man of her dreams—when she hadn't even been looking—she couldn't help but feel a little sorry for herself.

Because she *had* been looking. Actively, for over a year now. She'd found Mr. Maybe, Mr. Wrong, Mr. Right Now, Mr. Asshole and Mr. Possibly-Homosexual-In-Denial, but she'd yet to find her own better half. How unfair was that? Lena was still in college, hadn't figured out exactly what her mark was going to be, much less made it. Hell, she'd met Theo at a drive-thru, for pity's sake. Theo had gotten her French fries and she'd gotten his onion rings. They'd swapped accordingly and fallen in love.

Fried romance.

Delphie, on the other hand, had been out of college for four years, her business was in full swing, quite lucrative and fulfilling. Now she just wanted someone to share her life with. Was that too much to ask?

Thankfully her mother knew that Lena's impending wedding and all the festivities surrounding it were making Delphie even more aware of her own single status and unhappiness, and had limited what she'd asked Delphie to do.

She imagined she'd feel a lot less pathetic if she at least had a date for the wedding, but sadly that wasn't the case, either. Guys tended to get a little squirrelly when a girl invited them to a wedding. You either needed to know someone really well or not at all, otherwise it was a hard sell.

"So are you staying here then?" he asked, derailing her miserable line of thought.

"Er…no. I'm picking up the mail, taking care of the cat and generally keeping an eye on the place." She grinned.

"Your parents offered the hot tub and the beach as recompense and I happily accepted." She inwardly frowned.

Of course, now that he was here he could do it.

And she'd lose the flimsy excuse of semi-house-sitting to avoid the wedding festivities.

Not good.

No guy of her own, no date for the wedding and no excuse to stay away from the premarital hoopla.

And she was still naked in front of a perfect stranger.

She knew better than to ask if things could get worse, but couldn't keep from wondering all the same. It seemed to be that kind of day.

And it was that exact moment that she realized she'd forgotten something really important—something critical, even. She felt her face crumple into a wince.

A towel.

2

THOUGH THIS WAS NOT exactly the welcome home he'd imagined, he could do a lot worse than finding a beautiful naked woman in a hot tub, Silas thought. In fact, as far as homecomings went, this was a pretty damned good one.

Delphie Moreau had the most expressive face he'd ever seen.

It intrigued him.

For instance, over the past few seconds he could tell that she'd gone from being mildly worried to unquestionably miserable. Though he wasn't at all certain that he could help her in any way, he was suddenly hit with the irresistible urge to try.

A novelty, to be sure.

Seeing that unhappy expression on such a lovely face made something shift uncomfortably in his chest. Nonplussed, he shrugged the sensation off and tried to remember everything his mother had ever said about her. Honestly, he'd only half-listened when his mom had started in about Delphie. It was quite obvious that she'd had matchmaking on her mind, and Silas had assumed anyone that his mother chose for him wouldn't meet his approval.

He was cursing that wrong-headed conclusion at the moment, though, because given the way his blood had instantly heated and the rapidity with which it was pooling in his groin, Delphie was definitely an exception to that rule.

She was, quite literally, a wet dream.

She had a sweet, heart-shaped face with a sharp little chin, big blue eyes that were large and heavily lashed and a mouth that put him in mind of hot, frantic sex. What little he could see of her petite body was lush and creamy and decidedly feminine. With those shiny black curls piled atop her head and the smooth porcelain of her skin, she reminded him of one of the pretty dolls his mother kept in her curio cabinet.

Her ripe lips formed a hesitant smile. "Could I ask a favor?"

He nodded once, ready to retrieve the moon if she asked for it. "Certainly."

Impossibly, her cheeks pinkened further and she shrunk deeper into the water. Her voice, when she spoke, was small. "Would you mind getting me a towel?"

Silas felt a grin creep over his lips. "No problem."

He backtracked into the house, snagged the requested item out of the linen closet and then returned to the porch and handed it to her. He kept his eyes firmly on her face to keep from trying to sneak a peek at her bare breasts and congratulated himself on his success.

It was a hollow victory.

"Thank you," she murmured. She waited expectantly.

With a belated start, he gestured awkwardly toward the kitchen. "I'll, uh... I'll just go inside then." Smooth, Silas.

She dimpled gratefully. "I'd appreciate it."

Keenly aware of her every move—he heard the hot tub go off, the tell-tale splash as she left the water—Silas suddenly found himself quite thirsty. He sent a fervent thank-you in his father's direction when he found a lone beer in the refrigerator and made a mental note to buy more.

He'd just popped the top and was in the process of taking a hearty pull when Delphie ducked back into the kitchen. Looking mortified, but more confident, she'd wrapped the towel around what was quite clearly a very petite, very lush frame and held her clothes clutched to her chest. "I'll just go dress in the bathroom."

More torture.

It would have been better if he hadn't seen her undergarments, the red see-through lace, itty bitty scraps of fabric he could imagine shaping her lovely, milky white curves.

Two minutes later—after he'd had time to inspect the contents in the fridge and conclude that while Paula Deen could probably make a gourmet meal out of pickle relish, cream cheese and English muffins, it was beyond the scope of his talent—Delphie returned.

"Well," she said, seemingly at a loss. Her gaze darted around the kitchen, as if reluctant to meet his. "This has been interesting."

He chuckled and passed a hand over his face. "It's certainly added an exciting element to the homecoming story I'm going to tell when I get back," he said. He quirked a brow. "Do you mind if I tell the guys you were wearing a red bow on top of your head?"

Her laugh was quick and throaty, very pleasant. She pulled a small shrug. "Why stop there? Tell them I had a gift tag around my neck and a no-return policy."

She was quick, too. An admirable quality. "Excellent."

"No batteries required, either." She chuckled and arched a playful brow. "I'm sounding better and better, aren't I?"

"An easy sell, for sure," he said, his gaze skimming over her once again. A particularly sharp bolt of heat nailed his groin. "So you're across the street?"

She nodded. "Yep."

Silas leaned a hip against the counter top, content to study her. She had that kind of face, the sort that drew the eye and didn't want to release it. "How long have you been there?"

"Almost two years."

He inclined his head. "And is there an angry husband or significant other who's going to want to rearrange my face for finding you naked in my parents' hot tub?"

She blushed again, an action he found strangely refreshing. "Er...no."

He brightened. Maybe his Christmas was going to be merry after all, Silas thought, more than a little pleased with the change in his circumstances. Granted his parents weren't in town and this wasn't the homecoming he'd been expecting, but... He pushed off from the counter. "In that case, how about dinner?"

Her startled gaze swung to his. "Dinner?"

"Dinner, supper, the evening meal," he said, listing the various alternatives. "Whatever you want to call it. The fridge is bare and I've spent the last ten hours on a

plane eating complimentary peanuts and stale pretzels."
He grinned. "I'm hungry. Have you eaten?"

"No," she said. "I find that alcohol is a lot more effective if I drink it on an empty stomach."

That settled it, Silas decided. She was without a doubt
the most interesting person he'd met in a long, long time.

Quite possibly ever.

"So you'll join me?" he pressed. He gave her a smile—
the one that he pulled out when he really wanted to get
his way—and waited expectantly for her answer.

"YES," DELPHIE SAID after a moment's hesitation. Why
not? He'd practically seen her naked. What was dinner
after that? Furthermore, this was Charlie and Helen's
son, a man who'd been serving their country—risking
his life—since he'd gotten out of college. How could she
say no? What sort of neighbor or patriot would that make
her? Delphie wondered, knowing good and damned well
that the reason she was saying yes didn't have anything
to do with Silas's parents or being a good patriot.

She was a woman and he was *unbelievably* handsome.

He was also a potential wedding date, which had occurred to her while she'd been in the bathroom hastily
donning her clothes. Yes, she was being opportunistic,
and yes, she should be thinking more about her dear
neighbors who were going to miss seeing their son at
Christmas. But the shallow, vain part of her couldn't help
but think he'd look damned fine on her arm at the wedding. In fact, she wouldn't appear pathetic at all if he
went with her.

Glass half full, silver lining and all that.

Silas nodded, seeming pleased with her decision. "Excellent," he said. "Any suggestions?"

"What are you in the mood for?"

"My mother's orange rolls, actually," he confessed with a laughing sigh, "but I don't think I'm going to find those on the menu anywhere in town."

"Ooh, I know of the rolls you speak," Delphie said, following him through the house. "Your mother brought some over to me when I first moved in." He locked the door and pulled it shut. "Do you mind if we stop at my place so I can pick up my purse?" she asked.

"Not at all."

"And you're not opposed to driving? I've only had two glasses of wine, but for some reason it feels like I upended the entire bottle." It was utterly baffling. She hadn't noticed just how unsteady on her feet she was until she'd nearly done a face-plant against the door frame on her way into the house.

He chuckled. "That's because you were in the hot tub. It'll do it every time."

She turned to look at him over her shoulder. "Really?"

He nodded. "Really."

Delphie hummed under her breath and pulled a shrug. "Note to self—always drink in the hot tub. More bang for your buck."

She snagged her bag from beside the door and then walked next to him back to his car. He was even taller than she'd thought, Delphie noted, feeling particularly short beside him. Which, at five-foot-two, wasn't out of the ordinary, really. But for whatever reason, he seemed bigger than other men his height. It wasn't necessarily that there was more of him, but that his very presence seemed to need more room. Interesting.

Thrilling.

Ten minutes later they were snacking on hush puppies, sipping iced tea and waiting on their shrimp and grits. She liked the way his mouth moved when he talked, deep and unhurried, his voice a tantalizing drawl.

"So," he said, staring at her from across the table, his gaze twinkling with intrigued humor. "Do you often drink on an empty stomach?"

Ah. She'd known that little comment was going to come back to bite her on the butt. He waited patiently and seemed genuinely interested in her answer. His close-cropped dark hair had a slight wave and hugged his scalp and his eyes were so brown they created the impression of being black. It was quite arresting. High cheekbones created exaggerated hollows and planes on his face and his nose was appropriately proportioned and straight.

Ultimately, though, it was his mouth that did it for her. A bit full for a man, but masculine all the same, and there was a sensual quality to it that made her feel too itchy in her own skin. It crooked a little higher on one side, an endearing imperfection that somehow made it all the more sexy, all the more charming.

"Drowning a sorrow?" he pressed. "Recent breakup? On the outs with a friend? Someone outbid you on eBay?"

She laughed softly and looked away. "Worse," she said. "My little sister is getting married on Christmas Eve."

His keen eyes sparkled with a little too much understanding. "Ah," he said, lifting his chin. "Feeling left behind then? Like the ugly older sister your father can't unload even with two goats, a dairy cow and a good hunting dog?"

Her eyes widened and she laughed. "Not as bad as all that, thanks," she said. "Just a little melancholy. I'm happy for her," she told him. She squeezed lemon into her tea, then gave it a swirl with her spoon. "But I have to admit I'm not looking forward to the pitying glances from the various aunts and friends, as though I'm a failure compared with Lena's romantic success."

"So it's not that you're envious, you're just competitive?"

"A little of both actually," she admitted, impressed with his intuitive assessment. "But being alone during the holidays is hard enough without throwing a wedding into the mix." She chuckled and pushed a hand through her hair. "It compounds the pathetic factor."

He chuckled and shook his head as though the feminine brain was a mystery. "What is it about women and weddings?" he wondered aloud. "Your sister is signing on as chief launderer, cook, possible incubator and unpaid treasure hunter and you're going all gooey-eyed about it. Listen, it's a bad deal," he said with a deadpan expression, leaning forward as though he were imparting some serious advice. "In a week you're going to feel sorry for her and be patting yourself on the back for your narrow escape."

"Unpaid t-treasure hunter?" Delphie chuckled. Admittedly she got the other references, but this one was lost on her.

"Oh, you know," he said. "Honey, where are my keys? Baby, have you seen my vintage Lynyrd Skynyrd T-shirt?" He shook his head in feigned bafflement. "I've seen brilliant men who can spot bombs beneath a layer of sand get married, and suddenly can't find their asses with both hands anymore. It's amazing, really."

She didn't know when she'd laughed so much, Delphie thought, wiping her eyes. "Well, when you put it like that."

"Trust me," he said, as though confiding an important secret. "I know what I'm talking about. You should feel sorry for her. The romantic little fool has no idea what she's in for."

"I'll keep that in mind," Delphie said, chuckling. *Unpaid treasure hunter.* She mentally snorted, charmed all the same. "But I still wish I had a date."

"I'll go with you," he volunteered, much to her immense and relieved surprise. "We'll fill up on appetizers and make fun of everyone. It'll be fun."

Delphi stilled. Dare she hope? Could she be this lucky? "You don't have other plans?"

Another toe-curling smile. "Er...not anymore, remember?"

"But what about the rest of your family?" Why was she arguing with him? Isn't this what she'd wanted? *Shut up, Delphie.*

"They're still in Arkansas," he said. "My parents retired here, you know." He winced, looking momentarily bleak. "Unfortunately, there is no other family in town."

Her heart drooped for him, and she chastised herself for being selfish. "I'm sorry, Silas. This isn't at all the Christmas you'd imagined, is it?"

"No," he said slowly, releasing a fatalistic sigh. His gaze drifted over her face and settled hotly on her mouth. "But it's improving every minute."

Whoa.

Her nipples suddenly tingled and heat flooded her belly, then slid south and settled. She pressed her legs together to keep from squirming and mentally calculated the last time she'd had sex. Bleh. Higher math had never been her strength, but she knew from her exaggerated reaction to the man sitting across from her that A plus B in this instance equaled Too Damned Long.

"You'd seriously go to my sister's wedding with me?"

He cocked his head. "Is there going to be alcohol at this wedding?"

"Yes."

"And dancing?"

"Yes to that as well."

"And I'll get to dance with you?" he clarified, pinning her with that hot, dark gaze. "As much as I want?"

Pleasure bloomed in her breathless chest. "If you'd like."

"Sold," he told her with a succinct nod, as if it were a no-brainer.

Relief washed through her, taking away a large portion of the dread. "Thanks, Silas. You're sparing me more humiliation."

"No problem. Besides, I've got an ulterior motive."

A thrill snaked along her spine. She'd just bet he did. "Oh, really? What's that?"

"I'm hoping you'll reward me with a home-cooked meal," he said, surprising her. He popped another bite of hush puppy into his mouth. "It's been too long since I've had one."

She imagined it had. And any chance of his mother's Christmas dinner was down the drain now. No doubt he'd been anticipating that as much as seeing his family. For whatever reason, a meal shared always tasted better. Or it did to her, anyway. "Anything particular you'd like?"

"Fried chicken, mashed potatoes with gravy and macaroni and cheese," he said without preamble.

"Done," she told him, smiling. "Come over tomorrow evening and I'll hook you up."

Once again that dark gaze drifted across her face and settled on her lips. It was blatantly sexy, ridiculously thrilling and left absolutely no room for misinterpretation.

He wanted her.

Ulterior motive, indeed.

Something passed between them, an unspoken understanding, one that leveled the playing field and made intentions clear. She could have shied away—probably should have considering she'd just met him—and yet… she couldn't. More tellingly, she didn't want to.

Reckless? Potentially stupid? Most definitely. But there it was.

"I'll look forward to it," he said, his voice low and promising.

And from the way her toes were curling, so would she.

3

SILAS HAD NEVER BEEN one to squander an opportunity and, as he walked Delphie back to her door, he had every intention of making the most of this one.

Though the idea of going to a wedding on a date at all—much less a first one—was about as palatable to him as a colonic cleanse, in this case he instinctively knew that he wouldn't regret it.

In the first place, he'd be going with Delphie, the single most intriguing woman he'd ever met. And in the second place, he wasn't going to have enough time at home for this to get awkward. Thirdly, most significantly, she was interested.

He'd watched the flash of awareness kindle in her gaze the moment his eyes had connected with hers and he'd be lying if he tried to claim it was anything other than extremely gratifying.

Admittedly his romantic skills were a bit rusty—all part and parcel of his job—but he still knew enough about women to recognize when one was digging him and, much to his satisfaction, Delphie Moreau was every bit as into him as he was into her.

This brief relationship had the power to be very mutually satisfying and, just to make sure she knew what he was about and to confirm his own suspicions, he fully intended to let her know right now.

She paused at her door and turned to face him. Lamplight glowed golden over her jet-black curls and cast the side of her face in shadow. His breath hitched and a peculiar sensation moved through his chest, one that he'd never experienced before.

"Thanks for dinner," she said. He liked her voice. It was a bit husky, but musical. "I could've paid for mine."

He stepped closer and watched her lips twitch in a smile of recognition. "I asked you out," he said simply. "My treat."

She looked away to hide a smile, then glanced back up at him. Minx. "So that was a date?"

"Definitely. Our first."

She chuckled softly and gave him an admiring glance from beneath her lashes. "You work quick."

He pulled a lazy shrug, not bothering to deny it. What was the point? "I don't have much time."

A little sigh slipped past her lips and a furrow emerged between her sleek brows. "There is that."

"Am I reading this wrong?" Better to ask, he decided.

She considered him for a moment and he watched her gaze flicker to his mouth. "No," she said, seemingly coming to some sort of decision. She looked up at him again. "You're fun."

"Fun? That's all?"

"Fun's good," she insisted, laughing. "Everyone needs to have a little fun."

He was more than willing to give her a lot of it. And here was a small preview.

Silas slipped a finger beneath her chin, gratified when he felt her shiver, and tilted her face up for a kiss. The first brush of his lips across hers snatched the breath from his lungs and, though he knew it wasn't possible, he felt the ground shake beneath his feet. Startled, he drew back to see if she'd had a similar reaction, and she blinked drunkenly up at him, proof that she found him every bit as intoxicating.

It was all the confirmation he needed.

He bent his head again, this time laying siege against her mouth, and felt her instantly respond. She framed his face with her hands—a gesture that was as enflaming as it was tender—and slid her thumb beneath his jaw. Her sweet tongue moved against his, a mind-numbing seek and retreat that made him instantly hard and unreasonably hot. A low groan sounded in his throat and he wrapped his arms around her, fitting her small body more closely to his. She was lush and ripe and the plum-soft recesses of her mouth made him think of other soft womanly bits, particularly the generous mounds behind her lacy red bra and the even softer skin between her thighs.

He'd either been too long without a woman or this one held some sort of special appeal and, for reasons which escaped him, he didn't want to mine his mind for the answer to that question.

He just wanted her. More fiercely and more desperately than he'd ever wanted another woman.

That thought should have sounded an internal alarm loud enough to rattle his teeth and yet it didn't. He'd have to think more about that later.

Much later. Preferably when it was too late, when he was fitted firmly between her thighs, feeding on her marvelous breasts.

And with any luck, *she'd* be his Christmas present.

Sweet merciful heaven, Delphie thought as Silas's big hands roamed down her back and settled hotly on her rear end. She'd been kissed before and had even considered Mr. Wrong a champion kisser...but he didn't have anything on Silas Davenport.

For instance, Silas was one-hundred percent making love to her mouth and yet she could feel it quite keenly in another area farther south. Every time his expert tongue slid inside, her feminine muscles clenched, and with every movement of if his lips against hers, more heat seeped into her decidedly damp panties. Her goose bumps had goose bumps and if her nipples got any harder they were going to shatter. Every bone in her body felt as if it had melted, which was probably why she was practically sliding all over him, Delphie thought.

If she'd ever been so turned on by a mere kiss, then she couldn't recall it. Was it the alcohol? she wondered. Had it really been that much more potent?

No, she decided as he gave her rump a squeeze that made her cling even more tightly to him.

It was him.

He was big and hard and wonderful and when he held her, she felt unbelievably desired and protected, wanted and safe. As a woman who'd always felt more than capable of taking care of herself, it was a bizarre feeling, one that was strangely welcome, incredibly potent.

Aside from being damned good-looking and funny as hell, Silas Davenport had that other something special, that indefinable quality that gave him an edge over every other guy.

And she was cooking dinner for him tomorrow night *and* he was going to the wedding with her. The only thing that could make this day better was an orgasm, and she was dangerously close to getting that, too.

But not on the first date.

Breathing heavily, she reluctantly ended the kiss.

"Wow," he said, the admiration in his tone making her blush with pleasure. "I'd take you without the hunting dog," he teased.

Delphie chuckled. "Thanks," she said drolly. "I'll be sure to pass that along to my father."

He grinned down at her, his dark eyes twinkling with humor. "What time do you want me?"

She blinked up at him, momentarily panicked. She actually wanted him right now, but didn't think she was in the best condition to be making that decision. Was it inevitable? Oh, yes. She'd known that over dinner. But tonight?

His head dropped back and he laughed. "I mean for dinner," he told her.

Ah. Of course. She squeezed her eyes tightly shut as more color burst upon her cheeks. "Five work for you?"

"I'm available all day," he said, shooting a forlorn look across the street to the empty house.

A blatant ploy. "I'm sure you'll find something to do," she drawled.

From the look on his face, he thought he already had— *her*.

And the kicker? He was right.

In that instant she knew beyond a shadow of a doubt

that at some point before he left for Iraq again they were going to fall into bed together.

She wanted. She ached. She yearned.

And for reasons which escaped her, she felt bizarrely *secure* with him, for lack of a better description. It was as though a part of her that was always wound tight and on guard could relax with him, simply let go, and that feeling was so inexplicably wonderful she didn't know what to make of it.

Furthermore, the way her libido was humming, they'd be damned lucky if they made it to a bed. In fact, if this had been their third date—her usual absolute minimum before intimacy—he more than likely could have taken her right here on her front porch.

The thought was as disconcerting as it was thrilling, and should have set off an alarm strong enough to wake the dead.

Delphie merely smiled.

She was too excited to be spooked and too turned on to be cautious. Sometimes the best plan was no plan at all.

4

AT FIVE O'CLOCK on the dot, Silas rang Delphie's door bell. He'd been bored out of his skull *all day*. He'd taken care of some things around the house for his parents—a lightbulb had blown out in the carport and he'd fixed a loose step on the back porch—and had made a trip to the grocery store. He still needed to pick up a few Christmas presents for his parents and his sister, but had decided to pace himself, lest he run out of anything to do and embarrass himself by trying to hang out with Delphie all day.

Though he wouldn't have ever considered himself the sentimental Christmas type, Silas had discovered that he was missing more about the holiday than just his parents. He'd broodingly considered the absence of the Christmas tree and decorations and, after a few minutes of debate where he questioned his sanity, he dragged the decorations out of the attic and started putting them around the house.

The tree, the Nativity, the candle-holding Mrs. Claus who played "Jingle Bells," the battered wreath for the front door. He'd found the Christmas CDs and had plugged them into the DVD player and, in absence of the knowledge of how to make mulled cider, had lit a cinnamon candle he'd found in the kitchen. Once finished, he'd proudly inspected his handiwork and most definitely felt more of the holiday spirit taking hold.

Because he'd seen another person walking their cat on a leash down the beach, he'd picked one up and given it a try with Cletus.

To his delight, it had worked.

Initially the cat had looked at him as if he'd lost his mind, but after a few false starts Cletus had decided that he enjoyed being outside, even if he was tethered to a pesky human. Whether Silas's parents would thank him for this remained to be seen.

Delphie opened the door and smiled at him, making the breath seize up in his lungs and a strange ringing commence in his ears. "Hi," she said, a shy note to her voice that he found curiously endearing. The scent of fried chicken drifted to him and he inhaled deeply, dragging a little bit of her scent in with it as well. Vanilla and lemons, an intriguing combination.

"That smells delicious," he said, referring to her more than the meal.

"Come on in," she told him, widening the door to allow him entrance.

He held out a bottle of wine he'd picked up earlier when he'd been out. "For you," he said. She'd left her bottle on the back porch last night, so rather than risking a bad choice he'd simply bought the same thing.

"Thank you," she murmured, blushing slightly once more. She started toward the kitchen. "Have you had a good day?"

He trailed along behind her, enjoying the swing of her

hips. She wore a pair of black pants, a light blue sweater and a chunky necklace that drew the eye to her breasts. Oh, hell. Who was he kidding? She could be wearing a garbage bag and his eyes would be drawn to her breasts.

Because they were magnificent.

"I have," he confirmed. "I went to the grocery store for a few essentials—"

"Like beer," she interjected.

"Like beer," he confirmed. She uncorked the wine, poured him a glass, then handed it to him. "And I put up the Christmas tree and a few decorations. I taught the cat a new trick. Exciting stuff," he told her. "What about you?"

"I, too, had to make a run to the grocery store," she said, shooting him a smile. She started transferring dishes to the dining room table, her movements smooth and seemingly effortless. "And I worked a bit, of course."

"From home?"

She nodded. "Yep, which suits me just fine. After my first assessment, I can do a lot from right here."

And right here was lovely, he had to admit. Though there was plenty of color in her house, the furniture was mostly white. White boards covered the walls and ceilings, contrasting nicely with dark wide-plank pine floors. A couple of old porch posts were stationed on either side of the dining room, separating it from the living room, and she'd opted for open kitchen cabinets which were filled with lots of old dishes. Rather than a lot of pretty houses that were simply decorated for display, hers was livable and functional, accented with repurposed materials and reclaimed woodwork. After a moment, he said as much.

"This is really nice. Did you do some of it yourself?"

She gestured for him to sit and heap his plate, then chuckled once. "I did it *all* myself, thank you very much."

He felt his eyes widen. "All?"

"My dad was a carpenter," she explained, ladling gravy over her mashed potatoes. "Retired now, of course, but I spent a lot of time with him when I was younger."

Unbelievably impressed, he set his fork aside and stared at her. "Are you telling me that you know how to use power tools?"

She grinned and lifted a brow. "Do you want to see my nail gun?"

He shook his head and tore off another bite of chicken. "Forget the dairy cow, too," he said in wonder. "You are a gem among women. And you're a helluva cook," he added thickly around a mouthful of chicken. "This is amazing."

"Thank you," she told him, looking pleased. "So what about you? Had you always planned on joining the military?"

Silas laughed. "You're telling me you don't know the answer to that question? My mother hasn't given you everything but my pant size already?"

Her blue eyes twinkled. "Thirty, thirty-six."

He choked on a bite of mashed potatoes. "You're freaking kidding me," he said, stunned. "Tell me you guessed."

"She only mentioned it because you're such a hard fit," she told him.

Silas looked heavenward. Good Lord, what else had his mother told her? How he used to think that the bank tellers in drive-thru windows lived in those little boxes? How he'd once wanted a mustache like his father so much that he'd drawn it on with a Sharpie? How he'd been so nervous before his first day of school he'd puked all over his teacher's shoes?

His gaze slid to her once more and a bark of dry laughter rumbled up his throat. He had a terrible feeling he should have been paying better attention to what his mother had been saying about him to Delphie, because he was pretty damned certain she'd been listening when the Master Manipulator—better known as Helen Davenport—had been talking about *him*.

DELPHIE LAUGHED at his suddenly wary expression. "You don't have to look so worried," she said. "Your mother only ever had wonderful things to say about you."

"That's what I'm afraid of," he remarked grimly. "She's been doing the hard sell, hasn't she?"

Delphie felt her lips twitch and hesitated long enough for him to swear under his breath. "She's been very proud of you, that's all."

He rolled his eyes. "Nothing is more embarrassing than having your mother interfere with your game," he said with a put-upon sigh.

"You're doing well enough on your own," she conceded, quirking a brow at him.

He looked up at her and smiled, the grin eternally slow and lethally sexy and filled with so much heat she felt her toes curl once again. "That's good to know," he remarked.

"So what about me?" she asked. "You haven't been getting the hard sell on me?"

"I have." He winced. "But to tell you the truth, I didn't pay that much attention."

She felt a droll smile curl her lips. "Because anyone

your mother would pitch couldn't be someone you'd be interested in?"

He poked his tongue in his cheek. "Are you psychic or am I just that easy to read?"

"Neither," she told him. "I am diametrically opposed to anyone my mother suggests, as well." She took a sip of wine. "But you never answered my question."

"What was that?"

"Had you always wanted to join the military?"

He nodded. "Always," he confirmed. "The year I got a G.I. Joe for Christmas changed the course of my life," he joked, smiling. "Aside from being away from home, I love everything about it. I love knowing that I'm doing something that's honorable, that I believe in. That I'm standing in the gap, fighting for something bigger than myself, until the next group of like-minded men come along." He peered at her above the rim of his glass. "Sounds trite, I know, but…"

"It doesn't sound trite at all," she said, swallowing. It was noble and good and she was thankful there were men like him willing to serve.

"So no wedding festivities tonight?" he asked. "Don't they typically have a rehearsal and dinner or something?"

"Actually, no. A friend of Lena's is performing the service and it's very straightforward. She goes in, we follow. They say the I-dos and then we party."

He lifted one shoulder in a shrug. "Sounds simple enough."

"Instead of doing the stag party and bachelorette thing, Lena and Theo are partying together tonight, hosting their own intimate wake for the passing of their single days."

He nodded. "Interesting idea. They sound like a very... different couple."

Finished eating, she settled more firmly into her seat. She laughed softly and rubbed the bridge of her nose. "They're perfect for each other. It's disgusting."

"How long have they been dating?"

"Just a few months."

"So long enough for the new to still be there, but not long enough to discover any annoying habits." He nodded once. "Probably for the best."

She eyed him speculatively. "You sound like you've put a good deal of thought into this. Any particular reason you aren't married yet? Don't have enough land for the livestock you anticipate as a dowry?" she quipped.

Silas laughed again, the sound sexy and soothing, one that she knew she could easily get used to hearing. His gaze tangled with hers. "Honestly, I've just never met the right girl and haven't had time to truly look. I'm not opposed to it, if that's what you're asking. I'm not so attached to being single that I don't ever want to get married." He paused, looking thoughtful. "But I'd rather be alone than married to someone who wasn't right, you know?"

She did know. She had a couple of friends who'd rushed into marriage—more thrilled with having a wedding than having a husband—only to realize that the men they'd promised to love till death did them part weren't as wonderful as they had originally imagined.

He blew out a small breath. "And when I make a promise, then...I make a promise." A little frown creased his brow. "I think too many people go into a marriage believing there's a quick way out of it. That the vows are just pretty words, not the oath it's intended to be."

My goodness, Delphie thought, staring at him with a new appreciation. A man of his word. How novel.

He looked up and caught her staring at him, then an adorably self-conscious smile curled his lips. "What?" he said. "You think I'm old-fashioned, don't you?"

"I do," she said with nod. "And I think the world could use a lot more men like you."

Pity she wasn't going to have time to get to know him better, she thought, a pinprick of disappointment nicking her heart. Silas Davenport was handsome and funny, smart and charming and held on to antiquated beliefs that she happened to share. He was good, she realized. Genuinely good. And good guys were getting harder and harder to find.

Thankfully, though, she still had time to get to know him as well as she could.

She looked up then and caught him staring hungrily at her mouth, as though the dinner they'd just shared had been nice but not enough. Heat flashed over the tops of her thighs and a breathless gasp slipped out of her lungs. Her palms suddenly itched to touch him, to see if the skin on the back of his neck was as warm as it looked. If it could possibly taste as good as she'd imagined.

She'd been thinking about him all day. Anticipated seeing him again more and more with each passing second. She'd been keenly aware of her body, the way the air felt moving in and out of her lungs, the tight fit of her bra, the slide of silk over her hips. She'd worked, yes, but she'd also spent a great deal of time peeking out of her window, trying to catch a glimpse of him. And she'd spent just as much time watching the clock, waiting until the hour hand struck five and the countdown to having him had officially started.

Yes, she still had a little time to get to know him.

And if they were naked, then all the better.

5

SILAS KNEW THE EXACT moment he was going to get lucky. Something in her gaze shifted, became more open, less guarded…and a lot hotter.

"Thank you for dinner," he told her. "That's the best meal I've had in a very long time."

"You're welcome," she said. "It was the least I could do considering you're braving the wedding for me. You're going to make me look considerably less pitiable and for that I am forever grateful."

"It's nothing," he said, waving negligently. "I think you and I could find something to laugh at anywhere." He leaned forward. "And just think of all the material we're going to have to work with at a wedding. There's certain to be a crazy uncle, a drunken aunt and a too-blunt grandmother to provide entertainment." His gaze tangled purposely with hers. "And as an added bonus, I get to dance with you. Win, win," he told her.

"How did you know about Uncle Harry?" she quipped, her eyes widening.

"It's a given. There's always a crazy uncle at these things."

"Are you a good dancer?" she asked, her gaze lingering on his mouth again. Honestly, if she didn't stop looking at him like that, he was going to clear the table and have her for dessert.

He studied her for a moment, let his gaze drift over her face, along the slim line of her throat, the gentle swells of her breasts. And honestly, why didn't he do just that? They both knew that he wasn't here to eat fried chicken— he was here to make a meal out of her.

He stood and offered her his hand. "Why don't you turn the music up and find out?"

She visibly swallowed, then bit her bottom lip to keep from smiling. She knew where this was going. What sort of dance he really had in mind.

And she wanted it, too, otherwise he wouldn't be here.

With a simple inclination of her head, she picked up the remote control to the stereo and increased the volume. The music was bluesy and low, the perfect background for making love. The next second, she placed her hand in his and he drew her close, savoring the feel of her body next to his. Soft, warm, womanly. He inhaled, tasting her scent—musky with a citrusy finish. Something inside of him tightened and released, as though a lock had been thrown, the tumbler rolling into place.

She felt...*right*. Better. More significant than any other woman he'd ever held before.

"You smell nice," he said, whispering the compliment into her ear. Gratifyingly, she shivered and murmured a thanks. "Who is this?" he asked her, nodding toward the stereo. He wrapped his arm more snugly around her waist, knowing that it was going to make him harder and she was going to be able to tell. He could feel the tension gathering along her spine, her need pinging his, making it all the more potent, all the more intense.

"Marc Broussard."

"I like him."

She drew back and looked up at him. "I'm breaking my own rules for you, you know," she said, as if unable to prevent the disclaimer.

"Rules?" he scoffed playfully. "What rules?"

"I typically have to know someone better before I—" She struggled to find the right word.

"Make fried chicken for them?" he helpfully supplied the euphemism.

She chuckled, lowered her gaze. "Yes. I ordinarily have to know someone a little bit longer before I…make f-fried chicken for them." He loved her smile, the way her ripe lips curled just so. Her lashes were long and lush and painted shadows beneath her eyes. He loved that, too.

He grinned down at her. "So what you're trying to tell me is that I'm special."

"Something like that, yes," she confirmed.

"You're pretty damned extraordinary yourself," he told her. And she was. She was smart and creative, funny and warm-hearted. Aside from being unbelievably attracted to her, he genuinely liked her, Silas realized. She'd been an instant friend, which was rarer than this phenomenal appeal. He might have thought about that little realization and its significance if she hadn't chosen that exact moment to nuzzle her nose along his throat.

Sensation bolted through him, snapping the thin line of restraint he'd been holding on to. He drew back and kissed her, let his lips slide purposefully over hers, feeling the petal softness of her mouth against his. She bloomed, opening for him, and he slipped his tongue into her mouth, delving into the soft recesses, tasting her, sampling her, dragging her into the pit of lust he'd found himself in since meeting her.

She responded in kind, wrapped her arms more tightly around him, sliding her thumb along his jaw, behind his ear, into his hair. Her mouth was hot and languid, insistent and lazy, and he couldn't get enough of her, couldn't hold back. The intensity of the need—the unnamed emotion attached to the need specifically—should have terrified him, yet it didn't.

She breathed a sigh into his mouth that was part surrender, part relief, and with a little jump, wrapped her arms more firmly around his neck and her legs around his waist.

A minute later, she'd directed him to the bedroom and thirty seconds beyond that, he had her naked. Curly black hair spilled over a stark white pillow. Pale pink nipples pouted for his kiss. A smooth belly, the flare of womanly hips and a thatch of dark curls between her creamy thighs called to him.

Beautiful.

Achingly so.

Though he'd been sexually active since his teens and had never doubted his ability to please a woman, he was unaccountably nervous, felt like an anxious virgin hiding behind a large erection and more bravado than skill all over again. She was small and perfectly made, and he wanted to do this right, to make her thankful that she was breaking her rules for him. More than anything he knew he was going to want more of her *fried chicken* and, irrationally, he believed additional helpings were dependent upon this performance.

He bent and took a dusky nipple into his mouth, shaping her breast in his hand as he did so. She sighed a gratifying mewl of pleasure and tunneled her fingers into his hair. She arched up, giving him more, a silent offering, one he was more than willing to take. He licked a path to her other breast, circling the nipple with his tongue before pulling it deeply into his mouth. She made that noise again—the one that made him want to beat his chest and roar—and then slid her hands down over his back, tracing his spine.

The feel of her small, capable fingers against his skin sent gooseflesh skittering along the backs of his legs, and when her hand glided ever so innocently over his hip, then found its way between his legs, he almost came undone.

Or just came.

She worked him against her palm, skimming the tip of his engorged penis with her thumb, then clasped him once more and worked the skin along his dick from root to tip. Every stroke of her soft hand against him sent sensation hurtling through him, made his balls tighten and toes dig into the mattress. Taking a page out of her book, Silas slid his own hand down her abdomen, found the dewy curls between her thighs and deftly parted her nether lips. She was hot and wet against his fingers and the first brush of his thumb over her clit made her buck against his hand.

He smiled, rather pleased with himself.

She palmed his balls, pulling another hiss from between his teeth, and his smile capsized. She leaned forward and kissed his shoulder, dipped her tongue into the hollow of his collarbone—who knew that was an erogenous zone?—and then slid her wonderful lips along his throat. She nipped at his ear and worked herself against him as he slipped a finger deep inside her. She gasped again, every sound of pleasure an affirmation that this was right. She stroked him harder as he massaged her clit, then she shifted and lifted her hips.

"Please," she said. "I need—"

Truer words had never been spoken, Silas thought. He needed, too. He snagged his wallet from his pants at the foot of the bed and took out a condom, opened the packet and then swiftly rolled the protection into place. His gaze tangled with hers as he nudged against her, poised at the entrance of her womanhood. He didn't know what stopped him, why he paused. He only knew that it was imperative that she see him, that they commemorate the moment with a shared look. Her eyes were feverish and glazed, her mouth swollen and rosy from his kisses, her nipples erect and waiting. She was beautiful and perfect and right, and when he pushed into her, seated himself firmly between her milky thighs, he knew he'd never felt more at home anywhere.

And instinctively he knew he never would again.

DELPHIE'S BREATH ESCAPED in a long, desperate hiss as Silas came into her. He was big and hard and felt so unbelievably perfect. She'd heard of hot, mindless sex before, but had never truly had it until right this instant. From the moment he'd kissed her she'd completely lost control. She'd fed at his mouth, clawed away his clothes and squirmed shamelessly against him, utterly desperate to feel him inside of her. To put her hands on his bare flesh.

He loomed over her like a dark angel—black hair, black eyes and a smile that was as wicked as Satan himself. He looked at her as though he didn't know what to make of her, as though she were a mystery he had to solve, as though he desperately wanted a peek inside her head as well as a trip inside her body.

And she loved it. Relished it. Savored it.

She rocked her hips beneath him, taking him farther into her body and watched as he set his jaw. It made her feel powerful and less reckless because this was without a doubt the most out of control she'd ever been.

She didn't do this. She didn't *do* complete strangers.

But he didn't feel like a stranger. He felt perfect.

He bent his dark head and pulled her breast into his mouth once again, laving her budded nipple with his tongue.

Her feminine muscles clamped harder around him and a purely masculine sound escaped between his lips. It was music to her ears. She licked a determined path along his neck and breathed into his ear, then nipped at his earlobe and grinned when she felt him swell inside her.

He moved faster, pumping in and out of her, while feeding at her breasts. He was everywhere at once—on top of her, inside her. She found his mouth again, kissing him as he upped the tempo between their joined bodies.

She felt the first flash of impending release build in her sex and held him tighter. She grabbed the twin globes of his ass and drew her legs back, giving him better access.

He pushed harder, faster, then faster still and she could feel her breath getting stuck in her throat and she gasped and bucked wildly beneath him.

She needed— She wanted—

He reached down between them, found the little kernel of pleasure nestled at the top of her sex and pressed.

She came.

She dragged in a huge breath, but couldn't let it go. Lights danced behind her closed lids, every muscle in her body contracted and she fisted around him, coming harder than she ever had before in her life.

The orgasm was brighter, better and more satisfying than anything she'd ever experienced. She felt herself tighten around him again, then he set his jaw and pushed her harder, her tingling breasts absorbing his manic thrusts.

Three seconds later, he growled low in his throat and shuddered violently. His eyes closed, seemingly from the weight of pleasure, and a slow smile shaped his lips.

After a moment, he looked down at her, a wonderingly confused but satisfied look on his face. "Well," he said. "I'm glad we got that out of the way."

"Out of the way?" she repeated, feigning offense though she knew exactly what he was talking about.

He carefully withdrew, disposed of the condom with a tissue from beside the bed, then curled up next to her.

"Yeah," he said. "Because next time I intend to do a proper job of it."

She laughed and pressed a kiss against his naked shoulder. "You mean to tell me you didn't give me your best?" she teased.

She felt him chuckle beside her. "I can always do better."

If he did any better she didn't know if she'd survive it. "I like a man who wants to improve."

He slid a finger beneath the swell of her breast, making her shiver. "And I like a woman who's so into me she doesn't remember getting naked."

"How do you know I don't remember?"

"That telling frown I saw just a minute ago. It's the same look my dad gets when he walks into a room and then forgets what he went in there for."

What was the point in denying it? She didn't remember getting naked. She only remembered how nice it was after she'd gotten there. How much she'd loved the feel of him deep inside her, the delicious draw and drag between their joined bodies, the slip of his tongue along the base of her throat.

It was *wonderful*. Intoxicating. Potentially habit forming.

"You know what I think we should do?" she asked.

"What?"

"Take the rest of that wine and go get in the hot tub."

He chuckled. "Admit it. You just want see me naked."

She merely shrugged. "Turn about's fair play, right? You certainly got an eyeful last night."

"I didn't see anything," he said. "Though I wanted to," he qualified. "Damned bubbles."

"I was mortified."

He laughed softly. "I know. It was most entertaining."

"Thank you ladies and gentlemen," she said, deadpan. "I'm here every night. *Bada bing.*"

He nuzzled her neck. "You have the most interesting sense of humor."

She frowned, not altogether certain that was a compliment. "Is that a charitable way of saying that I'm weird?"

"No, it's a nice way of saying that you're fascinating."

She blinked, absorbing that statement, and felt a ripple of happiness eddy through her. She rather liked being fascinating. "Oh."

"You still want to go get in the hot tub?" he asked, pressing another kiss to the underside of her jaw. His hand found her breast and played lazily with her nipple. She felt him twitch against her thigh, rising to the challenge, as it were, once again. Her belly quickened in response, warmth engulfing her core.

"Nah," Delphie told him. "I've got wine here and you're already naked. Win, win."

"Come here," he said, laughing softly, rolling her toward him. "I'll let you have your wicked way with me."

As offers went, it was a pretty damned good one.

6

"THANKS SO MUCH for doing this," Delphie said the next day as they entered the church. She wore a red velvet dress with white fur trim and a matching Santa hat adorned with a sprig of holly. Her sister evidently had a unique sense of style and it was all Silas could do to keep from laughing at Delphie's pained expression when he'd gone over to pick her up this afternoon.

"No problem," he told her, smiling down at her. He just looked forward to taking it off her. He'd ended up spending the night with her last night and he'd awoken to the feel of a soft rump against his groin and a softer breast in his hand.

This could potentially be the best Christmas of his life.

She'd had a few wedding-related things to do this morning and he'd needed to get his Christmas shopping done, so they'd parted ways after a quick breakfast. It had been so easy being with her; he was trying to pinpoint the exact reason why that was.

Ultimately, he'd decided, it was simply her. She had no expectations, was funny and charming and the most responsive, enthusiastic bed partner he'd ever had. In fact, he could quite easily see himself becoming addicted to her.

Simply put, she was easy company and he enjoyed every minute he spent with her, in and out of bed.

That had never happened before. He typically either liked a girl well enough but found her lacking in the bedroom, or vice versa. This was the first time he'd ever found the total package.

How ironic that it was the girl his mother had been telling him about.

He watched the wedding party come down the aisle to the tune of "Jingle Bells," then everyone stood and the bride made her entrance on her father's arm to "Santa, Baby." He grinned and happened to glance at Delphie, who was looking as long-suffering as it was possible to be without appearing jealous of her sister, and she gave a helpless shrug.

Ten minutes later—after the bride and groom had promised to never let the sun set on an argument—the wedding was over and the reception had begun.

He quickly found Delphie and handed her a drink. "Too bad there's no hot tub to drink it in, eh?" he teased.

She downed the rum and eggnog in one gulp. "Hit me again," she said, shuddering. "Here comes my grandmother. I'm going to need it."

The old woman moved fast for her age, and her faded blue eyes fastened on Silas with a keen sort of awareness that made him acutely uncomfortable. It was as if the old woman had witnessed every depraved thing he'd done to her granddaughter last night and this morning and was going to share it with the room at large. "You must be Delphie's new young man."

"Silas Davenport," he introduced himself while Delphie shrunk with embarrassment. He wrapped his arm around her, drawing her closer to his side. "And I hope that she's as much mine as I am hers," he said.

Beside him, Delphie choked, but the ploy worked. The grandmother went from getting ready to give Delphie the you'll-get-your-turn-at-the-alter spiel to obvious happiness.

The older woman preened. "We're awfully proud of our Delphie."

"Of course," he said. "She's a remarkable woman. And she makes the best fried chicken I've ever eaten."

Delphie glared up him and flattened her lips to keep from laughing.

"Oh, she's a wonderful cook," her grandmother said. "She learned that from me, you know," the older woman went on, completely oblivious to the true meaning of the conversation. "I like to soak my chicken in buttermilk. Makes it more tender, you see. And the longer the better."

"That's right, Granny," she said, nearly choking. She darted a glance beyond the older woman's shoulder, pretending to see someone she needed to talk to. "Oh, look, there's Uncle Harry." She jerked Silas in her crazy uncle's direction. "I've been meaning to tell him something. See you later, Granny."

Looking a bit baffled, her grandmother merely smiled and nodded goodbye. As soon as they were away from her, Delphie whirled on him and giggled. "The best fried chicken you've ever had, huh?"

"Without question," he told her, smiling. He led her onto the dance floor, curling her into his arms as Bing Crosby's "White Christmas" suddenly drifted through the speakers. She smelled wonderful, he thought. Like a lemon pound cake—which was probably not all that complimentary, but delicious all the same.

"I'm quite flattered. You're not half bad yourself."

"Half bad?" he remarked, his eyes rounding as he sent her into a twirl. "Clearly I'm not trying hard enough."

"Yes, but you're steadily improving," she told him, "and that's what's important."

He wanted to take her right now, Silas thought. He wanted to flip that ridiculous dress up over her hips and slip into her from behind. He wanted to feel her breasts pebble against his hands and suck on her neck while he pounded into her, her sweet ass cradling his groin. He cast her a brooding glance. He'd even let her leave the hat on.

She saw him watching her and a wary smile shaped her mouth. "Do I even want to know what you're thinking?"

He purposely licked his lips, allowed his fingers to slip along the side of her breast. She gasped, her gaze finding his. "I'm thinking about fried chicken and the likelihood of having some right now."

She swallowed hard and he watched as her pulse fluttered wildly at the base of her throat. "Right now?"

He was suddenly so hard he could scarcely think of anything else. Red was her color. She'd put it on her lips as well, and the image of her mouth encircling him, sliding along his dick, was so vivid he actually stumbled over his own feet. "Right damned *now.*"

With a nonchalant shrug he'd remember forever, she threaded her fingers through his and tugged him toward the door.

DELPHIE WAS SO SHOCKED at herself she didn't know what to do. One minute she'd been enjoying Silas's quick but unsolicited rescue from her grandmother—he couldn't have said anything better had she scripted the line for him herself—and their ensuing dance. The next, he'd mentioned fried chicken, and her sex had started throbbing right along with her frantically beating heart.

Who gives a damn about the wedding? Delphie thought, and her breasts grew heavier and heavier with need. She just wanted to have the honeymoon over and over again.

With Silas.

She led him downstairs to a little-used bathroom and she'd no more than closed the door before she felt him behind her, lifting her dress, his hot fingers against the backs of her thighs.

A thrill whipped through her.

She bent over and parted her legs, then cast him a glance over her shoulder.

"I want you so bad I can barely think straight," he said, making the confession as he slid a finger against her slick folds.

She gasped and wiggled against him. "It's the fur on the dress, isn't it? It's sort of got a porn-star quality."

He laughed into her ear, then suckled her neck. She heard the telltale sound of a condom package tearing, the whine of his zipper and a second later she felt him pushing against her nether lips.

Her mouth opened in a soundless gasp and she felt her muscles clench, readying for him. She arched her back and bent forward, giving him better access. With a guttural groan of masculine satisfaction, he slid into her.

The breath hitched out of her lungs and she tightened around him and pressed her hands against the door. He slid out and pushed again and she could tell that he was holding back, that he was afraid of hurting her.

But that wasn't what hurt.

"Don't be gentle," she said, clenching her teeth against the need hammering against her. "Take me how you really want me."

He gave a startled little laugh and then bent forward and breathed into her ear. "I do like the fur," he said. "It's hot. And you look good in red. Like Santa's sexy little helper."

He grabbed hold of her hips and pounded into her. It was wild and manic, hot and dirty, and to her immense surprise, she found she really wanted it that way.

He did this to her, Delphie thought. He made her want him like this. He pistoned in and out of her, harder and faster, then faster still. She absorbed his thrusts and worked herself against him, arched her head back when it got to be too much and he bent forward and bit her shoulder, a light nip, but she liked it so much it made her vision blacken around the edges. He reached around and massaged her clit, upped the tempo and nipped at her neck.

"You're...improving," she gasped, feeling the first bit of climax dawning in her quivering, anxious sex.

"You know...what they...say about...practice," he said, taking her harder and harder. He was big and hard and wonderful and the only thing she regretted about this was not being able to put her hands on him. She loved the way he felt beneath her palms—the salty taste of his smooth skin, the texture of his male nipple against her tongue. She felt his tautened balls slapping against her aching skin, his huge hand on her hip and a masterful finger stroking her clit.

It was too much, too perfect, too…everything.

The orgasm swept her up, then pushed her down and her muscles clamped so hard she felt him jerk and groan behind her.

"Delphie," he breathed, her name a curse. "You're killing me."

She sagged against the door, her legs weak, and savored the lingering pulses of release. "Good," she breathed. "Because I don't want to die alone."

She meant it in the figurative sense, but realized the double meaning as soon as the words left her mouth. He came an instant later and held her tighter, then kissed the nape of her neck. "You won't," he said. "At this point I'm even willing to give up the goats."

Delphie laughed, missing him already.

7

THOUGH SHE'D INVITED him over for Christmas dinner with her family, Silas had ultimately refused. He tried to tell himself that he didn't want to intrude, but the truth was he was beginning to suspect he needed a little distance from Delphie to try to get his head back in the game.

Because at this point, he'd already lost it.

He'd known her three days, would be boarding a plane first thing in the morning and though he always dreaded leaving, it was never quite like this.

Right now the idea of being so far from Delphie made him feel utterly miserable, which was cause for concern on more levels than he cared to count.

He couldn't be this invested in someone he'd only known three days, could he? Surely not. Granted, it felt as if he'd known her a lot longer than that and she was by far the most interesting person he'd ever met. And the sex…

His balls tightened just thinking about it.

He couldn't get enough of her.

He looked at her mouth and instantly craved her. She made him crazy with wanting, and the perpetual need to slip out of his skin and into hers only worsened the more time they spent together. And, of course, he wanted to spend every second with her, so that wasn't helping matters, either.

He could tell that she'd hated leaving him this morning, but he'd assured her he'd be fine. He'd wrapped presents for his parents and sister and left them under the tree, and he'd picked up a little something for Delphie yesterday when he'd been out, as well. It was a small pendant made of blue sea glass that perfectly matched the shade of her eyes.

He'd just taken the bread out of the oven when he heard her knock at the door. "You cooked," she said, her eyes sparkling with delight. "You didn't have to do that."

"I wanted to," he said simply. "Although you're probably not very hungry."

Her gaze slid over him slowly as she set aside a bag and shrugged out of her coat. "Actually, I've been thinking about eating all day."

Her eyes lingered on his groin, alerting him to what exactly she'd been thinking of eating, and every bit of the moisture evaporated from his mouth.

"I've got a special Christmas treat for you," she said.

"You do?" Did that hoarse voice belong to him?

She gave him a gentle shove, sending him toppling onto the couch. "Yep."

She retrieved the bag she'd brought in and handed it to him. The scent of oranges and yeast and icing instantly enveloped him and he grinned. "You made the orange rolls?"

"I tried," she said. "I'm not sure they're exactly what you're used to, but…" She pulled a little shrug, then dropped to her knees in front of him. His zipper whined as he withdrew the sticky treat and she waited for him to take his first bite before she wrapped her hot mouth around his dick and sucked.

He came embarrassingly close to coming instantly and his eyes rolled back in his head.

She worked the slippery skin against her hand, licked and sucked and lapped and laved. She massaged his balls, paid particular attention to the tender area beneath the full head of his penis. From the unbelievably happy look on her face, she was enjoying eating him as much as he was loving the orange roll.

He'd never look at the dessert the same way.

As he popped the last bite into his mouth, she sucked harder. Then he came. Her eyes met his as she lapped him up, savoring the taste of his release.

"Silas?"

"Hmm?"

"Merry Christmas."

He dropped his head against the back of the couch and chuckled softly.

Oh, yes, it had been after all.

"I'VE GOT SOMETHING for you," he said later that evening, after he'd reciprocated her earlier gesture. Delphie was spent and boneless and dreading the morning.

"You do? You didn't have to do that."

"I know," he said. "That's what makes it a present."

She laughed against his chest. "I thought you'd just given me your present."

"I think you'll like this one better," he said.

She smiled. "Oh, I doubt that very seriously."

He tsked. "You haven't even seen it yet." He reached under the Christmas tree and pulled a small package out for her, then handed it to her.

Damn. Her gaze flew to his. He'd gotten her a *real* present. She'd just made him some orange rolls and given him a blow job. She hadn't expected this. "Oh," she said. "Thank you."

"Aren't you going to open it?"

Fingers trembling, she did just that. "Oh, Silas," she breathed. "Sea glass."

"I thought of you when I saw it."

"Thank you," she said, more touched than she could imagine. "It's beautiful."

"It's the color of your eyes."

"You don't have to flatter me, you know. I'm a sure thing."

He stared at her. "You need to learn to take a compliment."

Maybe so, but this felt as though it changed things. Their brief but glorious relationship had been fun and uncomplicated and she thought she'd done a good job of keeping her feelings in check. But this little token changed things, made her realize just how much she truly…cared for him.

In the morning he was going to leave again, which in theory had made him safe. But she didn't feel safe now, and he damned sure wouldn't be safe when he went back to Iraq.

She was going to worry and be miserable and there wasn't anything she could do about it. Too late she realized that this had never been uncomplicated, that she could never disengage her heart like that.

Silas Davenport, damn him, was special. He always had been, whether she'd been willing to admit it or not.

"Here," he said. "Let me put it on you."

She turned and felt his fingers brush the back of her neck. Another shiver eddied through her and she felt her eyes burn.

Oh, hell.

"Your parents are really going to hate that they've missed you," she said, looking for a subject change.

"I hate that I've missed them, too," he told her. "But I have certainly enjoyed spending time with you." He studied her, smiled. "You're fun."

She ducked her head and tucked a strand of hair behind her ear. "Thank you."

"See," he said. "This is what I love about you. You give me the best Christmas present of my life without batting a lash. I give you a compliment and you blush six shades of red."

"You know what I love about you?" she asked.

"I hope that it's something truly depraved," he murmured, his gaze drifting over her.

"I love how you feel...inside me."

"I can hook you up," he said, rolling on top of her.

Delphie leaned forward and licked a path up his throat. "Make it count, soldier. We're on a time line here."

He did.

8

"YOU SERIOUSLY DIDN'T have to do this," Silas said as they stood in the airport. He had his duffel packed, his papers ready. Everything was a go.

Only he didn't want to.

"Nonsense," she said briskly, a wobbly smile on her face. "You're a friend, Silas, and friends don't let friends drive themselves to the airport."

A friend. He knew that was true, but for the first time in his life he wanted to be so much more. He wasn't exactly sure when it had happened, but Delphie Moreau had burrowed under his skin and attached herself to his heart. Was he in love with her? Honestly, he didn't know. He'd never been in love before and had nothing to compare it to, no frame of reference.

But he knew he cared about her, that he didn't want to leave her and that the idea of anyone else eating his fried chicken set his teeth on edge and made him want to break things.

If it wasn't love, then it was damned close.

She'd made arrangements to return the rental to a place

in Folly Beach and had driven him to the airport herself. It meant that he got to spend more time with her, of course, but he suspected it was going to make saying goodbye all the more difficult.

Shit.

How had this happened? At what point had she become so damned important? His heart was beating so fast in his chest he was afraid it was going to burst right through. His palms and feet tingled and he had a horrible premonition that when he tried to walk away he wasn't going to be able to do it, that she would have to make the move first.

"Any idea when you'll get to come home again?" she asked. She posed the question lightly, as though it didn't matter, but her mouth was white around the edges and she shifted from one foot to the other, as though she was about to come out of her skin.

"My tour is up in two months," he said. "I'll definitely come home for a little while then."

She smiled. "Is it going to send you into a panic if I say I'd like to see you?"

Relief poured through him, loosening his tight limbs. "Not at all." He paused, darted a look at her. "I was actually hoping that I could call you, that you'd write."

She nodded, her eyes twinkling with tentative happiness. "I'd like that very much," she said.

Damn, this was hard. He had an entirely new appreciation for the guys who left behind wives and significant others now. This was horrible. Like lopping off an appendage.

She raised up onto her tippy toes and kissed him. Without hesitation, he wrapped his arms around her, lifted her off the floor and deepened the kiss. He poured every bit of his feelings into the mating of their mouths, showed her everything he didn't have the words to say. Catcalls and applause suddenly rang out and he reluctantly pulled away and rested his forehead against hers.

"Be careful over there," she said, her voice thick. Her eyes were bright with unshed tears she tried to keep him from seeing.

He nodded and made himself turn and walk away, and every step that took him farther from her became harder and harder to make.

Bloody damned hell.

WELL, THIS ABSOLUTELY sucked, Delphie thought as she watched Silas disappear into the security line. She told herself to move, but couldn't seem to get her feet to cooperate.

She'd realized late last night that this was going to be more terrible than she'd suspected. He'd mentioned his early departure and her heart had given a painful little squeeze. She'd ignored it then because she hadn't wanted to do anything that was a) going to clue him in to her sudden discomfort or b) ruin what was left of their time together by alluding to feelings it should be impossible to have.

She'd only known him three days. People didn't fall in three days. Did they? Rational, sane people? Ordinary levelheaded people? Not to say that she was any of those things—clearly she wasn't, otherwise she wouldn't have this huge lump in her throat—but it certainly lessened her ability to make fun of her sister's drive-thru love connection if it was the case.

The idea of not seeing him, not tasting him, not hearing that wicked laugh she'd grown so attached to made something in her chest twist and squeeze. She loved the sound of his heartbeat beneath her ear, the feel of his big hands sliding over her bare back. She liked kissing the soft spot beneath his jaw, loved the smell of his skin.

Two months before she'd see him again? Geez, it already felt like an eternity and he'd been gone less than a minute.

This sure as hell didn't bode well for the next sixty days.

With a deep bolstering breath, Delphie turned and started toward the exit.

"Delphie!"

Silas? Her heart leaped into her throat. She turned, only to see him running toward her. She frowned up at him as he skidded to a stop. "What are you doing?" she asked. "Aren't you going to miss your flight?"

"Not if I hurry," he said. His gaze searched hers and he seemed at a loss for the right words, which was bizarre in and of itself. He pushed his hand through his hair, looked away, then back at her.

"Silas?" she asked, confused. "Is something wrong? Have you forgotten something?"

His dark gaze latched on to hers. "Look, I know this is going to sound crazy, but I need to ask you something."

She nodded. "Okay."

"How do you feel about me?" he wanted to know. "You like me well enough?"

A strangled laugh broke loose in her throat at the absurdity of his question. "I think you know I like you well enough, Silas."

"And if I wasn't leaving right now, would you want to see me again on a regular basis?"

She nodded. Definitely. "I would."

"And if we were seeing each other on a regular basis, then we'd both want exclusivity, right?"

Exclusivity? Was he asking what she thought he was asking? "We would," she said haltingly. She felt a frown wrinkle her brow. "What are you trying to say, Silas?"

"I'm saying I don't want anyone else eating your fried chicken," he said significantly, the words so fierce they sounded as if they'd been pulled out by the roots.

She laughed and inclined her head knowingly. "And does that mean—"

His lips curled with wry humor. "Trust me, I won't be seeing anyone. I promise."

Delphie felt a smile slide over her lips as what he said fully registered. She laughed, her heart full with hope and the possibility of true love. "We just went from fun to serious, didn't we?"

He kissed her again, drew back and sighed. "All that means is that we're going to be having some serious fun when I return."

She smiled up at him. "Good," she said. "I only have one question."

"What's that?"

She hesitated, peeked at him from beneath lowered lashes. "Do you have a hunting dog?"

He guffawed. "No, but I'll get one. And the goats and the dairy cow, if necessary."

"Then we'll be farmers."

"So long as we're together," he said, shrugging as if that was the only thing that mattered.

And it was.

* * * * *

Sparkling Christmas kisses!

Bryony's daughter, Lizzie, wants was a *dad* for Christmas and Bryony's determined to fulfil this Christmas wish. But when every date ends in disaster, Bryony fears she'll need a miracle. But she only needs a man for Christmas, not for love…right?

Unlike Bryony, the last thing Helen needs is a man! In her eyes, all men are *Trouble*! Of course, it doesn't help that as soon as she arrives in the snow-covered mountains, she meets Mr Tall, Dark and Handsome *Trouble*!

www.millsandboon.co.uk

Come home to the magic of Nora Roberts

Nora Roberts

Christmas Magic

OVER 400 MILLION OF HER BOOKS IN PRINT WORLDWIDE

Identical twin boys Zeke and Zach wished for only one gift from Santa this year: a new mum! But convincing their love-wary dad that their music teacher, Miss Davis, is his destiny and part of Santa's plan isn't as easy as they'd hoped...

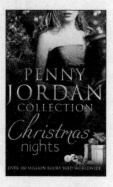

Mills & Boon® Online

Discover more romance at
www.millsandboon.co.uk

 FREE online reads

Books up to one
month before shops

Browse our books
before you buy

...and much more!

For exclusive competitions and instant updates:

 Like us on **facebook.com/romancehq**

Follow us on **twitter.com/millsandboonuk**

 Join us on **community.millsandboon.co.uk**

 Visit us Online Sign up for our FREE eNewsletter at
www.millsandboon.co.uk

WEB/M&B/RTL4

The World of Mills & Boon®

There's a Mills & Boon® series that's perfect for you. We publish ten series and, with new titles every month, you never have to wait long for your favourite to come along.

Blaze.
Scorching hot, sexy reads
4 new stories every month

By Request
Relive the romance with the best of the best
9 new stories every month

Cherish™
Romance to melt the heart every time
12 new stories every month

Desire™
Passionate and dramatic love stories
8 new stories every month

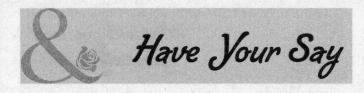

Have Your Say

You've just finished your book.
So what did you think?

We'd love to hear your thoughts on our
'Have your say' online panel
www.millsandboon.co.uk/haveyoursay

- 🌹 Easy to use
- 🌹 Short questionnaire
- 🌹 Chance to win Mills & Boon® goodies